MISS JULIA SPEAKS HER MIND
&
MISS JULIA TAKES OVER

MISS JULIA
— SPEAKS —
HER
— MIND —
&
MISS JULIA
— TAKES —
OVER

TWO NOVELS BY

ANN B. ROSS

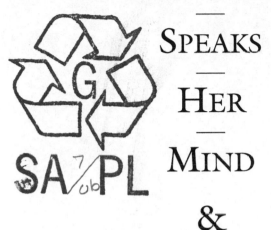

Garden City, New York

Miss Julia Speaks Her Mind

Acknowledgments

My thanks to all the Wordwrights, but especially to Elizabeth, Katie, Susan, Sally, and our fearless leader, Ted; to Boyd B. Massagee, Jr., Charles Waters, and Sharon Alexander, attorneys-at-law, all of whom proffered advice not always taken (so don't blame them); to Marion for his forbearance; and to Marian, Claudia, and John for never failing in their encouragement and support. My thanks also to the friend whose name I confiscated and, most especially, to Jennifer Robinson, Delin Cormeny, and Katharine Cluverius.

For Alice, Charles, and John Michael

Chapter 1

I'd just caught my breath after the shock of my husband's sudden passing when his last legacy showed up on my front porch. We'd buried Wesley Lloyd Springer some few months before that hot, still morning in August, and I hoped I was through signing forms and meeting with lawyers and shuffling through various and sundry legal papers. I declare, this business of dying has more legal aspects to it than you would think. The deceased never knows what you have to go through to get his affairs in order, and Wesley Lloyd's were in as much order as they could get. I thought.

Lord, it was hot that morning, and I recalled again how Wesley Lloyd had always put his foot down about air-conditioning the house, even when the Conovers had theirs done. Central air, too. Wesley Lloyd said it was a waste of money and, besides, fresh air was good for us. He felt that way only at home, though, because his office at the bank was kept cool enough for the three-piece suits he wore day in and day out. But I don't believe in speaking ill of the dead, even when it's the truth.

So I was sitting in my living room trying to get my mind off the heat by looking through a stack of mail-order catalogs. Making a list of the items I intended to call in for and having a good time doing it, since Binkie Enloe'd said I needed to spend some money. Sam Murdoch had agreed, and he ought've known since he was the executor of the will that had put me in my present more-than-comfortable position. Lord, there was more money than I ever knew Wesley Lloyd had, and it all belonged to me, his grieving widow. But a proud widow, too, and justly so, because I'd made such a fine and fortunate choice of husbands.

But I tell you, I thought I'd never get over the shock of finding Wesley Lloyd dead as a doornail, slumped over the steering wheel of his new Buick Park Avenue. Steel gray with plush upholstery, parked right out there in the driveway.

But I did, laying him to rest in a properly ordered Presbyterian ceremony as he would've expected. Then I had to suffer another shock when I found out how well-off Wesley Lloyd had been. Why, besides the bank his daddy'd left him, he owned half the county, seemed like, plus stocks and bonds and tax-deferred annuities, all of it making more and more money every day of the week. When the extent of his estate was laid out for me, all I could think of was how he used to hand me a housekeeping allowance every Friday, saying, "Make it last, Julia. Money doesn't grow on trees, you know." And all the time he was cultivating a whole grove! Well, a lot of good it did him, because I ended up with every penny.

Now, after forty-four years in blissful ignorance of Wesley Lloyd's activities, financial and otherwise, I had settled down to enjoy the benefits of widowhood and a full checkbook, both of which I was mastering with hardly any problems to speak of.

I looked out the window as a few cars passed by on Polk Street, headed down to Main. I declare, everybody and his brother seemed to have a telephone glued to his ear, though this town's not big enough to need BellSouth whenever you drive to the grocery store. Across the street the parking lot spread from Polk to the back of the First Presbyterian Church of Abbotsville, my church and the one Wesley Lloyd and his father, before him, had supported with their presence, tithes, offerings, and over-and-above donations. Advice, too, which was always taken but not always appreciated. Heat waves shimmered up from the asphalt lot as I took note of whose cars were parked over there. It was my custom to keep up with what went on around me and, since Mondays were Pastor Ledbetter's days off, I couldn't be blamed for wondering why he was meeting with several men on the session at the church. But far be it from me to be nosy.

I could hear Lillian humming along with the radio above the occasional clatter of pans out in the kitchen as she prepared my lunch. That was another thing that was different, now that Wesley Lloyd wouldn't be home for meals anymore. He'd liked a quiet house, meals served on time, and everything done right on schedule. I had already begun to enjoy a little freedom from that schedule, telling Lillian that we'd eat whenever either of us got hungry or she got the urge to put something on the table.

I licked a finger and turned a page in the Neiman Marcus Christmas catalog, wondering what Sam and Binkie would say if I ordered a few trinkets from it. I declare, some of the offerings were for people with more money than sense, a condition that didn't apply to me, I'm happy to say. I expect, though, that any number of people would've said it did if they'd known the full extent of Wesley Lloyd's prudence and foresight.

However. His prudence and foresight hadn't taken heart attacks into account. I knew as sure as I was sitting there he never intended to leave me in charge of everything he owned. I knew it as soon as Pastor Ledbetter came sidling up to me not two days after laying Wesley Lloyd to rest, telling me he knew I'd want to honor Mr. Springer's last wishes even if they'd never gotten written down. That was the first I'd heard that Wesley Lloyd had planned to make the First Presbyterian Church his main beneficiary, with Pastor Ledbetter and a member of the session as trustees who'd dole me out an allowance every month.

And speaking of which, you wouldn't believe the phone calls and circulars and brochures and letters on embossed stationery that had come to me from investment counselors, financial advisors, estate planners, and you name it, wanting me to turn my assets over to them. It didn't matter if it was a church, a college, a charity, or a businessman in an office, they all knew what was in my best interests. If I'd just let them take care of everything, I would be assured of an allowance dribbled out every quarter throughout my lifetime. Well, I'd been on an allowance for forty-four years, thank you, and having it all was better.

I reached over to close my wine velvet drapes against the morning sun streaming through the window—you have to watch that the sun doesn't fade your Orientals—and shifted in my chair to move out of the glare. A hairpin slid down my neck and, as I tucked it back in, I recalled how Velma had started talking during my last appointment, paying no attention to the business at hand, which was giving me a permanent. It'd just made me sick when I saw what she'd done. She said the curl would loosen up when it was washed, and besides, my hair was real fine, and I ought to know that hair texture changes with age, and was I taking any medication that would react with the solution. I declare, I wish just once in her life the woman would admit to a mistake and not blame me or my hair for coming out looking like a Brillo pad.

But some things you just have to live with. Like frizzy hair. And no children to comfort you in your old age, both of which can make you want to bury your head and cry.

But to look on the bright side, hair can grow out and children can grow up to squabble over inheritances, so I couldn't feel too sorry for myself. Not that I would ever deny a child of mine what was rightfully his. Or hers, but they might fuss among themselves. As it was, I was spared the shameful spectacle of a family split apart over who got what. I know what I'm talking about, because I've seen it happen too many times, more's the pity. I expect there's never been a will in the world that satisfied all the beneficiaries, so I couldn't feel too sad about being the sole survivor.

I sighed and turned another page, my attention so taken with the glitter of the catalogs that I nearly jumped out of my skin when the doorbell rang.

I went to the front door and looked through the screen at a woman standing there in heels too high, dress too short, and hair too yellow. All of it too young for the hard-living lines around her eyes and slick, red lips. A skinny little boy stood behind her hanging his head, and I thought she was selling something. Door-to-door salespeople do that, don't you know, take a child with them to make you feel guilty about turning them down. I opened my mouth to say "No, thank you," but she was already talking.

"I'm sorry to bother you," she said, hefting up the strap of her shoulder bag. I could see the sheen of perspiration oozing out from under her makeup as she took a deep breath and let the words pour out. "I wouldn't do this if I could come up with anything else. But I can't, and he didn't leave me no choice, and I got to make a livin'. You know how it is; well, maybe not. But I'm on my way to beauty school down in Raleigh. Learning nails? You know, acrylics and all? There's money in nails, and I just don't know what else to do."

I kept opening my mouth to tell her she had the wrong house, I didn't know her from Adam, but she didn't give me a chance. She pulled the child in front of her and gave him a little push toward the screen door. Sorry-looking little thing, scrawny and pale, standing there with a hangdog look to him and holding a brown Winn-Dixie grocery sack in both hands.

"This here's Wesley Lloyd Junior, though I guess," she said with a nervous laugh, "his name's not too legal, as nobody'd know better'n you. Wesley Lloyd Junior Springer is what I call him, it don't matter what's on his birth certificate, though his daddy's name's on it as the father. See, his name's right here." And she held out a piece of paper with the words "Certificate of Live Birth" across the top.

I could've been sleepwalking the way I opened the screen, took the paper, and read my husband's name on it. "Father: Wesley Lloyd Springer. Mother: Hazel Marie Puckett."

"I got to leave him with you," Hazel Marie Puckett said, pushing the little runt closer. "I got to depend on your Christian charity, 'cause Wesley Lloyd didn't leave me a red cent. I talked to that lawyer of yours, and she said not even the house I been livin' in some twelve years now. I'm broke, Miz Springer, and I'm not asking you for nothing but to look after my boy while I go get some trainin'. There's nobody else I can leave him with and, I mean, it's kinda like he's your stepson, idn't it? I'll be back to get him, six weeks, max, and I really hate to do it, but. Be a good boy, now," she said, patting him on the back, and using a foot to shove a pasteboard suitcase over beside him.

"Mind Miz Springer, now, you hear?" She gave him a quick kiss on the top of his head and tripped down the steps to a rumbling maroon-and-white car parked in front of my house. Burning oil so bad that thick fumes curled around my boxwoods.

"Miss! Miss!" I called, finally gaining my voice and hurrying out on the porch. "Come back here! You can't do this! I can't take this child! Miss! I'm calling the sheriff, you better get back here!"

But she hopped into the passenger seat, and the car sped off before she hardly had time to slam the door. Passenger seat, it came to me. Somebody else driving.

"What's all this yellin' about?" Lillian was at the door, her white uniform glowing through the screen mesh. You could mistake her for a heavyset nurse or waitress unless you noticed the run-over heels of her shoes that flapped with every step she took. She looked at me, and then we both looked at the boy.

I'd never seen such a pitiful-looking specimen. About nine or ten, I guessed, with lank brown hair hanging in his eyes, big horn-rimmed glasses down on his nose, pale skin dotted with freckles, shifty eyes that wouldn't look at either of us. He stood there with his shoulders slumped, the clip-on bow tie crooked on his thin cotton shirt and his shiny pants gathered high above his waist with a brown stretch belt. Wal-Mart special, no doubt. I looked him over good, ignoring Lillian standing there with her mouth open. I lifted his chin and studied his face, confirming what was as plain as day. My heart sank like an elevator as I gazed at Wesley Lloyd Springer, minus sixty-some-odd years. Looked just like him, but without Wesley Lloyd's self-confidence and leadership qualities.

I took a deep breath. "Lillian, look what else Mr. Springer left me."

Chapter 2

"Go call the sheriff," I told her as I turned back to the porch railing. I should've thought to get the tag number, but by then the car had roared down the street and turned right on Lincoln. A pall of black smoke drifted down in its wake.

Not hearing any movement behind me, I turned to see Lillian's arms around the little bastard, his head against her white nylon uniform. He turned loose of the grocery sack long enough to wipe the sleeve of one arm across his running nose, smearing his glasses even more. It was enough to turn your stomach.

Lillian looked at me like I'd lost my mind. "You can't call the sheriff on this pore little chile. What he done to you?"

"*He's* not done anything to me. Except be here. But I mean to report his mama." I crossed my arms against my chest and climbed on my high horse. "She can't just go abandoning a child on somebody's doorstep. I'll report her to the sheriff and the district attorney and anybody else I can think of. The idea of just dropping him off on me and leaving town. You're mighty right I'm calling the sheriff. If they hurry, they can catch her on the interstate and bring her back. This child's her responsibility, not mine!"

This tirade brought forth another wet snuffle from the little stray and another squinty-eyed glare from Lillian.

"Yessum, and I guess you want this whole thing on the front page of the *Abbotsville Press,* too, don't you? You thought of that? You thought what all this town gon' be talkin' and whisperin' and specalatin' about? You thought about what yo' preacher gon' say? An' all yo' church people? An' Miz Conover?"

Well no, I hadn't. Lillian had been giving me good advice for as long as she'd been with me, some twenty years now. We knew each other inside and out, and neither of us hesitated to say what we thought. Even so, we both knew how far to go without overstepping ourselves, so I guess that made us friends as well. LuAnne Conover accused me of being too friendly with the help, said I'd encourage thieving, which would lead to back talk and then, if I wasn't careful, to downright laziness. She said it's better to have a businesslike arrangement and keep my distance. But LuAnne had never been able to keep help more than six months at a time, so I didn't see her advice as all that sound.

Besides, Lillian was a capable, self-assured woman, unlike me, who had to ask Wesley Lloyd what I thought about most every subject. She had a lot of common sense, too, in spite of that gold tooth she had put in a few years back. In fact, I put more stock in what Lillian thought than I did LuAnne Conover, who had to tell anybody who'd listen how important her husband was. Leonard, a slump-shouldered, paunchy man who Wesley Lloyd never had much use for, was big in county politics. He had to run for half a dozen offices before he finally won one. Leonard's name on the ballot got to be such a joke around town that we all felt sorry for him and elected him a few years ago to some clerical office in the courthouse annex just to get him out of sight. When Wesley Lloyd told me to vote for Leonard, he'd said the clerk of court didn't have to be a lawyer or college educated or even acquainted with the law. So since Leonard qualified on all counts, I'd cast my ballot for him and now I had to put up with listening to LuAnne tell how lawyers and judges depended on him, and how influential his decisions were. To hear her tell it, the county's business wouldn't get done without Leonard being there to keep everybody straight. I didn't have the heart to tell her that Wesley Lloyd had also said that Leonard couldn't do much damage clerking in the courthouse, because he knew how to take instruction. LuAnne loved to bask in the glow of Leonard's job and, even though I'd been guilty of the same thing with Wesley Lloyd's position, I was now trying to get over it.

Lillian, however, had more sense than either of us. I studied what she'd said a few minutes, walking back to the railing and clenching it as my knees began to tremble. I knew she'd looked farther ahead than I'd been able to in my state of shock.

"All right," I said. "Go wake up Deputy Bates."

"I ain't gon' disturb that man's sleep. He work all night an' he need his rest."

I heaved a dramatic sigh and went into the house myself. "Well, at least do one thing without an argument," I said as I headed for the stairs. "Get that child inside before the whole town sees him."

Deputy Coleman Bates was my boarder, one that Sam Murdoch had strongly urged me to take in after Wesley Lloyd's demise. Not because I needed the money, because I didn't. But because Sam had said he'd sleep better knowing I had a man in the house. "There're a lot of wicked people out there, Julia," he'd said. "And a woman alone, especially one with your assets, would be an attraction to every thief, and worse, in this town." And he went on to point out that a deputy sheriff's car parked in my driveway would be a deterrent that no alarm system could match. So I'd fixed up the back upstairs bedroom, the one that opens onto the sleeping porch, which connects to the back staircase, and taken in a boarder. There was some comment about it at first, some speculation that Wesley Lloyd hadn't left me as well off as people had assumed. But soon after this young man moved in, I traded in Wesley Lloyd's Park Avenue, not wanting to be driving around in his deathbed, so to speak, for one of those little foreign coupes. Then I had the trim on the house touched up, and the drapes replaced in the living room, and on top of that, I made a sizable contribution to the church organ fund. That stopped the tongues wagging about my financial position.

I banged on Deputy Bates's door and called to him to get up, we had some bad trouble downstairs. I had no qualms about disturbing his rest, for he'd been in my house for a full six weeks and this was the first time I'd had to call on him. He'd told me that he left the Atlanta police force for a quieter, less stressful job here in Abbotsville, but I figured a little stress now and then wouldn't hurt him. So I banged on the door again.

I heard his feet hit the floor and a drawer crash open. The door sprang back, and Deputy Bates stood there in his boxer shorts, red and white stripes, with bleary eyes in his head and a dull gray pistol in his hand.

"What?" he asked, his eyes darting from side to side. "What's the trouble?"

"It's not that bad," I said, pointing at the gun. "You probably won't need to shoot anybody." The one who needed it was already dead.

He blinked at me, then shook his head. "Let me get some clothes on," he said.

I went back downstairs and out into the kitchen, where I heard Lillian bustling around. She had that abandoned child seated at the table with a huge slice of chocolate cake and a glass of milk in front of him. I took a deep breath and felt my mouth tighten into a sharp line.

"We're not entertaining company, Lillian," I said. "This child's moving on just as soon as I find somewhere to move him on to."

"Chil'ren get hungry," she said as she checked a pot on the stove. She wouldn't look at me, so I knew she didn't like the attitude I was taking. Too bad.

I ignored her and walked over to the table. I stood there, tapping my foot and looking at him as the anger in my heart turned my hands into fists. He slumped lower and lower in his chair until his face was about level with the second layer of the cake. The Winn-Dixie grocery bag was on the floor beside his chair.

"What do they call you, boy?" I demanded.

Tears flowed like a gushing stream out from under the smeared glasses, but he made no attempt to wipe them away. He held his hands in his lap and just sat there bawling without making a sound.

"Oh, for goodness' sake!" I said. "I asked you a simple question, so sit up straight and answer it."

His scrawny shoulders started heaving then, though he made an effort to pull himself up in the chair. Lillian decided to intervene then, though the Lord knows it didn't take much for her to make that decision.

"Junior," she said to me, and sharply, too. "They calls him Junior an' that ain't no way to talk to no baby."

I rolled my eyes at the thought of a nine-year-old baby. I knew I shouldn't be talking so hatefully, but every time I looked at that child I wanted to do some damage to somebody, and I couldn't reach the one who deserved it.

"Well, he won't be called Junior around here," I announced. "Not in this house, he won't. It's illegal, and as long as you're in my house," I said, turning back to the little sniveler, "which won't be for long, you'll be called Lloyd."

"Yes'm," he mumbled, sounding like he was underwater. Which he was.

"Okay, Miss Julia," Deputy Bates said, coming into the kitchen. As he walked through the sunshine streaming in the window, his gold-filled watch and the fine blond hair on his arms put me in mind of a Pawley's Island lifeguard, suntanned and sparkling with light, I'd once taken notice of. He'd put on a pair of blue jeans over the boxer shorts I'd previously been greeted with, and he was wearing cowboy boots, for the Lord's sake. Still, he made a fine figure of a man to be so young, with all those muscles filling out his white T-shirt. Nothing in his hands, I was happy to note. "What's the problem?"

"This," I said, pointing a finger at the child, whose blotched face screwed up again and overflowed with another torrent.

"How you doin', Bud," he said, nodding to the child, ignoring the river of tears and turning to Lillian with a grin. "Got any leftover coffee?"

"Pourin' right now," she said, her face beaming like it did whenever a man was around to feed. This one, in particular. She'd taken to Deputy Bates from the first minute he'd walked into the house in his dark blue uniform complete with badge, nightstick, pistol, walkie-talkie, and I-don't-know-what-all. You know how some women are.

I rolled my eyes again and sat down across the table from Deputy Bates. "If everybody's been served," I said after Lillian had set a steaming cup in front of him and put a fork in the child's hand, "I need some help here."

"Tell me," Deputy Bates said, and I did.

"That's some story," he said as I finished with an indignant shake of my head. "You didn't know anything about this?" He indicated Little Lloyd with a lift of his eyebrows.

"Nobody did! Not one soul. Did they, Lillian?"

"No'm," she mumbled, stirring a pan of corn like it needed all her attention.

"Did you know anything, Lillian?" I demanded, half rising from the chair. "Did you?" Fear and shame rushed over me like an ocean wave. I felt rolled over, turned around, and left with the gritty taste of sand in my mouth.

"Jus' talk, you know how peoples talk." She wouldn't look at me as she busied herself with moving pots around on the stove.

"You mean," I croaked, my hand on my heart, "that people *knew* what Wesley Lloyd was doing all this time, while I . . . I had no idea?"

I couldn't take it in, the thought that I'd been walking around town, going to church, the hairdresser's, the Winn-Dixie, holding my head up in oblivious pride while everybody else had known my husband—the banker, the church elder, the moneymaker, the leader of men—was philandering with a floozie. Faces of my friends, neighbors, church members, merchants—the paperboy, for the Lord's sake—flashed through my mind, all whispering, watching, tittering, and gloating. Some of them laughing at me, others feeling sorry for me. I didn't know which was worse.

Chapter 3

I sank back in my chair with a sinking feeling in my soul. "What in the world am I going to do?" I whispered.

"Let's think this out," Deputy Bates said. "First of all, the Department of Social Services can take Bud here. They'll look after him for a few days while we try to get a line on his mother. If we can't locate her, they'll find a foster home for him." He stopped and ran a finger across his mouth as he thought. "I guess there'd be a hearing when they do locate her. She could be declared unfit, maybe, and then he'd be a ward of the state. You'd have to testify, you know."

The child was watching him as closely as he could out of those glasses, taking tiny bites of the cake between hiccups. But when Deputy Bates said "ward of the state," Little Lloyd put his fork down and hung his head again. Lillian walked over to the table, the heels of her shoes flopping on the linoleum. She stood there with her hands on her hips as she looked me straight in the eye.

"You do all that, Miss Julia," she said, "an' ever'body know what they been 'spectin' be the gospel truth. You get the law an' the courts an' all in this, and it'll come out in the public, ever' bit of it!"

She was right. I could see myself telling a judge just how Wesley Lloyd Junior Springer had been sprung on me. The whole town would be slapping their knees. Wesley Lloyd had been too sharp a businessman for people not to enjoy his fall from grace. Even if he was dead and buried. As for me, I'd been too proud of him, and of myself, to be able to escape the eyes cutting in my direction as I passed, or the small, knowing smiles as people put up a pretense of the respect I was accustomed to.

"What am I going to do?" I whispered again.

"Well," Deputy Bates said, "I can put out some unofficial feelers, see if we can locate her that way. If she'll take him back, then that'll be the end of it. If she won't, or I can't find her, you can decide then whether to get social services involved. Not much you can do about it going public then, 'cause reporters watch the docket for interesting cases. And this would be interesting."

"You could look for her unofficially?" I asked, feeling some hope. "I mean, so nobody'd know why you were looking?"

He rubbed his hand over his hair and twisted his mouth. "I can try, but I can't promise much. I could do this, though," he said, sitting up in his chair. "I could sure nose around here, check arrest records, voting lists, run her name through DMV, see if there're any other, I mean, any relatives at all in town. Just do a general background check to be sure what she's claiming is true."

"Oh, it be true," Lillian said, looking directly at Wesley Lloyd's spitting image. " 'Less Mr. Springer had a brother don't nobody know about."

"Lillian, please," I moaned. Then with a sudden thought, the answer came to me. "That's it!" I said. "We'll say this child is Mr. Springer's nephew! We'll say he's his brother's, or his sister's, son, come to visit me. That'll do it, and it'd explain the resemblance, too." I laughed at the simplicity of it.

"Uh-uh." Lillian pursed her mouth, shaking her head. "That ain't gon' work. Ever'body knowed the Springer fam'ly ever since before Mr. Springer's gran'daddy give the land for that church 'cross the street. Mr. Springer growed up in this town and never left it 'cept for the time he went to that Davisum Collidge. Nobody'd believe he had a brother nor a sister, 'less they figure it was his daddy what had hisself a yard chile."

I hung my head and moaned again, knowing she was right. Wesley Lloyd had no cousins, either. He'd been a loner since the day he was born, and in this town that kept up with kinships going back a hundred years or more, the old men in the barbershop and on the bank corner would be telling and retelling any attempt to make a lie jump a generation.

"I don't want this whole town whispering about me, making things even worse than they are," I started, as humiliation bowed my head again. "Right now, I don't much care what they say about Mr. Springer, but anything they say about him makes me a laughingstock. I won't be able to hold my head up in this town again."

I felt my throat close up as tears blurred my eyes. I pulled a handkerchief from my pocket and covered my face, trying to get myself back under control. Every time I closed my eyes, that child's image flickered in my mind. And when I opened them, there he was in the flesh staring at me out of those fishbowl glasses. Breathing through his mouth, too. What had I done to deserve this?

"Miss Julia," Deputy Bates said, "it won't be that bad. Seems to me you're to be commended if you decide to keep this little boy until we find his mother. Besides, you haven't done anything to be ashamed of."

He was trying to be kind, so I managed a quavery smile at his innocence. "That's not the way it works, Deputy Bates," I said. "Don't you know it's always the wife's fault if a man strays? Or drinks too much? Or gambles? Or goes bankrupt? There's always something the wife's doing, or not doing, that pushes a man over the brink. That's just the way it is."

"Oh, surely not."

"It's the truth, and not much to be done about it, either. Especially now that Pastor Ledbetter is doing a series on how the welfare of the family hinges on the wife and mother." I took in a deep breath and occupied my hands with folding my handkerchief in pleats. "So. I might as well get used to the fact that all the telephone lines will be buzzing with gossip and rumors. Everybody'll be dredging up anything they can think of to excuse Wesley Lloyd and blame me."

"Womens be the worst when it comes to 'scusin' a man," Lillian said.

"That's right," I agreed, "and it's because they think if they're good enough, their husbands won't do anything wrong. As if that had anything to do with it. They can't admit that a man'll do whatever he wants, regardless of what kind of wife he has." I sniffed and dabbed at my eyes, the injustice of it all cutting to the quick. That child's watery eyes, so like Wesley Lloyd's, watched every move I made. Warily, as befitted his situation, I thought.

I made one last swipe at my eyes and squared my shoulders, self-pity giving way to a flood of anger. "And I'm living proof of it, because none of this is my fault! I haven't done one blessed thing wrong, because I did everything, I mean everything, just the way Wesley Lloyd wanted me to. Why, I didn't walk out of this house without his approval. I didn't express an opinion or even ask a question without looking to him first. The Bible says, 'Wives, submit yourselves unto your husbands,' and that's what I did, and this is the thanks I get for it! This whole mess is his fault, and he's the one who ought to suffer for it."

I could feel strength and determination coursing through me as I spoke. My back got straighter and I didn't feel like crying anymore. Lillian was squinting at me as the spoon she was holding dripped creamed corn on the floor. Little Lloyd stared at me, his mouth gaping open, and Deputy Bates smiled a little uncertainly.

"I know what I'm going to do," I said.

"Uh-oh," Lillian said.

"I can't wait to hear it," Deputy Bates said.

Little Lloyd sniffed and wiped his nose with his napkin.

"Lillian, get this child a Kleenex," I said.

"Here's what I'm going to do," I went on, feeling my way as I talked. "The first thing I'm *not* going to do is call any of those child welfare agencies. Keeping this child is my cross to bear, even though I don't deserve it, and it's the only way to get back at Wesley Lloyd. He hid this child for a decade, but I'm not hiding him. And I'm not going to hide my face, either. None of this is my fault, so why should I act like it is? There's not a reason in the world. They're going to talk no matter what I do, so I'm going to give them something to talk about. I'm going to hold my head up if it kills me, and I'm not going to protect Wesley Lloyd Springer from the consequences. This is his son, and everybody's going to know it, without any guessing. I'm going to flaunt this child before the whole town, so let the cookies crumble!"

"Uh, Miss Julia," Deputy Bates said, "how's that going to affect Mr. Springer?"

"Why, Deputy Bates, don't you believe in eternal life? You must not be a Presbyterian, because we believe the dead live on in one place or the other. And, believe me, Wesley Lloyd Springer's suffering now wherever he is. Nothing was more important to him than his good name, and I've lived my whole life trying to come up to his high standards. Well, I'm through doing that. I'm taking this child with me everywhere I go, and I'm going to make sure they know who his father was. Let them make what they will of it!"

"You thinkin' that's a good idea?" Lillian asked with more than her usual skepticism.

"You might ought to consider how that'll affect this little boy," Deputy Bates suggested. "I don't mean to tell you what to do, but it might be pretty hard on him." He shrugged. "Just something to think about."

The child's head had been swiveling from one to the other of us as we talked, and I wondered how much he knew or understood about his precarious situation. Not much, I decided, as I noted the dazed or addled or, have mercy, half-witted expression on his face.

I looked at him long and hard, taking in the streaked and splotched face, the crooked bow tie and glasses, the scrawniness of him, and felt my stomach churn.

"I've thought about it," I said. "And he has some choices. He can stand up for himself and face them down alongside of me. Or he can hide in a closet until his mother comes back. Or maybe he'd prefer to be turned over to the sheriff and social services." I leaned across the table to catch the child's eye. "You don't want to go to an orphanage, do you, boy? Answer me that."

"No'm." His shoulders shook with the effort to keep from crying.

"See there, he knows what's good for him," I said, feeling a sense of triumph now that I'd decided on a course of action.

"Miss Julia, quit scarin' that chile," Lillian rebuked me. "Eat yo' cake, honey, an' don't pay her no mind."

"And you quit undermining me," I told her. "Here's what we're going to do. Deputy Bates, you find out everything you can about this boy and his mother, but keep it quiet or some do-gooder official'll be on my doorstep wanting to take over. Lillian'll be helping me here with the child, and Little Lloyd!" He jumped as I turned to him. "You are Mr. Springer's only surviving child—Lord, I hope—and you're proud of who you are. You understand that?"

He nodded his head miserably, but I didn't have time for pity.

"I hope you know what you doin', 'cause you makin' trouble for yo'self and ever'body else, now," Lillian accused. "Mr. Springer didn't have no legal chil'ren, an' you might be makin' a bigger mess than you already got."

"He didn't have two legal wives, either," I snapped back. "But I'm stuck with what he did have, and I have to make what I can of it. This child is Mr. Springer's son, and sooner or later, credit will come to me for going above and beyond my Christian duty, and a few extra stars in my crown wouldn't surprise me, either!"

"Well, maybe," Lillian allowed, wiping her hands on a dish towel and trying not to roll her eyes. She knows how I feel about that.

"You're a pistol, Miss Julia," Deputy Bates said with a wide grin. "I thought Atlanta was hairy, but this'll be something to see."

Chapter 4

I'd about paced a rut in my hardwood floors before I was able to reach Sam that afternoon. I knew where he was, of course, but that didn't make the wait any easier. Sam had retired not long after Wesley Lloyd passed, right when I needed him the most, *to fish!* for the Lord's sake. He'd turned my routine affairs over to Binkie Enloe, so now I had two lawyers, one a young woman whose ability I'd doubted at first and the other that old man who'd rather fish than eat.

"One more call," I said to myself, "and if he's still not home, I'm going over there and sit on his porch till he gets there."

I looked out the window and saw Deputy Bates with the boy out in the backyard. He was supposed to be conducting an investigation, questioning the child and trying to get some details as to the Puckett woman's plans. Looked more like they were playing, though, than treating the situation with the seriousness it warranted.

As I stood there watching that unlovely child—I declare, only a mother could love him and, Lord, even she had taken off—I felt a twinge of pity for him before I could stop myself. It got even worse when I saw the child bend over in a fit of crying. Deputy Bates pulled him close and let him cry on his shoulder. I gripped the side of the sink and bowed my head, overcome with too many feelings that didn't make sense. Of course, I am tenderhearted when it comes to children.

Even though I intended to parade that child before the town, I was glad for the hemlock hedge around the yard that hid him from curious eyes. I knew I had to get myself together before going public with the pretense that he hadn't been the shock of my life. I looked out the window again and saw him take off those cockeyed glasses and wipe his eyes with the handkerchief Deputy Bates gave him. The child needed distraction and entertainment or he'd be dripping tears all over Main Street and everywhere else. There wasn't one thing around my house to play with, though, since Wesley Lloyd and I had never been blessed. Well, obviously, Wesley Lloyd had been. I'd just have to write some checks for swings and play toys so everybody would know how happy I was to have the little visitor.

I turned loose of the sink, sighing, and dialed the phone again.

"Sam!" I said when he finally answered. "Get yourself over here. I need to talk to you."

"Nice to hear from you, Julia," Sam Murdoch said in that smiling way of his that I didn't appreciate much at any time, and certainly not at this one. He'd gotten worse about it since Wesley Lloyd had passed. "What's got you so stirred up?"

"I'll tell you when you get here, so put up that fishing rod or whatever you're piddling with, and get over here. I've got more trouble than I can handle."

"Then it must be a doozy. I'm on my way."

I sat down on my Duncan Phyfe sofa in the living room to wait for Sam, who in spite of laughing at me half the time was a man I trusted. I used to think he'd been Wesley Lloyd's closest friend, but I was beginning to think that my husband hadn't had any close friends. Wesley Lloyd had played everything close to his chest, an admirable quality in a sharp businessman but likely to cause unexpected heart attacks, as he'd found out to his sorrow.

I'd known Sam Murdoch ever since I'd come to Abbotsville as a bride, and considered him and Mildred my friends. They used to come by on Sunday afternoons and we'd go for a drive together, Sam and Wesley Lloyd in the front seat, and Mildred and me in the back. That was before Mildred went to her reward some years back. The men had talked business and church—they were both elders—and we'd talked housekeeping and church, with a little whispered gossip to spice things up. Wesley Lloyd didn't approve of gossip.

Sam always ended the drive with a stop at the Dairy Queen for a chocolate-dipped vanilla soft cone. We all got one, except Wesley Lloyd, who had his in a cup with a spoon. Didn't want to drip on his three-piece suit. He was careful in everything he did, and at the time I took quiet pride in all his neat peculiarities. Like, for instance, he always stirred his iced tea seventeen exact times—I counted—each time with seventeen little tinks on the bottom of the glass.

The thing you had to know about Sam Murdoch, though, was not to trust his rumpled appearance and slow-moving ways. There were stories about him around town, like how he'd tell other attorneys from over in Charlotte or Raleigh, "I'm just a country lawyer up here in a country town," he'd say. And they'd come to Abbotsville for a court case, all patronizing and sure of themselves, until Sam took them on in open court. They'd leave town not knowing what hit them.

When Sam showed up at my door, his sweat-stained panama in his hands, I knew he'd walked the four blocks from his house. And in August heat, too.

"Get in here and cool off, Sam," I said, opening the screen for him. "I declare, it's foolish to be walking in this heat. It must be ninety degrees out there."

"Pretty warm, Julia," he said, coming into the living room. "Reckon Lillian's got any ice tea around?"

"Yes, and chocolate cake, too, which I don't suppose you'd refuse. Come on back to the kitchen; I want you to see something out there, anyway."

He followed me down the hall and out into the kitchen, settling himself at the table where Lillian and I'd had many a cup of coffee together. It struck me how natural it seemed to ask Sam back there, when it had never occurred to me to sit at that table with Wesley Lloyd. Wesley Lloyd had not been a kitchen kind of man. He'd had his meals in the dining room—"A place for everything, Julia," he used to tell me, "and everything in its place."

Since Lillian was nowhere around, I glanced out the window and saw her outside with Deputy Bates and that child. So I got Sam his iced tea and a slice of cake. Then I sat down across from him and told him about the heavy burden that had been laid upon me that morning.

He ate and nodded, frowned a few times, and then said, "I'm sorry you had to find out this way, Julia."

That took the wind out of my sails. Any lingering hope that Wesley Lloyd's nefarious activities weren't widely known went with that wind.

"Why didn't you tell me?" I said, wavering between screaming my head off and crying myself sick.

"That's not exactly the kind of story to take to a wife," he said. The pity I heard in his voice nearly broke me in two. "And besides," he went on, "I didn't know it for a fact; I just strongly suspected it. Nobody with any sense would come to you with a story based on rumor."

"There're a lot of people in this town without much sense," I said. "That's why I'm surprised no one told me, or even hinted at it."

"People're afraid of you, Julia," he said, his eyes beginning to smile again.

"Afraid, my foot. How can anybody be afraid of me?"

"You're a woman with a strong sense of right and wrong, and you don't mind telling the difference to anybody who'll listen."

"It's all a sham," I whispered, digging out my damp handkerchief. "All I've ever done was parrot Wesley Lloyd. I've never had a thought or opinion of my own, I realize that now. Maybe if I'd had enough sense to think for myself, I'd have found out about him long before this.

"I need to know something, Sam. Why in the world didn't he provide for that woman and her child in some way before he passed? Didn't he care about them? How did he think she was going to get along, raising the child by herself? It's just not like him to be unprepared for a contingency."

"I tried, Julia," he said. "I kept after him for years to get his affairs in order. I don't mean specifically for the woman, although like most everybody I'd heard the stories. But all he had was that standard will that you and he made out, what, twenty years or so ago. Remember that? He came in wanting a will for himself and one for you, each leaving the other everything. Just your basic kind of will until, he told me, he could plan one out in detail."

I could feel my face turning white and my eyes getting bigger. "Do I remember it? Like it was yesterday! That was right after Papa died and left me twenty-five thousand dollars, my share from the sale of the home place. Sam," I said, as a hot pain shot through me, "those wills were for his benefit! He wanted to make sure he got everything I had if I went before he did. That's the truth, isn't it? He didn't count on dying first, did he? And, Lord help me, I didn't think twice about signing whatever he put in front of me." The pain in my chest stopped the flow of angry words. I closed my eyes and took a deep breath. "I know he didn't intend for it all to come to me. He never trusted me with anything financial, so I don't understand why he didn't change his will later on."

"I don't understand it either, Julia. When I stopped practicing law, that was one of the things I told Binkie to get on to. See if she'd have more luck in getting old W.L. to update his will."

"W.L.," I said with a rueful smile. "He never did appreciate you calling him that."

"Too uptight for his own good. You know, it's crossed my mind that one reason he kept putting off making another will was that he'd have to admit to this woman. Maybe he couldn't bring himself to tell me why he would include her and the child. That's why I thought Binkie might be able to do it."

"Binkie'd never have had a chance with Wesley Lloyd," I said, waving that consideration away. "He wouldn't've confided in anybody who, in his opinion, was untried, much less a woman, no matter how capable. But, Sam, he wouldn't have had to admit to anything if he'd made some provision for them outside of a will. You know, bought her a house and set up some kind of fund for the child. Why couldn't he have done that?"

"Julia," Sam sighed, "I hate to speak ill of the dead, but here's my opinion. I think W.L. just couldn't turn it loose. He had to control it all, and that's a failing of a lot of successful men. But," he went on, "tell me this. Why're you so worried about them? You aren't feeling guilty about it all coming to you, are you? Or feeling sorry for that litte boy out there?"

"Neither one!" I said, pushing back my chair and getting to my feet. "The idea! I'm not feeling guilty about the one nor sorry for the other. No, I'm just mad as thunder, because if he'd provided for them outside of the will, I'd never have known about them. Since I never knew how much he had in the first place, I wouldn't've missed what he did for them. I tell you, Sam, if he had to get involved with that woman, it seems the least he could've done was to've kept them out of my life. Now here I am stuck with that illegitimate, illegal, and . . . and unwanted child out there!"

I paced back and forth, wringing my handkerchief until I calmed myself enough to sit back down. Sam put his hand over mine, but I was too exercised to be so easily comforted.

"And here's another thing, Sam," I said, intent on learning as much as I could about the man I'd spent forty-some-odd years with. "Do you know anything about him planning to leave anything to the church?"

Sam put both hands on the edge of the table and leaned back in his chair, tipping it off the floor. He smiled and shook his head. "Not from him. Never a word of any intention like that. But I heard plenty about it while I was on the session. Seems W.L. hinted around about it to Larry Ledbetter, and Ledbetter took it to heart. He's been planning how to spend that windfall for years and, since W.L.'s death, the whole session's been discussing new building plans. That's one reason I resigned."

"You what?" I couldn't believe I'd heard right. "You can't resign from the session! You were elected, Sam. How could you resign?"

"Easy," he said. "I just did it. I thought things would change when the church began to rotate elders, but they haven't. Bunch of old coots on there now who haven't had an idea of their own since nineteen-fifty. I got tired of fightin' 'em."

"Well," I said, not quite able to take it in. I'd never heard of anybody resigning from the session except for a terminal disease or a move out of town. "Well," I said again, "I guess I shouldn't be surprised at anything you do, Sam Murdoch."

I got up and walked to the window, maybe hoping my problem out there had disappeared. But there he was, sitting on a garden bench with his head down and that grocery sack hugged to his chest. Deputy Bates was leaning over, his elbows on his knees, talking to him. I watched as the boy shook his head, then a bit later nodded at something Deputy Bates said. The child hadn't been raised right, which didn't come as any surprise.

"What am I going to do, Sam?" I turned away from the window as I realized how much I wanted Sam to approve any course of action I took.

"I take it you're planning to keep the boy?"

"I don't have much choice, though Deputy Bates is going to do everything he can to find that woman." I fumbled for my handkerchief as the injustice of it all flew through me again. "I ought to sue her! And I just may do it, if he ever finds her."

"Careful with that kind of talk, Julia," Sam said, very carefully himself. "The last session meeting I attended, there was some discussion of suing you."

"Me! What on earth for?"

"Money. Some on the session, a good many, in fact, think there's a better than even chance of laying claim to some of W.L.'s estate, based on what Larry Ledbetter calls verbal commitments to him. He seems to think that a promise made to a member of the clergy ought to carry more weight than a twenty-year-old will." Sam paused, studied his empty plate, then looked me straight in the eye. "I'll tell you this, Julia, when a preacher and his session decide the Lord needs a new building, there's very little that can stop them. Except how to pay for it, and that's where they figure you come in. So I want you to watch yourself. Don't imply anything, don't promise anything, and, above all, don't sign anything."

Well, that really took my breath away, but at the same time a reassuring thought entered my mind. "That's why you resigned, Sam, isn't it?"

"Since I'm the executor of the will, I couldn't very well be party to an effort to have it set aside. I won't deny that money's important, but the idea of a church suing one of its own members to get it is more than I can stomach. Especially if that member is a helpless widow woman." He grinned until I had to smile back.

"Huh," I snorted, "I'll show them a helpless widow woman, and I'll show them a few Scripture verses, too. 'Ye shall not afflict any widow or fatherless child,' Exodus twenty-two, twenty-two, and that's just one. So with you and Binkie Enloe on my side, to say nothing of the Lord, I'm surprised they'd even consider such a thing."

"Oh, they'll try to get some big firm out of Raleigh or Atlanta, but they won't have any luck. The only way they could overturn that will is to come up with a later one."

"They're a bunch of fools," I pronounced, "and I can't worry about them now. I've got too much else on my mind."

"I know you have, Julia, and I'm sorry for it. I don't want to add to your worries, but it does surprise me a little that this Puckett woman hasn't thought of suing. She'd have a better chance than the church at a share of the estate. If she can document what she claims."

"She told me she'd talked to Binkie, so maybe she has thought of it."

"Well, you'd better talk to Binkie, too, and let her know what's going on. For all we know, she's not left town to study nails but to consult an attorney. Leaving the boy with you might be her way of getting on your soft side, make you recognize him or feel sorry for him. In case the suit doesn't turn out so well for her."

"That's the most foolish thing I ever heard," I said. "How in the world could anybody think I'd give a flip for a child like that? That's beyond my comprehension. No. No danger of that, but, Sam, this whole situation's a pure tribulation to me. Tell me what I ought to do."

"Seems to me you've already thought it out pretty well. Let's hope Coleman can find his mother, and she can make better arrangements. If she can't"—he shrugged his shoulders—"well, you're doing the only decent thing you can do. I hate to see any child get put into the system. But, Julia, be careful, people don't like too much flaunting. You may not care what they say about W.L., or you, but they could hurt that little boy out there."

"Just let them try," I said, wringing my handkerchief until it was stretched out on the bias. "If I take that child under my wing, they'll have to deal with me first!"

"Well, I sure wouldn't want to tangle with you," Sam said. Then, rising from his chair, he added, "Unless it was on my terms."

I never spent such a miserable night as I did the first night that child was in my house. I was so edgy and shaky that I couldn't bring myself to do anything for him.

"Lillian," I said, "would you please stay a little longer and get that child to bed for me? I just don't think I can touch him or anything that belongs to him."

"You better get over that," she told me. "If you gonna do like you said and put on a good show, you got to make out like you glad to have him. And that means takin' care of that baby."

"I know it. I know it. You don't have to tell me. I declare, my mind is so jumbled, all I can think of is how bad that child needs a haircut. Now, with all I have to worry about, you'd think something besides a shaggy head of hair would be weighing on my mind." Appearances are important, I've always thought, but to tell the truth, it was *my* appearance with that child in tow that was bothering me.

"Huh," she said, heading back to the kitchen, where the boy was waiting. "Jus' get him one, and that be it. Another worry'll pop up to take its place."

There were plenty of worries waiting in line, I thought, as I heard the two of them go up the stairs. Lillian put fresh sheets on the bed in the room across the hall from mine, tucked the child in along with his paper sack, and, before leaving for her own house, told me to go to bed and quit worrying.

Easy to say, for it was the worst night of my life, and I'm including the night I found Wesley Lloyd draped over his steering wheel, his eyes and mouth wide open as if he'd had the surprise of his life.

I'd been sleeping the sleep of the just when I heard his car pull in the driveway about midnight, no different from any other Thursday night for ten years or more. Wesley Lloyd believed in routine, and his never changed from sunup to sundown. Except on Thursdays, when I thought he worked late to prepare for the Friday morning meetings in the boardroom of the Springer Bank and Trust. I'd turned over and waited to hear the car door slam, the jingle of his keys, and his heels clicking on the cement walk. But I'd heard nothing.

After some little while of lying there wondering what was keeping him, I'd put on a robe and gone downstairs to see about him. I tell you, when Wesley Lloyd's routine changed, it had to be for a good reason. And it was, because he was dead as a doornail. Right in our driveway. In his new Buick Park Avenue. Steel gray with . . . but I've already told that.

It was awful and I never wanted to go through another experience like it. I didn't intend to, either, since I didn't plan to marry or bury another husband. Well, the burying part hadn't been so hard, what with the way this town and my church comfort the bereaved. They came with piles of food and flowers and donations to my favorite charity, and somebody sat with me every minute of the day ready to fulfill my every wish. I felt like the star of Wesley Lloyd's funeral. Queen for a day or two, until they figured it was time for me to manage on my own. And I'd done that with Lillian's help, and Binkie's. Sam's, too. In fact, it'd been so easy that I didn't know why in the world a widow woman would ever remarry. You might find out what kind of man you were yoked to after it was too late to do anything about it, like I had.

Not that I'd've known what to do if I'd known what Wesley Lloyd was up to before he passed on. But all through that long night as I stared in the dark on my lonely bed, thinking about that child across the hall, I kept telling myself I'd have done *something*.

But you have to know about something before you can do anything about it. And I didn't know a blessed thing until the results of it showed up on my doorstep. Blindest woman in North Carolina. Believed everything anybody'd ever told me, especially if it was a man doing the telling. That's the way I was raised, Southern and Presbyterian. But no, I take that back. I only believed it was gospel truth if it came from Larry T. Ledbetter, my preacher, or Sam Murdoch, my lawyer, or Wesley Lloyd Springer, the man I'd been married to for forty-four years.

I'd been proud of that. Proud that I was married to a man of means and position, one of the few men left in the state who owned his own bank, and solid as a rock, too. Both him and the bank. People trusted him with their money and, I gave him credit, their money was always safe in the Springer Bank and Trust.

We had a good marriage. I thought. He'd found me at my papa's home down in South Carolina, when he was looking at some new ways of running the bank his daddy had left him. Wesley Lloyd was a progressive thinker even then. He was a churchgoer, too, and that's where I met him—after Sunday services at my home church. He was always in church whenever Sunday rolled around, didn't matter where he was or what he was doing. "Sunday's the Lord's day, Julia," he told me. "And the Lord's house is where we ought to be on it." So there he was, shaking hands with the preacher, and then with me, as soon as the benediction and the seven-fold amen was over that Sunday so many years ago.

I was the oldest girl in the family, the last one left. My two sisters had already married, and everybody figured I'd be a spinster the rest of my life. Twenty-three years old, unmarried, and no prospects. Sounds pitiful today, doesn't it? Why in the world I didn't think of going out on my own and making a life for myself, I don't know. But that was another small town, choked to the gills with the traditions of the past. I'd gone a while to the teacher's college at Winthrop, but when Papa needed help at home, guess who was picked? When Papa said, "Jump," I was always the first one in the air. I knew he'd have preferred one of my sisters—have you ever noticed how the one who wants to please never does?—but he was stuck with me. Until Wesley Lloyd Springer showed up.

Sounds like a love story, doesn't it? Well, it wasn't much of one, but I was grateful for it. Wesley Lloyd never was one for romance and sentiment and all the things you read about. He was a businessman, knew what he wanted and how to get it. That's the way he proposed to me. Everybody thought it was a whirlwind romance because it all came about so fast. But Wesley Lloyd, being some years older than me, always had his head on his shoulders.

"I need a wife of a certain character and background," he'd said to me. We were sitting in the front parlor of Papa's house, and I was studying the half-carat solitaire in its blue velvet box that he'd handed to me. "I have a position to maintain," he went on as he pulled his gold watch from his vest and glanced at it. That was a habit that never left him. Time is money, he always said. "And I need a wife who'll keep my house and be a helpmate in my town. I'm not what some would call wealthy, but you'll never want for anything."

I took the ring out of the box and turned it round and round. Then I tried it on, and the fact that it fit seemed a sign to me. I was always on the lookout for signs so I'd know the right things to do. I accepted Wesley Lloyd's proposal without any of the bells and music I'd heard at the picture show on Saturday afternoons. And I didn't miss it. My sisters had married with stars in their eyes, and after only a few years their eyes had dimmed with the despair of niggling over every penny. I prided myself on making my choice based on sensible grounds and figured, on the basis of our mutual levelheadedness, that Wesley Lloyd and I made a good match. I wanted my own household with a man who could afford it, and I got exactly that.

He brought me to this house forty-four years ago, and I guess I'll live here till I die. But I'll be blamed if I'll die hanging over the steering wheel of a Buick Park Avenue. The house was new then. Brick, two stories with a front veranda that provided an unhampered view of all the comings and goings at the First Presbyterian Church. Only a couple of blocks from Main Street, so I've been situated in the middle of everything. Wesley Lloyd said he built the house for his bride, and I remember being so pleased and proud. It took a while for me to realize he'd built it before he ever met me. But that was Wesley Lloyd for you, always thinking ahead, always prepared. I thought.

I fit into this town like I'd been born to it. Wesley Lloyd Springer's wife had a built-in place, and I slid into it like butter on a biscuit. I learned right quick that everybody in Abbotsville had the same respect and high esteem for Wesley Lloyd that I had. It didn't matter that other men towered over him or that they had deeper voices and stronger muscles. When Wesley Lloyd studied a loan application, there wasn't a bigger man in town. People listened to him and heeded his advice, and not just in his office at the bank. Town commissioners consulted him, lawyers telephoned him, businessmen pleaded with him, and the First Presbyterian Church of Abbotsville didn't spend a penny without his approval. He was a leader of men, and everybody knew it.

And, oh, I'd been so proud of who I was. Julia DeWitt Springer. Wesley Lloyd Springer's wife.

Dumbest woman in town.

Chapter 6

It's a wonder I slept a wink that night. How could I with my husband's bastard child in my guest room right across the hall? I'd never been so torn up in my life. The idea of Wesley Lloyd betraying me, breaking his vows, living a life of hypocrisy, fornicating not once but, I now realized, every Thursday night for years upon years.

And who knew if the Puckett woman was the first, or even the only, one? My whole life, everything I'd relied on and believed in, was like dust under my feet. I told myself that there was not one thing I could do about the past, that I had to clear the fog I'd been living in and face everything clear-eyed and levelheaded. I had to call a spade a spade and let the chips fall.

When daylight finally came, I got out of bed with my mind made up and my resolve thoroughly firmed.

There was one thing I could and would do—flatly refuse to sugar-coat or whitewash what that man had done to me. Wesley Lloyd had been a hypocrite of the first order, but there was no reason for me to be. A whited sepulchre was what he'd been, clean on the outside but rotten to the core. Oh, I was mad at him, mad at what he'd done to me and mad that he didn't have to live with the disgrace. During that long night, I had come to an understanding of how easy it would be to wring a husband's neck.

Now if you think those boiling feelings came from love and jealousy, you'd be wrong. I always thought I loved Wesley Lloyd; after all, I was married to him, wasn't I? But I didn't give a lick about that. I raged at him, not out of love or because of his betrayal of the marriage bed, but because he'd demanded such a high level of conduct from me, lecturing, criticizing, and quoting Scripture at me, and all the while he was jumping weekly into another woman's bed.

Don't get me wrong; there was no other bed I wanted to jump into, Lord, no. Too old for it, for one thing. But it was the *principle* of the thing.

I moved from ranting and raving at him to cringing in humiliation at what the town was going to do with this juicy item. It was going to take everything I had to hold my head up and ignore their smirking faces. I just wished Wesley Lloyd could be there to see how strong I was going to be. I'd show him a thing or two about strength of character. After all, I was already doing things he'd never credited me with the ability to do. Like keeping records. And writing checks. And balancing my checkbook.

Binkie Enloe, at that first meeting I'd had with her, could hardly believe how Wesley Lloyd had protected me from the harsh realities. I was sitting there in her law office in my gray crepe, my Red Cross shoes, white because Labor Day was still a while away, clutching my pocketbook in my lap while Binkie explained the facts of finance to me. She'd looked at me over the gold-rimmed glasses she used only for close work and said, "Miss Julia, I didn't know there was a woman in the world who didn't know how to write a check." "Yes," I'd said with a prideful smile, "Mr. Springer always took good care of me." Binkie blew out a breath, then commenced to show me how to write checks and keep records, and it was ever so easy. I don't know why Wesley Lloyd thought I didn't have a head for figures.

———

By six-thirty that morning I was dressed and ready to march downtown to Binkie's office. It was going to be a long wait until eight when she was usually behind her desk. I started downstairs and found the boy sitting on the stairs, dressed in the same chintzy clothes he'd had on the day before, including the clip-on bow tie. I hadn't heard a peep out of him all through that long night, now here he was, up and dressed, with his suitcase and Winn-Dixie grocery sack beside him.

I stood two steps above him and looked him over as he hunched against the wall. He slid the grocery sack closer to clear the stair, and glanced quickly up at me. The sack looked flat and half empty, rolled down the way he had it, but he seemed to like having it close by. I'd heard about little boys' treasures, so I didn't want to think what might be in it.

"Up pretty early, aren't you?" I asked. What do you say to a nine-year-old first thing in the morning?

"Is my mama coming back today?" he asked.

I took a deep breath, not knowing exactly how to answer him. But the truth is always the best. "Not likely," I said. "Now come on to the kitchen. Lillian'll be here soon and we'll have breakfast. Leave your things here."

He followed me down the stairs and into the kitchen, scrunching his shoulders so that he reminded me of a little old man. He looked like Wesley Lloyd, but he didn't act like him. Wesley Lloyd had not been a tall man, but he stood as straight as a poker and walked with purpose, shoulders back and heels clicking.

I pointed Little Lloyd to a chair while I started the coffee. The day looked to be a fine one, sun shining, birds singing in the backyard, impatiens heavy-headed with a sprinkling of dew. The world was going on as if the earth hadn't shifted under my feet since I'd stood at that same window yesterday morning.

I poured two cups of coffee and set one before the boy. He looked quickly up at me and then down again. Lillian needed to get out the Windex and clean those glasses. I shoved the cream and sugar beside his cup and said, "Fix it the way you like it."

He poured cream to the top of the cup and stirred in two spoonfuls of sugar. Leaning over, he tasted the coffee with the cup still in the saucer, screwed up his face, and put in two more spoonfuls. Not much of a coffee drinker, I thought as I sat down across from him and occupied myself with my own cup.

I couldn't look at him except out of the corner of my eye and then I realized he was watching me the same way. We had little to say to each other, and I wished I'd turned the radio on while I'd been up. I racked my brain to come up with something to talk about, believing that ease of conversation is the mark of a cultured person.

I put down my cup and said, "Have you had a movement since you've been here?"

Coffee sloshed over into his saucer. "Ma'am?"

"Your bowels. Have they moved yet?"

His eyes veered wildly behind his glasses as he looked from one side of the kitchen to another. "Yessum. A little."

"Well, you need to have a good one today. I've always found that you can handle problems better if you have regular movements on a daily basis. I have some Ex-Lax if you need it."

"No'm, I don't need it."

He kept his head down over his coffee, and that was the end of the conversation. I gave up trying to draw him out. A little later he ventured to ask where Deputy Bates was. I told him Deputy Bates worked nights and would be home in a little while to go to bed, so we couldn't be running and jumping and making a lot of noise. That seemed to satisfy him, but it was a relief when Lillian came in the back door. She put the *Abbotsville Press* on the table, then looked sternly at me.

"You givin' that chile coffee?"

"And why not? He could use a little perking up."

She shook her head, then began pulling out bacon and eggs. The boy turned out to be a picky eater, which I'd noticed the night before at supper. He tried everything without complaining, but it was plain that he didn't have much appetite. I made a mental note to get him a tonic from the drugstore. And a haircut at Buddy's.

At seven-forty-five, I stood before the hall mirror and adjusted my hat. Then, taking my pocketbook, I left the house for Binkie's office. I got to the sidewalk, then turned back. Might as well face the music from the start.

"Little Lloyd!" I called from the front door. "I want you to go with me."

He came, carrying his grocery sack, but he looked more like he was headed for a dentist's office than a lawyer's. Miserable looking, if you want my opinion, but it wasn't my fault.

"You want to leave that sack here?" I asked, thinking he'd look a lot less trashy without it.

"No'm." He clutched it to his chest, so I rolled my eyes and started off again.

"Stay right with me, now," I said. "We've got business downtown."

He walked by my side, but a half step behind, those shoulders hunched over so bad that I was beginning to worry about his posture as a grown man. You can freeze in unattractive ways, you know.

It was too early to meet anybody on the sidewalk, but several people in cars waved to me. I could see them adjust their rearview mirrors to get a better look as they passed.

Binkie took us right in, with hardly any waiting. If you have enough assets, a lawyer will make time for you without fiddling around with appointments and such like. Binkie Enloe kept a severe expression on her face, but it was still mighty young looking, which was no surprise since she *was* young. She made up for it with those glasses that she'd snatch off when she wanted to make a point. She wore dark suits with plain linen blouses, and tried to tame her curly hair with a severe cut. It didn't work. By midday her head would be a tangled mess of curls. I expect that flyaway hair was one reason for her serious demeanor. I've always found that you have to compensate in other ways when your hair won't behave. But Binkie was all business, and I don't know what I would've done without her those past few months. In spite of having felt she didn't know enough to get in out of the rain when Sam first sent me to her.

"You know who this is, don't you?" I asked before I got sat down good. "His mama said she'd talked to you."

"Well, yes, she did," she said, cool as a cucumber. Not much flustered Binkie Enloe. "How did you end up with him?"

When I told her how the Puckett woman just left him and took off, she raised her eyebrows. Totally shocked.

"Well," she commented. "I see. You plan to keep him until she's found?"

"What else can I do?" I demanded. "Don't swing your legs, Little Lloyd." He was sitting in one of Binkie's big chairs, his legs dangling in the air.

"Well, you could—"

"No, I couldn't," I said, interrupting her. "I know you're going to say that I could turn him over to social services, but all that'll do is look like I'm trying to hide from the truth. And the talk will be just that much worse. No, I'm going to face the town with the facts. And if it hurts Mr. Springer's reputation, then so be it.

"Now. Sam Murdoch told me to tell you what's going on, so that's what I'm doing. And I want to know how many people are planning to sue me. This boy's mother? My own church? Who else?"

"Nobody, at this point," she said. "I'm getting inklings about the church, but you don't need to worry about them. Promises and/or intentions don't mean anything. Mr. Springer's will names you as the sole beneficiary, and that's that. The church can't do anything but threaten and gnash its teeth." She smiled a little at the thought. Little Lloyd sniffed wetly from his chair behind me. I reached in my pocketbook and handed him a Kleenex. "As for Ms. Puckett," Binkie went on, "she gave no indication she was thinking along those lines. But I'll have to tell you, Miss Julia, she might have a good case with the proper documentation of her claims."

"My Lord, she's got a birth certificate with Mr. Springer's name on it, big as life! What else does she need?"

"Birth certificate information is usually taken by a nurse from the mother. That information is as good as the mother's word. But if she can show with receipts and so forth that Mr. Springer supported the child as his own, then she's in a pretty strong position."

"But she didn't say a word about laying any claims! In fact, she said she wasn't asking for anything but for me to take care of him until she got some training so she could support him herself. Binkie, I'll tell you this, I don't want to be sued. Mr. Springer, regardless of his *intentions,* left everything to me, and I intend to keep it."

"All right," she said, nodding like she agreed with me, and I knew she did. Fair is fair, after all. "There's not much we can do, unless and until somebody serves you with notice of a suit. Now on to other business while you're here. You've got First Union and Wachovia banks putting out feelers to buy the Springer Bank and Trust. They're interested, but not willing to commit at this point. They're hoping you'll come down on the price, but the Springer Bank is worth every penny we're asking. I'm going to approach one or two others, and see if that won't stir them up a little. I'll make as good a deal as I can for you. You don't want too much cash, for tax reasons, but we'll want a good stock exchange. Does that still suit you?"

"As long as the bank we deal with is in good shape, it does. I don't want a lockbox full of worthless stock if one of them pulls a savings-and-loan stunt."

She smiled that quick smile of hers, and studied her papers. Then she studied Little Lloyd for a minute. Finally she shook her head at this living testimony of a hypocrite. "Keep me informed," she said. "If you hear from Ms. Puckett, I want to know about it."

I thanked her and left, Little Lloyd tagging behind. I got to the door of the reception area, then turned around to Mary Alice McKinnon, behind the desk. Pleasant young woman who always put me right through to Binkie whenever I called.

"Mary Alice," I said, turning the child by his shoulders, "I want you to meet Mr. Springer's son. This is Lloyd Springer. Say hello to Miss McKinnon, Lloyd."

He ducked his head, while Mary Alice gasped and turned red. She managed a word or two of greeting, because she's from a good family, but it was clear she was impressed with my truthfulness.

Out on the sidewalk, I said, "Now, see, that wasn't so hard. Let's go get a fountain Coke at the drugstore."

Chapter 7

When we were through with the pause that refreshes, I marched the child down the block to Buddy's Barber & Expert Depilatory Shop. Buddy Whitesides had two chairs in the front where he and Arlo Turner wielded razors, scissors, and electric clippers. And flung around clouds of talcum powder with their little whisk brooms. In the back, separated by a gray flannel curtain, Alva, Buddy's wife, had a chair where she ministered to those with hair in unsightly places. You couldn't've paid me to go back there.

Both Buddy and Arlo were working on two men I didn't know, farmer types, when we walked in. And sitting in one of the maroon Naugahyde and rusted-chrome chairs was Leonard Conover, of all people, waiting his turn. He looked up from his magazine when the bell over the door tinkled, then he slammed the magazine shut and shoved it under a stack on the table beside him.

"Why, Julia," he said, his face turning an unappetizing red. "I didn't expect to see you here."

"I didn't expect to be here, either. But here I am because this boy needs a haircut. Buddy," I said, turning to the owner, "which one of you does the best haircut for a child?"

"Oh, we're both good," he said, clippers suspended as he looked from me to the boy. "Either one of us will do you a fine job. That a little friend of yours?" He nodded toward the boy.

"You could say that," I said, sitting down by Leonard and motioning Little Lloyd to take a seat, too. "How are you, Leonard? How're things down at the courthouse?"

"Good, good, I stay busy." He kept looking across me to the boy, curious as a cat. I should've said something right then, because if you want something to get around town, just tell it in a beauty or barbershop. But I held my peace for the time being.

"Yes," Leonard went on, his fair complexion gradually returning to its natural state, "besides all I have to do at the courthouse, church business is taking up a lot of my time. Lots of plans. Yes, lots of plans. Takes a lot of work." He nodded his head for emphasis.

"I don't doubt it," I said. Leonard had never been known as a ball of fire even before he became a civil servant. I rested my hands on my pocketbook in my lap and fixed a steady gaze on Buddy so he'd hurry up and get to us.

"You know, Julia," Leonard said, half turning in his chair to get my attention. I noted the fine graying hair that barely covered his scalp, the soft weight of his shoulders, and how he spread out in the chair, and wondered if LuAnne minded. But then, once married, you take whatever the results turn out to be. "I'm not supposed to say anything about this," he told me in a confidential whisper, "because it's just in the planning stage. But the church has grown so much that we've just got to consider a building program. I've been thinking, and it's just my idea, but now, with Wesley Lloyd gone and all, you might be ready to move to a smaller place. You ought to think about donating your house to the church. We could sure use the space, even if it's just for parking."

I turned and looked at him. I clamped my teeth together and said, "You want to tear down my house so you can park cars over there for one hour each week? Leonard Conover, not in a million years."

He raised and lowered a shoulder, then slumped back in his chair. Leonard was used to having his ideas shot down. "It was just a thought for, you know, well, when the house gets to be too much for you."

Arlo was shaving his customer's neck while Buddy snipped around his client's ears, their attention on us more than on their work. It made me cringe to think of a slip. Contrary to what I'd always heard about conversation in a barbershop, there was very little going on in this one. Too busy trying to hear Leonard and me, and trying to figure out what I was doing with a child who looked awfully familiar.

"Don't plan on that happening anytime soon. Buddy," I said, "I don't mean to hurry you, but some people have things to do." He nodded and snipped faster as I added, "We don't all work at the courthouse, you know."

"Now, Julia," Leonard said, heaving himself up in his chair for another approach, "you don't have any idea what I do at the courthouse, and I hope you never have to find out. But you ought to consider that Wesley Lloyd never wanted you to be burdened with responsibility. What he left is too much for one person, 'specially for somebody who's never had experience handling estates and such like. Believe me, I know what I'm talking about. I sure wouldn't want LuAnne to be burdened like you are."

I stared at him. LuAnne was as likely to be burdened with Leonard's estate as she was with the Publishers' Clearing House Sweepstakes grand prize.

"You don't think I'm capable?"

"Well," Leonard said, and exchanged knowing smiles with Buddy and Arlo. Three barbershop tycoons. "You're not getting any younger, Julia."

There was a bulletin for you.

Buddy flipped the cape off his customer and started flicking talcum powder around the poor man's neck.

"Come on, Little Lloyd," I said, taking his hand. "Mr. Buddy will take you next."

I helped Little Lloyd up in the chair and onto the board that Buddy put across the arms to raise him to the right height. "Take your glasses off," I said, and then to Buddy, "I don't want it shaved, buzzed, or styled. I want a decent haircut that gets the hair out of his eyes and off his neck. In fact, you can give him one just like you used to give his daddy."

Recognition of the boy and confirmation of their suspicions froze every man in the place. Arlo's eyes bugged out as his jaw dropped. His customer frowned, trying to make sense of what was going on. Leonard sat in his chair like he was paralyzed with shock. He kept opening and closing his mouth, his lips making a smacking noise each time they met. The voice of some country music singer on the radio yearning for commitment did little to fill the embarrassed silence.

"Well, get on with it," I said to Buddy, who stood with his hands held up in the air like a surgeon.

"Yes, ma'am, okay, we'll give this boy a fine haircut." He jerked around, picked up a comb, dropped it on the floor, fumbled for another one, and gave me a sick grin as he finally got started on the boy's head.

Some people don't know how to act when the truth stares them in the face.

By the time we started home, after meeting any number of people downtown, I was drained to a fare-thee-well. Telling the truth, which I'd forced myself to do after nearly falling down on the job in the barbershop, can really take the starch out of you. Little Lloyd felt the same way, because he scuffed his feet all the way home and I had to speak to him about it.

"Pick up your feet, Little Lloyd," I said as we walked down the sidewalk on our way home. "Here, let me have your hand, and smile so everybody'll see how happy you are."

He gave me his hand and said, "I don't much think I am."

"Well, of course not, what with your mother gone and all. But you have to put up a good front so people won't know your personal business and talk about you. And that reminds me, we should've gotten you something to play with. What do you enjoy doing?"

He thought for a minute, then said, "I like to put puzzles together. And I like to listen to music."

"I used to like puzzles myself. We'll have to get us some and work them together. What kind of music do you like?"

"All kinds, but I like Tim McGraw and Sawyer Brown best. My mama, she likes Dwight Yoakam. She likes to watch his videos."

"Do tell," I murmured, not having an idea in the world of what he was talking about. "Here we are," I said, turning into the front walk. "I declare, we've had a time of it. And the day not half over yet."

———

There was still a long day in front of me, because LuAnne Conover was sitting there ensconced in one of my wine velvet Victorian chairs. She hopped up as soon as we got in the door, flapping and waving her hands with the thrill of it all.

"Julia, oh, Julia," she said, running to my side like I needed help to get in the door. "Oh, I just heard this terrible news; I just can't believe it; tell me it isn't true! Oh, Julia, I just feel for you so much, I don't know how you're bearing up. How are you, anyway?" She was speaking to me, but her eyes, bright with curiosity, were fastened on the boy.

"Sit down, LuAnne," I said, trying to get my hat off my head. "I'm all right, but it looks like you need some help. Didn't Lillian offer you anything?"

"Oh, I couldn't eat a thing. I'm just too upset by all this, and *suffering* with you, Julia. Tell me now," she said, sitting beside me on the sofa and leaning practically in my face, "just what all happened. You wouldn't believe all the stories I've heard this morning!"

"Oh, I probably would," I said, sighing. I knew the town about as well as it could be known, and Mary Alice, along with everybody else we'd met, except maybe Leonard, who'd never been able to put two and two together, would've been on the phone as soon as my back was turned. "By the way, this is the subject of all you've heard." I looked over at Little Lloyd, who was still standing by the door. "Say hello to

Miz Conover, Lloyd, then run on in the kitchen and ask Lillian for your lunch. If you didn't spoil your appetite with that cherry Coke."

He ducked his head and mumbled something at LuAnne before scurrying out of the room. I would've corrected his manners, but LuAnne's were worse. She just stared at him with her mouth open.

"I wouldn't have believed it if I hadn't seen it!" she gasped. "Somebody told me you had that boy, but I told them, 'No, Julia wouldn't do that.' What in the world are you thinking of, Julia? How can you stand to have that child in your house? I tell you, if Leonard pulled a stunt like that, I wouldn't take in his"—she paused, looked around, and whispered—"bastard."

"You do what you have to do, LuAnne," I said, "which is what I'm doing. Now, I want to ask you something. Did you know Wesley Lloyd was keeping that woman?"

"Oh, Julia, everybody knew it. Well, I mean," she corrected herself, "it's been talked about for years. You know how these stories get around."

"Why didn't you tell me?"

"Why, you know, I just didn't believe it." She laughed a little nervous laugh and quickly cut it off when she saw the look I gave her. "And nobody did, believe me, they really didn't. Or maybe they thought you knew and didn't care. Ann Landers says the wife always knows, and everybody should MYOB."

"My Lord," I moaned, holding my head in my hands.

I heard the telephone ring and Lillian's voice as she answered it. I didn't want to talk to anybody, including LuAnne. But on she went.

"Julia, everybody's upset over what you're doing and, I have to tell you, they're wondering if maybe you're not thinking too clearly."

"Oh, I mean," she said as I lifted my head and glared at her, "we all know you've been under a strain, what with Wesley Lloyd's passing and all. It's just been too much for you, and you need to sit back and let your friends take over for you. Leonard was saying just the other day that there are legal remedies."

"Legal remedies? What are you talking about, LuAnne?"

"Why, all your problems, of course. Leonard sees this type of a problem every week or so, and the decisions he has to make just tear him up."

I leaned my head back against the sofa and closed my eyes. "Have mercy," I prayed just loud enough for LuAnne to hear, as well as the One addressed. If I were fool enough to let Leonard Conover make decisions for me, I'd need not only mercy but shock treatments, too.

"Now, Julia," LuAnne went on, "I'm here to do anything I can for you. You just go up and lie down, and I'll answer the door and keep a record for you. People are going to want to come by or call to see how you're doing."

"Nobody's died here, LuAnne! And I don't need to receive people who just want to satisfy their curiosity. I'm too busy to see anybody anyway, so you can run on home and look after Leonard."

"Well," she said, and I could see her feelings were hurt. Too bad, because mine were, too. "I just thought you'd want a friend beside you in your time of trouble."

"My time of trouble was all those years when Wesley Lloyd was gallivanting with that woman. I could've used a friend then, but I didn't have a one in this town."

"I can see you're upset, Julia, and I don't fault you for it." She got up and stood by me, her hand on my shoulder. "I'm praying for you, and so is the whole prayer chain. I started it right before I came over here."

"Thank you," I whispered. What else could I say? The Presbyterian Women's Prayer Chain transmitted news of sickness, accident, death, divorce, pregnancy, teenage problems, bankruptcy, and anything else you could name, and did it faster than a streak of summer lightning. Well, it was no more than I expected, having activated the prayer chain myself any number of times when I'd heard something that needed to be prayed over and passed on.

When LuAnne left, Lillian came into the living room where I still sat trying to collect myself.

"I made you some soup," she said, setting a tray on my lap. "I'm feeding that little boy in the kitchen, then he gon' help me peel apples for a pie. Eat somethin' now. You gon' need it, 'cause that was yo' preacher callin'. He want to know can you walk over to the church. He want to counsel with you."

"I guess I could use some counseling," I said. "Thank you, Lillian. I'll eat this and go on over there."

I'd been a Christian all my life and a Presbyterian for most of it. The way I was raised and who I married hadn't offered much choice in either matter. Not that I'd ever expected or wanted a choice. Still, neither Wesley Lloyd nor I had ever been the type of person who needed counseling. Now I found myself hoping that my preacher could comfort my hurting heart and help me accept the burden laid on me by Wesley Lloyd.

We'd had this preacher four, no, about five years now, and he'd settled in fairly well. Larry Ledbetter was his name; not Lawrence, but Larry. Have you ever noticed how many preachers and evangelists have little-boy names? Just open up the *Abbotsville Press* most any day and you'll find Jimmys and Johnnys, Billy Earls and Ronnies advertising their services at some local church, usually with somebody named Dawn or Tammy or Debbie singing and playing the piano or the saxophone or some such thing. You'd think grown men would put aside childish things, including childish names.

That's why I liked the Presbyterian church; we believed in doing things decently and in order. When you went to church, you knew exactly what you were going to get. We didn't want to be surprised or entertained. And, Lord knows, we didn't want anything changed.

Take that time we had an interim pastor who changed the order of worship so that the offering plates were passed right after the sermon instead of beforehand during the anthem. You'd have thought he'd instituted something indecent. It upset a lot of people who'd been accustomed to digging out a dollar bill or their pledge envelopes as soon as the choir director stood up. I didn't think it was a good idea, either, but not because I was against change. I just thought the pastor was taking a big chance in passing the plates right after he'd finished preaching. I mean, what if he'd had an off day and his sermon hadn't been too good? I wouldn't risk it myself.

Wesley Lloyd spoke to him about it, and pretty soon the order of worship went back to the way we'd always done it.

But as soon as Pastor Ledbetter accepted our call, he saw the lay of the land right away and didn't make a false move. He was a quick study when it came to latching onto the men of power and agreeing with them. Contrary to most of the new breed coming out of our seminaries, he was a dyed-in-the-wool Calvinist, which meant he was as good as Wesley Lloyd at finding Scripture verses to support his opinions. He and Wesley Lloyd saw eye to eye on just about everything, and if they didn't, why, you'd never know it from Pastor Ledbetter. He picked up right away that Wesley Lloyd didn't like confrontations or arguments about the way the church was run.

I'd noticed recently, though, that Pastor Ledbetter had a freer look about him, both as a pastor and as a pulpiteer. More expansive, maybe, in the way he moved and sermonized, the last of which he'd do at the drop of a hat or a greeting on the street. I thought I knew what he was feeling—something close to being loosened from the ties that bound.

After walking across the parking lot, I found it a relief to step inside the air-conditioned church. I went through the fellowship hall and on into the preacher's office suite. Norma Cantrell, Pastor Ledbetter's secretary, always acted like she was doing me a favor whenever I wanted to talk to him. As I walked into her office, she glanced behind me and tried to crane her neck to see out in the hall. She was looking for Little Lloyd, I knew, and I was glad I'd left him at home. She liked to make out like she was so professional, but she was the biggest gossip I knew. That's why she liked her job, since every Presbyterian in trouble sooner or later ended up talking to the preacher. I'd warned Pastor Ledbetter about her talkative tendencies, but he'd just patted my shoulder and told me he'd take care of it. Ever since then she'd flounced herself around anytime I was in her office, not that anybody with all that weight ought to do any flouncing. So I knew the preacher had confided in her, and that's when I stopped confiding in him.

Still, he was my pastor and he'd done a good job burying Wesley Lloyd. The sermon had been all I could ask for, telling all the good deeds Wesley Lloyd had done for the church and the community, and making me feel proud.

But I wasn't feeling proud on this visit, just broken and humble. I longed for some spiritual comfort for the double bereavement that was now my lot.

Norma patted her teased hair with one hand and, with the other, fingered the pearl necklace that was attached to the earpieces of her glasses. "Afternoon, Miss Julia," she said, reaching for a pencil to show me how busy she was. "Are you here to see Pastor Ledbetter? He's pretty busy right now."

"He just called me to come over, Norma, which you know because you probably dialed the phone for him. Tell him I'm here, please."

She aimed a glare at me that was unbecoming in a church setting, lifted the phone receiver, and pushed a button. It wouldn't have taken her two steps to walk to the door of his office, but no, she had to use that push-button phone.

She turned her head away from me and practically whispered, "Mrs. Springer is here. Shall I ask her to wait?"

She must not've gotten the answer she wanted, because she pursed her lips before hanging up. About that time, Pastor Ledbetter opened his door and stood there filling that space and the air around him with his ministerial presence and authority. Charisma, I think it's called, and he'd preached a whole sermon one time on all the meanings of the word. He loved to call on his seminary training to instruct us in the Greek language. He'd made it plain that being charismatic for Christ didn't mean you had to speak in tongues, which is something main-line Presbyterians don't hold with at all.

"Come in, Miss Julia," he said in his hearty voice that aimed to make me feel welcome. "How are you? It's good to see you on a day besides a Sunday."

"I'm over here on Mondays for the Women of the Church meetings and on Wednesday nights for prayer meeting," I reminded him. Did he think I only showed up on Sunday mornings?

"Oh, I know, I know," he said, smiling his wide smile. "Just joshing you, Miss Julia. Have a seat, now. Here, let's sit in these comfortable chairs." He closed the door behind us and indicated the two wing chairs beside a bay window. They were fine chairs, upholstered in cream damask, that were bought instead of a swing set for the children's playground.

I sat down and smoothed out the skirt of my Leslie Fay shirtwaist. I felt edgy, like I always did when a preacher wanted to see me. It was like being called to the principal's office, even though I couldn't think of a thing I'd done wrong. I halfway expected to hear about building plans and my contributions thereto, especially since Leonard Conover had spilled the beans. What I wanted from him was some commiseration and prayer over the intolerable situation Wesley Lloyd had left me in. I was ready for some pity.

"Now, Miss Julia," he said, templing his hands before him and looking into my eyes with deep concern. He crossed his feet at the ankles and leaned toward me. I could feel that charisma I was telling you about, and I thought again of how powerful a pulpiteer he was. Why, he filled out a pastoral robe to an outstanding degree, and made a commanding figure behind a pulpit. He liked to stretch out his arms and grasp each side of the podium as if he had to keep the thing from flying off above the congregation.

"Now, Miss Julia," he said again, sorrow dripping in his words and pulling his mouth down. "What's this I hear about you?"

I was having queasy feelings that felt strangely like guilt, but for the life of me, I couldn't think why.

"Why, I don't know. What have you heard?"

"Ah," he said, searching my face intently. Then he nodded as if he'd confirmed something. "It's hard to remember things, isn't it? But short-term memory loss is a natural result of aging, just the Lord's way of helping us cut our ties to worldly things."

"There is nothing wrong with my memory, short- or long-term. I asked what you'd heard, because rumors fly so thick in this town I didn't know which one you'd come in contact with."

"Just to remind you, then, I'm concerned about this child, the one you've been introducing around as Mr. Springer's son."

"Oh, Pastor," I said, with some relief that he wasn't going to start in about how the Lord needed more parking spaces. "You don't know how I need your prayers, for I've never had such a shock in my life. You can imagine. It's about broken me in two to learn about Mr. Springer's waywardness. I'm trying to do the Christian thing, even though it's the hardest thing I've ever done."

"I understand," he said in a soft, understanding voice. I felt tears spring to my eyes at the compassion I heard. I could put on a steely face for the curious and the ridiculers, but kindness just about crumpled me up.

"Yes," he said, "I can imagine what you're going through. Emotional turmoil plays havoc with our ability to rightly discern a situation. You must be very careful, Miss Julia. Unscrupulous people can take advantage of your trusting nature, as I am led to believe is happening to you right now, and it's confusing your mental processes. For instance, we don't always know what the Lord's will for us is in unusual circumstances. And what we think is the Christian thing to do may not be at all. That's why I wanted to counsel with you."

My eyes dried up and I felt confused. "I don't understand," I said. "I thought I was doing the Lord's will."

"Well, it's a delicate matter, but I'm sure we can straighten this out and you'll be able to handle things a little better after we talk. You see, Miss Julia, Mr. Springer was highly thought of in this town, indeed, in this whole section of the state. To say nothing of our beloved church. I can't tell you the contributions he made to everything he cared about, and it seems to me that we should be careful about anything that would be a blot on his good name."

"I'm not following you," I said, but my insides were beginning to knot up on me.

"I'm saying that your running around town proclaiming that child as Mr. Springer's son is unbecoming to a fine Christian woman like yourself." He leaned so close that I could smell the breath mint and hear it click against his teeth. "It helps nothing," he went on, "to besmirch Mr. Springer's reputation, which you're perilously close to doing. Why, you know that the Springer family donated the very land this church is on and contributed greatly to this sanctuary."

"Yes, I know it." My hands twitched on the arms of the chair, and I clasped them in my lap.

"And there's a Sunday school room named for your husband, and all the hymnals have his name stamped in them because he donated them."

"I know that, too." Wesley Lloyd's rings—the ones he'd put on my finger with an oath of fidelity—were cutting into the palm of my hand.

"But, Miss Julia, you may not know that the session is seriously considering a Family Life Center, a building that would strengthen family ties by providing our members with a place for all kinds of activities. We're thinking of a gymnasium, a video arcade room for young people, a study room, and several other possibilities to make the church the center of our lives," he said, pausing and studying me awhile. He lowered his voice to a confiding whisper, "And our plan is to name it the Wesley Lloyd Springer Activities Center."

I couldn't believe it. Little Lloyd's face with its running nose, smeared glasses, and open mouth blended with Wesley Lloyd's as I pictured an oil portrait hanging in their activities center for all to see. "I don't think Mr. Springer's name should be associated with such a thing," I managed to say, "considering the activities he was engaged in."

"Miss Julia, Miss Julia," he said, chiding me as if I were a child. "See, that's the very thing I'm talking about. You are not grasping the essence of what I'm saying here. And this inability will only get worse as time goes by. You might consider and earnestly pray about granting someone trustworthy your power of attorney so you won't have to struggle with all these complex matters."

"Sam's taking care of all the complex matters."

"I know, but as soon as the estate's settled, everything will revert to you. And frankly, Miss Julia, I don't think you want that burden. And, if I may speak lovingly, I'm not sure you'd be able to handle it."

He had a point. I wasn't sure I'd be able to handle it, either. I couldn't depend on Sam forever, and Binkie was getting so busy she might not want Wesley Lloyd's affairs dumped in her lap. I probably could've worded that better.

"Who would you suggest, Pastor?"

"Not a lawyer," he said, as if he knew my thoughts. "Lawyers can tie you in knots, giving you first one side of a question and then the other, and letting you make the final decision, and charging you for every minute. You need to consider someone who is, first of all, a Christian, and second, someone who is a strong, stable, family man. One who has proven that he's able to care for those under his protection. I would suggest someone in this church who has proven his ability through consistency and diligence. Someone who would be able to see through these devious attempts to gain access to the Springer estate through guile and subterfuge, as is being done even now by way of that child you've so unthinkingly taken in."

"Maybe I'm still not following you," I said. "Are you saying that I ought to deny that child's lineage, when anybody who looks at him can tell who his father was? Are you saying that I ought to lie about it?"

"Oh." He laughed and shook his head at my density. "Not lie, Miss Julia. Just not saying anything is not lying. Mr. Springer did so much good in his life, and will do even more in the future, that I think we can afford to overlook some, ah, human foibles. After all, what is a Christian but one whose sins are forgiven?"

My nerves were about to jump out of my skin by this time. I kept thinking that I wasn't hearing him right, but every time he opened his mouth he said something even more unbelievable. "You want me to deny this child's very existence, is that it?"

"Well, we really don't know for sure whose child he is, do we?" He looked at me for a long minute, frowning with concern. "I'm worried about you, Miss Julia, truly worried. I fear that you haven't thought through all the ramifications. It seems to me that you need responsible, spiritual guidance to prevent, shall we say, a rash action on your part. For instance, have you thought that the child could have a claim on Mr. Springer's estate? And your recognition of him can't do anything but help that claim? Why, it's possible that a good lawyer could take the entire Springer estate away from you and give it to that unknown child. Now what kind of stewardship would that be if you let that happen?"

Now I understood. Anytime a preacher starts talking about stewardship, he's talking about *your* money and *his* plans. Especially his building plans. It's hard to fathom the lengths some of them will go to fill the collection plates. Why, not too long ago I heard about a preacher in Chapel Hill who had an ATM installed in his church. But then, as Wesley Lloyd used to say, that's Chapel Hill for you.

"Let me ask you something, Pastor," I said, steering him back to my concerns. "Did you know about Wesley Lloyd's adultery?"

"Well," he said, smiling, as he sat back in his chair and looked off over my head. "I don't think that's a subject for us to be discussing. I'm sure it makes you uncomfortable, and gossip, which is all it was, is beneath us, don't you think?"

"So you did know."

"Let me counsel with you seriously here, Miss Julia." He leaned forward again, resting his arms on his knees and putting an earnest look on his face. "Some men, certain men, carry a heavy burden in life. They have great and terrible responsibilities. We don't understand this, but in many ways they are held to a different standard than the rest of us. Think of David and his many wives and concubines. He was guilty of adultery and even of murder, yet the Lord delighted in him. You see what I'm saying here? We have to overlook and forgive those men who have more to offer than the average person."

I don't know why I'd never noticed how coarse the skin of his face was or how close together his eyes were. "I do see what you're saying," I said. "You're saying that wealthy men can commit sins that would condemn a poor man. And you're saying that you're afraid that little boy will get the money you want for the church. Do I have it right?"

"No, no," he said, still smiling like he was dealing with a half-wit. "You mustn't see it like that. I'm just trying to protect Mr. Springer's name, and yours. And the church's. Mr. Springer was so closely associated with First Church of Abbotsville that anything that smears him smears us, too. We need to work together here, Miss Julia. I think you'll feel much better when you learn to accept the Lord's will in this matter. Now, why don't we have a prayer together?"

He raised his face toward the ceiling and closed his eyes. When he opened his mouth to call on the Lord, I stood up and walked out.

When I stepped into Norma's office, she quickly stuffed a napkin in her desk drawer and closed it. Krispy Kreme doughnut aroma filled the room.

"Through already?" she chirped. "I thought you'd have a whole lot more to talk about."

"Don't think, Norma," I said as I traversed her office to the outside door. "It doesn't take long to discuss adultery when the pastor's for it."

I glanced back to see her mouth drop open, so I said, "You've got sugar on the front of your blouse," and walked on out.

Chapter 9

I don't know how I managed to walk across the parking lot and then the street and up the steps to my front porch with my limbs trembling like they were. Somewhere in one part of my mind I was aware of the way the hot asphalt sucked at my shoes with each step I took. And I knew I waited on the curb for a UPS truck to pass before crossing the street, but the roaring in my head kept me from concentrating on anything but getting to the wicker rocking chair on the porch.

I sank down in it, thankful for the wisteria vine that covered one end of the porch. Nobody could see me there, and maybe a few minutes of privacy would settle me down.

My preacher! A man of God saying the things he did. And comparing Wesley Lloyd to David, of all people, who, as everybody knows, had dabbled in somebody else's bed, too. But that didn't excuse Wesley Lloyd. And if it did, then everything I'd ever heard from a pulpit, read in the Bible, and believed in all my life meant absolutely nothing.

I curled my hands on the arms of the rocker and pushed off with a foot. I rocked and thought, and rocked and thought some more, taking stock of my situation. It had never entered my mind that my pastor wouldn't support me in this trying situation. How many times had I heard him preach on how hard it is to do the right thing? Doing the right thing, he'd preached many a time, goes against the natural grain of the sinful heart. So I knew that acknowledging the child was the right thing to do because it was the hardest thing to do. And Pastor Ledbetter should've seen that and encouraged me in it.

That's all right, I told myself, rocking faster. I knew that most of the church members would take whatever position Pastor Ledbetter did. A congregation wasn't called a flock for nothing. So I was going to have to gird my loins to walk into that building for the worship service with Little Lloyd. I had a few more days before Sunday, and I determined to prepare myself for it and not shirk my duty to raise up a child in the way he should go, even if I had only a little while to do it in. The church might abandon me, but it was my church and I'd not abandon it. Preachers came and preachers went, but we Presbyterians continued on.

I got up finally and, with knees still atremble, walked back to the kitchen. Lillian took one look at me and reached for the coffeepot.

"That preacher wadn't no help, was he?" she said, pouring two cups and bringing them to the table.

"Not only no help," I said, easing myself into a chair, "he just made things worse." I told her the gist of the conversation in the preacher's office. "And he had the gall to tell me it was the Lord's will to take his advice!"

"Law, law," Lillian commiserated. "Preachers is sometimes the worst ones for knowing the Lord's will. Seems like they's bad about mixing up their ownselves' will with the good Lord's. I seen it many a time. You 'member me tellin' you about that preacher we had at the Shiloh AME Zion Church? The one what got mixed up with the lead singer in the choir? It was a mess 'fore we got rid of both of them, what with the lead singer's husband wantin' to shoot the preacher, and the preacher sayin' he was bein' led by the Lord." She leaned back and laughed. "All us knowed what he was bein' led by, and it sure wadn't the Lord!"

I smiled, wrapping my hands around the coffee cup. "I'm beginning to think that that's what a lot of men are led by," I said, somewhat embarrassed at talking about such earthy matters.

"Where's that child?" I suddenly asked, not yet used to having another person in the house to account for.

"I sent him upstairs to rest awhile," she said. "He kinda droopy, seem like. I hope he's not gettin' sick on us."

"Oh, me," I said, hanging my head at the thought of another complication in my life. "I'll go call the drugstore right now and have them deliver a tonic. I meant to do it before this, and while I'm at it I might as well call the Western Auto and see if they have a swing set they could put up out in the back."

"That boy too big for a swing set," Lillian informed me. "Besides, Deputy Bates say this morning when he come home that he gonna put a tire swing on that big tree out there, if you don't mind."

"Why, no, I guess I don't," I said, though a few days ago the thought of a tacky tire swing in one of my trees would've struck me as the equivalent of a whitewall planted with red salvia in my front yard. "A tire swing would be fine, if he wants to do it. Lillian, I think I'll go up and lie down for a little. This day's worn me out."

I tiptoed up the stairs, not wanting to disturb the rest of Deputy Bates, who'd worked all night. I got to the head of the stairs and noticed that the guest room door was ajar. Without thinking, I pushed it open, not really intending to check on the boy, because I didn't much care if he was resting or not.

His bed was empty, and my first shocked thought was that he'd run off to find his mother. My second thought was that I'd had about as much trouble from that boy as I could tolerate, and to call the sheriff to start a search for him was more than I could face.

I headed toward the back hall to Deputy Bates's room, not at all reluctant now to wake him again. But there, right outside Deputy Bates's door, was Little Lloyd, sound asleep on the floor, his knees curled up around that Winn-Dixie sack. I reached down to wake him but turned around instead and brought a pillow and a summer blanket from his room. I put the pillow under his head and spread the blanket over him, and he hardly stirred. Then I went to my bedroom and closed the door. He could sleep wherever he wanted to. His daddy certainly had.

But I couldn't sleep. I couldn't even rest my eyes. Every time I closed them, I pictured myself walking into church, come Sunday, with that stray child while everybody craned their necks and whispered behind their hands. I knew what they'd be saying. They'd be saying that Julia Springer was finally getting her comeuppance, and they'd be happy about it. I cringed at the thought, even though I hadn't done anything to be ashamed of. The Bible says that children suffer for the sins of their fathers, but it doesn't say a thing about wives suffering for the sins of their husbands, more's the pity. I lay there, getting more and more nervous and edgy. So I got up and went back downstairs.

"I'm going out for a while," I told Lillian. "I just have to get out of this house and do some thinking."

"Well, you be careful," she said. "You ain't that good a driver to be goin' here, there, and everywhere."

That didn't deserve an answer, so it didn't get one. I took my new car out of the garage and just started driving. It was a new experience for me to drive with no destination in mind and no need to be back before Wesley Lloyd got home. So I drove out of town, taking the two-lane roads throughout the county, searching for those with little traffic. I drove slowly, looking at fields and orchards, finding packinghouses and neat farmhouses along the rolling hills. I drove into areas I'd never been in, discovering small communities along the French Broad River and Briar Creek, inching along behind farm trucks and seeing tractors trailing plumes of red dust out in the fields. I circled the county, avoiding the interstate because in my state of mind I might get on it and never come back. Of course, I hadn't done too much driving on the interstate, since whenever we'd gone anywhere, Wesley Lloyd had always taken the wheel. That was his job. Mine was folding maps.

But that's what I felt like doing now, just getting on that fast track and driving and driving until I'd outrun all my troubles.

I'd not been paying much attention to the details around me, just automatically registering the rows of apple trees, loaded with fruit, and the few cars and trucks that passed me. My mind was heavy with grief and busy weighing the options, the possibilities, the "what-ifs" of the unthinkable mess Wesley Lloyd had left me.

I stopped at a crossroads, where Craven Gap Road intersected with Jessup and, since there was no traffic, let the car idle for a few minutes while I decided which way to go. The sun was edging down behind the mountains in the west, turning them purple and lengthening the shadows of the trees along the road, and I began to feel a little anxious about the lonely countryside. I needed to head toward home.

A deep, rumbling noise suddenly filled my little car, scaring and confusing me. All I could think of was a crop-dusting airplane about to land on the road, with me in the way.

I looked from one side to the other, trying to determine where it was coming from. Then I glanced in the rearview mirror and nearly had a heart attack. The chrome grill of a huge truck was right behind me, right on my bumper, towering with growling menace over my little car. I stretched to see better, and could hardly see a thing through its darkened windshield. Two figures, maybe. I couldn't be sure, but since I was blocking the road, I quickly pulled out into the intersection, took a right, and headed toward town. The truck followed, staying a few yards behind, where I was able to get a better look at it. It was black with a row of yellow lights on a bar across the cab, but the unnerving thing about it was the oversize wheels that jacked the body of the truck up above everything else on the road. Why in the world would anybody want a thing like that?

I thought the driver would want to pass, so I slowed down. So did he. Then I went a little faster, but still within the speed limit because I didn't want him to think I was afraid. And I wasn't, I just didn't understand the menace I was feeling from him. Night was quickly coming on, so I switched on the headlights. So did he, only his were all yellow, the ones over the cab and the fog lights on the front.

As it got darker, the truck blended into the night and all I could see in the rearview mirrow were those strange yellow lights floating above the road. I didn't like it at all. I felt lonely and scared, although the truck had done nothing but stay right with me at every turn I made.

And it stayed with me until I reached the highway leading into Abbotsville. I pulled into light traffic, relieved to be among other cars on the streets and by gas pumps and at drive-up windows at Hardee's and pulling into Wal-Mart's. I looked back several times, but the truck was gone. I'd been foolish to worry. It had probably been a young man and his date heading for the movie theater, with no thought of me at all. We'd both just been going in the same direction.

Still, I was glad when I finally pulled into the driveway at home. Welcoming light from the windows spilled out onto the yard, and before I could help it, I felt a lifting of my spirits. There was more than a lonely and empty house waiting for me.

Lillian had already fed Deputy Bates and Little Lloyd their suppers, so I had to endure her fussing and complaining while I fixed a plate for myself. She'd been worried about me, which, though aggravating to listen to, gave me comfort that somebody cared.

"I was 'bout to get Deputy Bates to put out one of them pointed bulletums on you," she told me.

"You've been watching too much television, Lillian. Now, where is Deputy Bates? I want to know what he's found out."

"That chile don't need to hear you two talk about his fam'ly like I know you gonna do," she said, taking a carton of ice cream out of the icebox. "He like this chocolate swirl kind." She dipped a hefty spoonful into a bowl and took it to the living room where little Lloyd and Deputy Bates were watching a rerun of *Baywatch*. I would've put a stop to that, for fear those half-naked young women would inflame the boy's senses, but I just couldn't summon the energy.

Deputy Bates came into the kitchen and sat down across from me. "Well, Miss Julia," he said, "I'm not sure I've got anything for you, but I have been asking around. There's nothing on a Hazel Marie Puckett in anything I ran. But a good bit on Pucketts in general. I asked my lieutenant if he knew any Pucketts, and he said everybody in the department knows several of them. Seems they're one of those families that are in and out of trouble all the time. At least, some of them are."

"What kind of trouble are we talking about?"

"Domestic disturbances is a big one. Drunk and disorderlies, DWIs, fights, disturbing the peace, you name it. Years ago, they were into bootlegging, now they're growing marijuana. They all come from down around Benson's Gap in the southwestern part of the county. There're several families down there, all kin to each other, and if they're not fighting with their neighbors, they're beating up on each other. My lieutenant said that if I haven't been called down there yet, I soon will be."

"Lord," I said, "it's worse than I thought."

"Not necessarily," he said, shaking his head. "Remember, I didn't find anything on this woman. There're always some few in families like that who break out of the pattern. And she has no arrest record, at least not in this county."

"I just can't imagine Wesley Lloyd going to the end of the county into a group of people like that every Thursday night. You didn't know him, but I'll tell you that doesn't sound like something he'd do." Even as I said it, I realized that nothing I'd learned that he had done sounded like something he would do. So much for knowing someone.

"Didn't you tell me the Puckett woman mentioned a house she'd been living in?"

"That's right!" I said. "She said he'd not even left her the house she'd been living in for ten years or more. Now, if we could find that, maybe a neighbor or somebody could tell us more."

"Call your lawyer," he said. "If everything came to you, then it should be on a list somewhere. We ought to be able to figure out which property it is with Bud's help. I couldn't get much out of him, though I tried. He just said they lived out in the country and he rode a bus to school. But he ought to be able to identify the house if we get him in the right area."

"You'd think a child would know where he lives," I said.

"I got the feeling that she kept him pretty close to home," Deputy Bates told me. He picked up the salt shaker and turned it around, thinking over the problem. "Seems his mother did most of her shopping over in Delmont, and of course he went to one of the county schools. Looks as if she made an effort to stay out of Abbotsville."

"I just wish Wesley Lloyd had made an effort to stay *in* it." I stirred lima beans around on my plate, not at all hungry, but needing something to occupy my hands. It was humiliating to talk to Deputy Bates, or anybody, about what my husband had done, and how he'd gone to such lengths to keep me from knowing about it. But of course it wasn't just me he'd wanted to keep in the dark, but everybody who'd thought he was a fine, upstanding man.

"I'll get up early tomorrow afternoon," Deputy Bates said, "so if you'll call your lawyer and get a list of the county properties Mr. Springer owned, we'll take Bud and look for the house."

"All right," I said. "I don't know what good it'll do me to find where she lived, but I'll at least see the scene of the crime."

Chapter 10

The list I got from Binkie had been winnowed down to residential properties in the county, but it was lengthy enough. Deputy Bates drove my car, with me beside him and Little Lloyd in the backseat with his grocery sack.

"I can't wait to get there," he said, snapping his seat belt on. "You'll like my house. It's real nice."

"I'm sure it is," I said, and cut my eyes at Deputy Bates, who was intent on his driving. I didn't want any smirks about who had bought the house, and why. Not that Deputy Bates was given to smirking, but you never know. I craned my neck toward the backseat and asked, "You sure you can't give us any directions?"

"No'm, I never been this way before," Little Lloyd said. He was looking out the window as Deputy Bates drove us first toward Benson's Gap and the several small communities along the river. I had to do something about that child, and teach him to look at people when he spoke to them. But maybe it was just me he couldn't face, which was understandable because I could hardly face him.

From the road, we looked at unpainted or peeling farmhouses, an inordinate number of them with sagging sofas on the porches and rusting farm machinery in the yards. Deputy Bates slowed down as we passed each one so Little Lloyd could get a good look.

"That look familiar?" he'd ask, and then, "Think we're getting close?"

Each time the boy shook his head, until we came to a cluster of frame houses around a grocery store and a post office with a dusty flag hanging limply on its pole.

"There it is," he cried, pointing ahead of us.

"Which one, Bud?" Deputy Bates asked.

"There! At the very end. Maybe my mama's there." He hiked himself up to lean on the front seat so he could see through the windshield. He was breathing through his mouth in little gasps, fogging up his glasses.

We turned into a dirt driveway that led to a small white-painted house with a railed front porch. A high hemlock hedge enclosed both the front and back yards, and a huge oak tree shaded most of the house. Right in front of us was a closed two-car garage with a short breezeway connecting it to a side door of the house. Deputy Bates turned off the ignition, and the three of us sat there listening to the tick of the engine as it cooled off. Everything else was quiet, no movement anywhere, no road sounds. My heart hurt as I thought of the many times my husband had pulled into this drive and into that garage, and then slipped, unobserved, into the house where the child who was breathing down my neck was conceived and raised.

"That's my house," he said. "It's real nice, ain't it?"

"Isn't it," I corrected.

"Yessum, it is."

I took a rasping breath and said, "Well, let's see if anybody's home."

We climbed out, Deputy Bates pulling back his seat so Little Lloyd could get out. He ran to the front steps, calling, "Mama, Mama, I'm home!" I hoped she was.

Little Lloyd opened the front door and walked right in, while we followed behind him. As we crossed the porch to the open door, I could hear his feet running through the house and his voice calling his mama becoming more and more shrill. Desperate, maybe, and I couldn't blame him. The house was empty, not a stick of furniture, not a piece of clothing. Nothing.

The boy came back into the front room, his face a picture of despair. I could've felt sorry for him if I hadn't been so put out with that woman for going off and leaving him.

"Come here, Bud," Deputy Bates said, pulling the boy to him. "Your mother said she was going to Raleigh, remember? She's learning a trade and then she'll be back to get you. It makes sense that she'd take her furniture with her, or maybe she's stored it for when you'll be back together. Don't cry, now. This doesn't mean anything."

Well, maybe, I thought. That woman ought to be strung up for leaving her child with strangers the way she'd done.

"Since we're here, I guess we ought to look around," I said, taking note of the smallness and sparsity of the rooms. No matter how nice Little Lloyd thought it was, his father had certainly not squandered money on his little love nest. I could've felt some shame over his stinginess if I hadn't been busy trying to picture him in it.

The rest of the house was as bare as the front room; not even the kitchen appliances had been left. Deputy Bates looked in all the closets, checked the ceilings for access to an attic, which he didn't find, and then went out through the breezeway to the garage.

"Y'all stay there," he called as the boy and I started to follow him. "Go back out to the car, and I'll be there in a minute."

I wasn't interested in an empty garage any more than I was in an empty house, so it suited me to put my hand on Little Lloyd's back and turn him around. The sooner the child got out of there, the better, it seemed to me.

We sat in the car with the windows rolled down, waiting in the afternoon stillness for Deputy Bates. It was hot and humid, with butterflies flitting among the shrubs by the porch, insects chirping, and Little Lloyd sniveling in the backseat. I handed him a Kleenex from my pocketbook, but I couldn't think of a thing to say to him. We both had our problems.

"What if my mama don't ever come back?" he said, trying to choke back the tears.

"She will. I wouldn't worry about that." But of course that's what I was doing.

"But I mean"—he stopped, his throat thick with misery—"I mean, what if something's happened to her and she can't come back? I don't know what I'd do."

My land, the child thought I'd turn him out cold on the streets. Where did he get such an idea?

"Well, for goodness' sakes," I said. "If something's happened to your mother, which I very much doubt, you'll stay with me until better arrangements can be made. So you don't need to worry about that."

I hoped I'd reassured him on that score, but I wasn't about to commit myself to any long-term child care, no matter how pitiful the child. I was glad to see Deputy Bates close the front door of the house and walk over to the car. He got in and started it up, his face closed and thoughtful.

"Anything in the garage?" I asked as he backed down the driveway.

"Well, no cars. Just some oil spots and a few odds and ends." He caught his bottom lip in his teeth, and glanced in the rearview mirror at the child, who was scrunched up in the corner of the backseat. "Miss Julia, I'm going to stop at that grocery store down the road and get us all a Coke. It's hot as . . . well," he said with a quick grin, "pretty hot."

"Suits me," I agreed. "I could use a Co-Cola, and I expect Little Lloyd could, too."

Deputy Bates parked in the shade of a tree in the packed dirt parking area in front of the store. Tin signs, weathered and rust-streaked, advertised Winston cigarettes and Peeler's milk. A hand-lettered sign on the screen door announced that fresh farm eggs and homegrown tomatoes were available. While we waited for the drinks, I got out of the car and sat on a bench under the tree, hoping for a breeze to cool me off. Lord, it was hot and heavy. I took last Sunday's bulletin from my pocketbook and fanned myself with it. Little Lloyd stayed in the car, looking with miserable eyes at the front of the store.

Deputy Bates handed him an icy bottle through the window, then came and joined me.

"Miss Julia," he said, in a tone that made me look closely at the frown on his face, "I'm going to let you take that little boy and drive back home. I'll wait here for Sheriff Frady and some of the others, then ride back to town with them."

"What? Why is Earl Frady coming out here?"

"I called him," he told me, turning his steady gaze on me. "I found something besides oil stains in that garage; maybe nothing, but it looked like blood."

———

It wasn't enough to have that worry on my mind all the way back to town. As soon as we pulled into the driveway at home, I knew something was wrong. Lillian was sitting on the back steps with her hands over her face. She sprang up as soon as she saw us.

"What is it now?" I wondered aloud.

She was at the car window before I got the keys out of the ignition, and the sight of her face made me forget about blood on a garage floor.

"Oh, Miss Julia!" she cried as I got out of the car. "You not gonna b'lieve . . . I didn't know what to do! I been waitin' for you to get home. Oh, Law, I ain't never!"

"What in the world, Lillian?" I put my arm around her shoulders. "What is wrong with you?"

"I just went to the store, like I always do, an' I locked the doors. You know I always lock the doors. An' I didn't even know it till I got the groceries put up, 'cause the kitchen ain't messed up a bit. But then I went in the front room, an' I couldn't b'lieve it!"

"What are you talking about?"

"Somebody been in the house, that's what I'm talkin' about! Tore it up, too. Least the front room's all tore up, I didn't look no further. I come out on the steps to wait 'cause *Unsolved Mysteries* say don't touch nothing when somebody break in yo' house."

"My Lord," I breathed, feeling dizzy with all the implications. I put my hand on the car to steady myself. "Come here, Little Lloyd, and hold my hand. We better go see what the damage is." He gave me his hand, and I tried not to think how many times he'd rubbed it across his nose. He held his grocery sack in the other. "Come on, Lillian."

"We ain't s'posed to touch nothing," she warned me.

"I'm not going to touch a thing. But I want to see how much of the house they've been in, and see if anything's been stolen. And I need to get to the telephone to call the sheriff." Except he was at the other end of the county, along with Deputy Bates.

Lillian was right. The house had been ransacked, drawers pulled out of the desk and sideboard, with papers and silver dumped on the floor. The sofa cushions were on the floor, and the chairs tipped over. My needlepoint pillows had been hurled across the room, knocking over a lamp that lay shattered on the floor.

"Oh," I said, holding to the back of a chair. "My *Gone With the Wind* lamp! Who did this? Who in the world is responsible for this?"

We went upstairs, my feeling of trepidation confirmed at the sight of the bedrooms. My dresser drawers had been turned out on the floor and on the bed, with underclothes strung everywhere. Clothes from the closet were piled on the floor, and shoe and hatboxes emptied and discarded. Even the bathroom cabinets and the linen closet had been cleared. It looked like someone had just swept his arm along the shelves, knocking everything to the floor. Soap, bath crystals, talcum powders, cologne, towels, washclothes—everything had been flung to the floor and walked on. A full roll of toilet paper was stuffed into the commode, along with the red rubber bag that had to do with my personal hygiene. The lemon scent of Jean Naté was almost strong enough to mask the putrid smell of the semisoft clump of you-know-what on my white Royal Cannon towels.

"My land," I gasped, holding my hand over my mouth. "This is unbelievable." I pulled Little Lloyd away from the door. He didn't need to witness such an affront to sensitive natures.

"That the worst thing I ever seen," Lillian said. "What kind of person do somethin' like that? We better call the police."

"I'm going to," I said, pulling Little Lloyd out of the room. "But let's check the other bedrooms first."

They were the same. Little Lloyd's room was worse than mine, if that was possible. The mattress had been pushed off his bed, where it leaned half on the floor. His clothes were on the floor and his cardboard suitcase had been cut and stomped. We stood there surveying this senseless damage, and I could feel Little Lloyd's damp hand closing tighter on mine.

"I'm real scared," he said.

"Don't be," I said. "Let's go to the kitchen, and I'll call the sheriff. Little Lloyd, don't you worry. Somebody sick and evil did all this, but they won't do it again. Don't you be afraid; I'm going to see to it."

Chapter 11

While I called the sheriff's office, Lillian paced the kitchen, wringing her hands in her apron. She cried and apologized for going to the store, taking all the blame on herself. Little Lloyd stood next to me, his eyes big with fright.

"They're sending somebody," I said, hanging up the phone and hearing the nervous words pour out of my mouth. "I told them to contact Deputy Bates, too. Now, Lillian, sit down and get yourself together. This was not your fault, and I don't want to hear another word about it. Looks to me like it was either somebody looking for something in particular, or vandals who just like to tear things up for the sake of it. I didn't see a thing missing, did you? Television's still here, and so is my silver. I'll have to go through the papers in the desk, but I can't imagine anybody'd want canceled checks, can you? Sit down, Lillian. You're making me nervous. We've got to think about who could've done this. Did you see anything missing? How you reckon they got in?"

She finally took a seat at the table and wiped her face with her apron. "I 'spect they climb up the back stairs. Didn't you see Deputy Bates's door standing open with the glass broke out?"

"You're right. I did see it, but I was still thinking of what was in my bathroom to make much sense of anything else."

It wasn't long before two sheriff's deputies arrived to look through the house and begin making a report. Would you believe they wanted to know my age? As if that had anything to do with what'd happened. Sheriff Earl Frady drove up soon after with Deputy Bates, and everybody had to tell their stories all over again. I was asked a dozen times if anything was missing, but the more I went through the house with one or the other of them, the more I was sure that not one thing had been taken. I was close to the end of my patience, what with uniformed officers trooping in and out, poking here and there and asking one question after another, until I saw one leaving with a large plastic bag held out at arm's length. Deputy Bates asked if I wanted my towels back, but I told him not to bother. I appreciated them taking that calling card out of my bathroom, and I knew Lillian did, too.

By the time they all left, I'd had about as much excitement as I could stand. Lillian called two of her granddaughters to come help her straighten up the mess in the house, and I was grateful for them. Deputy Bates stood in the kitchen with a worried look on his face and a cup of coffee in his hand.

"Little Lloyd," I said, "go out in the yard and play. You've been cooped up in the car or the house all day, and you need to be outside for a while. Here"—I reached into the pantry—"take this bag of Oreos. We may not have much supper tonight."

He looked up at me through those thick glasses in a way that gave me a start. His eyes were so much like Wesley Lloyd's sometimes that it was like looking at my husband before I ever met him.

When he left with his cookies, I turned to Deputy Bates. "What in the world's going on here? First you find blood in that child's house and now this house's been broken into. I'm beginning to feel something bad's going to happen every time I turn around. You don't reckon whoever did this to my house was somebody you arrested, do you?"

"I doubt it, Miss Julia. I haven't been here long enough to make anybody that mad at me. But to catch you up on the other, we had the crime-scene unit down at Bud's house, and preliminary tests confirm that it is blood. Human or not, we won't know until we hear from the SBI lab. There wasn't a lot of it, some spattering and a long smear on the wall. And a little pool on the floor, which was still sticky. That means it got there fairly recently, although the humidity in the closed garage may've had something to do with that. I've got bad news for you, though. If it's human blood, you're going to have to tell Sheriff Frady how you came to have Bud with you. We'll have to track down his mother, using every method we have, to be sure, first of all, that it's not her blood since she was the last known tenant of the house. And as far as we know, you were the last person to see her around here. Tracing her is going to open a whole can of worms for you."

"A can of worms is right," I said. I leaned against the kitchen counter, tired to death of all the complications that Wesley Lloyd had left me. "You know there was somebody with her when she left here. I told you she wasn't driving the car, so I wasn't the last one to see her."

"I know. But we don't know who that was. We don't know if she went straight to Raleigh from here or whether she went back to her house. We don't know if the blood was in the garage before she brought Bud here or if it got there after she left him. We don't know anything, and won't, until we find her. I just want you to be prepared. You're going to have to tell the investigating officers everything that's happened. And be prepared for the possibility that Bud's mother knows something about the blood in her garage. Or that it's hers."

"Oh my Lord," I said, holding on to the counter. "You don't think something's happened to her?" I was ashamed to admit that my first thought was of being stuck with that child forever, in spite of reassuring the child to the contrary not three hours earlier. "That poor woman," I said, quickly getting my mind in the proper frame.

"It's too early to know. But for now I'm going to the hardware store and get some more locks for your doors. And a pane of glass for the broken one upstairs."

"Go to Prince's Hardware," I told him, "and charge it to my account."

I went into the living room to help Lillian and her two grands, but she told me to keep out of their way. So I went outside to the backyard and sat with Little Lloyd in the glider. I folded my hands in my lap and sighed.

"You want some Oreos, lady?" The child held the package out to me.

"Don't mind if I do," I said, taking one. "But call me Mrs. Springer, not lady. That sounds like you don't know who I am."

"No'm. I mean, yes'm." He nibbled a cookie all the way around, then started back at it like a mouse, taking tiny bites until he had only a little nubbin of the center left. Wesley Lloyd had had peculiar eating habits, too.

It made me nervous to watch him, so I said, "Don't you want to play?"

"No'm, I don't much feel like it." He turned his head toward me when he spoke, but still wouldn't look me in the eye.

I didn't feel much like talking, so we ate Oreo cookies and listened to the birds in the trees.

Before long, Lillian stuck her head out the back door and called me in. "You got company," she said. "Miz Conover and Mr. Sam and yo' preacher, they all here to see 'bout you."

I sighed and got up, telling Little Lloyd he'd be better off to stay outside. "If you haven't already learned it," I said, "news gets around fast in this town. I wouldn't be surprised if the nine-one-one line wasn't connected to the Presbyterian Women's Prayer Chain."

I was glad that Lillian and her girls had started with the living room, because it was straightened enough to receive company by now. They were all there: Sam, sitting at his ease in a chair, hat on his knee and a concerned look on his face; LuAnne, chirping around in her usual excited state; and Pastor Ledbetter, standing by the front window like he was daring the burglar to try it again.

Pastor Ledbetter and LuAnne started toward me, talking at once, asking how I was, what was stolen, did I know who'd done it. Sam stood up when I came into the room, but he hung back waiting, I guess, to get a word in edgewise.

"Everybody's fine," I assured them. "Have a seat now. I appreciate your concern, but it's nothing. Just vandals, most likely."

"I don't doubt it," Pastor Ledbetter pronounced. "There're no morals left anymore. And it's going to get worse before it gets better, as the Bible tells us. The closer we get to the millennium, the more of this kind of thing we can expect. It starts with the breakdown of the family, Miss Julia, which is why it's imperative for you to get that child back with his own family. You don't want to be standing in the way of a united family, and my counsel is to get that boy back with his kin. All this trouble dates from the time you agreed to take him from his mother."

Sam frowned, opened his mouth, then turned away from the pastor like he had to get himself under control. I took a deep breath, not wanting to admit that I, too, had wondered if the break-in had had anything to do with Little Lloyd. But I just shook my head, realizing it was too much trouble to straighten the preacher out on the matter of me taking a child from his mother. I'd hardly had a choice.

So I just said, "I appreciate your concern, Pastor, but please remember that I wasn't the one who had a family to break up in the first place."

"But it's incumbent on all of us," he said, "to put into practice family values. *Biblical* family values."

I couldn't understand why he was blaming me for a break-in at my own house and a breakdown of all families everywhere. I'd had enough of it.

"Which biblical family would you be talking about?" I snapped, having in mind all the adultery, fratricide, incest, murder, multiple wives, envy, and downright meanness displayed by any number of families in the Bible.

"Oh, Julia," LuAnne said, reaching for my hand and patting it. "You're all upset."

"Of course I am, LuAnne," I said, snatching back my hand. "What do you expect after somebody's been through my papers and underclothes and closets and drawers? Sam, have a seat. I don't see anything funny about it." I said that because he was smiling a little, even though his eyes were grave with concern.

"I don't see anything funny, either," he said, but by then I figured he'd seen the humor of somebody going through my underclothes. Drawers, too. That was Sam for you. "What does Coleman say about this, Julia?"

"He's helping with the investigation," I said, "and it's too early to know anything yet. But I want you to know that having a sheriff's deputy boarding in my house sure didn't deter this burglar."

"True enough," Sam said, and got a faraway look in his eyes, so that I knew he was thinking things over. Probably coming to the same conclusion I had, that somebody had wanted something bad enough to risk breaking into and entering this particular house.

After I assured LuAnne and Pastor Ledbetter that everything was under control, I walked out on the front porch to see them off. I wanted them gone so I could talk freely with Sam. LuAnne said Leonard was waiting for her to fix his supper but she could come back later and sit with me.

"No need for that, LuAnne," I said firmly. "I'll be going to bed early. It's been a hectic day, and I'll see you at church tomorrow anyway."

When she realized that Pastor Ledbetter intended to linger, she let herself be persuaded to drive off. The pastor still had something to say to me, even though he knew Sam was waiting in the living room.

"Miss Julia," he said, his voice taking on the tone of a doctor breaking the bad news. "I have to urge you again to give up this plan of keeping that child with you. This terrible occurrence ought to serve as a warning that something's wrong about it all. You don't know what you've got yourself caught up in, and you could be putting yourself in some danger."

I longed to unburden myself to him and be guided by his advice, but I knew his agenda already and it didn't fit with mine. Sometimes, a lot of times, we know what is right without anybody telling us. And I knew it was right that I look out for Little Lloyd whether the blood in his garage or the state of my house had anything to do with him or not.

"Pastor," I said, "that little boy had nothing whatsoever to do with my house getting broken into. It was vandals, plain and simple. Besides, he was with me and Deputy Bates when it happened, and one thing has nothing to do with the other."

"I'm not accusing the child, Miss Julia. All I'm saying is that once we head down the wrong track, we open ourselves up to all kinds of mischief. You're putting yourself between this child and his mother, and that's just wrong. We have to do everything we can to keep families together, not break them up, don't you agree?"

Well, no, I didn't. I'd heard of too many families that needed to be broken up—cruel fathers, drunken mothers, drugged boyfriends, battered wives, and so on and so on. But I'd heard Pastor Ledbetter on all those subjects from the pulpit and, according to him, prayer and a good dose of family values would cure them all. To my way of thinking, about the only thing that would cure them was a baseball bat.

"Sam's waiting for me, Pastor," I said. "He probably needs to discuss some of Wesley Lloyd's business matters. Thank you for coming." I turned and walked back inside.

"Sam," I said, shutting the screen door behind me, "do you think I'm breaking up that child's family?"

He laughed. "Julia, the child's father is dead and his mother's abandoned him. Don't let Ledbetter confuse you. The child has no family, unless it's you and Lillian and Coleman. Use your head, woman."

"I'm trying to, Sam. But I declare, it's swimming by now, and you don't know the half of it." And I told him about the blood in the garage and what Deputy Bates had said about having to tell the sheriff everything. "Now, I reckon the social services will try to put Little Lloyd away somewhere. Busybodies, every one of them, and government interference, too. What would this town say if I let that child be treated like a pauper while I enjoyed Wesley Lloyd's proceeds? I tell you, it's none of their business who's looking after that boy."

"We can probably fix it, if it comes to that," Sam said. "I don't know why you wouldn't qualify as a foster parent, if they insist on following the letter of the law. Let's don't worry about that now. I'll talk to Binkie Monday morning, and we'll see what we can do."

"Well, that'd relieve my mind a good bit. I've got enough to worry about without that on top of everything else. I'm telling everybody it was vandals who broke into the house, Sam, but I don't think it was. And neither does Deputy Bates. We think somebody was looking for something. I just don't know what it could be. Everything I'd consider to be of value was left alone." I leaned my head back on the sofa and stared at the ceiling. "Why now, is what I want to know. What do I have in this house that hasn't been here forever?"

Sam looked at me out from under his eyebrows while he turned his hat around in his hands. "Not a thing, Julia," he said, "but that little boy out there."

With that worrisome thought in mind for the rest of the evening, I let Little Lloyd stay up until he was so sleepy he could barely stumble up the stairs. We were all on edge, afraid to walk from one room to another without someone with us. I put up a good front for the child's sake, but to tell the truth, I was still jittery at the thought of some stranger in my house, rummaging through my things looking for who-knew-what.

Lillian offered to stay the night, but I sent her on home. She was too scared to sleep a wink in my house, even though it was unlikely that anything else would happen. Especially after all the official coming and going throughout the afternoon. I'd have felt better, though, if Deputy Bates hadn't had to work, but he told me that he and every other officer on duty would be patrolling the area. And several times during the night I saw the gleam of a spotlight sweep across the house and yard. My tax dollars at work, and I was grateful for it.

As I climbed the stairs after checking the doors half a dozen times, I hoped Little Lloyd wouldn't lie awake listening to every noise in the house, like I knew I would. I left both our doors open so he'd feel safer, but toward morning, when I decided to get on up, I found him curled up in the hall next to my door. The child must've had an affinity for hardwood floors.

I decided against Sunday school that morning, figuring Little Lloyd didn't need to face a dozen nosy nine-year-olds who'd been filled with all their parents' gossip. His week had been hard enough, to say nothing of mine. I knew LuAnne would be in her element without me in the Lula Mae Harding class that morning. She'd be able to tell everybody about the boy and the break-in in every graphic detail. The members of the Lula Mae Harding class were firm on the matter of details, saying that we needed to know every little thing so our prayers would be effective. As if the Lord was sitting up there without a clue, waiting for us to tell Him what was going on. I knew He'd get an earful today.

I laid out Little Lloyd's clothes, some I'd bought for him on Deputy Bates's advice. Khaki pants, white shirt, navy blazer, and a red-and-blue-striped tie. He dressed himself except for the tie, which I took in hand. I tied it and pushed the knot up against his collar, then stepped back to consider my handiwork. One end hung below his belt while the other stopped at his breastbone.

"That won't do," I said, undoing it for another try.

"I could wear the other one," the boy said.

"That clip-on thing? No, you couldn't. When you go to church, you wear the best you have." I stopped myself from saying anything else about his clothes and, by extension, the one who'd selected them. The child wasn't responsible for either.

"Hold your head up, and I'll give it another go," I said, measuring the ends again. "I declare, this thing has a mind of its own."

"It sure is pretty, though," he said, as if to make up for its waywardness.

"Yes, it is, and it looks handsome on you. There!" I said, giving the tie a final tug. "Look in the mirror. I think we've got it."

He studied his reflection some little while, touching and smoothing the tie, with an expression that was solemn as a judge.

"I wish my mama could see it," he finally said. "She likes pretty things. I thank you for it, Miz Springer."

"You're welcome, I'm sure. Now let's go before we're late."

I handed his jacket to him, then stopped to adjust my hat. Wearing a hat to church makes me old-fashioned, I know, but it also makes me obedient, according to Paul and Pastor Ledbetter.

"Before I forget," I went on, "you do know how to act in church, don't you?" For all I knew, the child had never darkened the door of a house of worship.

"Yes'm, I do." He frowned in thought as his glasses slid down his nose. "Sit still. Be quiet. Pay attention. And behave myself."

He looked over his glasses in my general direction, fuzzily searching for confirmation. "Very good," I said. "That's advice to live by." I stopped dead in my tracks. I'd been sitting still, staying quiet, paying attention, and behaving myself all my life, and look where I was now. "On second thought," I said, "one of these days, when you're old enough, I want you to be able to think for yourself. Now, are you ready?"

"Yes'm."

I wasn't sure I was, knowing what we'd be facing. But I'd set my course and was determined to see it through.

"Remember now," I cautioned as we went down the stairs, "be polite to everybody, but don't answer any questions. Let me do the talking."

"Yes'm."

I closed the front door behind us, and we walked across the porch and down the steps.

I brushed a piece of lint from his sleeve and said, "There're a lot of people who just thrive on gossip, don't you know, so don't let them bother you."

"No'm."

With a hand on his shoulder, I stopped him when we reached the street. "Look both ways before you cross."

"Yes'm."

I must say the child was amenable to instruction, but that did little to calm my nerves as we made our way toward the church and two hundred or so pairs of avid eyes.

As we went along the sidewalk, one car after another pulled into the parking lot and people began to stream into the church. A few men, deacons mostly, stood around the back door smoking their last cigarettes before the service. There was a holly bush there that was about dead from all the cigarettes crushed out and buried in the mulch around it.

On Sunday mornings, I always walked around front so I could go in the main door, which was only fitting for a formal service. But when we got to the corner, I almost turned around and went back home. There was that gaudy marquee that Pastor Ledbetter had put up one week exactly after Wesley Lloyd was interred. He'd wanted it for ever so long, but Wesley Lloyd had put his foot down, saying we were Presbyterians, not Baptists, and that a marquee advertising sermon topics was inappropriate and unacceptable. But Wesley Lloyd wasn't around anymore, and there was nobody able or willing to tell the pastor nay. So it was up, blaring forth his name and his topics, changed once a week, and everybody welcome. I declare, it set my teeth on edge, and especially that morning. Pastor Ledbetter's topic for the service was "Woman, the Bedrock of the Family."

But I went into the marble-floored narthex and prepared to lead Little Lloyd to my usual seat, four pews from the front and on the center aisle. I put my hand firmly on his shoulder, just as I used to put it in the crook of Wesley Lloyd's arm. This was partly to keep the child from scuffling along behind me and partly to give him a squeeze if he started to wipe his nose on his sleeve. "Head up, Little Lloyd," I whispered.

We marched down the aisle, side by side, just like Wesley Lloyd and I used to present ourselves. This time, though, I turned my head neither to the left nor to the right, but I knew people were craning to see and I heard the buzz of whispers. I cut my eyes over to the side and saw LuAnne Conover's about to pop out of her head. And I saw Mamie Harrison pointing at us, whispering furiously to her husband, who was deaf as a post. I'd timed our entrance so there'd be no chance of anybody talking to us, and as soon as we were seated, we all had to get to our feet again as the choir entered the chancel singing the processional, and Pastor Ledbetter in his black robe stepped up to the podium.

I endured that service. That's the only way to put it. Little Lloyd began fidgeting after the first fifteen minutes, so I found a pen and whispered for him to draw something on the bulletin. Then I gave him a Life Saver and a Kleenex.

Pastor Ledbetter started off with how the Lord had burdened his heart all week long over the duties of women and mothers, and women who tried to be mothers but who weren't. Every word he said was aimed at me, and I knew it. I sat there staring up at him while he droned on about how Christian women were becoming tainted by the world and abandoning biblical precepts, taking on responsibilities that they were never designed to assume, making decisions, financial and otherwise, that they were not qualified to make. And all of this was leading to the worst crisis the church had ever experienced.

I didn't take my eyes off him, and after the first few minutes, he looked everywhere but at me. He had the podium, but I had the better of him. Several times he lost his place and had to repeat himself. Then he got a second wind when he came to the climax of his sermon.

"All my remarks to this point," he declaimed as he stacked his note cards preparatory to winding up, "have been laying the groundwork for us to consider with prayerful hearts the recent action by the General Assembly. An action that opens the door to the acceptance and *the approval* of homosexuality in our beloved church. This is just the latest step in the headlong rush to wipe out the biblical underpinnings of our faith. Beloved, this is indicative of the lengths liberals will go to if we give them an inch. And it all began twenty-five years ago when the General Assembly permitted women to be ordained and to become officers of the church."

He paused and looked out over the congregation, his eyes sweeping left to right and up to the balcony. You could've heard a pin drop.

"Now I know," he went on, lowering the tone of his voice to keep our attention, "what I've just said won't sit well with some of you, especially those women who have served as officers in this church. But hear me out, if you will. I'm giving you an example of what can and will happen when we ignore the clear teaching of Scripture. Whether we like it or not, the Scriptures teach that only men are to serve as deacons, elders, and pastors. Paul writes to Timothy that an officer should be the husband of one wife, a clear indication that he did not envision women as deacons or elders. Even more to the point, Paul writes further to Timothy that he does not permit a woman to teach nor to usurp authority over the man, but to be in silence. Now, that's a hard thing to accept, for it is a fact that women have served well and faithfully in all offices throughout our denomination. But that's not the point. The point is that we have been going against the teaching of God's Holy Word. And look what it's led us to: homosexuals in our schools, in our military, and in our pulpits. Beloved, we must be in complete submission to the Lord's will if our church and our nation are to survive."

I tried my best to tune him out, tired of church politics that pitted one group of men against another group of men over women's role in the church. I already knew Pastor Ledbetter's position. He held that women's duties consisted of covering their heads, their mouths, and their casserole dishes, and I'd done all three about as long as I wanted to. But when he tied all the woes of the church to women officers, I could've wrung Paul's neck, and Timothy's, too, for giving men like Pastor Ledbetter justification for their prejudices. And don't tell me, as he'd done before, that a woman's submission elevates and ennobles her. I knew all about submission, and all it had gotten me was the humiliation in khaki pants sitting next to me.

When that interminable sermon was over, I grabbed Little Lloyd's hand and headed down the aisle. People were crowding out of the pews, but they gave us a wide berth and I knew they'd picked up on who'd been the pastor's target. Several smiled at me, their eyes drawn like magnets to the child with me. Others talked animatedly with their neighbors, keeping themselves too occupied to notice us. Yes, and when I got to the door, there was the pastor shaking hands with people as they left. I expect he thought I'd sneak out one of the side doors, but I marched up to him, ready to give him a piece of my mind. I managed to get Little Lloyd right up in front of him.

"Little Lloyd, this is Pastor Ledbetter, who's taken such an interest in your welfare," I said, and loudly, too. It stopped the conversation around us and held up the line as well. "Pastor, it was a privilege to hear your sermon this morning, but I'll have to tell you that I don't think the Lord's burdened your heart quite enough on the subject. You might want to consult Him on the duties of husbands and fathers, and men who try to be both in different households. And if permitting women to be officers in the church is what started us on the slippery slopes of sin, I'd like to know what mountaintop the church was sitting on for the two thousand years men had it to themselves."

I heard several women gasp at my outspokenness, but I didn't care. I took hold of Little Lloyd's hand and left, breathing hard but with my head held high.

I was so mad it took a few minutes of fierce walking before the car parked in front of my house registered in my mind. An old maroon-and-white vehicle with fins and a tilt in the back end. A rusted fender, too.

"My Lord, Little Lloyd," I said, clasping his hand harder and feeling my heart lift, the first time that'd happened in a number of days. "I believe that's your mama's car!"

"It is! It is! She's come back for me!" He turned loose of my hand and began running for the house.

Chapter 13

"Wait! Watch for cars! Little Lloyd, don't you cross that street till I get there!" I hurried after him and we hastened across, up my front walk and onto the porch. My heart was racing with the anticipation of telling that woman what I thought of her. I intended to lay her low, but I didn't get the chance to do it.

A man was sitting in my rocker, hidden by the wisteria vine, with no sign of Hazel Marie Puckett.

The sight of him slowed Little Lloyd's steps and stopped mine. He was of a husky build, not tall, but solid as a wall. His hair, blacker than his eyebrows or the carefully shaved outline of a goatee and mustache, was slick with pomade or gel or some such. One lock curled on his forehead. He wore a suit, grayish green, a white shirt, and a tie that was splotched with green and maroon colors. And white socks, for the Lord's sake. He wore a large gold watch turned to the inside of his right arm and a heavy gold ring on each middle finger. A soft leather Bible, with gilt-edged pages, was clasped to his chest. I pegged him for a preacher of some kind—well, the slick kind—before he opened his mouth. But far be it from me to be critical.

He stood up, a smile of welcome on his face, when we stepped up on the porch. Little Lloyd edged close to my side.

"Miz Springer," the man said with great solemnity as he bowed in what I can only describe as a deferential way. "I'm here to offer my humble apologies for the disgraceful way my niece, Hazel Marie Puckett, has conducted herself and to convey the deep gratitude of all the Puckett family for your kind acts of Christian charity, praise God. All of us, myself not the least, will be forever in your debt for taking Junior in and caring for him like you done. I'm here to relieve you of that burden and to take Junior back into the fold of his loved ones, who have sorely missed him."

Well, hallelujah, I thought, and couldn't help but smile at my most unlikely looking savior.

"Forgive me, ma'am," he went on before I could reply. "Let me introduce myself, though I would hope you'd already recognized me from the *Fanning the Flame* program, televised each and every Tuesday evening from nine till ten over WCHR, channel eight, coming with the power of God into thousands of Christian homes in Western North Carolina and the Upstate." I shook my head and mumbled that I didn't watch much television. He smiled like he recognized me as a potential viewer and contributor. "I'm the Reverend Vernon Puckett, known far and wide as Brother Vern, which I would be honored to have you call me." He held out his hand, which I shook, noticing how sweaty it was. Still, it was a hot day.

"Have a seat, Mr. Puckett," I said, "and tell us where this boy's mother is."

"Well, she's down in Raleigh," he said, sighing, lowering himself into the rocker, his thighs bulging like hams. I don't generally notice such intimate details of a man, but polyester makes for a snug fit. He pulled out a large handkerchief to mop his face. "I declare, that girl has been a trial to all us Pucketts, and I'm sure I don't have to tell you why, Miz Springer." He glanced up at me with a penetrating look, letting me know that he knew all about her connection to Wesley Lloyd. "Now, as you may not know, the Lord's work takes me all over this state and into others as well. I been in the great state of California, lo these many months, and I tell you, Miz Springer, that place needs the Word of God as bad as anyplace I ever been. Wherever I get a call, I go, praise God, He keeps me busy. As it happens, I been called to hold revival services all next week at Bethany Crossroads Baptist, and that's right outside Raleigh. It was the Lord's doings, Miz Springer, 'cause we got a call from Hazel Marie not two days ago, asking if any of us was down that way could we bring Junior to her." He turned his eyes, black as raisins, on Little Lloyd and said, "You want to see your mama, boy?"

"Yessir," Little Lloyd answered. He stood beside me, his hand gripped to the arm of my chair. Excited and pleased, no doubt.

"Well, then," Brother Vern said, slapping the floppy Bible on his knee, "go get what you come with and we'll be on our way. I got to be down there by nightfall for an early morning telecast, praise God. Got to be up with the chickens!" He threw his head back and laughed, showing me large, artificial teeth. I didn't much care for the man. Something about him was a little too smooth and practiced for my taste. But then he was a television personality, so I guess he had a bit of the actor in him. Most preachers do.

Little Lloyd hesitated beside my chair. I couldn't understand the child. Here was an answer to both our prayers, a way to his mother for him and a way out of this mess for me.

"Go on, boy," I said. "Put everything in that suitcase I gave you, your new clothes, too. I want you to have them. Your mama's sent for you and I expect she can't wait to see you."

"Will you tell Deputy Bates 'bye for me?" he asked, cutting his eyes toward his uncle. Great-uncle, I guess.

"Of course," I assured him. "He'll probably want to come see you when you get back to town."

He gave a quick smile and dashed into the house. I heard his feet pounding up the stairs. I sat back, thankful that this child from the wrong side of the blanket was being taken back to it. I turned my attention back to the man beside me in time to see a broad smile wipe out the frown he'd directed at the boy.

"Mr. Puckett—"

"Uh, uh, uh," he admonished me, wagging his finger to and fro.

"Brother Vern, then," I said. "I hope you give your niece a piece of my mind for me. I never heard of anybody dropping off a child on perfect strangers before. Especially in these circumstances, as you've indicated you know about."

"Indeed I do," he said. He leaned forward in that confidential way that all preachers seem to learn in seminary. I got a whiff of a dark, musky cologne, and noticed the gleam of a jeweled cross in the center of his tie. Zircons? Diamonds? Surely not. I leaned back out of the aroma field as he went on. "I don't mind telling you that when I learned some years back of how my niece was living, I was shocked to my innermost soul. I prayed about that situation, I can't tell you how many times I laid it before the Lord, and I talked to her and I pled with her, and all to no avail. And I prayed for you, too, Miz Springer, and I didn't even know you."

"Well, I declare," I said, touched in spite of myself.

"Yes, that girl has caused us all untold heartache, but I know she loves that boy. And a mother's love overcomes the worst of sins, praise God."

"Maybe so, but what am I thinking? You and Little Lloyd can't go off on that long drive without a thing to eat. It'll take just a minute to put something on the table. And while I'm at it, I'll see what's keeping that child." I got up to go to the kitchen, but he was on his feet faster.

"No need, ma'am, no need at all. I plan on stopping at the Burger King out by the interstate. We'll eat as we go, praise God for the conveniences provided for His people. I'm really pushed for time, and

Hazel Marie is anxious for us to get there. I thank you for the offer, though, praise God."

Little Lloyd came out on the porch then, with his suitcase in one hand and his blazer in the other. His glasses had slid down on his nose and he looked out over them in a dazed and addled way. The child must've been blind without those thick lenses. I'd intended to get him some better-fitting ones if he'd stayed much longer. But at least he was leaving with a good haircut.

"Well, Little Lloyd, we'll miss you," I said, sure the Lord would forgive me for the lie. But what else are good manners but lies? "Lillian's going to be upset when she comes tomorrow. And Deputy Bates won't know what to do with that tire swing back there. I hope you'll come back to see us." Well, lightning didn't strike the first time.

"Yes'm," he mumbled, ducking his head and looking ready to cry. Taking in his look of misery, I felt a sudden twinge of pity. Not that I cared about the boy, you understand, but it was just that I didn't know how his mother could look after him. I did have a certain responsibility here, however little I'd wanted the care of him.

"You know, Mr. Puckett, I'm a good mind to keep the boy till I hear directly from his mother. Not that you wouldn't look after him," I added at the sharp glance he gave me. "But you have your hands full already, what with your television shows and revival services, and what if you miss connections with his mother? You can't be dragging a child all over the countryside, keeping him up late, feeding him fast-food hamburgers and I don't know what all. Yes, I think the boy should stay here."

I glanced from one to the other, saw Little Lloyd's indecision and Brother Vern's startled look.

"Oh, no, that won't do." Brother Vern raised his hand like he was stopping traffic. "Beg your pardon, Miz Springer. I didn't mean to speak so sharply. But, you see, I'm under commission to get that boy to his mother. I promised her and, well . . ." He stopped, shook his head, and narrowed his eyes. "I'll tell you the truth, Miz Springer, you don't want to cross that woman. There's no telling what she'd do and, believe me, you don't want to find out."

"Well, if you put it that way," I said, images of my ransacked house flitting through my mind. But it couldn't have been the Puckett woman. She was in Raleigh, wasn't she? "I declare, I don't know what to do. What do you think, Little Lloyd?"

"He wants to be with his mother," Brother Vern pronounced. "Don't you, boy?"

"Yessir, I—"

"Thank the nice lady, then, and let's get on the road." Brother Vern pushed himself up from the rocker, a gleam of sweat on his face, and buttoned his suit coat. Double-breasted, too, which was not the best choice for a man of his girth. He tucked his Bible under his arm and walked toward the steps. He was ready to go.

"You sure you have everything?" I asked the boy. "Coloring book and crayons? A book to read on the trip?"

"Yes'm, I've got everything." He lifted his head and stared at me hard, frowning as he looked me straight in the eye like Wesley Lloyd used to do. Not at all like the retiring child who'd been moping around my house for days.

"Well, what about—?"

"I got everything in my suitcase," he said, his eyebrows wiggling as he frowned and squinched his eyes and carried on until I thought something was wrong with him. Then he surprised and shamed me by saying, "Thank you for letting me stay. I'm sorry for all the trouble."

"Why," I stammered, "no trouble. It was nice having you around." And while I waited for lightning to surely strike that time, I realized I'd spoken with a smidgen of truth.

Brother Vernon Puckett picked up the suitcase and, with a firm hand on Little Lloyd's back, guided him down the steps and out to the car. I stood watching them, waiting for the relief of a burden being lifted and not feeling it. The car started with a roar and black smoke billowed out the tailpipe.

"My Lord!" I exclaimed, stunned at my density. *Somebody* had been driving this very same car when the Puckett woman had hopped into the passenger seat hardly a week before. Who'd been driving then? How had Brother Vern ended up with it?

"Wait!" I cried, running down the steps and waving at them. The car roared off, Little Lloyd's face looking back at me through the side window. They turned right on Lincoln and were lost to sight, black smoke drifting down around my boxwoods.

Before I could turn back to the house, a deep, growling rumble reverberated in my head and filled the empty street. I looked around, unable to tell where it was coming from. Then I saw a black pickup, hiked high on monster tires, edging around the far corner of the block and rolling toward me. My Lord, I thought, my heart pounding like sixty, that's the very truck, or its twin, that followed me the other night. The very same yellow lights across the top, the same tires, the same black windows. As it passed within ten feet of me, I saw an orange lightning flash painted on the door. I watched it pass, too unnerved to move, as it went slow enough and loud enough to deafen me. I watched it turn right on Lincoln, and heard the sound of that awful motor fade away like thunder in the distance.

I hurried back to the porch and hid myself in the wicker rocker behind the wisteria, shaken by the coincidence. If that's what it was. I sat there staring off at the empty street, worrying about Little Lloyd, wondering if the truck was after him and not me at all.

A wisp of black exhaust curled along the steps, and I felt more lost and lonesome than I had even during the time of my recent bereavement.

Chapter 14

Later in the day I tried to read the newspaper, even the "Over 50" section that was supposed to appeal to people like me but didn't, trying to fill the long Sunday afternoon that stretched out before me. The air was still and hot, the house quiet and so lonely that I wondered what I'd do with myself from then on. My throat felt closed and tight, and it got worse whenever that child came to mind, which was more often than I wanted to admit. Where was he, what was he doing, and why did I care?

Well, I didn't, I reminded myself. He was no longer my problem, if he ever had been. I folded the papers and then my hands, and looked around the empty room. Maybe I'd replace the velvet draperies with something lighter, maybe re-cover the furniture. Maybe a decorating project would take my mind off my recent troubles. Maybe it wouldn't.

I was glad to hear a knock on the front door around four o'clock, and even gladder to see Sam standing there.

"Come in, Sam," I said, opening the screen door for him. "I know you'll rejoice with me that my problems have all been solved."

"How'd you manage that, Julia?" He settled himself in one of the Victorian chairs by the fireplace. His familiar bulk seemed to fill the room and the lonely afternoon. I noticed how his hair had lightened, and how blue his eyes seemed in contrast.

I took his hat and placed it on the marble-topped chest, then took a seat on the sofa. "His uncle, or rather his mother's uncle, was waiting for us after church. He'd heard from Hazel Marie and she wanted him to bring Little Lloyd to her down in Raleigh. I guess she found a place where she could have him with her. They left about twelve-thirty, quarter to one, something like that. They're well on their way by now."

I looked at my watch, wondering where on I-40 East that child would be. I hadn't been able to get his face, staring at me from the car window as they left, out of my mind. Nor that business with his eyebrows before they left.

"That does solve your problem, then," Sam said. He paused, studying my face then; in that mind-reading way of his, he went on. "So where's all that rejoicing you mentioned?"

"Well, the thing is," I said and stopped to finger a button on my dress, "I began to have second thoughts about letting him go, and Little Lloyd didn't seem all that thrilled about it, either. I didn't really notice it at the time, because *I* was so thrilled to have him go. I mean, he wanted to see his mother, I know that. But there was just something about the way he acted, now that I've had time to think about it, that makes me wonder about the whole thing.

"And, I might as well admit it, I didn't have my wits about me enough to question Brother Vern. That car, for one thing."

"Why don't you start over," Sam said, "and tell me from the beginning. Who's Brother Vern, and what's worrying you about the car?"

So I told him, and the more details I laid out, the more I realized how wrong I'd been to let the child go off with somebody I didn't know from Adam.

"But the boy knew him, didn't he?" Sam asked.

"Yes, he did. He just didn't seem to like him very much, but I could be wrong. What I should've done, Sam," I said, standing up and pacing the floor, "was to've found out where the Puckett woman is. Then I could call her and make sure the boy gets there all right. That's what I *should've* done. Now there's no way to know where he is or where she is. Or where Brother Vern is, for that matter. I should've stuck to my guns. Instead, all I could think of was getting Wesley Lloyd's child out of my house and out of my life. Totally self-centered, that's what I've been."

"You're too hard on yourself, Julia. You were willing to look after the boy—"

"Yes, but I didn't *want* to. That's the difference between the letter of the law and the spirit of it. It's the attitude of the heart that counts, Sam, and you know it as well as I do. And," I said, taking a deep breath, "I better tell you about that deformed truck, too."

When I finished, Sam was so agitated, he stood up and put his hands on my shoulders, bringing me to a stop. "Julia, why in the world were you driving around the countryside by yourself after dark?"

"Because I wanted to," I snapped. "Sam Murdoch, Wesley Lloyd treated me like a ten-year-old all my life, and I'm not going to be treated that way by you or anybody else again."

He dropped his hands. "You're right and I apologize. I'm just worried about you, Julia. Will you allow me that?"

I pretended to think about it, then nodded and said, "Yes, you can worry, but give me credit for having some sense."

Wesley Lloyd would've told me to act like I had some, but Sam smiled and said, "I give you more credit than you know, Julia."

Not knowing how to respond to that, I changed the subject. "What should we do about that child?"

"First thing, now that you don't have to worry about social services taking him from you, let's ask Deputy Bates to contact the Raleigh police to locate the Puckett woman. They can confirm that the boy's there and being cared for. Nothing will come back on you except a little reassurance."

"Good, let's do that. Deputy Bates worked late this morning, but he ought to be up any time now. In fact, let's go out to the kitchen and I'll put on a pot of coffee for him. He'll need something to eat, too. Would you like some eggs for your supper?"

"Don't mind if I do," he said, following me down the hall. "But, Julia, I didn't know you could cook."

"Anybody can scramble eggs, for the Lord's sake," I said, though if the truth be known, I wasn't much of a hand for any kind of cooking. And didn't care to learn.

———

I had another restless night, in spite of Sam's suggestion and Deputy Bates's willingness to make an official inquiry into Hazel Marie Puckett's whereabouts. The sheriff would be interested, too, he'd told us, since she was wanted for questioning about the blood on her garage floor and walls. Deputy Bates hadn't been too happy to learn that Little Lloyd was gone. I'd seen disappointment and concern written all over his face, and his response had rankled me.

"I'm going to miss that boy," he said.

I took that as criticism and snapped back, "Well, I won't. How do you think I felt, having that illegitimate child underfoot every day, all day long?"

My eyes welled up, and Sam said, "Now, Julia."

That wasn't much help, because I had been remiss in letting that child go off. They knew it and I knew it, but what could I have done when his own kin showed up to claim him? A lot of things, as it turned out. I could've wakened Deputy Bates, for one. I could've questioned Brother Vern, for another. I could've asked, even demanded, that he give me her address. I could've gone upstairs with Little Lloyd and made sure, out of his great-uncle's hearing, that he wanted to go with him.

Oh, there were a lot of things I could've done and should've done, and now I had to live with it all. I got up sometime in the middle of the night and walked across the hall to Little Lloyd's room. The empty bed made me realize how empty my house was, and maybe my life, as well.

I was just a selfish old woman with nothing but a few million dollars to her name. No husband, no children, nothing to look forward to but more of the same. Even the thought of writing checks and buying things couldn't lift my spirits.

I cried. Sitting there in Little Lloyd's room, not a light on in the house, an old, slightly blue-haired woman who'd thought of nothing but herself all her life. Yes, I cried.

But not because I missed the boy, not at all. He'd been nothing but a reminder of Wesley Lloyd and, I hate to say this, I wasn't missing *him.* It was because I was worried about the child and because I'd been lax in looking after him. If I could be assured that he was safe with his mother, I could put the whole week behind me and get on with my life. I might even plan a tea and invite all the women of the church. Wesley Lloyd hadn't been gone a year yet, but there was no reason I couldn't entertain if I wanted to. It'd show everybody that I could still hold my head up. So I went back to bed and filled my mind with cucumber sandwiches and layered cream cheese sandwiches, and cheese straws and petit fours and flower arrangements and linen napkins, planning the most elaborate tea anybody'd had since Lula Mae Harding had her last one before she passed and the ladies' Sunday school class named itself after her.

Sam arrived that Monday morning about the same time Lillian did, one at the front door and the other at the back. We all ended up in the kitchen, drinking coffee and eating the toast Lillian had fixed. She wouldn't sit at the table with us because she'd once told me that it wasn't right for her to visit with my company. I didn't care, especially since Sam wasn't real company, but she busied herself around the stove, getting a big breakfast ready for Deputy Bates when he got off duty. She listened to us, though, and made her opinions known by the expressions on her face. She hadn't liked it one little bit that I'd let Little Lloyd go off with "somebody callin' hisself his uncle."

"What you do that for, Miss Julia?" she'd asked. "That baby need lookin' after, not let go off with ever' Tom Dick that come by."

I said, "It was his mother's uncle, not any Tom, Dick, or Harry. So don't blame me for his own mother's neglect and carelessness."

"That be a pitiful excuse," she'd told me.

Sam stirred his coffee, then reached over and put his hand on mine.

"I went by this morning and talked to Sheriff Frady. Just laid it all out for him. I don't have to tell you he was mighty interested in the relationship between you and the boy. Then he called in this lieutenant and I had to tell it again. That lieutenant is sharp. He put it right together with the blood Coleman found at the boy's house."

"I'd have thought Deputy Bates would've already reported it all," I said, surprised at where Deputy Bates's loyalty seemed to be placed.

"No, apparently Coleman just explained that the boy was staying with you and that the three of you had driven out to check on the house. He let them assume that the Puckett woman knew you and that you had agreed to look after the boy. He was trying to keep social services out of it."

"I hope he won't get in trouble over it."

"I doubt it. He could only tell what he knew for a fact, and that's what he did. Still, he respected your wishes to keep the boy out of a foster home. But, Julia, you're going to have to talk to them yourself. That lieutenant, what's his name, Peavey, he wants to know what you know and what you suspect about the whole situation. He's treating the Puckett woman as a missing person and, after hearing what I had to say, is about ready to treat the boy as one, too."

"But he's with his uncle!" I protested. "Great-uncle, I mean. I know, I know. Lillian, quit looking at me that way. I know I shouldn't have let him go off, but what was I supposed to do?" I wanted to cry again. Instead, I refilled our cups. It was all so unfair. I hadn't asked to be betrayed by my own husband, and I hadn't asked to have his bastard dumped on my doorstep, and the Lord knows, I hadn't asked to be blamed for it all, either.

"Nobody's blaming you, Julia," Sam said, reading my mind again. "Tell you what. Why don't you go fishing with me tomorrow?"

Lillian started laughing, and I glared at her. "Yes, and I can see me going fishing with you, Sam Murdoch. First off, I've never fished in my life and, second off, if this town didn't already have enough to talk about, that would do it."

"It'd be good for you, Julia, and who cares if the town talks? The men would just wish they were in my shoes, and the women would be jealous of you for landing the handsomest man in town."

Lillian laughed out loud. "Don't sound like no fishing I ever heard of."

"You two," I said, feeling my face redden. "I've got enough worries without adding you to them, Sam Murdoch."

"Ah, Julia," Sam said, cocking his head to the side and lowering his voice. "I don't want to be a worry to you. I want to help you, if you'll let me. Getting away for a few hours out on a lake would make all the difference in the world. You'd like it, I promise."

"No, and that's that," I said, refusing to look at him. "You can fritter your time away if you want to, but I have things to do."

"You better listen to him, Miss Julia," Lillian said. "Not too many men knocking on yo' door that I been noticin'. 'Specially not one like Mr. Sam."

"You tell her, Lillian," Sam said, smiling now. "Tell her she's letting the best man she'll ever know slip through her fingers."

"That's about right," Lillian agreed, with a long look of warning at me.

"The subject is closed," I said, tired of being teased. I was in no mood for it.

I heard Deputy Bates's car pull in and was glad to see him come in the back door. He looked tired, but maybe he'd turn the conversation to something more sensible. Lillian and Sam took on over him, Sam pulling out a chair for him and Lillian hurrying over with coffee.

"I'm fixin' you two eggs over light, sausage, and grits. That all right with you?" she asked him.

"Sounds great," he said, twisting around to turn off his walkie-talkie that was giving out bursts of static and a jumble of words from somebody with a real bad cold. "What a night," he went on. "I'm glad to have it over with."

"Lotta calls?" Sam asked.

"Man, yes. A robbery out at the Motor Inn. Three fights down on Mercer Avenue, and speeders all over the county. Then an Alzheimer's patient walked out of a nursing home. Had to get the trackers and dogs out, but we found him. It just never stopped."

"What you need," Lillian declaimed as she flipped eggs, "is a little honey in yo' life." Then she laughed so hard I was afraid she'd break the yolks.

Deputy Bates grinned and said, "What makes you think I don't already have some?"

She whooped then and told him she could tell when a man had a little or a lot or none at all, and he was in the last category. Sam sat there laughing with them, but to me the conversation was getting a little too racy. It was my kitchen, after all.

"Has there been any word on Little Lloyd or his mama?" I asked, and everybody got serious again.

"Not a thing," Deputy Bates said, going after his breakfast like he hadn't eaten all night, and he probably hadn't. "We put out a description of the car and notified the state troopers to watch for it, but there's been nothing. The Raleigh police're going to check all the beauty schools down there as soon as they open this morning to see where the Puckett woman's registered. Other than that, there's not much else we can do. Oh, yeah, Lieutenant Peavey's going down to Benson's Gap sometime today and question some of the Puckett clan. He knows a bunch of them, arrested most of 'em at one time or another, and if anybody knows anything, he'll get it out of them. Lillian, if it's not too much trouble, I believe I could eat another egg."

"No trouble a'tall," she said, beaming like she did when anybody appreciated her cooking. I didn't tell her that he'd eaten four of mine the night before.

When Deputy Bates finally pushed his plate away and praised Lillian to the skies, more than she needed, to be honest about it, he took a deep breath.

"Miss Julia," he said, "Sheriff Frady's coming over this morning to ask you about Little Lloyd and his mother. It'd be best to go ahead and tell him everything."

"Sam's already warned me," I told him. "And I don't plan to leave anything out. I want that boy found so I can quit worrying and get some sleep. I'll tell you this, though, I am certainly glad I didn't try to hide the fact that Little Lloyd is my husband's son. It'd be so much worse if I had, because I'd have to reveal it now anyway. See, Lillian? Sometimes I do know what I'm doing."

"*Some*times," she admitted.

I heard car doors slam out front, and my heart gave a lurch inside my chest. I'd never been questioned by law officers before and I wasn't looking forward to it. It could be about as bad as being counseled by my preacher. Earl Frady wasn't much, but he represented a lot, even if I did know his wife went on a spree now and then, and only stayed out of jail because none of his deputies was willing to arrest her.

Sam stood up with me and said, "Come on, Julia, let's go let them in."

Then Deputy Bates got up and Lillian folded her dish towel as they came to join Sam and me. The four of us went to the living room to greet the sheriff.

Chapter 15

I'd known Earl Frady for all the eighteen years he'd been sheriff of Abbot County, and he still looked like a none-too-prosperous shopkeeper in his brown polyester suit and black wing tips. He smiled his quick, nervous smile when I came to the door, and smoothed the thin hair over the bald spot on his head. He looked even more uncomfortable and unprofessional than usual, standing shoulder high to the big, sharply uniformed man behind him.

I opened the screen for them, and Deputy Bates introduced Lieutenant Wayne Peavey. He was far and away the largest man in the room, towering over us and unnerving me, what with those dark glasses that reflected my image without giving away anything of himself. He had a thin, firm mouth that looked as if it would split his face if he smiled.

None of us had to be introduced to Earl Frady; he'd been getting elected every four years like clockwork. Not because he knew so much about law enforcement, but because he knew county politics and county politicians inside and out. And because he knew enough to hire professionals, trained and experienced deputies, to keep the peace. And because he had enough sense to leave them alone and let them do it. That was enough reason to keep returning him to office.

He showed up only when he thought something might make the newspaper or when, like now, somebody important might be involved in a crime.

We all took seats except Lillian, who leaned against the double opening to the dining room. She'd placed herself behind Lieutenant Peavey, but where I could see her. Deputy Bates took the piano bench, and Sam pulled up a chair next to Sheriff Frady. We looked at the sheriff, waiting for him to start, but the big lieutenant cleared his throat and took out a little notebook. Then he commenced questioning me about everything that'd happened since Hazel Marie Puckett showed up on my porch.

Lillian frowned every time he opened his mouth.

Right at the start, Sam interrupted to state in no uncertain terms that I was answering questions only in a spirit of cooperation, and that if the sheriff had anything else in mind, my attorney of record had to be present. Lillian crossed her arms and nodded in agreement.

"Nothing like that is on our mind," Sheriff Frady said, straightening out one leg and plucking at the stretchy material to get enough slack to go over his knee. "We just need to know the sequence of events leading up to the break-in here Saturday. In broad daylight. That's mainly what we're investigating, and to see if Mrs. Springer's discovered anything missing."

"Mind your questions, then," Sam said, giving the sheriff a squinty-eyed look.

Sam was a Democrat, born and bred, and so was Sheriff Frady, who knew which side his bread was buttered on. The sheriff nodded at his lieutenant to continue, while he leaned back in his chair and looked around like the proceedings had nothing to do with him. And they didn't.

The lieutenant took me step by step through the past week, making notes as he went. After I went over in detail how the boy had left my house the day before, described Brother Vern and his car, and declared that as far as I knew, Hazel Marie Puckett was filing nails down in Raleigh, he closed his notebook and stood up.

"All right, Mrs. Springer," he said as I craned my neck to look up at him. "We don't know what happened in that garage. Neighbors tell us that the woman and her son lived there, but they're both missing. Seems the place belongs to you, and the boy was here with you, so there's a connection to you whichever way you look at it. And not only was there blood in that garage, we also found a couple of teeth. We're waiting on the investigation report to confirm if we're dealing with human substances, but we still don't know who they belong to or how they got there."

"Well, I don't, either," I said.

"No'm, I guess not, but what we found hadn't been there much more than twenty-four hours, and from what you've told me, nobody knows where you were Friday afternoon."

"Why, Friday afternoon I didn't even know where that house was, much less that it belonged to me. And I told you I was driving around. All evening for some three hours. Ask Lillian. Ask Deputy Bates. They were both here when I came in." Deputy Bates had been leaning his arms on his knees, staring at the floor. He looked up and confirmed my statement with a nod. Lieutenant Peavey didn't notice.

"But according to you, nobody saw you during that three hours."

"Well, the black truck did."

Lieutenant Peavey aimed those black sunglasses at me and said, "What black truck?"

So I told him. He shrugged one shoulder, and didn't even open his notebook. "Black pickups all over the place. You need a better witness than that."

"Now, just a minute," Sam began, getting to his feet. "Are you accusing Mrs. Springer of having something to do with all this? I told you, Earl," he said, turning to the sheriff, "and I'll tell you again. If you want to use anything said in this room, you're in trouble. Mrs. Springer has not been represented by counsel, and I warned you about it before you began."

"Now, Sam," the sheriff said, getting up and edging toward the door. "We're questioning everybody and, so far, nobody's been charged with anything."

"I should hope not," Sam said. "Since, so far, you don't have any charges to file. What crime has been committed except for a break-in right here? Is Mrs. Springer a suspect in that?"

"No, no, of course not," the sheriff said, aiming a hard look at his lieutenant, who ignored him. "We just have to, you know, cover all the bases."

The lieutenant turned to me. "You're not planning any trips out of town, are you? I may want to talk to you again."

When they left, Sam was fuming at the idea of me as a suspect in a crime without a habeas corpus, or delicti, or some such. I didn't pay much attention, because my head was in a swirl again. That child had turned my life upside down when he entered it, and was still doing it now that he was out of it.

————

It had just gotten dark good that Monday night, about nine o'clock, and I was hoping for a good night's sleep. Though now that my whereabouts last Friday had been called into question by the authorities, I didn't have much hope for it.

I went into the kitchen to heat some milk for a cup of Ovaltine, figuring that might help. Then, on second thought, I put the pan up and took down Lillian's cooking sherry. That ought to do it, I thought. Presbyterians aren't supposed to use alcohol, but a lot do. Not Wesley Lloyd, though, who was a teetotaler by conviction, which meant that I didn't either. However, it came to me as I tasted the vile stuff that the ABC store ought to have something better, since so many people seemed to like it. I resolved to take myself down there and buy something decent to drink. I didn't care who saw me, either. Just to get a little something to help me sleep, you know. And to aid the digestion. Nothing wrong with that, since Paul told Timothy to take a little wine for his stomach's sake. If you can find a verse of Scripture to back you up, even Presbyterians will leave you alone.

I was just putting the bottle back when I heard a scratching at the back door. Then two little taps. I froze. Scared to death. Who could be at my back door that time of night? Anybody I knew would come to the front and yoo-hoo along with the tapping.

I hesitated, trying to think what to do. Get to the phone? Scream my head off? Run through the house and out the front? *In my bathrobe*? Stay real quiet and pretend I wasn't home?

Lord, it wasn't possible. I was directly in line with the window in the door, and whoever was out there could see me, plain as day.

I grabbed the sherry bottle by the neck and went to the door. I flipped on the porch light and nearly fainted.

I couldn't get the door open fast enough, and when she stumbled through it, I wished I had fainted.

Hazel Marie Puckett fell against me and clung so that I was looking right into her poor smashed and swollen face. "Miz Springer!" she gasped. I held her upright, feeling the frailness of her bones. "I'm sorry to bother you," I think she said. Her words were so slurred I had trouble understanding her. "I need to see Junior. Please, I have to see him."

"Sit down, sit down," I cried, putting my arm around her waist and guiding her to a chair. "What happened to you? You look terrible!"

Her eyes were almost swollen shut. Her mouth was split and swollen out of shape. Dried blood caked the corners of her nose and mouth, and her whole face was blue and yellowish-green with the worst bruising I'd ever seen. Her nails were dirty and broken, and right from that I figured she hadn't been in Raleigh at beauty school. Her dress was torn and streaked with dirt, and her bare feet were scratched and filthy. All in all, she was a mess.

"What happened to you?" I asked again, as tears poured out of those battered eyes. Fresh blood leaked from her split mouth, and she put a hand up to cover it. "Have you been drinking?" I demanded.

"Oh, no'm. I . . . an accident. I've been in an accident. Please, Miz Springer, I got to see Junior."

She wasn't in any shape to see anybody but a doctor, and I wasn't ready to admit that her Junior was in Raleigh looking for her. I took out some ice cubes and wrapped them in a dish towel.

"Here," I said, "put that on your face. It'll help the swelling. Have you been to the hospital? You may need some stitches around your mouth."

"No'm, it's all right. Just some teeth," she said, pressing the ice pack to her face.

"Teeth! You lost some teeth? You need to see a dentist, and right soon, too. You want to take care of your teeth. I go twice a year. Every year. Whether I need to or not." I was chattering, but I did that any time I got upset and this was one of those times.

"I need Junior," she said into the towel. "Please, is he in bed? I just need to be sure he's all right."

"Well," I said, taking a deep breath. "Of course he's all right. It's just that somebody's wires have got crossed. 'Cause he's in Raleigh, looking for you."

"Raleigh!" She looked up from the towel with the most stricken look I'd ever seen. "But . . . he's supposed to be here! With you, where he'd be safe. I left him here, he can't be gone! Tell me, Miz Springer, please tell me he's here with you."

"Hush, now," I comforted, "he's all right. Your uncle picked him up yesterday to take him down to you."

"You mean . . . Brother Vern? You mean Brother Vern's got him?" The look on her face made my heart sink.

"Well. Yes."

"Oh, God," she sobbed, and her whole body seemed to shrink into itself. "How could you let him go? I counted on you to take care of him."

"Now just a minute, miss," I said, taking immediate umbrage at being blamed for one more thing on a long list. "You left him here with not so much as a by-your-leave. You didn't tell me word one about where you'd be, and you called Brother Vern to come get him and he did. Was I supposed to keep him from his own uncle? Great-uncle?"

She shook her head. "I didn't call nobody, wasn't able to. And 'specially not him. I thought Junior'd be safe here."

"He would've been, if you'd told me what was going on," I said. I don't mind saying that I was on the defensive. I hadn't felt right about Brother Vern ever since they'd been gone, and I hated being told that not feeling right about him was the right feeling to have. "I'm not a mind reader, you know. And if you'd had the courtesy to tell me not to let Little Lloyd go off with, *I remind you,* one of your own family, then I wouldn't have let him go. What else was I supposed to do?" Seemed I'd been asking that an awful lot lately.

"I'm sorry, Miz Springer," she whispered, burying her head in the towel again. That blond hair needed washing, and a new color job, too. "It's just, well, Brother Vern's been looking for something since Friday. He tried to get me to tell him about it, but, Miz Springer, I didn't know what he was talking about."

"He tried to get you . . . ?" Light dawned in my slow mind. "Are you telling me you weren't in an accident? Are you saying that Brother Vern did this to you?"

She shook her head, but kept it in the towel. "No, but he let somebody else do it."

"Thay Lord," I gasped, and sank into the chair beside her. "And him a preacher! I can't believe this."

"Being a preacher don't mean a thing, Miz Springer," she said. "Or calling yourself a Christian, neither."

"Well, child," I said, shrinking up a little myself. "You're not telling me a thing I don't already know.

"Why did Brother Vern want Little Lloyd so bad?" I asked.

"Who?"

"Little Lloyd, the one you call Junior," I snapped. "I hope you don't expect *me* to call him Junior."

"Oh," she said. She lifted her head out of the towel and took a deep breath. Then doubled over with a gasp, holding her side. "My ribs. I think something's broke inside."

"I'm calling a doctor," I said, getting up to go to the phone.

"No, please." She touched my arm, stopping me. "We've got to find Junior. I've lasted this long, I can keep going till we find him."

I studied her a minute, looking at the various colors of the bruises and the blood that was dried and cracked on her face. That beating had not been recent. I didn't know how she'd managed to last without medical treatment, but she wasn't dead from it, so maybe she could keep going.

"All right, then," I conceded. "But we've got to get you in better shape."

"Maybe," she said, pointing at the sherry bottle still gripped in my hand. "Maybe a little of that would help."

I gave it to her and watched her turn it up. She took several long swallows straight from the bottle. When she came up for air, she coughed and sputtered and had a hard time getting her breath back.

"Shit! What is that stuff?"

"Watch your language in my house, miss," I told her. "And keep in mind that beggars can't be choosers."

"Yes'm, sorry. I thank you for it." She turned away, trying not to gag.

"Come on over to the sink," I said, helping her get up. "I'll fix some warm saltwater so you can rinse out your mouth. That'll help that missing tooth."

"Teeth," she said, pulling back her lip to show me where two had once been.

I thought I'd start gagging, too, but I got her to the sink. When she finished rinsing her mouth, I gave her some aspirin and started her toward the stairs.

"A good, hot shower will make you feel better," I said.

"But I have to find Junior."

"Listen to me," I said, stopping on the landing and taking her by the shoulders. "You're in no condition to find anybody. You can't even think straight, and straight thinking is what we need right now. So you just come on with me and get yourself cleaned up and feeling better. Then we'll decide what to do."

By the time I got her out of the shower, dried off, and into one of my gowns, it was all I could do to get her into Little Lloyd's bed. She was out on her feet. Pretty tired, I guessed. To say nothing of four aspirins and a fair slug of cooking sherry.

I closed her door, but left mine open. I lay in bed, thinking about this turn of events, wondering if I should call Deputy Bates or Sam or who. Nothing they could do that night, though, as dead to the world as she was.

I'd wait till morning, then try to get more out of her, like why did Brother Vern have her beaten half to death, and why did he want Little Lloyd, and what in heaven's name was it all about?

I finally went to sleep and dreamed about tires as tall as my head trying to run me down while I searched all over creation looking for that child.

Chapter 16

It was not a restful night. I came awake fully about five o'clock and got on up, with that child still on my mind. He was all I could think of, for he'd been wandering in and out of my dreams most of the night. And, Lord, what was I going to do about the woman across the hall? I thought about calling the sheriff, or telling Deputy Bates, and just washing my hands of the whole mess. On the other hand, it would be worth keeping her around just to see Pastor Ledbetter's face when he heard of it. Maybe I'd remind him of David's harem, and see if he would excuse Wesley Lloyd then.

And at that thought, I began to feel downright dejected again. My house had become a way station for Wesley Lloyd's second family, people popping in and out, and me not knowing who to trust and who not to.

One thing I did know. I'd been tricked again, and this time by that preacher in sheep's clothing. Wesley Lloyd Springer had tricked me, just pulled the wool over my eyes as slick as you please, and now Brother Vernon Puckett had done the same thing. They'd taken advantage of my trusting nature, and I was getting mad as thunder, not only at them, but at myself for being so easy to fool. It wasn't going to happen again, believe you me.

And in the bed right across the hall was the loose woman who'd slept with my husband for untold numbers of years, and here she was sleeping now in my house. If Wesley Lloyd hadn't been six feet under, all he'd have to do would be to walk from one bed to another.

The thought made me sick to my stomach. I needed my morning coffee.

I put on my robe and tiptoed down the stairs to the kitchen. Strange, I thought, to start the day with pictures in my mind of Wesley Lloyd with that woman, yet the night before when she'd stumbled into my house with the evidence of a beating all over her, I hadn't given one thought to Wesley Lloyd. And what they'd done together.

I made the coffee and sat at the table with a cup of it before me.

Thinking. Trying to understand what was going on. Trying not to worry about Little Lloyd. A hard thing to do, now that I knew his mother was worried sick about him.

It's funny about women and children, isn't it? There was Hazel Marie Puckett, with no money, no home, and no husband. Yet she had a child. And here I was, a respectable married woman with everything to give to a child, and the Lord hadn't seen fit. This was just one more situation where I wondered what in the world He was thinking of.

I'd fully expected, within a decent time after being married, to welcome a blessed event. But it hadn't happened and I hadn't questioned it. But Wesley Lloyd had. He'd announced one morning a few years into our marriage that I had an appointment with Dr. Monroe to find out what was wrong with me. I didn't like it, but who was I to question Wesley Lloyd's decisions?

I won't go into too much detail about what that doctor did to me, but you wouldn't have liked it, either. They put me up on a table and stuck my feet in these metal contraptions; then the doctor pulled on the bottom sheet and said, "I'm going to scoot you down, now." And when he did, my knees splayed out on each side, and I thought I'd die when he threw up the sheet and sat down on a little stool to get a good look. And that nurse of his was right down there getting an eyeful, too. And in the midst of that, another nurse opened the door so that anybody in the hall could get in on the picture show. I'm not going to describe how Dr. Monroe poked, prodded, and mashed around down there. Nor where he put his fingers.

It was a mortifying experience, and I decided as soon as they let me off that table they'd never get me back on it. If that's what it took to have children, I'd just pass altogether.

And wouldn't you know it, the very next Sunday there was Dr. Monroe waiting in the narthex to usher us to our pew. I couldn't look him in the face, especially when he smiled and squeezed my arm, so pleasant and genteel with that pink rosebud in his lapel. Humiliating, was what it was, after what he'd looked at and fingered and handled on his examining table. And I didn't like the way he shook Wesley Lloyd's hand and asked how things were going.

That did it for me as far as seeking help from medical science. As a predestinated Presbyterian, I had reason not to go messing around with what wasn't meant to be. I told Wesley Lloyd that I'd just do what Sarah and Hannah and several other barren women had done, and depend on prayer alone. He couldn't very well argue with that, since that was what he was always recommending to me. I figured if the Lord wanted me to have a child He'd give me one.

Coffee slopped out of my cup as Little Lloyd's pale little face came to mind. I stiffened in the chair and said aloud, "But, Lord, I didn't mean give me one *this* way."

The night was slowly giving way to morning, with the gray shadows of shrubs and trees taking shape in the yard. I heard the chirping calls of birds break the stillness of the night. Early birds getting their worms. Which reminded me that an Oreo would taste good with a second cup of coffee. That was not the kind of breakfast that Wesley Lloyd would've approved of, but as we've all noticed, he was no longer around to pass judgment.

I went to the pantry and commenced rummaging around to find the cookies. Lillian liked them, too, and we'd been known to hide the last few from each other. I moved cans of Luck's beans and Campbell's soup, and jars of Jif peanut butter and Hellmann's mayonnaise, and sacks of Lily Maid flour, Dixie Crystals' sugar, and Yelton's cornmeal, but I couldn't find the Oreos. I was determined, so I went through the folded grocery sacks that Lillian saved and, bless Pat, I came across one with something in it.

"Lillian, you sneaky thing," I said to myself, smiling at the thought of her searching for the Oreos I was fixing to eat.

I reached in the Winn-Dixie sack and pulled out a picture book. I stood looking at it for a minute, coming to realize that I was holding Little Lloyd's precious sack. The one he always had with him, the one he slept with, the one he never let out of his sight, the one I'd never thought in a million years he'd go off without. I'd thought it held a little boy's treasures, that's what Lillian had told me. And she'd also told me to keep my hands out of it, and here I was holding a child's well-used picture book that'd been hidden away among the empty sacks. I should've put it back right then. The child had a reason for leaving it there, even though I couldn't think why in the world he would've.

But, as I'd already discovered its contents in all innocence, I opened the front of the book and read the inscription. In for a penny, in for a pound. I recognized my husband's heavy, confident penmanship. He'd written: "For your birthday," and signed it with his full name, "Wesley Lloyd Springer." I sighed, my heart heavy with the thought of my husband's rich private life and my barren one. I turned to the title page. *Aslan's Book of Pictures.* Wesley Lloyd had no more an idea of what a child wanted for his birthday than I did. But I think I would've picked out something better than a book about lions.

I heard Lillian on the porch and felt guilty for plundering through somebody else's belongings. Then I thought better of it. Lillian should know about this so she wouldn't gather up all the empty sacks and throw them out.

"What you doin' up and in the pantry?" she asked as soon as she came in the door.

"Come see what I found," I said, holding out the book. I told her how I'd come to find it, without mentioning Oreos. "I was looking for a pencil," I said.

"Well," she said, "you just put that book back where you found it."

"I intend to."

"You know what it mean, don't you?"

"What?"

"It mean," she said, "that he want to come back. When you leave something you loves somewhere, it draw you back to that place."

"Lillian, you know better," I said, putting the book in the sack and folding down the ends the way Little Lloyd had left them.

"I don't mean it act'ally draw you. I mean it what you *want* it to do. That chile left here intending to come back, 'cause he left what meant the most to him."

"Well, I declare," I said, touched in spite of myself. "I do believe you're right. I can't think of any other reason he'd leave it. He certainly put a lot of stock in this sack, or what was in it, or both. And, Lillian, he found a good hiding place for it. I would've never thought to look here, if I was looking for it. So," I said, thrusting the sack under the empty ones, "back it goes, and it can wait right there for him."

I closed the pantry door and sat down at the table. "Get some coffee and come sit down," I said. "I've got something else to tell you."

When she was settled, I told her about our new houseguest and her pitiful condition. She punctuated my recitation with a series of "No's!" and "You don't mean it's!," but I finally got it told and admitted I didn't know what to do next. Which was no surprise to her.

"That chile in trouble, an' his mama, too," she declared. "What we gon' do 'bout it, Miss Julia?"

"I wish I knew. I'll take something up for her to eat, it'll have to be something soft or liquid, Lillian, two of her teeth have been knocked out. Maybe when she eats a little, she'll be able to help us decide what to do."

"Soup," Lillian said, getting to her feet. "I'll heat some soup and crumble up some sody crackers in it. That be good for her. You pour some milk. She'll need building up.

"Now, what I want to know," she went on as she put a pan on the stove, "is what you gon' tell Deputy Bates? He be here pretty soon."

"I don't think I'll tell him anything," I said. Then, at her quick glare, hurried on, "At this time. He's in a bad position, Lillian. The sheriff, or rather that big lieutenant, wants to question Miss Puckett and that could take all day when we could be looking for Little Lloyd. If I tell Deputy Bates she's here, he'll have to report it and no telling what that would lead to. If he doesn't know it, he can't report it. So, I'm just thinking of what's best for him."

"Uh-huh," she said. She poured soup in a bowl and crumbled in saltines until it was a thick mush. She put the bowl, a spoon, a napkin, and a glass of milk on a tray. I added a bottle of aspirin.

"You take this on up to her," Lillian said, "and I'll fix his breakfast. Go on, now, I think I hear his car turning in. And put yo' clothes on, too. Sound like we got lots to do soon as Deputy Bates close his eyes."

I hurried upstairs with the tray, wanting Deputy Bates to think I was still in bed. Hazel Marie Puckett groaned when I touched her shoulder. Lord, she looked worse in the daylight.

"Shhh," I whispered. "Here's something to eat, but we have to be quiet. There's a deputy sheriff in the house."

Her eyes flew open, as much as the swelling would allow, and I could see the fear in them.

"Is he here for me?" Her mouth was so misshapen that she could hardly form the words.

"Should he be?" I asked sharply, realizing again how little I knew about her.

She shook her head. "You never know."

Well, that was the truth, especially after my run-in with Lieutenant Peavey. "Eat," I told her, "but be quiet about it. Deputy Bates lives here and pretty soon he'll be sleeping right down the hall."

When she'd finished the soup, I helped her across the hall to my bedroom and ran a hot bath for her. Deputy Bates would think it was my morning ablutions. I told her to soak out the soreness while I dressed. I gave her some of my underclothes and then went to the closet to pick out a dress for her. When she came out of the bathroom in my slip, hunched over against the pain in her ribs, I had three for her to choose from. None of them Sunday dresses, just my good, everyday shirtwaists. She looked at them for quite a while.

Then she said, "Do you have anything else?"

"What's wrong with those, I'd like to know?"

"I'm sorry. I just meant, maybe some jeans or shorts."

"There're some things," I informed her, "that ladies don't wear. And jeans and shorts are two of them."

"Sorry," she said, and picked up the first one and put it on. It was maybe a size too big for her, but she was skinny to start with, and it was somewhat longer than she was accustomed to wearing, which wasn't a bad thing. I started looking for some slippers that would fit.

We heard a tap on the door, and Lillian stuck her head in. "He gone to bed," she said, sidling in and closing the door behind her. "I come to fix you up," she said to Hazel Marie, holding up a roll of Ace bandage.

So we helped Hazel Marie undress again, and Lillian displayed another of her unsung talents as she wrapped the bandage around the chest of the woman who'd had my husband's arms around the same places.

Chapter 17

As soon as Lillian finished, Hazel Marie Puckett swallowed hard a few times, then clapped a hand over her mouth.

"Sick!" she gasped, clutching her ribs with one arm and scrambling for the bathroom. She made it to the sink before soup, saltines, milk, and aspirin came spewing out.

I went to the far corner of the room, as far from the sound of it as I could. I'm sensitive to things like that, don't you know, and I couldn't bring myself to go in and help her. I moved the curtains aside and looked down on the street. Cars passing, people going to work, two runners panting and sweating as they pounded by on the sidewalk. Normality everywhere except in my house. Help me, Lord.

I heard water running in the bathroom, and Lillian comforting Hazel Marie. I turned back as Lillian led her toward the bed. She wiped Hazel Marie's face with a wet cloth, then pulled down the covers on the bed.

"Lay back down, now," Lillian told her. "You too weak to be doin' anything. You need a doctor." She glared at me.

I sat down on the side of the bed, trying not to think about how this woman was now in my bed. Wesley Lloyd's bed. But I had to put first things first, and that little boy was the first thing.

"Miss Puckett," I said, "I know you don't feel good, but I need some answers and I need them now. We're both concerned about Little Lloyd, and if you're out of commission, as it seems you are, I need to know how to proceed in finding him."

"Please," she said, "please find him."

"We will. Now, listen to me and give me some straight answers. Who was driving that car when you left Little Lloyd here?"

"Brother Vern," she said, her voice weak but determined. "He was going to take me to Raleigh—I didn't lie to you about that. I had a place in beauty school, and Brother Vern had just come home from preaching somewhere out in California. He was all tore up about Wesley Lloyd's passing. He didn't know about it until he got home, and he offered to drive me down so I could get a new start."

I nodded. "So why'd you change your plans?"

"I didn't change them." She put a hand over her eyes, but I could see tears leaking down her face and into her hair. "I thought we were on our way, but as soon as we left Junior here with you, he told me he had to see some people on church business and it wouldn't take long." She dabbed at her eyes with the corner of my three-hundred-count Egyptian cotton sheet, took a deep breath, and continued on. "He drove way back in the hills, up near the edge of the national forest, I think. I'd never been up there before, but we ended up at a couple of trailers. Single-wides, and the sorriest bunch of people I'd ever seen. Just trailer trash, with outhouses and filth all over the place."

I thought to myself that they must have been a motley crew indeed, since her own people were considered pretty sorry. But I didn't say anything.

"So what happened then?"

"Well, he kept making one excuse after another for not leaving, kept having meetings with the people living there and telling me he was on the Lord's business and I'd have to be patient. And all the while, he was counseling me—that's what he called it—reading the Bible and praying over me."

"Uh-huh," I said when I heard the word "counseling."

"I didn't know what was going on," Hazel Marie said, looking first at me and then Lillian. " 'Cause he kept asking about Wesley Lloyd, how he died, was he saved, had he been right with the Lord, and had he straightened out his affairs before he faced judgment. I didn't know, Miz Springer, I swear Wesley Lloyd never talked about anything like that with me. You have to believe me!" She commenced crying again, burying her face in the sheet.

"Oh, I believe you," I said. "He never discussed things like that with me, either. But don't worry about him being saved. He was a Presbyterian and therefore one of the elect, which makes me wonder about the election process. But that's neither here nor there. What happened then?"

"Well, Brother Vern kept on at me, saying that Wesley Lloyd had promised to provide for me and Junior. He thought I was holding out on him, told me I was being selfish and ungrateful, and I had to re-spect the hierarchy of order that the Lord instituted because woman is the weaker vessel. It just got worse and worse, and he's got a temper,

Miz Springer, a temper you wouldn't believe. I thought he was gonna hit me right there, but the Lord stayed his hand."

"I don't understand," I said, though I'd heard Pastor Ledbetter expound on that hierarchy more times than I cared to recall. In a family, according to him, children are under the wife, and the wife is under the husband, and the husband alone is answerable to God. But I couldn't figure where uncles came into it. "Did he think he had a right to whatever you had?"

"Yes, ma'am, but that's kinda the way it is in our family. The men take care of the money, if there is any, even if it belongs to the women. And since my daddy's dead, and I don't have a . . . Well, you can see how he figures it's his place to look after things for me. But I don't have any things for him to look after."

"Thay Lord," I said, about to roll my eyes until I realized that my situation hadn't been much different from hers. Except for the violence. But then, I'd never refused Wesley Lloyd anything. "So how'd you get away from him?"

"I kept asking to go, telling him I had to be in Raleigh, and he'd promised. Finally, after a day or two, I forget now how long it was, I just decided to walk outta there. I didn't know where we were, but I thought I'd just walk till I come to a road and follow that. Soon as I started out, though, some of those people took hold of me and wouldn't let me leave."

"Well, I never," Lillian said. "Don't tell no more till I get back. You need some liquids in yo' stomick. Jes' lay right still while I go get you something to drink."

She came right back with a glass of chipped ice, a spoon, and a can of ginger ale.

"Suck on this," she commanded, shoveling a spoonful of ice into Hazel Marie's mouth. "An' soon as yo' stomick feel settled, we'll start on this drink."

"Go on," I urged. "What happened then?"

"Well, Brother Vern was still trying to get me right with the Lord, he said, so things wasn't too bad. Except I couldn't leave. He preached at me till I thought I'd go cross-eyed. He just would not believe that Wesley Lloyd hadn't left me anything. All I had was three hundred dollars for beauty school. I offered him that and he took it, then he went on and on about Wesley Lloyd's papers. I didn't know what he was talking about, and still don't. I swear I don't.

"The next thing I knew, he told me to get in the car. That was Friday, I think, Friday evening. He drove me to my house, I mean the one I'd been living in, and, Miz Springer, I got such a shock when we pulled in. Two of my cousins, twice removed, was moving my furniture out, Jerome and Donnie. They just loaded it up in a U-Haul and a pickup. I tried to stop them, but they wouldn't listen to me. Said Brother Vern'd told them they could have whatever they could move. They come from the other side of the family, and that whole bunch is not worth a hill of beans."

I almost smiled as I thought of the pot and the kettle, but I didn't. "So they took your furniture?"

"Yes'm, every stick," she went on, wiping her eyes and taking a quivering breath. "I tried to get Brother Vern to make them quit, but he told me that your lawyer was going to take possession if the family didn't get it first. He said he'd looked through everything I had and couldn't find Wesley Lloyd's papers, and he'd run out of patience."

She turned away and hid her face. Lillian reached over and patted her on the arm. "Now don't you worry, honey. You safe here with us."

I rolled my eyes at that, and asked Hazel Marie, "So what happened then?" I asked.

"He talked awhile to my cousins. Then he left."

"And?"

"They beat the shit outta me," she said.

My mouth tightened as the shock of the word resounded in Wesley Lloyd's bedroom. I was not accustomed to such language. However. What she said seemed to be pretty much the truth.

"Brother Vern come back sometime later," she went on, "but, Miz Springer, I couldn't give what I didn't have. And he said if I wasn't gonna be obedient like I was supposed to be, he'd just have to keep Junior away from me. Said I wasn't fit to raise a child, being outside of God's will like I was. Miz Springer, I was alayin' in that garage, hardly able to get my breath and hurtin' so bad I thought I was gonna die, and he said he'd just keep Junior till I decided to submit to the Lord's will. And he left me there, bleedin' and hurtin', and I knew he was going after my little boy."

She was sobbing by this time.

To give her a chance to collect herself, I told her how we'd gone to her house and how Deputy Bates had found blood all over the garage, and teeth, too, and how, when we got back to town, we'd found that my house had been broken into.

"It had to've been Jerome and Donnie," she said. "Maybe Brother Vern thought you had Wesley Lloyd's papers."

"I do," I said. "Or rather my lawyer does. But there's nothing concerning you or the child in them. I'd know it if there was."

"I bet he tear up the house 'cause Little Lloyd wadn't here for him to get ahold of," Lillian said. "That man's mean as a snake. But, honey, how you get from that place to here in the shape you in?"

"Walked and crawled," she said. "I was afraid to try to get a ride, lookin' like I do. Afraid somebody'd call the law on me. And afraid Donnie and Jerome would be looking for me, too. So I went through fields and woods, hiding out in the daytime and come into town after dark, so afraid he'd get to Junior before me. And he did." More crying.

I felt bad about it all. There I'd been so anxious to be rid of the child, and blithely let him go off while his mama was walking miles to get to him. I felt real bad.

"Drink some of this," Lillian urged, holding out the glass of ginger ale. "I 'spect you keep it down now."

"I still feel sick," Hazel Marie said, "but I got to get up and look for Junior."

"The problem is," I said, "is where're you going to look? You think Brother Vern took him to Raleigh, like he told me?"

She thought for a minute. "No. He just told you that to get Junior away from you. No, he's still around, 'cause he thinks I've got something of Wesley Lloyd's. Oh, me," she said, as she began to untangle herself from the sheets. "I feel like I'm gonna throw up again."

Lillian helped her to the bathroom, saying, "This girl need some medicine or a doctor or something."

"Not a doctor," Hazel Marie said. "I'll be all right."

"Watch after her, Lillian. Get her into one of my gowns while I walk downtown to the drugstore. I ought to be able to find something that'll make her feel better."

I put on my hat, hung my pocketbook on my arm, and commenced walking. Perkins Drugs was only two blocks away on the corner of Polk and Main, so I could walk it quicker than I could find a parking place.

I marched down the sidewalk, intent on my errand, going over in my mind what purchases to make for the Puckett woman. Miss Myrtie Gossett came walking toward me, that ugly tote bag on her shoulder, and wanted to stop and talk. I waved and passed on by. I had no time for gossip. Besides, I was the hot topic, so she couldn't tell me anything I didn't already know.

Troy Beckworth was leaning on the door of his insurance office, hoping for a calamity that would scare up some business for him, and I do mean scare. He'd taken to advertising on the Asheville television, warning people about the dangers of flooding from the sea surge of hurricanes, and us two hundred miles from the coast and three thousand feet above sea level.

"How do, Miz Springer," he said.

"Sea surge," I replied. "For the Lord's sake." And passed on by.

And when I went into the drugstore, who should I run into but Norma Cantrell in her big hair and a turquoise pantsuit. She was getting a prescription filled instead of taking care of the pastor's office, which is what she should've been doing.

"Why, Miss Julia," she said, patting that hair to be sure it was still a foot high. "What you doing in the drugstore?"

"Minding my own business," I said, looking at my watch. "Particularly since I'm not supposed to be working in anybody's office."

She huffed a little at that, but her salary and the preacher's came out of my pledge and I had a right to demand a day's work for a day's pay.

I went about my business of picking out the things on the mental list I'd made. A box of straws, a bottle of Extra Strength Tylenol, another Ace bandage, and a hot-water bottle for the soreness. I carried it all to the counter by the cash register where Norma was standing. She pretended she wasn't interested, but she eyed everything I put down, and I saw her trying to get Buck Tatum's attention by making little sideways jerks of her head at my pile of merchandise. He kept on counting pills, and I went back down the aisle.

After considering all the places where Hazel Marie had been messed up, I picked up two more hot-water bottles. I don't like those heating pads with electric cords that plug in the wall. They're all right if you're holding them to a sore place while you're sitting up, but try turning over in bed.

I took the hot-water bottles to the counter and with a look at Norma dared her to say anything. I stood there tapping my fingers on the counter, trying to think of what else I needed.

"Uh-huh," I said, turning on my heel and catching a glimpse of Norma's avid stare. I paid no mind as I went looking for a tube of Ben-Gay. Good for muscle soreness and stiffness. I added some Q-Tips, Band-Aids, and Mercurochrome. Then, on the Puckett woman's request, a bottle of foundation to cover her bruises. Cover Girl, which seemed apt.

When I got back to the counter, I called Buck to come help me. I needed one more thing.

"I'll be through here in a minute, Miz Springer," he said from behind his drug counter. "Just getting a few things together for Miz Cantrell."

I didn't mind waiting a few minutes, but Norma said, "Oh, that's all right. Go ahead and wait on Miz Springer. I'm in no hurry." She turned and looked me straight in the eye. "Pastor Ledbetter sent me." Letting me know she was on the job.

"All right, then," Buck said, "what can I do you for, Miz Springer?"

"I need some paregoric."

Norma's eyebrows went up like they were on springs.

"Can't do it, Miz Springer. Have to have a prescription now."

I rolled my eyes at that. Somebody's always changing rules that've worked well enough for years. I said, "And just what are people supposed to do when they need relief? Call a doctor and pay his bill, too?"

Buck and Norma exchanged knowing glances, as if they thought I was blind or too crazy to notice.

"Well, now, Miz Springer," Buck said, pulling at the tail of his white jacket. He loved to dispense medical information along with his pills. He'd wanted to be a doctor or a veterinarian. I couldn't remember which, but they wouldn't let him in.

"It's a controlled substance now," he informed me. "Too many people self-medicating themselves with it. Want me to call your doctor and get a prescription for it?"

"No, if I need it bad enough I'll call him myself." I wasn't ready to explain to a doctor why I wanted a prescription for a painkiller. "Just give me a large bottle of Pepto-Bismol for now."

Norma couldn't stand it any longer. "What're you going to do with all that stuff, Miz Springer? If you don't mind me asking."

"I do mind, Norma," I said. "But since you have, I'll tell you. Instead of letting the church tear down my house, I'm going to turn it into a home for injured cats and dogs. And when they're better, I'm going to let them run around in the church parking lot. So be prepared to do some scooping."

I paid for my purchases and left the drugstore, aware of Norma's squinty-eyed appraisal following me down the sidewalk.

Chapter 18

Lillian and I doctored on Hazel Marie for some time when I got home with the medical supplies. I kept hoping she'd drop off to sleep, but every time her eyes began to close she'd think of Little Lloyd and start crying again. And every time I turned around Lillian was handing her another drink. If it wasn't ginger ale, it was a milk shake or a glass of lemonade, saying she had to have something on her stomach. It's a wonder she didn't begin to float. After a while, she ate a slice of dry toast and kept it down, which relieved me considerably.

She kept wanting to get up and look for the boy, but we convinced her that the best thing she could do was stay in bed until we knew where to look.

I volunteered to call all her relatives down in Benson's Gap, and we decided that I'd pretend to be somebody wanting Brother Vern for a preaching service and not mention Little Lloyd at all.

"That's the best way to do it," I said. "We don't know how many others are in this with him, but I'll bet that wherever the Reverend Vernon Puckett is, the boy is, too."

"He may have him hid somewhere," Lillian said.

"Don't create problems," I told her. "Besides, if I find Brother Puckett, you better believe I'll find Little Lloyd. I'll have that man in jail so fast his head'll swim. The idea of lying to me to get that child. To say nothing of ransacking my house. I tell you, he'll think twice about messing with me again."

Hazel Marie slept most of the afternoon, except for the times Lillian woke her with another glass of something to drink. During that time, I spoke to more Pucketts than I'd ever known existed. At first it was hard to do, unaccustomed as I am to lying. But after a while, I about convinced myself that the little church I'd made up really needed Brother Vern's ministry. Most of the people I spoke to had that local mountain twang, and I found myself following along.

"I'm alookin' for Brother Vernon Puckett," I'd say. "They's a need for his preachin' in our church, 'cause it's about to split in two, and we need a revival real bad."

That certainly got more cooperation than when I said something like, "I wonder if you could tell me, please, where I might find the Reverend Puckett."

But none of them knew where he was. Or if they did, they weren't telling.

After that disappointment, I had another idea. It was Tuesday, and Brother Vern's telecast was supposed to run at nine o'clock that night. Unless he canceled out and ran a substitute in, we'd know he was in Spartanburg for at least an hour.

When I told Hazel Marie what I'd come up with, she wanted to head down the mountain right then and wait for him to get to the studio.

"No," I said. "If he sees you before he starts his program, he'll just drive off. You ought to wait and see if he's on live and not just running a tape. Which he might be, if he thinks you're able to get to him."

When Lillian heard what we were going to do, she announced that she was staying to watch, too. So we kept Hazel Marie in bed in my room until Deputy Bates was up and gone, and then we helped her downstairs. I'd offered her either my cotton chenille zip-up robe or my blue satin wraparound with lace inserts, the one I kept in case I ever had to go to the hospital. She chose the blue satin, and why wasn't I surprised?

"Come to the kitchen first," Lillian told her. "You need to rinch yo' mouth again with salty water. An' I fixed you another milk shake to put some meat on yo' bones."

Hazel Marie brought the milk shake into the living room, and Lillian made her comfortable on the sofa with pillows behind her back. I turned the television on and we all leaned forward to watch the *Feeding the Flame* program, coming to you live with Brother Vernon Puckett, the anointed of God, preaching with Holy Ghost power the good news of the Gospel.

And there he was, in a royal blue suit and matching tie with a white dove on it. His hair looked wet and slicked back, except for that little curly swirl on his forehead. He made a big thing of attaching what he called a lavaliere microphone to his lapel, laughing and pretending he didn't know how it worked. Just your average workingman, unfamiliar with technical devices. Uh-huh, and those one-eight-hundred numbers running across the screen in front of him.

"Pray with me now, all you brothers and sisters in the telecast-viewing audience," he started out, but not a one of us bowed our

heads. *"Lord, we ask that You send the devil packin' tonight, and let your angels just camp around us so we'll be in a frame of mind to receive your blessin', praise God, amen.*

"Now then," he went on, hardly taking a breath. *"I want you-all to know that a special blessin' is comin' to you tonight. I don't want to say I'm happy about this, you know how it is, but Brother Winslow, who has the next hour after us, has taken sick, and we're prayin' for you, Brother Winslow, but the good people here at the station has asked if I can go on for two hours instead of my usual one."* He paused, looked around, and put this surprised look on his face. *"Can I go on for two hours? Brethren, I can go on for ten hours! It don't take no effort for me to preach just as long as somebody's out there to listen! But now, before I get revved up good, let's hear from Sister Rubynell. Come on out here, Rubynell, and backin' her up is the Glory Boys Band; take a bow, boys. They all down here from up in Shelby, North Carolina, and we thank you for it."*

Hazel Marie sat up and said, "He's going to be there for two hours, and I can be there in that time. I'm going to Spartanburg and make him tell me where he's got Junior."

"Wait," I said, waving her back. "You don't have a way to get there, and we don't know yet if this is a rerun. Let's be sure this is live before you do anything."

By that time, Sister Rubynell had appeared in what looked like one of my housedresses, and she was a sight to see. Her hair was silvery white and teased so high that Norma Cantrell's couldn't hold a candle to it. She looked about my age, with a few more pounds on her and a whole lot more wrinkles. In spite of that curled mass of hair, she wasn't wearing a lick of makeup except for a thick layer of blue eye shadow. The contrast was jarring, to say the least.

"That woman look like she been rode hard and put up wet," Lillian said, frowning at the screen.

She sounded it, too, because when she opened her mouth, without so much as an introduction by the band, she came out with a loud, piercing rendition of "Will the Circle Be Unbroken?" Fingernails on a chalkboard, I thought, turning down the volume. But she evermore got into it, at one point snapping her fingers and saying, "Pick it up, boys," in spite of their flailing away to do just that, and she didn't miss a beat. She had a set of lungs on her, I gave her that.

I cut my eyes over at Lillian and Hazel Marie to see how they were taking this, not wanting to offend anybody by saying what I was thinking. Lillian's church likes hand-clapping, foot-tapping music sung on key by rich voices, so she was sitting there with a frown on her face. Hazel Marie, on the other hand, was watching intently and nodding her head in time to Sister Rubynell's screeching. We Presbyterians like semiprofessional choirs to do our singing for us, with only a few congregational hymns to mumble our way through.

"Thank you, Sister, and all you Glory Boys," Brother Vern sang out on the last twang of the electric guitar. There was a smattering of applause as the camera panned across an audience of a dozen or so people sitting on folding chairs.

"Now, I want all you folks in the telecast-viewing area to listen up, 'cause I got some good news and I got some bad news," Brother Vern said. *"The bad news is, there's a devil loose out there lookin' for whoever he can devour. Make no mistake about it, he don't want no New York strip with A.1. sauce and he don't want no strawberry shortcake neither. He craves the souls of men. And women's and children's. Don't matter to him, he'll take 'em all. But the good news is, JEE-sus was hungry, too, and you know what he ate? Help me now, He swallowed up death. Praise God, He took death and swallowed it whole and not a one of us has to be afraid of the devil's appetite no more. Listen to me, now, 'cause I'm agonna tell you all about it. Just as soon as I wipe my face here."*

He laughed in that folksy way of his, and took a large white handkerchief from his pocket. He mopped the sweat from his face, which was glistening in the television lights.

"All right, lissen to me now," he went on as he paced back and forth. *"You got to have JEE-sus in your heart. Wait a minute, wait a minute. Lissen here, you don't have to mix up a cup of Kool-Aid or hitch a ride on Hale-Bopp to find Him. Nossir, that ain't the way to do it. All you have to do is say, 'Come on in, Jesus,' and that's it. Wait a minute, don't turn that dial, all you gonna see is somebody trying to sell you a car or a double-decker hamburger. You don't need that, so stay tuned 'cause I got lots more to tell you.*

"But first, I want you to meet a real special guest right here in the studio with us. He come all the way from Memphis, Tennessee, to tell us about a special ministry that God has called him to. Come on over here with that television camera." As Brother Vern moved to the side, he kept looking over his shoulder to be sure the camera had him in view. He pulled up a chair beside a sofa where a very wide woman was sitting. She held a toddler on a lap that looked full of an unborn child. Beside her was a wisp of a man, bald head shining, who was holding another toddler. Between them was a little older child.

"This here's Brother Stedman Jones and his good wife, Sister Leesie. Welcome to the Fanning the Flame *program, good people.*

Now, folks," Brother Vern said, looking directly into the camera, *"Brother Stedman and Sister Leesie take to heart the Lord's commandment to be fruitful and multiply, 'cause they got, count 'em now, sixteen children, praise God!"*

The camera panned quickly across a row of children bunched up behind the sofa. Lillian shook her head and said, "Sixteen head of chil'ren. How they feed 'em?"

The camera came back to Brother Vern, who leaned toward his guests and said, *"What's the Lord got you doing now, Brother Stedman?"*

"Glad you asked," Brother Stedman said, unrolling a narrow two-foot long piece of paper. *"I want everybody to call in right now to get this special gift for only twenty-three dollars, plus postage and handlin'. See, it's a bumper sticker that tells everybody where you're goin'. And, believe you me, it ain't to no Wal-Mart's."*

"What that thing say?" Lillian asked.

"It says," I said, squinting against the glare of the television lights on the shiny paper, " 'Warning! Driver May Disappear at Any Moment.' What in the world does that mean?"

"It's talking about the Rapture," Hazel Marie said, surprising me no end. "You know, when all the believers will be taken up in the air." I vaguely remembered hearing something about that from a visiting evangelist in First Church. But most of us mainline Presbyterians are post-dispensationalists, or so Wesley Lloyd told me.

"I declare," I said, turning my attention back to the set.

"Hear that, folks?" Brother Vern took one end of the banner and held it up high. *"Put one of these on your bumper, and you'll be doing your neighbors a favor, telling them to watch out for cars going every whichaway when that final trump sounds. In the twinklin' of an eye we'll be swept right up outta our sports-utility vehicles and our pickups and our living room recliners, ain't that right, Brother Stedman? Now, why don't you tell us what all you been doing over in Memphis. I know you been busy."*

"Yessir, I sure have," Brother Stedman said, and I thought of those sixteen children and figured out what he'd been busy doing. *"Besides running off these bumper stickers, I been workin' on them abortion clinics. I've closed down two of 'em and been put in jail three times, praise God. I need your prayers real bad, 'cause you got your liberals, and your secular humanists, and your homasexals, and they're all dead set against me."*

"Well, you got my prayers, Brother," Brother Vern assured him. While Brother Vern went on, it came to me how some Christians

seemed to always need to have something or somebody to be against. If it wasn't desegregation, it was women's lib. If it wasn't sex education, it was secular humanism. And if it wasn't one-worlders, it was just plain Democrats. Now it was abortionists and homosexuals who were ruining the country and destroying Christianity. Well, I had more faith in the Lord of Calvin and Knox than to get carried away over that unlikely possibility. He'd been running things since the beginning, and I didn't figure He'd have much trouble keeping a lid on things in this day and age. Besides, we didn't have any abortion clinics in Abbotsville. Or homosexuals, either.

"Now," Brother Vern said, drawing my attention back to him. *"Brother Stedman, I want to give our telecast viewers a good look at your fine family. Smile, young'uns, you're on* Candid Camera! *Come on, put the camera on ever'one of 'em, praise God for the stars in your crown, Sister Leesie."*

That poor woman had sat all through this with a smile plastered on her face, without a word to say for herself. Of course, nobody had given her a chance to speak, and she was probably too tired anyway. I kept wondering how she got all those children fed, washed, and dressed to make their appearance on television.

"Look!" Lillian yelled, jumping up and pointing at the screen. "Look right there!"

"What is it?" I strained to see what she was pointing at.

"It's Junior!" Hazel Marie came off the sofa, holding her ribs and spilling her milk shake all over my Oriental. "It's him! Brother Vern's got him in that family! He's right there, don't you see him?"

"It is him," I said, seeing that little pinched face with the thick glasses sliding down his nose. All the children were smiling and posing for the camera like they'd done it a hundred times before, while Little Lloyd stood in their midst looking lost and forlorn. I noticed that he had on his clip-on tie because, I was sure, he didn't have anybody to make the knot in his good one.

"I got to get down there," Hazel Marie said. "Miz Springer, I hate to ask you, but could you loan me enough money for a taxi? I'll pay you back if it takes me twenty years."

"A taxi? To Spartanburg? That's forty miles from here, and I certainly will not." I stood up and clicked off the television. "We'll take my car. Get yourself together and let's get started."

Chapter 19

"Wait for me," Lillian said. "I'm goin', too, but I got to get this milk shake up."

"Leave it," I said, "we don't have time to be cleaning rugs. It's forty miles down there, and he's going to be on the air for"—I looked at my watch—"another hour and a half. If we hurry, we can be down there about the time he's through."

"Oh, please, let's hurry," Hazel Marie said. She was so jittery that the blue satin robe was shaking and shimmering around her.

Lillian looked at her and then at me. "You want me to go get her clothes?"

"No," I said, "it takes too long to get her dressed. You two go on out to the car, and I'll lock up the house."

I got my pocketbook, checked the cash in my change purse, turned out the lights, and hurried outside to the garage. Hazel Marie was already in the passenger seat, while Lillian stood waiting for me.

"You want me to drive?" she asked.

"I do not. I'm perfectly capable of driving this car."

"Well, I know you don't see too good at night."

"Neither do you," I said. "Besides, I do have headlights, so get on in and let's go."

She pulled back the driver's seat and started cramming herself into the narrow backseat, moaning and groaning as she did. "Whew," she said as she plopped in, "this ain't built for no normal person."

Hazel Marie had her hands clasped in her lap, staring straight ahead, willing us to get started.

I drove through town, seeing only a few cars at that time of night, but half blinded by the headlights of the ones we did meet. By the time we got to the interstate I'd learned not to look right into them. There were only a few headlights way off in the distance when I got ready to merge, so I was able to do it without having to fit in between a stream of cars.

"Miz Springer," Hazel Marie said softly and a little hesitantly, "you don't have to stop and look on a ramp. You can just go on out in the nearest lane. If you don't mind me saying so."

"I'm doing the driving," I reminded her, but I considered what she'd said. I thought you always had to stop and look both ways when entering a main road.

After a while Lillian said, "How fast you goin'?"

"I'm almost up to the speed limit."

"Well, get on up there and a little over," she said. "We got to get to that place 'fore he go off with that boy again."

"Oh, yes, please let's do," Hazel Marie said.

"Now look, you two, I want to get there as quick as you do. But I want us there in one piece, so spare me the comments."

"I probably could drive," Hazel Marie said, "if you need me to."

I glanced at her, hunched over with the pain in her ribs. "You can't hardly straighten up, much less take the wheel of a car. I'll get us there, don't worry. And in plenty of time, too."

In fact, night driving wasn't as hard as I'd thought it'd be. There wasn't a lot of traffic, and what there was came in bunches that whizzed on past us.

"Uh-oh," Lillian said as a flash of lightning lit the southwestern sky. "Look like a cloud comin' up."

"Heat lightning, most likely," I said. Still, it worried me. I could do without one of our fierce mountain storms that usually followed a heat spell like we'd been having.

For long stretches, we were the only car on the road. The four-lane highway dipped and climbed, ran past the Continental Divide, and curved between high cliffs before streaming down the mountain to the flat country below. Our headlights cut a tunnel through the night as lightning occasionally flashed behind a cloud ahead of us. I thought I could hear the tires humming on the pavement, then realized it was Hazel Marie moaning. Or praying.

"I jus' thought of something," Lillian said, leaning forward between the front seats. "What that chile doin' in that fam'ly? Reckon Brother Vern give him away?"

"Oh, don't say that," Hazel Marie cried. "Surely he wouldn't do that."

"He might," I said. "He might want him where he'd be out of your reach, and mine. But don't you worry about it. We know Brother Stedman lives in Memphis, and from what he said about his activities there, I don't expect we'd have any trouble tracking him down."

"I want to get Junior tonight. I just don't think I could stand it if we miss him."

"We'll get him," I said, with as much assurance as I could muster. I wasn't ready to drive to Memphis that night, but I'd do it if I had to.

"I jus' thought of something else," Lillian said. "Do anybody know where we goin' when we get to Spartanburg?"

Trust Lillian to say what had just occurred to me. That studio on television had seemed so real that I guess I just thought we could drive down the mountain and straight to it.

"I think I know where it is," Hazel Marie said. "I was down there one time when Brother Vern had the idea of a family band. The Puckett Pickers or the Pickin' Pucketts, he couldn't decide which, but it didn't work out. He said music was supposed to be to the glory of God, but we couldn't stay in tune long enough to glorify anybody."

"I declare," I said, wondering what other talents Hazel Marie had. Besides those Wesley Lloyd had appreciated.

"I jus' thought of somethin' else," Lillian said.

"For goodness' sakes, Lillian," I said, "what now?"

"We might ought to have a plan of some kind. I mean, do we go inside an' grab him? Or do we wait till he come out an' scoop him up then? Better think about what we gonna do."

So we all thought for a mile or so, considering the best way to snatch a child who'd been snatched from us. I wished I could think of some way to trick Brother Vern the way he'd tricked me, but I couldn't. I looked over at Hazel Marie, but all I could see in the glow of the dashboard lights was an intense frown on her face. She was either hurting bad or thinking hard. Maybe both.

"Uh, Miz Springer," she said, scrunching up her shoulders so that I thought her pain had gotten worse. "I hate to ask this, but you reckon we could stop for a minute?"

"You want to stop?" I took my foot off the gas and got a blaring horn from a lumber truck that passed us so fast it shook the car. I speeded up a little to keep from getting run over, and asked, "You going to be sick?"

"No'm, it's just that I got to, well, pee-pee, and I don't think I can hold it any longer."

"*Pee-pee?*" I almost laughed, then remembered what she could've called it. "Lillian, help me look for a filling station. I haven't seen one for miles, but we ought to come up on a sign pretty soon." But the roadsides were dark, and there were no exit signs ahead that I could see.

"I can't wait, Miz Springer. I got to go real bad."

"Well, I don't know what I can do. I can't make a filling station with a bathroom just appear out here on the side of the road."

She moaned.

Lillian said, "Be quicker to jus' pull over an' let her go beside the car."

"Why, that's plain trashy," I said. "Lillian, this is your fault, making her drink all day long."

"Ain't nobody gonna see her, so jus' pull on over. When you got to go, you got to go, an' don't matter if it do be trashy."

I didn't like it, but I pulled over onto the edge of the road. After fiddling around on the dashboard, I found my blinker lights. Hazel Marie had the door open before we stopped rolling good, and Lillian shoved out after her.

"Squat down right here," she told her, "an' I'll stand so cars comin' up can't see you."

"I don't even care," Hazel Marie said tightly, hiking up my satin robe and hunkering down beside the car.

"Reckon they's any snakes out here?" Lillian said, almost stopping Hazel Marie in her tracks, so to speak.

Suddenly a blast of light hit us. We were lit up like the sun had come up at ten o'clock at night. My heart nearly stopped when I heard the whooshing sound of air brakes behind us. A big truck, with running lights over the cab and a pair of headlights that put us on display for miles around, pulled up behind us.

"Thay Lord," Lillian said. She spread her skirt out to screen Hazel Marie from view.

"Hurry up. Hurry up," I urged. "My Lord, he's getting out!" I saw the shadowy figure of a man climb down from the cab and walk over to my window.

"You ladies need any help?" he asked, leaning down to look across me at Hazel Marie's head, which she was covering with one hand. I gave her credit. I couldn't see much of him, but he wore a baseball cap and had a powerful masculine odor to him. Probably been cooped up in that truck for miles on end.

"No, but thank you for stopping," I said. "We're all right, just a, you know, a necessity stop."

"Well," he said, grinning and spitting on the road, "I know how that is, but you ladies need to be careful along here. They's been somebody 'long this stretch with a blue light that ain't no police."

"Hurry up, Hazel Marie," I said.

"I'm tryin'," she said.

"Where you ladies goin'?" the trucker asked.

"We goin' to Spartanburg," Lillian said. I glared at her, trying to stop her from telling a stranger our business. "You know where they's a television station down there?"

"You mean that Christian broadcastin' one? I know where that is. If y'all're headin' there, you can follow me. I'm goin' to the interchange and on up to the Milliken plant on I-85, an' we'll pass right by it."

Hazel Marie popped up right then, straightening out her satin negligee. She said, "Oh, thank you, thank you. That's wonderful. We'll follow right behind you."

The trucker stood up to look at her over the top of the car. Then he leaned down to look at her through my window. He couldn't decide which view he liked best, but I doubted he'd seen many beat-up blondes in satin negligees on the side of the road before this. But I could've been wrong.

"Lemme see can I get back in this car," Lillian said, crawling over Hazel Marie's seat. "We needs to be there real soon, Mr. Truckin' Man, so don't spare the gas."

"Now, just one minute," I said. "We don't need to go too fast. Are you in, Miss Puckett? Reach over and get the door, Lillian."

"This ain't gonna be no problem," the trucker said, squatting now so he could get a good look at Hazel Marie through the window. "Just get behind me, stay a coupla car lengths away, and the slipstream'll do the rest. Y'all got a CB in there?"

"I don't think so," I said.

"Well, I won't lose you, and when we get to your exit, I'll blink my lights and blow the air horn in plenty of time for you to make your turn. Just stay in the same lane I'm in all the way down." He straightened up and began walking back to his truck. Then he turned around and came back. "I hope you don't mind me askin', but are y'all some kinda gospel-singin' group?"

I nearly choked, picturing Lillian in her white nurse's uniform, Hazel Marie in my blue satin robe, and me in my Leslie Fay shirtwaist singing gospel songs on television.

"Nossir," I said and, figuring we needed to provide some explanation for ourselves, went on, "we're going down for a healing service." Forgive me, Lord, but it was the only thing that seemed to fit us all. I don't hold with lying as a usual thing, but the ox was just about in the ditch.

"Aw, I'm real sorry to hear that," he said. "Don't you worry none; I'll get you there." He gave Hazel Marie a tender look, a change from what he'd been giving her.

"We need to hurry," she said. "The program goes off at eleven, and I just got to get there before then."

"You'll make it if I have anything to do with it." He ran to his truck, put it in gear and pulled out around us, tapping his horn as he went.

I followed, and it was as easy as he said because I didn't have to watch all the other traffic. He did it for me. All I had to do was click on my turn signal when he did, change lanes when he did, and stay right behind him.

"Uh-oh," Lillian said.

"What now?"

"They's another big ole truck comin' up behind us. He might want us to get outta the way."

"I don't think so," Hazel Marie said, gingerly turning to look back. "No, they've put us in the rocking chair."

"In the what?"

"We're between two eighteen-wheelers an' they won't let anybody else in. He must've called out over his CB an' told him we need to get there in a hurry."

Across the way on the interstate, two big trucks going west on I-26 blew their horns and blinked every light they had, which was plenty. After a while, a car pulled up alongside of us and just stayed at our speed, every person in it gawking at us.

"What them folks want?" Lillian asked. They were worrying me, too.

"See that antenna?" Hazel Marie pointed at the car. "They got a CB, so they've heard about us."

"Good Lord!" I gasped as bright lights lit up the car beside us, and a horn blew a blast that sounded like Brother Stedman's last trump. Another big truck came rushing up behind the car, getting right on his bumper. This new truck kept blinking his lights and blowing that horn. The driver of the car spurted on past us like a bat out of you-know-where. Scared to death, and I didn't blame him.

The third truck then eased up until the trailer was even with us, and we moved on down the interstate with one truck in front, one behind, and one to the side of us.

"They got us in the pen," Hazel Marie said. "Thank you, Lord." She leaned back against the headrest, and seemed to relax for the first time since we'd started.

That was the easiest driving I'd ever done, and I resolved to get myself one of those CB radios and from then on call for an escort every time I went anywhere.

We rolled on down I-26 eastbound, the third truck occasionally pulling ahead to let a fast car pass, then easing back beside us. When we got to the I-85 interchange, I didn't even have to worry about getting on the right exit ramp or merging with the heavier traffic. I just leaned that little car in the curve right along with our trucking friends and let them clear a path for us.

"I think I see it," Hazel Marie said, pointing ahead of us. "See those red lights high up over there? I bet that's the tower."

"I can't look," I said, "but you must be right. He's moving us over to the outside lane. Yes, and there go his lights. Y'all watch for the exit."

The lights on the truck in front of us were blinking like a nervous Christmas tree, and the horn started blowing. I flipped on my turn signal to let him know he could let up, I'd gotten his message.

"There it is!" Lillian yelled. "Slow down! Turn off! Turn off 'fore you miss it!"

"Blow your horn back at him, Miz Springer," Hazel Marie said.

"I can't do everything at once," I cried, slowing down, straining to see the exit, blowing my horn, and hoping the truck behind wouldn't climb over us. When we were safely on the exit road, every truck on both sides of the interstate blew their air horns and flashed their lights. Truckers' prayers for poor Hazel Marie, I guess. Lord, forgive me for lying by indirection, but she could use whatever prayers she could get.

The broadcasting studio was a squatty cement block building with that steel-strutted edifice, blinking with red lights, towering above it. A weed-choked wire fence enclosed the parking lot, with a security light on a pole at the open gate. A half-dozen or so cars were parked in the uneven asphalt lot, but we didn't see any people. One yellow bulb burned over the entrance to the building, and there was a weak light coming from a small window high up beside the door.

"It sure looks closed up. Wonder if anybody's in there," I said, trying to decide the best place to park.

"Somebody's there," Hazel Marie said. "The studios don't have windows, that's why it's so dark."

I knew that.

"I'll park by the side of the building while we decide how to go about this," I said.

"If you don't mind, Miz Springer," Hazel Marie said, "park over in that far corner. I got to pee-pee again if we got time."

I rolled my eyes even though nobody could see me, and drove over to the darkest corner in the lot. Hazel Marie slid out of the car and I was treated to the slithering of satin and the top of her head again as she crouched down beside the open door.

"She losin' a lot of fluids," Lillian said. "We ought to stop on the way home an' get her a drink."

I said, "Don't even think about it."

"Woo-oo," Hazel Marie sighed as she eased back in her seat. "That's a relief. I was 'bout to pop."

"All right, now," I said. "We're here, and Brother Vern's program'll be over in about ten minutes. What're we going to do?"

"I'm gonna sneak in and get Junior," Hazel Marie said.

"You ain't gonna do no sneakin' in what you got on," Lillian reminded her.

"I'll go in," I said. "Little Lloyd'll come when he sees me. He knows me."

"Uh-huh," Lillian said. "An' that Brother Vern know you, too. You think he jus' gonna let you come take that chile by the hand an' walk outta there? Ever'body in there workin' for Brother Vern, an' all he got to do is yell, 'Stop that woman!' an' they stop you."

"Well, what do you suggest we do?" I asked, edgy now that we were there without knowing what to do next.

"I bet those truckers would've helped us," Hazel Marie said. "Wish I'd thought to ask 'em. We coulda told them my little boy was kidnapped by a crazy snake handler or something." Once lying starts, it just keeps growing, which is why I'm against it as a general rule.

"Huh," I said, "too late now." But I shivered at the thought of a bunch of wild truck drivers crashing in on a live television program. Sister Rubynell'd really have something to screech about, to say nothing of all those children in there. "We better think of something quick."

"Brother Vern don't know me," Lillian said. "Lemme outta this car. I'm goin' in an' get our little boy."

Chapter 20

"Okay," I agreed, because I couldn't think of a better way. "Miss Puckett, let Lillian out on your side. Then if you can manage it, see if you can get in the backseat. When she comes out with Little Lloyd, we won't have time to get you in and out of the car."

She nodded and opened the door again. When she was out, hunched over and holding her rib cage, Lillian crawled out beside her. Then, whimpering with pain, Hazel Marie managed to get over the seat and into the back. She groaned as she settled into the seat. A flash of lightning lit up the weeds along the fence, as well as her drawn face, frowning with pain.

"Lordamercy!" Lillian yelped as a roll of thunder followed the flash. "I got to get outta this 'fore I get struck down."

She started toward the station, but I stuck my head out the window and called to her in a loud whisper.

"Lillian, Lillian! Come back here a minute."

She came to my window and leaned against the door. "What you want?"

"Take this," I said, rummaging in my pocketbook. I held out two new hundred-dollar bills from among several that I kept on me in case I needed anything. And also because Wesley Lloyd had never given me more than fifty dollars at a time. "I didn't see any of your people on that television show, so you may have trouble getting in. Tell whoever you see that you work for somebody who's too feeble to get out of the car, but who wants to contribute one of those bills to Brother Vern's ministry, and to buy a bumper sticker from Brother Stedman with the other one. Don't give them to just anybody. Make them let you inside where Little Lloyd can see you."

"That's a good idea," she said. "Money do talk. And open doors, too."

She hurried toward the building, shoes flapping on her heels. I admired her courage, knowing how frightened she was of lightning. To say nothing of knocking on a door belonging to white people in the middle of the night.

"As soon as she's in, I'll pull up right in front," I told Hazel Marie. "We'll keep the car door open, so all they'll have to do is jump in."

"Keep the motor running, too," Hazel Marie said through clenched teeth. Those she had left, that is.

We watched as Lillian tried the door at the front of the building. Then she began pushing a buzzer, and for a long while I thought no one was going to answer. When the door finally opened, we could see her talking to someone for what seemed like several minutes. Finally, she held up the two bills and the door opened wider. She went in and it closed behind her.

"She's in!" I eased the car up beside the front of the building, keeping the headlights off. I reached over and opened the passenger door wide.

My hands trembled on the wheel as I wondered what was going on inside. I slid my left foot onto the brake pedal so the other one could rest on the accelerator, ready for takeoff. Other than the rumble of thunder, Hazel Marie's painful breathing, and the muted roar of traffic on the interstate, everything around us was quiet.

"I hope nothing goes wrong," Hazel Marie said. "She's been in there an awful long time. What if he wants to put her on TV? He does that sometimes, just picks somebody out to interview as the Lord leads him."

Lightning flashed again, closer this time, and heavy raindrops began to spatter on the windshield. I looked out to my left, seeing the rows of cars on the interstate and dreading the moment of merging again.

"Lillian won't go on TV in her work dress," I said. Then to keep my mind off what was happening inside, I asked, "Where did Brother Vern go to seminary?"

"He didn't. He was working for the World of Boots and Shoes when the Lord called him to preach. He got the call right between the Bass Weejuns and the Converse high-tops. He says fitting shoes on people's feet gave him more training in misery than any seminary could."

I left that alone, since Hazel Marie's soft voice told it so matter-of-factly. Far be it from me to disturb anybody's faith.

"Well," I said, "I guess it takes all— Oh! here they come!"

The door of the building flew open and Little Lloyd ran out with Lillian right behind him. Several men and a pack of children, pushing, shoving, and yelling, ran after them.

"Get in! Get in!" I threw back the passenger seat and Little Lloyd practically flew over it to land in the back.

"Mama! Mama!" he cried, lunging for her. She reached for him and pulled him close.

"Sweetheart," she said. "Oh, baby, are you all right?"

"Careful, Little Lloyd, your mother's hurt. Hurry, Lillian!"

She was in and trying to get the door closed. Men, teenagers, and little children swarmed around the side of the car. One of the men held on to the door while Lillian tugged and strained to get it closed. She screamed as somebody reached in to pull her out of the car. I stomped the gas pedal so hard the tires spun on the asphalt. When I took my other foot off the brake, the little car practically leapt in the air. The momentum swung the door wider, then slammed it shut, flinging the man holding it to the ground.

The chain-link fence loomed before us, coming at us fast. I jerked at the wheel, spinning it around, feeling the car swerve and rock on its frame. Before I knew it we'd turned completely around. Practically in our tracks. I heard screams, but they were all coming from inside the car. People, some of them children, ran from one side of the lot to the other, arms waving, trying to get me to stop. They scattered as I came back at them.

"Miz Springer!" Hazel Marie yelled. "Watch out!"

"What you doin'?" Lillian cried. "Don't run over them people!"

"I can't find the gate!"

"Turn on the headlights!" Lillian yelled.

That helped. I found them and the gate and sped out onto the access road.

"Oh, my Lord," I said, "how do I get over there on the interstate?" Bumper-to-bumper traffic moved along beside us, separated by a ditch of weeds and a metal railing.

Hazel Marie had her arms around Little Lloyd, but she sat up straighter to look out the windshield. "There's a ramp right up there past the rise. You can get on there."

My stomach dropped as we sailed over the rise and down the ramp to the interstate. One car after another, a continuous line of headlights and taillights, filled both lanes of southbound traffic. I didn't let it bother me, though, since Hazel Marie had told me how to manage an entry. I zoomed toward the nearest lane, looking neither to the right nor the left.

Little Lloyd screamed. Lillian called on Jesus, but I just sped up and slid the car into the traffic. I'd never heard such blowing of horns and screeching of brakes. I paid no mind.

I breathed a sigh of relief as we moved along with the traffic. Lillian's hand was practically white where she was gripping the armrest.

"Anybody following us?" I asked.

Lillian turned around and said, "Only 'bout two million cars, but I can't see who's in 'em."

"Well, let's hope for the best. Little Lloyd, are you all right? We're glad to have you back." The amenities done, I said to Lillian, "Help me look for the windshield wipers; that rain is peppering down now. I wish this car wasn't so new so I'd know where things are."

"You know where you goin'?" she asked as I finally turned the right knob and got the wipers going.

"No, Lillian, I don't. I just know we're going away from Brother Vern. Other than that, I'm just driving and doing the best I can."

"We'll go to Atlanta if you keep on this way," Hazel Marie said. "Watch for a Greenville exit and come off on that. We can get back to Abbotsville that way."

"My Lord!" I said as the roar of a heavy motor surrounded us and bright headlights behind us nearly blinded me. I reached up to adjust the rearview mirror. "What's that truck doing so close to us?"

"I can't see nothin'," Lillian said, as she twisted in her seat and shielded her eyes with her hand. "He mighty close, but he don't look like one of them trucks we had before."

"Lemme look," Hazel Marie said, and I heard the intake of her breath as she tried to turn around. "Pull out in the other lane, Miz Springer, if you can, and I'll try to get a look at him from the side."

I twitched the car over into the fast lane and got a horn blast from another car for my trouble. I had the turn indicator on, so it shouldn't've been a surprise. I speeded up, though, and lost the glare of headlights through our rear window.

"I see him!" Hazel Marie yelled. "Oh, my goodness, that's Jerome's pickup. I know it is, see how high it's jacked up."

A jacked-up truck rang a bell that I didn't want to hear.

"Look at them wheels," Lillian said. She'd turned completely around to kneel in the seat. "What he doin' with them big wheels on a pickup?"

"Truck pulls," Hazel Marie said, as if that explained anything. "I didn't see his truck back at the TV station. I don't know what I'd of done if I had."

"Maybe it was parked in the back," I said. "But if it's the same truck I've seen before, it has a habit of appearing out of nowhere. The question now is, how do we get away from him?"

"We got to think of something," Hazel Marie said. "Miz Springer, we can't let him catch up with us. He's pulled into our lane now! Oh, God, don't let him catch us."

"Mama?" Little Lloyd said.

"Don't worry, Little Lloyd," I said, "he hasn't caught us yet, and if this car lives up to the claims they make for it, he won't."

"What you gonna do?" Lillian asked. "Outrun him all the way to Atlanta, Gee-A?"

I said, "Think of something, somebody."

"One good thing," Hazel Marie said, "we can't miss that pickup. It stands out even in the dark. Miz Springer, try and get back in the outside lane, but stay with some other cars so he can't tailgate us again."

"I hope you have a plan," I said.

"Don't turn on your blinkers," she said. "We don't want to give him any warning. Just scoot on over whenever you can, and let's hope he loses track of which car we're in."

I did, but nobody liked me doing it. People can be so rude about blowing their horns. I just blew mine back.

"All right," I said, "I'm over here. Did he follow us?"

"You look, Miss Lillian," Hazel Marie said. "Me and Junior're gonna scrooch down so he'll only see two heads in the car, and maybe he'll think it's not us."

"He still in that other lane," Lillian said, "and they's a whole lot of cars around him an' us."

"Good," Hazel Marie mumbled from the floorboard. "Miz Springer, take the first busy exit into Greenville, then turn into the first street you come to on the right. Park on that street and cut your lights. If he follows us off the exit, maybe he'll keep on going."

I couldn't argue with the plan. It sounded like something that'd worked for her before, and it did again. We came off the interstate with several other cars, and as we left the ramp, Lillian said the pickup was still trying to get in the exit lane.

I parked the car on a dimly lit side street, turned off the lights, and kept the motor running. We sat there in the dark, listening to each other breathe and Little Lloyd sniffing.

"There it is!" Lillian pointed as the monster truck, black as the devil, passed at the end of the street. Jerome didn't slow down, apparently trying to catch up to where he thought we'd be. The roar of the truck's motor reverberated down the side street. I shuddered at the sight and sound of it, for it had to be the same truck I'd seen twice before. Now, thanks to Hazel Marie, I knew who was in it and, as she would've said, it scared the . . . well, pee-pee out of me.

"Lord," I said under my breath, "that thing could run us off the mountain and nobody'd ever know."

"What we gonna do if it come back at us?" Lillian asked. Her hands twisted in her lap, and I felt a twinge of guilt for putting her in this dangerous situation.

"We're gonna be gone," Hazel Marie said. "Miz Springer, ease on out now and get back on the interstate. We'll go back the way we came, now that he thinks we've gone this way."

I pulled out slowly, easing out of the side street and heading across the overpass to enter the interstate on the opposite side. More heavy traffic, but there was safety in numbers so I didn't mind it so much.

"This is not going to fool him long," I said.

"Yes'm," Hazel Marie said, "but by the time he figures it out, we ought to be far enough ahead to make it home all right."

"Well, an' that's another thing," Lillian said. "What we gonna do when we get home? If he really after us, ain't no being home gonna stop him."

"We can get help there," I said, trying to reassure her. And me. "If we have to, we'll sic Deputy Bates and Lieutenant Peavey and Binkie Enloe on him. We'll be all right once we get there. I just don't want to be driving alone on that mountain with him right behind us."

"Look, there's that TV station 'cross yonder." Lillian pointed past my face, but I was too busy to look. "They's still some people out in the parking lot. Talkin' 'bout us, I 'spect."

I heard some whispering between Little Lloyd and his mother, then he stuck his head up between the front seats. "Miss Lillian, I want to thank you for coming to get me. And you, too, Miz Springer. Me and my mama really 'preciate it."

"You so welcome, honey," Lillian said, patting his hand.

"Some things are just right to do," I said, then fearing that I'd sounded ungracious, changed the subject. "Lillian, tell us what happened when you went in there."

"Well, first thing, I didn't think I was gonna get in. They didn't like somebody knockin' on they door that time a night. But them big bills you give me changed they minds, like it would anybody's. That first man what come to the door, he wanted me to give 'em to him, but I say, 'No, I got my 'structions an' they got to go dreckly to Brother Vern and Brother Stedman.' He keep tellin' me they on the air an' can't be 'sturbed an' I keep tellin' him I wait for 'em. Finally, he let me go in the studio, but he tell me to stay over in the corner outta the way till Miss Rubynell sing again an' then I can hand over the donations. That suited me, 'cause everybody so busy they forget about me, an' I stood there lookin' 'round for our little boy an' wonderin' how can I get him to see me."

"I saw you, Miss Lillian!" Little Lloyd said, so excited that his glasses almost fell off. "I couldn't believe it was you over in that corner. I didn't even see you come in."

"Well, the next thing I had to worry 'bout was you sayin' somethin'. You know, out loud, that'd let everybody know what was up."

"But I knew better, didn't I? I didn't say a thing, did I?" He was bouncing on the seat and I almost said something to him, but thought better of it with his mother there. I declare, I didn't know the child had that much life in him, which is just as well. I can't stand a nervous, talkative child, can you?

"You sho' didn't, honey. You did it just right. I jus' put my finger on my lips to shush you an' then motion you to come on to me."

"And you know what else I did, Mama? Miz Springer, guess what I did then? I whispered to one of the big kids that was on the show that I had to go to the bathroom and he said okay. And I just got up and left and Miss Lillian followed me. And then we ran, didn't we, Miss Lillian!"

"We made us some tracks, all right!" Lillian said, laughing.

I have to confess that I admired Little Lloyd's quick thinking, in spite of having to hear about it at full volume. Not many nine-year-olds would have their heads on so straight.

"I'm real proud of you, baby," Hazel Marie said, "and so glad to have you back."

We were all quiet as I maneuvered the car through the loop to put us back on I-26. The traffic thinned out as we began the climb toward Abbotsville. Nobody spoke, thinking either about our close calls or about Jerome, one.

There were no bright-beamed headlights behind us, so I leaned back and began to relax, keeping my hands lightly on the steering wheel. In spite of everything that'd happened and in spite of the fact that we were safely on the way home, not a one complimented me on my driving. Even though I really had the hang of it by then.

"Uh, speaking of going to the bathroom," Hazel Marie said.

"Just hold your water," I said. "I'm not about to stop on the side of the road with that Jerome after us. I'll come off on the next exit and we'll look for a cornfield."

I don't know why they thought that was so funny, but they laughed about it all the way home.

We all had a slow start the next morning, except for Lillian, who was up before seven getting breakfast for Deputy Bates. We didn't want him guessing we'd been tooling around two states in the middle of the night. I'd cautioned her before we'd gone to bed, saying we all needed to get our stories straight before telling anybody about our nighttime activities.

"Lieutenant Peavey told me not to leave town," I reminded her. "But what he don't know won't hurt him."

I got up about eight and checked on Hazel Marie and Little Lloyd in his room.

"I think I pulled something loose, Miz Springer," Hazel Marie said as she tried to sit up. "I'm awful sorry to be so much trouble. But I got my baby back, thanks to you and Miss Lillian, and I'll be all right."

"You stay right there in bed," I told her. "Here's some Tylenol, and if that doesn't help I'm taking you to the doctor today. Little Lloyd, run down and let Lillian give you some breakfast, but don't wake up Deputy Bates."

"Yes'm," he said, a brighter, happier child than I'd seen before. Not much improved in looks, though, I'll have to say, since he inherited so much from Wesley Lloyd.

———

"Did Brother Vern treat you all right?" I sat at the kitchen table with Little Lloyd while Lillian puttered around the sink. I noticed that so far he'd not retrieved his Winn-Dixie sack; at least it wasn't in his lap or by his chair.

"Yes'm, it was all right," he said, giving me quick glances like he was still afraid to look me in the eye. "I thought he was taking me to my mama."

"I thought so, too, or I'd've never let you leave with him. I want you to know that. But he didn't hurt you, did he?"

"No'm."

"What did he want with you? Did he ever say?"

"He said my mama wouldn't let him have something my daddy gave her. He thought I knew where it was, but I don't even know what it is."

Lillian said, "That man up to no good, if you ast me."

"Amen to that," I said. "Little Lloyd, I want you to stay inside today, either with me or Lillian. Your mother's not feeling well, so she needs to stay in bed.

"Lillian, I don't want to scare this child, but Brother Vern and Jerome Puckett may not be through with us. If you see that truck, or hear it, let me know. I want us all to stay close until we see what they're up to."

"This baby's not gonna be outta my sight," Lillian said. "Come on over here, honey, le's us make some biscuits for when Deputy Bates have his supper."

He got out of the chair, smiling, and went to her. For the first time since I'd known the child, and for just the briefest time, he didn't resemble Wesley Lloyd in the least.

———

The front doorbell rang as I started to leave them to it. Lillian and I looked at each other, then at Little Lloyd, whose face had gone white.

"It's nobody; don't worry," I said. "Jerome's not going to come to this house and announce himself. Lillian, you and Little Lloyd stay in here. I'll see who it is, and get rid of them as soon as I can." Unless it's Sam, I amended to myself.

It wasn't. It was Pastor Ledbetter, smiling confidently and not at all abashed over the outcome of our last meeting. Standing beside him was a short, thin man in a blue-and-white seersucker suit, the kind Wesley Lloyd wouldn't't've been caught dead in. The man had a few strands of reddish hair combed carefully across the bald area where his hair had receded to a remarkable extent. He smiled without showing any teeth, stretching the thin mustache into a straight, dark line between his mouth and his nose. Milky blue eyes stared at me through gold-rimmed glasses, and it took me a minute to remember my manners.

"Why, good morning," I said, tearing my eyes away from the nondescript little man who had such a mesmerizing stare, and focusing on Pastor Ledbetter. He was looking too friendly for me to expect another lecture on a woman's responsibilities. That took a serious mind and a long face, but if he brought up Wesley Lloyd's estate again, I decided I'd transfer my membership. Maybe to the Episcopal church, where grown men get down on their knees. Which a lot of men, including the Presbyterian kind, ought to try. "I wasn't expecting you, Pastor, but do come in."

"Miss Julia," Pastor Ledbetter said, smiling broadly as he ushered in the stranger and followed him. "Sorry not to call first, but I wanted our newest member to meet you, so we just stepped across the street to introduce you. Dr. Fowler, this is Miss Julia Springer, who is one of our most active members. I don't know what First Church would do without her."

"How do you do, Mrs. Springer," the man said, shaking my hand. "Pleased to meet you. I'm Dr. Fred Fowler."

I don't trust people who have to make sure you know their titles, do you? And I've noticed that people with honorary titles are the worst offenders, so my guard went up another foot or so.

I got them seated and asked if they cared for anything to eat or drink. No, they both said, this was just an introductory meeting, which struck me as strange since Pastor Ledbetter had never made such a to-do over a new member before. At least to me, he hadn't. They sat side by side on my sofa, the little man smiling what seemed to me a secret smile, like he knew something that gave him pleasure, and Pastor Ledbetter giving me his broad, outgoing one.

"How've you been feeling, Miss Julia?" Pastor Ledbetter asked. "A little run-down lately?"

"No," I said cautiously, wondering at his concern. "Can't say that I have. I've been too busy to worry about how I'm feeling. How about you, Pastor, you feeling all right?"

"Oh," he said, laughing and glancing sideways at Dr. Fred Fowler, who sat with his eyes glued on me. I hadn't seen the man blink yet. "Nothing wrong with me an afternoon of golf wouldn't cure."

"Well, an afternoon of golf would cripple me," I said. Both seemed to think that was an exceptionally amusing thing to say. "Do you have a family, Dr. Fowler? I'd like to meet them and welcome them to town."

"No, I'm sorry to say. The Lord hasn't led me in that direction, but maybe I'll meet someone here."

"Maybe so, but I'm afraid there's not much to choose from in Ab-botsville," I said, thinking of the dearth of available women in their fifties. "Are you planning to practice in Abbotsville, or have you come here to retire?"

"Oh, I don't have any plans to retire. I like my work," he said, crossing one leg over the other like he was perfectly at ease. I wasn't, because those eyes of his had a strange, penetrating look to them. If he thought he was going to get me up on another table in those metal contraptions again, he had another think coming. He studied me for a minute and said, "What would you think if I opened my practice in Abbotsville?"

"I wouldn't think much one way or the other," I said. "I'm not the one to ask. The Chamber of Commerce, maybe, or some of the other doctors could help you. But you're not a young man, if you don't mind my pointing it out. Aren't you starting out a little late in life?"

His smile stretched out broader, still with no teeth showing. I wondered if he'd needed braces as a child and hadn't gotten them. Dr. Fowler and Pastor Ledbetter glanced at each other, and Pastor Ledbetter raised his eyebrows.

"No," Dr. Fowler said, "I've been in practice for a number of years over in Chattanooga, but I'm feeling the need for a change. Have you ever felt that way, Mrs. Springer?"

I twisted my mouth, glancing from one to the other of them, wondering at the strangeness of the conversation. I tried to make allowances, though, because even some educated people have poor social skills. "No, I can't say I have. My feeling is that if you move around too much, people think you're flighty. It's especially bad where doctors are concerned, as I expect you know. People always wonder about a doctor who picks up and moves somewhere else; they wonder if something's wrong with him. I hope I haven't offended you, but the way people are couldn't be news to you."

"No, indeed," he said, putting his hands together and resting his fingers against his chin. "Mrs. Springer, I can see that you're a discerning judge of people, and I'd like to speak with you again, if I may. Could you spare some time to, well, just sit and talk every now and then?"

"I'm not sure. I'm pretty busy these days, but I'd like to help you if I can."

"I'm sure you'll manage it," Pastor Ledbetter said, rising to his feet. Dr. Fowler followed, holding his hand out to me as my preacher kept trying to get a commitment. "You could meet over at the church," he said, resting a heavy hand on my shoulder. "You can show Dr. Fowler around and tell him about the church and the town and yourself, as well." Pastor Ledbetter turned to the doctor. "She knows all the local history."

"It would be a pleasure," Dr. Fowler said. "Can we say ten o'clock this Friday?"

"I'm not sure I can do it then," I said, feeling uneasy over their combined efforts. "In fact, I'm sure I can't this Friday. Maybe sometime next week, or maybe Pastor Ledbetter can find somebody else to talk with you."

"I'd really rather it be you, Mrs. Springer," Dr. Fowler said, holding my hand and giving it a little squeeze. He wasn't that young, but he was too young to be flirting with me. I'd heard of men who preyed on wealthy widows regardless of age differences. I drew my hand away and stepped back.

"It's got to be you or nobody, Miss Julia," Pastor Ledbetter said in his heartiest manner.

I smiled and walked them to the door. "Maybe you should prepare yourself for nobody," I said. They both thought that was a clever thing to say, and they left smiling and shaking their heads.

I watched them walk across the street, Pastor Ledbetter leaning over the shorter man, talking nonstop and gesturing with his hands. I crossed my arms and shook my head. This beat all I'd ever seen. I couldn't wait to tell Lillian that my preacher was now playing Cupid. I leaned against the door and laughed to myself. I might even tell Sam, too.

I turned back into the living room, still smiling. I don't care how old you get, the least hint of a man's interest is enough to lift up your heart. I hate to admit it, but it's the truth even when it's from a man so unlikely as to slightly turn your stomach. Wonder what makes a woman so dependent on a man's good graces? There was little about Dr. Fowler that appealed to me, except that I seemed to appeal to him. And that was enough to brighten my outlook considerably. I'm just as foolish as the next woman, I guess.

I sat down in the chair by the front window and looked across the street at the church. It stood there, benign and holy, with its spire reaching toward heaven. A place of sanctuary and worship, yet there'd been so many upsets and hurt feelings and cliques and intrigues and downright battles in it, you wouldn't believe. And something was going on over there now. If I could only figure out what.

Leaning my elbow on the arm of the chair, I studied the problem. Pastor Ledbetter, unlike our previous preachers, had never been one to be guided or instructed or counseled by anybody. Except by Wesley Lloyd, who was no longer around to make his will known. So, what Pastor Ledbetter wanted, he got. And now, I realized with a start, what he wanted was a money-eating monument to family values, whatever they were, that he called an "activities center." An activities center built with the assets of Wesley Lloyd Springer, that widely known paragon of traditional family values.

I jumped from the chair so fast I got a catch in my back. *That's* what was on the preacher's mind. That's why he was over here making me feel I was in the inner circle. Drawing me in, that's what he was doing.

But how did Dr. Fred Fowler, newcomer and special friend of the pastor, fit in?

I walked the floor, rubbing out the crick in my lower back, trying to figure how Pastor Ledbetter's mind worked. Not an easy job, unless you understood that he never gave up on anything. He had the patience of Job, because I'd seen him work his will in spite of opposition from the session. But only since Wesley Lloyd had passed, of course. So it stood to reason that he still had building on his mind.

Maybe Dr. Fowler had money to burn. Doctors make it hand over fist, don't you know. Maybe Pastor Ledbetter was thinking that, with contributions from Dr. Fowler and, if he couldn't break Wesley Lloyd's will, from me, he could break ground any day.

That was it, I was sure of it. Get Dr. Fowler and me together, make us feel *chosen* to donate to the church, and he'd get what he wanted. The man would stop at nothing to do the Lord's work as he saw it. It made no difference if somebody else saw the Lord's work in a different light. Pastor Ledbetter had a hot line to heaven and nobody could tell him it might be a party line.

Well, he was just going to have to dial in again, because I wasn't about to be manipulated by the likes of him. The thing to do was to find out if Dr. Fowler was in on the plan or if he was being played for a fool like I was. Some way or another I needed to get close to the good doctor and see if his interest was in me as a woman or in me as the means to a pile of bricks with a commemorative plaque on it.

And they'd given me the perfect way to go about it.

Chapter 22

"Lillian," I called toward the kitchen, "I'm going over to the church."

"What for?" she yelled back, but I was already out the door.

I hurried across the street and the parking lot, hoping to catch Dr. Fowler before he left. If I could get him off in the bowels of the church by himself, I ought to be able to find out whether his interest was in me or my pocketbook.

When I swung open the door to the fellowship hall, I saw the two of them, still talking, at the far end near Pastor Ledbetter's office suite. Their eyes lit up when they saw me.

"Miss Julia," the pastor called, coming toward me with his hand out. "I hoped you'd change your mind. I was just telling Dr. Fowler how much we need your input and he's so anxious to get to know you better."

"Well," I said, "I find I have a little time this morning, so, Dr. Fowler," I said, turning to him, "if you still want a tour of the church, we can do it now."

"Indeed I do," Dr. Fowler said. "I'd be delighted to have a lovely lady show me around. Here, take my arm and let us proceed."

Now that's a gentleman for you. I put my hand in the crook of his seersucker-clad arm, smiling at him and wishing I could smile up at him, instead of across and maybe a little down. But beggars and widows can't be choosers, and I confess to a little glow at the thought of any kind of interested party, even if the party was on the short side.

"Splendid," Pastor Ledbetter said, showing his teeth in a wide smile. "I couldn't ask for a better arrangement. Now y'all take your time. Nothing's going on in the church right now, no meetings or anything, so just wander around as long as you want. I'll do some work on my sermon, then come track you down about twelve and we'll see about lunch."

"That's fine," Dr. Fowler said, staring at me as he spoke. "Miss Julia and I are going to explore this magnificent building. Aren't we, Miss Julia?" And he patted my hand as it still rested on his arm.

"Yes, and I'll begin by pointing out that we're now in the fellowship hall, where we have prayer meeting on Wednesday nights with covered-dish suppers. A Boy Scout troop used to meet here, until a former pastor put a stop to it on the grounds that they weren't Christian enough." I waved my free hand around the large basement room, linoleum-floored and stacked with folding tables and chairs along the walls.

Dr. Fowler and I climbed the stairs to the sanctuary on the main floor, with him holding doors for me and watching each step I took. Those strange eyes didn't miss a trick.

As we stood at the back of the empty sanctuary, I was struck again by how spacious and elegant it was. White walls with cream-painted moldings, deep red carpeting down the center aisle that attracted any number of brides because of its processional value, red velvet pew cushions donated by a group with bony backsides, eight large Williamsburg brass chandeliers, double pulpits, choir loft with rows of organ pipes on either side. A beautiful and worthy place to worship the Lord, and considering what it cost to build and furnish, it ought've been.

We strolled up the aisle, arm in arm, and I pointed out the pew where I always sat. I showed the doctor one of the hymn books with Wesley Lloyd's name on a sticker inside the front cover.

"You must miss him very much," Dr. Fowler said tenderly.

"Not especially," I said, feeling I should be truthful in the Lord's sanctuary, and assuming that Dr. Fowler had been apprised of some of Wesley Lloyd's inclinations.

"Well, the heart closes over pain and begins to heal itself," Dr. Fowler said, "and I expect that's happening to you." He seemed so sympathetic to my plight that I gave him credit for being a better physician than his looks suggested.

We walked behind the choir loft, glancing, as we passed, into the practice rooms where dark red choir robes hung in rows. Then we strolled down the hall and into the new Sunday school building. By that time, Dr. Fowler had taken my hand from his arm to hold with his own. He had our hands clasped up close to his side. I pretended I didn't notice the change, chattering on about how this building had been attached to the original one, and how many Sunday school rooms it had, and how many members used it, and so on and so on. You know how I get when I'm nervous.

"Miss Julia," he said, slowing his steps and leaning slightly toward me. "Julia, you just seem so much at home here. I can tell that you are in your element, right here in this sacred place."

My heart, or something, fluttered. What a nice compliment, since I'd always considered myself a deeply spiritual person. And this doctor was the only one who'd recognized it. He was exceptionally perceptive, and I predicted he'd do well in his new practice. But this wasn't getting the information I needed, so I stopped that train of thought.

"I want to show you the chapel," I said, moving with him down the hall. "It's a very small sanctuary that was donated by the Belcher family, and it got away with Wesley Lloyd something awful because he didn't think of it first. See, here it is." I opened a door with my free hand, and we looked into the beautiful room, shimmering now with the morning sun streaming through the stained-glass windows.

"Lovely," he breathed.

I nodded in agreement, then realized he was staring at me. I declare, I'd not had so much attention directed my way since Wesley Lloyd's funeral. I felt an unfamiliar tremble work its way down deep inside of me, and I had to work to pull myself together.

Still and all, it'd been such a long time since I'd been in proximity to a man that I believed I'd be forgiven for enjoying a tingle or two. Who would know? Wesley Lloyd hadn't been interred all that long but, let's face it, his mind hadn't been entirely centered on home life for some little while.

"The church provides for a lot of the needs of its members," I said, subduing a tremble in my voice. "But Pastor Ledbetter seems to think we need a new building for family activities."

"Family activities are very important," Dr. Fowler said, his voice lowered to match the holiness of the place, his eyes searching mine, "especially in this day and age. Now, dear lady, what else do you have to show me? I'm entirely in your sweet hands."

I swear, which I hardly ever do, my knees started to buckle. My mind was telling me that Dr. Fowler wasn't all that attractive—short, skinny as a rail, red hair, pale skin, and wispy hair, what there was of it, had never been to my taste—but my senses were being powerfully moved and not by the thought of building plans. And here was a man looking deep into my eyes, breathing in little gasps and saying the sweetest things. He could be appealing, in the right light, to any neglected woman.

"Why don't we walk over here," I said with a little quiver, as he covered my hand with both of his. "I want to show you the bridal parlor. We have a lot of weddings in the chapel, small weddings, you know, and especially second weddings." I believe I actually tittered as we walked into the parlor. "I mean, people who are marrying for the second time. Widows, and the like."

"Lovely," he said again, and glanced at me.

It was a lovely room, done all in shades of green—carpet, walls, draperies, upholstered chairs and love seat. Very soothing and inviting. Wesley Lloyd had contributed toward the furnishings, especially the gilt-framed portraits of former pastors and leading lights of the church, which included his father and grandfather.

"I can see," Dr. Fowler said, rubbing his hand over mine, "how this room would mean a lot to someone just beginning a new marriage. Second marriages can be very fulfilling."

I took a deep breath and breathed out through my mouth. "It's a little warm in here," I said, fanning the bodice of my dress as discreetly as I could. "They don't keep this building very cool during the week."

I indicated the portraits on the wall, which was all I could manage at the time, and we walked slowly around the room. Dr. Fowler read the brass plate on each one, all the while keeping me close to his side.

To tell the truth, I thought the feelings that were coursing up and down inside of me had been banked years ago along with the ashes of my marriage, but skinny little Dr. Fowler was proving virile enough to stoke my fire. And don't talk to me about age. If you haven't lived sixty-some-odd years maintaining a ladylike deportment in all areas of life, you don't know what'll suddenly turn on when you least expect it. Age and deprivation are powerful stimulants, and, if you don't believe me, wait till it happens to you.

Dr. Fowler turned away from the portrait he'd been studying and caught his breath as he brushed against me. He backed against the wall, still holding my hand, and I stepped closer before I could help myself. Drawn by animal magnetism and Old Spice. I leaned in for a bigger whiff. I'd always been a fool for Old Spice.

"Oh," I whispered.

"Julia," he said, his voice strident with urgency.

I pulled his hand up to the middle of my bosom, without letting it touch anything important, and leaned into him. Excitement thundered like a drum in my head.

"Miss Julia!" His eyes darted around the room.

"Don't worry. We're alone," I whispered, wishing he had enough hair for me to run my fingers through. In fact, there were a lot of things I wished were different about him but, if I kept my eyes closed, I could concentrate on my feelings and not on his looks. It'd been a long time since I'd felt anything close to such heady emotion, and I wanted to make the most of it as long as he was willing. Which he certainly seemed to be.

"I . . . I know we are." His voice squeaked, high and shrill. But passion can do that to a man.

He twisted his hand in mine, but I held on tight and put my face against his neck, wet now with perspiration. A man in heat. I'd about forgotten what one was like.

"Miss Julia . . . please," he gasped, turning his head so I could snuggle closer.

Lord, when a man is so carried away that he begs for your favors, a woman can be forgiven for having her spirits lifted.

"Shhh," I whispered, not realizing I was so close to his ear.

He squawked. I have to be honest, that's what he did, and it almost closed me down. But I'd read that in the throes of passion some men make strange noises, some cry out, and others hold their peace. Wesley Lloyd had been in the last category, and I found it interesting to be tangling with a different sort this go-round. It takes all kinds, don't you know.

"Miss Julia," he whispered, frantically wiggling his body between me and the wall. "I *must*—"

"No, wait," I said, understanding now what the word *fast* meant.

"You don't understand," he said, putting his free hand on my waist and turning me toward the love seat.

"I believe I do," I gasped. Lord, I wished the man looked a little better, but I was running a fever by that time. Finding out about Pastor Ledbetter's plans had gone completely out of my head.

I closed my eyes tighter, letting the darkness bring Wesley Lloyd's preferences to mind. He preferred to conduct our business in the dark and by feel.

As Dr. Fowler clasped my waist tighter and pushed himself away from the wall and against me, I felt his rising interest.

"I have to . . ." he croaked, pushing me backward. "I *really* have to get—"

The door slammed open, and we both jumped about a foot. Away from each other.

"What in *the* world?" Pastor Ledbetter stood there, bug-eyed and open-mouthed.

"*. . . out of here!*" Dr. Fowler bellowed. He ran to the pastor and edged behind him. "The woman's crazy, Larry, just like you said. My God, she practically ravished me!"

Dr. Fowler's flushed face glared at me. He patted his straggly hair and pulled his suit coat together. With trembling fingers, he buttoned it closed.

"This . . . this woman," he went on, his voice quaking with outrage. "Larry, you wouldn't believe."

"Yes," Pastor Ledbetter said, sorrow pulling at his long face and slumping shoulders. "Yes, I would. I saw it for myself. Miss Julia, what are we going to do with you? You know we can't have this sort of thing. And in the church, too. I am so disappointed in you, and so very sorry for you."

"I couldn't control her, Larry," Dr. Fowler said, finally getting his breathing under control. "I tried to get away, but I've never seen such a deluded patient walking around free before."

Mortification swept over and through me, as I reinterpreted Dr. Fowler's words and actions of a few moments before. My Lord, what a fool I'd made of myself.

I did the only thing I could. I fainted.

———

When my eyes popped open, I was lying on the green velvet love seat in the bridal parlor, my head flat and my legs dangling over the arm of the sofa. Pastor Ledbetter sat on a straight chair next to me, fanning my face with a legal-size envelope.

"I think I'll just lie here and die, Pastor," I said as the humiliating memory flooded my mind.

"No, no," he said soothingly. "You mustn't say that. You've allowed Satan to have the upper hand, Miss Julia, and now you have to fight back. He's left you with a sickness of the soul."

"You think so?" I covered my eyes with my hand, so tired and unnerved I couldn't bear the light.

"Oh, yes. Dr. Fowler says so."

I shuddered. "Where is he?"

"He's gone, don't worry. He thought he ought to leave in case his presence caused a, ah, recurrence."

"Little danger of that," I mumbled, and turned my face into the sofa. "I just don't know what got into me. I thought . . . well, it doesn't matter now what I thought."

"Miss Julia, I know you were acting out of character, and that you weren't in control of yourself. Dr. Fowler thinks you need therapy before it happens again."

"Therapy?" I turned to face him, keeping my hand over my eyes but looking at him through my fingers. "He thinks I'm that bad off? What's wrong with me?"

"Have you ever heard of"—he lowered his voice to a whisper as he leaned over me—"nym-pho-*man*-ia?"

"Nympho . . . *oh!*" My heart skipped and thudded, and I clutched at my chest as he pronounced the name of my affliction in broad daylight. The word I'd only heard whispered about and guessed at, the word that was tinged with dark, voracious appetites. I could hardly get my breath.

"Do you understand me, Miss Julia?" he demanded. I just lay there, staring at the ceiling, trying to take it in. "We are talking mortal danger here, and something has to be done. You are not only risking your own soul, but also the soul of any man you come in contact with. You can't play around with something like nympho-*man*-ia. I've studied up on it, along with other sins of the flesh, and I know what I'm talking about."

"What does it mean?" I whispered.

"Opinions differ, Miss Julia." Pastor Ledbetter sat back in his chair and shifted into a teaching mode. "Some so-called experts say you're born with a natural inclination for unnatural acts and can't be changed. Others say it's a learned response to childhood trauma, an arrested state of emotional development, and that it's a normal, alternate lifestyle. Of course, Christians know better, don't we? We know it's sin, which can be overcome by exercising the will and being forgiven through grace. Afflicted people can choose to live normal, decent lives. And that's what you want to do, isn't it?"

"Oh, yes, I do. And, Pastor, I've always lived a normal, decent life. I really have. I couldn't've had this condition all my life and not known it, could I? This just had to've been an error in judgment, an aberration, or something."

"No," he said, so forcefully that I cringed against the cushion. "You have to call it what it is. It is *sin,* and nothing less. You have to admit it and face it head-on. You may've been able to hide these impulses even from yourself, but now, with the grief of Mr. Springer's passing and the upset of that errant child, you've allowed this, this *debauchery* to rear its ugly head. Dr. Fowler is practically a stranger to you and look what happened with him. Who can tell what you'll do with somebody you know?"

He was right. If I could go after somebody as unappetizing as Dr. Fowler, there wasn't a man in town safe from me. The thought of flinging myself on Brother Vern or Leonard Conover or Lieutenant Peavey caused an ominous rumble from my stomach. Then I thought of Sam, and covered my face again.

"Pastor, don't tell anybody about this," I begged as tears streamed down my face onto the velvet love seat. "Please promise you won't tell. I'll get some help. I'll do anything, just don't tell anybody." I clutched at his hand, pleading with him and trying to stop his infernal fanning. "Especially Norma Cantrell. She'll blab it everywhere."

"Listen to me now," Pastor Ledbetter said as he pulled a large handkerchief from his hip pocket and gave it to me. "I'm not going to tell a soul. But you must promise me to get some help, and I firmly believe you can be helped. With prayer and obedience to the Word of God and Christian counseling, this problem can be overcome. But, Miss Julia, you must have someone trustworthy look after your affairs while you're so incapacitated."

"Binkie's doing that," I said, trying to blow my nose from a prone position.

"Miss Enloe's not a member of our church, and I think your guardian should be someone with the same values that you have."

"Guardian?" I said, struggling against the velvet to sit up. "You think I need a guardian?"

"It's the usual procedure in cases of this kind, all perfectly legal and aboveboard. A guardian would be appointed to protect your interests, and it would be for your own good, Miss Julia. I don't want to see you put away by court order, which could happen if you do this again and it becomes public."

"Public," I repeated. I swung my feet to the floor, testing my balance and the floor's stability. "Pastor, I'll do anything to keep this from becoming the talk of the town. And don't worry about it happening again. I'm staying away from red-headed men, for one thing. So as far as therapy and a guardian are concerned, I've got to give that some thought."

"Don't take too long, I beg you," he said, sitting back in his chair and observing me. "It would be better for all concerned if you did this voluntarily. If it comes to a hearing, your condition will become public knowledge. As an ordained minister of the Word, I can't continue to ignore a sin committed before my very eyes. You need to know that the Lord has already burdened my heart about you and some of the decisions you've made long before today."

Mercy, I thought, as my eyes rolled back in my head. When you're threatened with the leading of the Lord, you're in real trouble.

"I'd appreciate it if you'd call Lillian to come get me," I finally managed to say.

"I'll walk you home, or maybe I'd better drive you across the street."

"No. Thank you, anyway." It was all too much for me. I started crying again, wanting only to curl up in a corner of my house with a sack over my head. "Call Lillian for me. Please, I just want Lillian."

Chapter 23

As soon as Lillian showed up, Pastor Ledbetter told her I'd had a weak spell and needed to be watched carefully. She took one look at me and got me out of the church. She walked me across the street and into the house and, before I knew it, I was in bed with a cold cloth on my forehead and a lunch tray on my lap. And she did it without any questions or fussing or mumbling under her breath, much less any eye rolling. She was a tower of strength, which I badly needed.

"You can take the tray, Lillian. I can't eat."

"You better eat something," she said. "What happened to you, anyway?"

"Oh, Lillian, it was awful." I reached up and pulled the cloth over my eyes. I didn't know how I could ever face anybody again after mortifying myself the way I'd done.

"A weak spell can't be that bad, 'less you fall and show more'n you want to," she said as she stood with her hands on her hips. "What you need is a doctor and you better see one fast."

"I know, and I will. Just as soon as I get my strength back."

"Well, then, you can start with this soup. Liquids is what you need." That was Lillian's remedy for everything. She held out a spoon, and when I didn't take it she said, "You want me to feed you?"

"I do not." I pressed the cloth tighter to sop up the overflow. "Just let me rest a little, then I'll eat."

When she left for the kitchen, pictures of what I'd done during the past hour tormented my mind until I thought I'd throw up with the shame of it all. Worst of all, Pastor Ledbetter and that awful Dr. Fowler knew how I'd acted up, and they were going to make me go tell somebody else about it. How could I go into some doctor's office and say, *"Sorry to bother you, but I'm a nymphomaniac"*?

I ran through my mind all the doctors in town. As far as I knew, none of them specialized in sudden and uncontrollable fits of physical appetite. And they were all men, and what if I had an attack of it while I was being examined?

I moaned aloud.

And if they wrote me a prescription for the condition, would Buck Tatum fill it and know what I was being treated for?

I writhed with mortification. And sloshed soup all over the tray.

What I needed was an expert, a confidential expert who wouldn't blab all over the place.

An expert, I thought, and snatched the cloth off my eyes. Lord, there was an expert right across the hall, if I could only ask her. But I couldn't. I couldn't confide in anybody. Not Hazel Marie, not Lillian, not Binkie nor Sam. No one could know, and I determined to do whatever it took to keep my affliction a secret.

My head swam as I tried to think through this sudden change of life. Pastor Ledbetter'd said I needed a guardian, but what did that mean? Just someone to manage my money, or someone who'd follow me around all day to keep me from attacking every man I met? And he'd implied, or maybe he'd said, that if I didn't appoint one myself he was going to take steps. Public ones, too.

Lord, I'd thought that child showing up on my doorstep was as bad as things could get. I was wrong. What in the world was I going to do?

My head snapped up as the answer suddenly came to me. I'd heard Pastor Ledbetter say a million times that prayer could move mountains, and here was the perfect test. I'd pray like I'd never prayed before and depend on the Lord to cure me so I wouldn't need a guardian.

Then I remembered what the pastor had said about it being a matter of will, which, coming from a Calvinist, didn't make sense. How could you exercise free will and, at the same time, have your life planned, plotted, and predestinated?

If I wasn't careful, I'd give myself a headache with such theological problems. I had to keep it simple. I'd pray my heart out, and I'd steer clear of men, all shapes and sizes of them. Yes, I'd pray for a cure and, while I was at it, I'd pray that the Lord would keep the mouths of those two shut. And if that didn't work, I'd deny it till my dying day.

———

"Now, what was that about, I wonder?" I hung up the phone with hands shaking so bad I had to hide them from Lillian. In an effort to appear normal, I'd made myself come down to the kitchen. I didn't want to alarm Lillian by hiding in bed all day.

Little Lloyd was standing on a stool at the sink while Lillian showed him how to shuck corn for supper. I'd just assured her that I was fully recovered from my weak spell when the phone interrupted us.

"What?" she asked. "That wadn't that Brother Vern, was it?"

"No, not him," I said, frowning with concern. "It was LuAnne Conover, wanting to know how I'm feeling."

"What you troubled 'bout that for?"

"Because she was calling to ask the state of my health, that's why. She usually has a dozen things to talk about, not how I'm feeling. You want a glass of tea, Lillian? Little Lloyd? I declare, before another summer gets here, I'm going to air-condition this house."

"The whole thing?"

"The whole thing."

"I been meaning to ast you 'bout one of them little units for the kitchen," she said. "But the whole house'd be better. Sometime it get so hot, I have to open the Frigidaire and stand in front of it."

My land, I thought, no wonder the electric bill's so high.

I put my tea on the table and sat down, listening to Lillian tell Little Lloyd how to get the silk off the ears. Then, still frowning, I propped my elbow on the table and rested my chin on my hand. Unbidden images of the fool I'd made of myself flooded my mind, so that I had to hold on to the table to keep from crawling under it. Gradually, my thoughts centered less on my shameful actions and more on Dr. Fowler's responses to them. Mercy, I thought as I suddenly sat up straight, I couldn't have mistaken that. It'd been a long time since I'd been in a face-to-face situation with a man, but you certainly don't mistake a thing like that.

Anger flashed through me like one of Troy Beckworth's sea surges. They'd blamed it all on me, said I was crazy, called me a . . . well, a you-know-what, and all the while that man had been as interested as I'd been. And then denied it, and said I needed a guardian. And therapy, of all things.

I squinched my eyes together, recalling Pastor Ledbetter's opportune arrival. My Lord, could they have planned it all?

I couldn't believe such a thing of my pastor, but then, a good many men had been doing things I couldn't believe. I wasn't a nymphomaniac, couldn't possibly be. Not and crawl into a lonely bed every night, even when Wesley Lloyd had been in it.

Those two had been playing with my mind, and they'd done a pretty good job of it. Well, I'd show them a thing or two. Sam still had control of Wesley Lloyd's estate and it would take months to get that settled. Until then, no one else could lay a hand on it. And as far as a guardian for me, I'd go them one better and appoint two. Between Binkie and Lillian, I ought to be well looked after, even if I didn't tell them why they needed to watch me. And, just to be on the safe side, I'd watch myself whenever a man came around.

The doorbell rang, putting me to the test then and there.

"I'll get it, Lillian," I said, halfway hoping it would be Pastor Ledbetter so I could let him know that Dr. Fowler's actions hadn't been so innocent, either. I'd tell him I suspected a conspiracy between the two of them, and that I just might sue their pants off. Well, not that, exactly.

On my way to the door, I stopped dead still in the dining room. I couldn't threaten them with a thing. All they had to do was tell one person, and the news of my so-called affliction would be all over town by nightfall. I'd never live it down.

The doorbell rang again, bringing me to myself, as well as to the unwelcome presence of Lieutenant Peavey.

I invited him in, gathering my strength to put on a good show of being pleased to see him. He'd intimidated me even before I had so much more to hide. I offered him a chair, and I took one across the room where I hoped he'd be safe if my condition suddenly flared up. No telling what I might do if Pastor Ledbetter's diagnosis had been anywhere close to accurate. I figured it was better to err on the side of caution until I could get a second opinion.

I tried not to look too closely at Lieutenant Peavey, but he seemed bigger than anything in the room, including the mahogany breakfront with my collection of mother-of-pearl oyster plates.

"Mrs. Springer," he started, taking out his little notebook and clicking his pen. "I'd like to ask you a few questions about a matter that's recently come up."

"My lawyer's not here."

"That's all right, but you can call him, if you feel you need him."

"Her."

"Ma'am?"

"My lawyer. It's a her, Binkie Enloe."

"Well," he said, twisting his neck like his collar was too tight. Binkie had that effect on people. "Well, she's a good'un. But, Mrs. Springer, I guess I misspoke myself. I'm here not so much to question you as to pass on some information and see if it has anything to do with what happened here last week."

I sat up at that. "What information?"

"Our department, along with several others in the area, has been notified by the Spartanburg Sheriff's Department that a child, a little boy, was kidnapped last night."

My eyelids fluttered. "Kidnapped?"

"Yes, all the surrounding law-enforcement units are working on it, and they'll probably call the FBI in before long. Seems a black female walked into a television studio down there, and took the child before anybody knew what was happening. When I saw the name, Puckett, I figured it might be one of our Abbot County Pucketts."

"Why, that's terrible," I said, wondering if he could hear my heart pounding away. "Lieutenant, excuse me for just a minute. I left something on the stove and I need to turn it off before it burns." I got up and hurried toward the kitchen. "I'll just be a minute," I called back.

I slipped through the kitchen door and closed it behind me. "Lillian," I hissed, motioning to her. "Don't say a word; don't say anything. You and Little Lloyd get over here quick."

"What you want?"

"Shhh, I told you, don't say anything. Get in the pantry. You, too, Little Lloyd, get in here." I pushed them both into the pantry and closed the door behind us.

"What is it? What is it?" Little Lloyd jittered around so much that his glasses went cockeyed on him. Then he clutched at Lillian.

I patted his shoulder. "Don't worry," I told him. "We're going to look after you, but you two need to stay in here and not make a sound. No matter what you hear, you've got to stay quiet."

"What's goin' on out there?" Lillian asked. Whispered, rather. "Who was that at the door? Was it that Brother Vern?"

"No. Worse than him. It's Lieutenant Peavey, and all the police in two states are looking for Little Lloyd."

I clamped my hand over her mouth. "Don't scream. Stay quiet. I'm going to get rid of him before he finds out we've got this child and takes him away from us. You're not going to scream, are you?"

She shook her head, her eyes rolling as much as mine ever had. She grabbed my hand and jerked it away. "I ain't about to do no screaming. What you think I am? Now, you ain't gonna turn this chile over to the law, are you?"

"Of course not. Why do you think we're in the pantry? Little Lloyd, you stay right here with Lillian and don't be afraid. We'll figure out what to do as soon as he leaves."

I went back into the living room, apologizing for having to interrupt the lieutenant's flow of information. "You know how it is," I said. "When you've got several pans on the stove, you have to watch them like a hawk. I declare, I do love to cook." If he believed that, he'd believe anything.

"Now, tell me more about that poor little kidnapped child," I said, smoothing my dress as I sat down.

"I'm trying to establish if the child who was taken in Spartanburg was the same one who left here Sunday. The one you told me about yesterday. What was his name?"

"Wesley Lloyd Junior Springer. Puckett, I mean Puckett."

"Which is it? Springer or Puckett?" He was making notes in his little book.

"It's complicated, Lieutenant. I think he's known as a Springer, but legally he's a Puckett."

"I don't understand."

"I don't either."

He shook his head, frowning as he studied his notes. "Could you describe the child you know? The fax we got didn't have much of a description. About nine years old, wearing glasses, sandy hair."

"Sounds close," I said, thinking that I could show him a picture of Wesley Lloyd and he could get a fairly accurate description of the child. But then, I could've produced the child himself. "Do they have a description of the person who took him?"

"African-American female in a nurse's uniform, heavyset but not fat. Quick on her feet, they said. Got into a car that tried to run over the people chasing them, so she had at least one accomplice."

"Accomplice," I repeated, hoping he didn't notice the tremor in my voice. "What kind of car?"

"New, dark-colored, possibly foreign make," he said. "That's the best they could do, 'cause the car didn't have any lights on and witnesses said the driver tried to run them all down. One scared bunch of people, from what I understand. The officer I talked to said there were a lot of children appearing on a program at the time. The parents were convinced that it was a liberal plot to kidnap one of theirs to stop their ministry. Pretty confusing, I gather. A dozen kids taken to the station, all crying and terrified. Parents demanding police protection, and it was a while before the officers determined who'd been taken. Turned out to be this Puckett kid, but the uncle who claimed to be his guardian couldn't or wouldn't give them much information." I could tell he was watching my reaction, at least those dark aviator glasses were trained on me like a double-barreled shotgun. "It's a strange situation."

"Very strange," I said, making every effort to look straight back at him. "I hate to hear it anytime a child's been kidnapped and I hope to goodness it wasn't the little boy who visited me. But I understand there're a lot of Pucketts."

"They are that," he said, closing his notebook and standing. "Well, Mrs. Springer, if you hear from the boy you know, call me so I can at least eliminate one of them."

"I'll surely do that, but as far as I knew on Sunday, he was going to Raleigh to be with his mother." That was certainly what I believed to be true on Sunday. "You were going to find out if he made it, weren't you?"

"Right. I'll double-check that today. Well, I 'preciate your time, Mrs. Springer."

"You're quite welcome," I said, walking him to the door. "I'd like to know how this turns out. I do hope you find the child. And whoever took him."

"We'll find 'em," he said, that mouth set in a hard line. I looked away, determined not to notice mouths anymore. "One thing I can't stand is somebody who'd hurt a child. I don't know how you feel, Mrs. Springer, but most of us in law enforcement are glad to have the death penalty in this state."

"Ah," I swallowed hard. "So am I." I hoped my face didn't look as bloodless as it felt. I closed and locked the door behind him, then ran to the kitchen.

Chapter 24

"Come on out," I whispered to Lillian and Little Lloyd. "But stay away from the windows. I don't want anybody to see you."

"How'm I gonna cook supper and stay away from the windows?" Lillian said, holding on to Little Lloyd and peeking around the pantry door.

"I just want to make sure he's gone and not coming back. I'll tell you, Lillian, I never knew that it's just as hard to keep quiet about the truth as it is to tell an outright lie."

"I ain't worrin' 'bout lyin', I'm worrin' 'bout goin' to jail," she said.

Little Lloyd said, "I don't want you to go to jail, Miss Lillian."

"Don't you worry," I said. "Nobody's going to jail, least of all Lillian. I mean, if anybody goes, we all will."

"My mama, too?" Panic washed over Little Lloyd's face as he clutched at Lillian.

"Miss Julia, you scarin' this chile, an' me too."

"I'm sorry, I'm sorry. I was just thinking out loud. Now, let's get ourselves together. Lillian, do you think Miss Puckett would be able to get along by herself?"

"She can't hardly get outta bed by herself. You not aimin' to put her out, are you?"

"No, no," I said, waving my hand. "I thought, if she could manage it, I'd take her and Little Lloyd off somewhere till this all blows over."

"This ain't gonna blow over," Lillian reminded me. " 'Specially since they got the police in it. How you reckon they knowed to be lookin' for him?"

I was afraid she'd ask that. "Well," I said, "the fact of the matter is, somebody down there reported it. Claimed the boy's been kidnapped."

"Kidnapped!" I was surprised they didn't hear her down on Main Street.

"Shhh, not so loud. Now, look, it's not so bad—"

"Don't tell me it's not so bad. It can't get no worse!"

"Actually, it can. They have a description of you as the one who kidnapped him."

"Oh, Jesus!" She grabbed Little Lloyd and hugged him to her, almost suffocating him in the process. "What we gonna do, Miss Julia? You know I ain't no kidnapper. I jus' get this baby back to his mama where he belong. Oh, Jesus!"

"Lillian, Lillian. Listen to me now. This is certainly an unexpected turn, but we're going to handle it. They don't know it was you, just somebody like you, and they don't know that Little Lloyd is here, or his mother, either. They're not even thinking of looking here for either of them."

"They gonna be lookin' for me an' this chile ever'where an' they not gonna stop till they find us." She wiped her eyes with her apron, then clasped Little Lloyd again. "But don't you worry, honey, you worth all this worry an' then some."

He didn't look convinced. And I certainly wasn't.

"Here's what we're going to do," I said, with more assurance than I really felt. "Much as I hate to do it, I'll have to get Sam over here, and Binkie."

"How Miss Binkie gonna get us outta this mess?" Lillian asked. "They say she smart, but I went in an' got this chile an' you drove the getaway car, an' this the evidence right here in front of us." She rubbed her hand across the head of the "evidence."

"You forget, Lillian, that his mother is right upstairs. How can he be kidnapped if he's with his mother?" I stopped, remembering Lieutenant Peavey'd said that Brother Vern had claimed to be Little Lloyd's guardian. If that was true, and who knew what legalities Wesley Lloyd had entered into, then Hazel Marie could be a party to kidnapping, too.

Surely not, I assured myself; Wesley Lloyd wouldn't've had anything to do with somebody like Vernon Puckett. I groaned, because I'd never thought he'd have anything to do with somebody like Hazel Marie Puckett, either.

"Little Lloyd, were Brother Vern and your daddy friends with each other?"

"I don't know," he said.

"Well, I mean did they visit together? Talk about things together? Anything?"

"No'm, 'cept one time right before Brother Vern went off to California, he was talking to my daddy out in the backyard." He untangled himself from Lillian's arms and pushed his glasses up.

"Well," I said, "what did they talk about?"

He squinted his eyes and gazed off above my head, thinking hard. "I heard Brother Vern say my daddy ought to take everything into account. And my daddy told him it wasn't any of his business, and that he'd make arrangements when he got ready to. Or something like that."

"Sounds like Wesley Lloyd," I mused aloud. "So, as far as you know, they weren't what you'd call friends?"

"No'm, Brother Vern didn't come see us much 'cause he was always preaching somewhere. And my daddy worked real hard and couldn't be home much, either."

Lillian and I looked at each other over his head, and I shook mine at the way this child had been raised.

"Sooner or later," I said to Lillian, "the lies have got to stop. But not till we know what we're up against. If anybody finds out we have Little Lloyd, the police will send him right back to Brother Vern or to social services, one. And I'm not going to let that happen, even if it means lying my head off."

———

"He suspects us, I know he does." Hazel Marie lay in bed, her hair a mess of brassy tangles on the pillow. The bruises on her face had faded to near the same yellow tint. Still swollen, though, around her eyes and mouth.

"No, I don't think so," I said. "Lieutenant Peavey might be wondering a little, since he picked up on the Puckett name. However," I said as I tucked in the sheet at the foot of her bed, "if they're treating this as a kidnapping, we could be in big trouble. I just wanted you to know what we're up against now."

"I don't think I can stand anymore." She turned her face away as the tears started again. "I don't know how it could be kidnapping when he's my own little boy. I'm about at the end of my rope."

"Get hold of yourself," I told her as I snatched a Kleenex from the box and handed it to her. "If there's one thing I've learned in all this, it's that you have to stand up for yourself. Nobody else is going to do it for you, least of all the people you ought to be able to depend on." That was as close as I wanted to get to discussing Wesley Lloyd.

"You are so strong, Miz Springer," she said, dabbing at her sore face with the tissue. "I wish I could be like you."

I snorted at that and told her to get some rest. As I walked downstairs, it came to me that I was strong, if that's what I was, only because I had the money to back it up. If I'd been like Hazel Marie, without a penny to my name, I'd be overwhelmed and ready to give up, too. A pitiful commentary, but there it was.

I stopped on the stairs as my knees began to tremble. Money wasn't going to protect me from my sickness, or sin, or whatever it was as long as Pastor Ledbetter held it over my head. Regardless of Wesley Lloyd's estate, I wasn't any stronger or safer than that poor, pitiful woman in my guest bed. In fact, I might even've been worse off because of it.

———

In spite of the fluorescent lights overhead, the kitchen had begun to take on a greenish glow by late afternoon. An ominous growl of thunder swelled overhead as a swirl of limbs from the nandina bushes scraped against the window behind the table. I looked out to see the light green undersides of leaves on the poplars as the wind swept through the branches.

"It's coming up a cloud," Lillian said worriedly. "No tellin' what gonna happen next. Honey," she said to Little Lloyd, "don't you get close to the windows, lightnin' be coming with that wind." He moved a chair beside the pantry and sat very still, his hands clasped between his knees.

"It does look bad out there," I said, and cringed as lightning clicked close by. Thunder boomed around the house barely a second later. "Close," I said. "I better unplug the television."

From the front window of the living room, I could see a sudden downpour of rain falling like a sheet, streaking the panes. Lightning continued to pop around the house, while thunder crashed and rolled. I shuddered and pulled the drapes. As the room darkened, I reached to turn on a lamp, then drew back as another flash of lightning warned me away.

As I started back to the kitchen, I heard running steps on the front porch and the doorbell ringing. I peeked out the window before going to the door. Too many people had been showing up to hand us more problems.

"Binkie, what in the world!" I threw open the door and held the screen for her. Her hair and clothes were soaked, and she stood there trying to dry her face with a wet Kleenex. "Come in! What're you doing out in this storm? Get in here and dry off."

"Sorry to drip on your rug, Miss Julia. I'll just slip my shoes off, they're wet through." She was laughing and gasping for breath. In spite of looking like a drowned cat, Binkie had some color in her cheeks, and her eyes were sparkling. "I haven't been caught in the rain in I don't know how long! And I haven't run like that in a long time, either! Wow, I'm wet to the skin! Just look at me!"

Her skirt and blouse were plastered to her form, making her look even smaller than she was. In fact, she looked more like the young girl who used to ride her bicycle past my house on her way to the picture show. She'd always call out and wave if she saw me in the yard or on the porch. Big personality, that girl, even back then. Since coming back to Abbotsville to practice law, Binkie'd had to work hard to be taken seriously. Everybody wanted to pat her on the head. Patronizing, you know. Some of the locals actually tried it, and ended up with a nub instead of a hand. She called herself Elizabeth T. Enloe now, but she'd always be Binkie to me.

"Let's get you dried off," I said. "Why in the world are you out in this storm?"

"I was on my way back to the office from the courthouse." She smiled and pushed her hair out of her face. "And just decided to walk on over here. Thought I could make it before the rain started, but I missed it by a mile, didn't I?"

She looked up and past me, smiled again, and I turned to see Deputy Bates come into the living room from the hall.

"Sorry, Miss Julia," he said, turning toward the kitchen. "Didn't know you had company."

"No," I said, holding out my hand and backing away. I didn't want him in the kitchen because I hadn't had time to prepare him for Little Lloyd's return. Well, to be honest, I hadn't had time to prepare whatever story I was going to tell as to how we'd gotten the child back. And of course I didn't want him too close to me, either, since I didn't know at what age a man might stir up my condition. If I had one to stir, that is. "I want you to meet Binkie Enloe, one of the best women lawyers in town. Binkie, Deputy Bates."

Binkie gave me a quick glance, chilling me for a minute, and I didn't know why.

Deputy Bates walked over and shook her hand. "One of the best lawyers, period," he said, and then I did know why. "She's raked me over the coals in court a few times." But he smiled when he said it. And so did she.

"Let me get some towels," I said. "Keep her company for a minute, Deputy Bates, if you will."

"Coleman," he said, his eyes still on Binkie.

"What?"

"Coleman. Call me Coleman." He was still looking at her, but he was speaking to me. I think.

"Coleman," Binkie repeated.

I hurried into the kitchen and told Lillian to send Little Lloyd upstairs to his mother.

"I thought you not tellin' no more lies," she said.

"I'm not. It's just too soon and I don't know what Binkie's doing here. I've got to feel her out before we spring Little Lloyd and Miss Puckett on everybody. Now just get the boy upstairs, and stay quiet about everything."

She grumbled about it, but she sent the boy up the back stairs, promising him chocolate cake for dessert.

Binkie was standing by the door, water dripping on the floor from the hem of her skirt. The room was dark, that sort of dusky dark of a late afternoon storm. Rain fell steadily outside, but not as hard as before. Deputy Bates had his hands in his pockets, looking down at Binkie, a smile on his face.

"Come on back to the kitchen," I said, not wanting to offer one of my velvet upholstered chairs to a sodden guest. "Binkie, we need to get you out of those wet clothes."

Deputy Coleman Bates watched as he followed Binkie to the kitchen, and she was a sight to see from the back, what with her wet skirt molded to her hips and thighs. Deputy Bates, I mean Coleman, almost ran into the kitchen door.

Lillian walked back into the kitchen and started to make a fuss over Binkie, declaring she had to get out of her wet clothes before she caught her death.

"I'll run get one of Miss Julia's robes for you," she said, "then we'll put your clothes in the dryer."

I took Binkie to the downstairs bathroom, where she disrobed and rerobed in my blue satin robe that Lillian had cleaned since its trip to Spartanburg. I don't know where Lillian's mind was, the heavy chenille one would've been more appropriate and considerably less form-fitting. By this time, I felt like I was clothing half the women in town.

I declare, I never knew what that blue satin was capable of, but when she walked back into the kitchen, Deputy Bates, I mean Coleman, couldn't take his eyes off of it. It'd had the same effect on the truck driver when Hazel Marie was wearing it. Binkie was embarrassed and hurriedly sat down, wrapping it close around her. She clasped the neckline to keep it from gaping, which it was inclined to do.

"These'll be dry in a few minutes," Lillian said, bundling up Binkie's wet clothes. "Who wants coffee? Or lemonade, or what? Got some chocolate cake, too."

Lillian passed around the dessert plates and poured coffee. It was the first time I'd seen Coleman ignore any food Lillian put in front of him. He was paying a lot of attention to Binkie, though.

"Thanks, Miss Lillian," Binkie said, then looked across the table at me. "Miss Julia, I know you wonder what I'm doing, calling on you this time of day. I could've asked you to come to the office, but I thought it'd be better to talk here."

That sounded serious. I glanced at Lillian as she stopped in the middle of the room and lifted her eyebrows. What did Binkie know, and who'd told her?

"What?" I asked, fearful of her answer.

"I wanted to see how you were doing," Binkie said. She glanced at Coleman, then looked back at me. "Would you rather we talked about this in private?"

"I don't think so, since I'm doing fine. Why'd you think I wasn't?" The only thing to do was brave it out and deny everything. I tried a laugh, but it was a weak one. "What is this? Everybody and his brother is suddenly concerned about my health. First Pastor Ledbetter, then LuAnne Conover, and now you." I looked around at all of them as they looked back at me. "Why, Binkie? What've you heard?"

"I've had a few phone calls," she said, clipping her words as she did in her office. "And, since you're my client, I wanted to be sure you were all right. I see you are, so that's all there is to it."

"No, that's not all there is to it," I said, about ready to break down with the strain. "Somebody's telling tales, and I want to know what it's about. Now, what's supposed to be wrong with me? Heart attack? Gallbladder trouble? Brain tumor?" *Nymphomania?*

"Nothing like that," Binkie said. "Don't be concerned about it. It'll die down."

"Binkie Enloe," I said, "that's not good enough. I want to know what's being said because whatever it is, it's not true."

"Well," she said with some reluctance. She scraped up some chocolate icing with the side of her fork, looked at it, then at me. "This is just street talk, but I've heard that you might be slowing down. You know, getting a little forgetful, a little confused. All perfectly normal after a certain age."

"Me?" My mouth dropped open, not knowing if this rumor was tied to my recent shameful display or if it was something new. "They're saying I'm getting senile? Is that it? That's it, isn't it?"

Lillian stood stock-still in the middle of the room, and Coleman listened with a bemused smile on his face. But this time it was for me and not Binkie.

"Lillian," I said, "did you hear that? Am I senile? Do I look confused to you? Do I forget things?"

"No more'n you ever did," she said.

"Who's saying these things, Binkie? Where'd you hear them?" I swallowed hard, wondering if Binkie would help them put me away. By this time, I didn't trust anyone.

"A couple of people from your church called me. They were concerned, wanted to know what they could do to help."

"Thay Lord," I said, slumping in my chair. "And they sent you to check up on me?" Pastor Ledbetter had promised not to tell, but it crossed my mind that he might've felt the Lord leading in a different direction.

"No, not me," she said, slicking a strand of hair behind an ear. "I'm looking after your interests. Somebody else is trying to determine how competent you are."

"Who?"

"Your pastor, Mr. Ledbetter," she said. "And some psychologist from a Christian counseling service. A new member of your church, I believe."

"Dr. Fred Fowler? Is that who you're talking about?" I gasped and buried my face in my hands to hide the red flush that burned through my skin. My Lord, that peaked little man was a mind expert and he'd said I was crazy. And no wonder, after what I'd done to him.

And my pastor knew all about it, maybe suspected something lurking in my character even before I'd given them proof. I jerked my head up, recalling my earlier suspicions about the two of them. Maybe they'd planned that fiasco at the church. And how had Pastor Ledbetter even known to read up on nymphomania, and him a man of God, unless somebody had put it in his mind? It certainly wasn't covered in any theological library I'd ever seen.

I narrowed my eyes, thinking *entrapment*.

"Do you know what they're going to do if they decide I'm failing before their eyes?" I wanted to fall on my knees and beg Binkie to save me, but I didn't want to tell her why I needed saving.

"I'm not sure, Miss Julia," Binkie said. "But there's nothing they can do without a competency hearing, which, I warn you, is not hard to get. I want you to watch what you do and say around them. Don't give them any ammunition, so to speak. You can call me anytime you get concerned about anything. Now, Lillian, if my clothes are dry, I'd better head on home. The rain's slacked off some."

Chapter 25

I sat there, too stunned to be hospitable, and let Lillian get her clothes. I had enough awareness to note that Binkie was a sight in her wrinkled linen, but she wouldn't let Lillian plug in the iron.

I was still sitting and staring into space while Coleman insisted on driving her home, still sitting and staring when they said good-bye and left, and still sitting and staring when Lillian came to the table and stared back at me.

"It ain't like you to take this sittin' down," she said. She put her hands on the table and leaned over toward me. "I thought you gettin' some gumption since Mr. Springer passed and left you more'n anybody can spend in a lifetime. Now you actin' like you used to when he was alive, all shriveled and shrunk up, takin' whatever anybody hand out and scrungin' down in yo'self. That preacher ain't got no hol' over you, so what you doin' actin' like you doin'?"

"Oh, Lillian," I whispered. Tears stung my eyes, and the pain in my chest spread out to burn in my throat. "Seems like everybody's got some kind of hold over me. And my pastor . . . It just hurts, that's all."

"It can't hurt if it ain't so. All you got to do is show 'em yo' mind as good as it ever was."

"I thought I was already doing that. But there's a lot you don't know, Lillian."

"I know all I need to know, an' then some. Ain't nothin' wrong with yo' mind and you know it. Law, Miss Julia," she said, straightening up and shaking her head, "ain't nobody get the best of you yet. Why you think anybody start now? Now, get outta that chair an' help me get some supper for Miss Hazel Marie and that little honey upstairs."

By the time we'd fixed trays to take to them, Coleman had called to say he was eating with Binkie and wouldn't be home till late. Which was pretty quick work on somebody's part. So Lillian and I fixed trays for ourselves and carried them all up to Miss Puckett's room.

"A picnic!" Little Lloyd cried. "I've never had a picnic before!"

"Well, you have one now," I said, and busied myself distributing trays, helping Hazel Marie sit up in bed, and fussing at Lillian for not wanting to eat with us. "Sit down and eat, for goodness' sake," I told her. "If, that is, you're not too good for us."

"I'll eat with you, Miss Lillian," Little Lloyd said, hopping off the bed where he'd been sitting with his mother.

"Well, come on over here, honey," she said, "an' put yo' tray on this desk next to mine."

"I declare, Miss Lillian," Hazel Marie said, "I believe you're gonna steal my little boy away from me."

"No'm, I'm not gonna steal him, I'm jus' gonna love him up for you." Lillian patted his shoulder and he smiled like he couldn't be happier.

"Speaking of stealing little boys," I said, "what're we going to do about Brother Vern and this kidnapping charge? We can't keep you two shut up in this room forever."

"I know, Miz Springer," Hazel Marie said, leaning back against her pillow and staring up at the ceiling. "And I want to thank you for everything you've done for us. You, too, Miss Lillian. I ought to be able to get out of your hair by tomorrow, if you can put up with us one more night."

I put down my fork. "And just where're you going to go?"

"I don't know. Back to my mama's house, I guess. Her new husband won't like it, what with his three kids there already, but I don't know what else to do. Junior'll have to start to school pretty soon, so I'll have to settle somewhere and find me a job."

Silence settled over the room, and I felt Lillian glaring at me. "There's no need to make a hasty decision," I said. "Besides, just going off on your own won't solve the problem if Lillian's arrested for kidnapping."

"Lord, don't say sucha thing!" Lillian stopped eating and stared at me.

"I'm sorry," I went on. "I didn't mean it that way. What I meant was, we may all have a charge of kidnapping hanging over us and we need to take care of that before going our separate ways. Now, Miss Puckett, think hard. Could Mr. Springer've made your uncle Little Lloyd's guardian and you not know about it?"

"No, ma'am! He wouldn't've done that."

"Well, as long as the police think he did, we can't just announce the boy's whereabouts and go on about our business. I want you to think now. Did Mr. Springer indicate in any way that he might do that? Could he've told or just implied to Brother Vern that he was going to do it?"

"No way, Miz Springer," Hazel Marie said. She moved her tray off her lap and sat up as straight as she could manage. "Wesley Lloyd wouldn't've done any such a thing. He always said I took good care of Lloyd, and besides, he couldn't stand Brother Vern."

That was one thing I could still agree with Wesley Lloyd about.

"All right," I said. "If you're sure about it, then we can admit we've got the child and the police can't take him away from us. If Brother Vern raises a fuss, we'll demand to see a legal document. Then we'll turn around and accuse him of kidnapping."

"How you do that?" Lillian asked. "You the one let this chile go off with him. That ain't no kidnapping."

"You're splitting hairs, Lillian," I said. "The least he's guilty of is false pretenses. Anyway, what we need is something to hit him with to counteract his charges against us. Miss Puckett, you haven't had enough to eat. You're skinny as a rail, as it is."

"Brother Vern's looking for something," Hazel Marie said, picking at a cucumber slice. "I told you how he kept wanting to know what Wesley Lloyd left us, and how he was going to use Junior to make me give it to him. I still don't know what he thought I had, 'cause I don't have anything."

"He probably thought you had a bank account," I said. "Or maybe the deed to your house. There's no telling what he thought, and from my recent experience, there's no telling what Wesley Lloyd could've actually done.

"Now, if you're sure we're safe from Brother Vern, the thing to do is bring in Lieutenant Peavey and tell him to call off the Spartanburg police and the FBI. We'll tell him all about Brother Vern. After we accuse him of everything we can think of, not even social services would put a child in his hands. But before we do that, I think I better talk to Sam and Binkie, just to be on the safe side."

———

I went down to the kitchen the following morning, way before my usual time of rising. Switching on the coffee, I pulled my robe closer against the coolness left by the thunderstorm. Wesley Lloyd'd had firm ideas about living on schedule. There's a time, he'd often said, for sleeping and a time for waking. Of course, his Thursday night bedtime didn't stick to the schedule, but I guess he didn't count that, since he'd likely been in bed part of the time at Miss Puckett's house.

One of the nice things about being a widow, though, was that you could pretty much do what you wanted to without getting any cold looks or sharp words about it. I found I liked going to bed and getting up whenever the spirit moved me. And I liked not having somebody asking if I was sick or if my conscience was hurting me if I broke that somebody's routine.

So, I sat there in the quiet kitchen, drinking coffee and considering all the things that I needed to straighten out: what to do about Hazel Marie and Little Lloyd, what to do about Lieutenant Peavey and the kidnapping charge, what to do about Pastor Ledbetter and the threat he held over my head, and how to fix Brother Vern's little red wagon.

I stiffened and looked around the kitchen. I'd heard something, a scratching or scuttling sound. I thought of the night Hazel Marie'd shown up at the back door, and tiptoed over to peek outside. Nobody there, but as I turned toward the table I heard it again.

The pantry, I thought. My next thought was mice. And I shuddered at that thought. I stood still, listening. The refrigerator clicked on, but nothing else stirred. I wasn't eager to confront a mouse, but neither did I want to eat anything that'd been rodent-nibbled. I looked around for something to throw and grabbed a saucepan by the handle.

I crept to the pantry door, leaning against it and listening. Nothing. But I had heard something, so something was in there. I jerked open the door.

"Scat! Shoo! Get outta there, you nasty things!" I cried, holding the pan high.

Nothing moved. I lowered the pan, thinking maybe Pastor Ledbetter was right on the money in more ways than one. Maybe I was beginning to hear things now. I started to turn away, but then I heard a definite hiccup and a muffled sob.

"Who is that? Who's in there?"

Little Lloyd answered from behind a stack of Bounty paper towels. "It's me. Please don't shoot."

"Don't shoot!" I exclaimed, and started laughing. "Child, I'm not going to shoot you! What're you doing in there? Come on out here and talk to me."

He edged out, ducking as he emerged from under a shelf. He wore the cowboy pajamas I'd bought him, and he had his Winn-Dixie sack in his hand. His hair, mussed from sleep, stood up at various points on his head. His glasses were crooked on his nose.

"I'm sorry," he sniffled, wiping his teary face.

"What're you sorry about? I don't care if you want to sit in the pantry at five o'clock in the morning, but sitting at the table is more comfortable. You want some coffee? Or a glass of milk?"

"Maybe some coffee, if you don't mind." He stood there in his baggy pajamas with his paper sack clutched to his chest, and I noticed a fine tremor running across his shoulders.

"Are you cold?"

"No'm. I just didn't want to bother you."

I poured a cup of coffee and set it on the table.

"You couldn't bother me, Little Lloyd," I said, pulling out our chairs. "Come sit down. I'm glad to have your company."

"Yes'm." He sugared and creamed his coffee with a heavy hand and, as he stirred, I wondered how he could drink the concoction. But to each his own.

I said, "Don't tell Lillian I gave you coffee, okay?"

He glanced up at me, saw me smiling, and smiled back. "Okay."

"So," I said. "We've got to get you and your mother settled, don't we? School's going to start pretty soon."

"Yes'm."

"You looking forward to living with your grandmother?"

"No'm, I don't reckon I am."

"Oh? Why not?"

"I don't know." He shrugged and looked around the kitchen. "I like it here."

"Well," I said, surprised, "I'm glad you do. But I expect you'll get used to whatever your mother decides on, don't you think?"

"Yes'm, pro'bly so."

We sat in silence, drinking our coffee and waiting for daylight. I couldn't think of anything else to talk about except the things that were worrying me, which weren't fit to share with a child.

He set his cup down and straightened his shoulders from their habitual slump. His eyes darted around from me to the table and back again. He took a deep breath. "Miz Springer?"

"Yes?"

"If somebody gave you something to keep, what would you do?"

"Why, I guess I'd keep it. Wouldn't you?"

"Yes'm, I would." He lifted the cup with both hands to his mouth, and blew on the hot coffee. Then he set the cup down without drinking.

He said, " 'Cept, maybe you'd need to know how long to keep it. Wouldn't you?"

I made a show of considering the question, twisting my mouth in deep thought. "I suppose so. You mean, I take it, if this somebody hadn't told you when to give it back?"

"Yes'm, but more than that. I mean, what if you can't give it back?"

"Ah," I said. "Like, if somebody gave you something to keep and you happened to lose it?"

"Oh, no'm!" He looked at me, eyes wide at the very thought. "No'm, I wouldn't never lose it."

"Well, I was just speaking hypothetically, you know."

"What? I mean, ma'am?"

"Hypothetically. Just in general, so to speak. I didn't mean to suggest that you would." Though of course that's what I'd assumed the conversation was about.

I said, "Let's start over. You want to know what I'd do if somebody gave me something to keep for them. I haven't lost it, but I can't give it back. And you want to know how long I should keep it?"

He nodded, watching me intently. Talking to a child wasn't proving all that hard to do.

"Let me think," I said, patting my mouth with my fingers and studying the problem. "I need some more information. It's not broken, is it? That's not the reason you can't give it back?"

"No'm."

"And you still have it. You haven't given it to anybody else."

He shook his head solemnly, from side to side.

"In other words, you've taken good care of it. Oh, I know. You've grown attached to it and don't want to give it back. Is that it?"

"No, ma'am, I don't want it anymore. I just don't know what to do with it."

"Well, just tell whoever gave it to you that you can't keep it any longer. That's what I'd do."

He slunk down in his chair, his head tucked into the collar of his pajamas like a turtle. "I can't. My daddy gave it to me."

Oh, Lord, and here I'd thought I was doing so well playing a game with this strange child.

"Well," I said, "that puts a different light on it. I guess, if he didn't tell you how long to keep it or who to give it to, he meant for you to have it. Yes, I'm sure he meant for you to keep it for your own."

The gold watch that Wesley Lloyd wore in a special pocket came to mind, the one with a heavy gold chain with a Rotary pin on it. But no, they'd taken that off him and given it to me when they closed the casket after the final viewing. Maybe it was a check or a large bill.

"If it's money, Little Lloyd, I can assure you that your father would be proud of you if you put it in the bank. That way, it could earn even more, and I know that's what he'd do with it."

"No'm, it's not money." He slowly turned his spoon around on the table. His hands were small, frail-looking like his mother's. It occurred to me that the child was deeply worried about this problem. It wasn't a game to him.

"All right," I said, leaning down to catch his eye. "Here's my advice. Talk it over with your mama. I expect she'd know what to do."

"I thought about that." His voice was so low that I had to lean even closer. "But my daddy gave it to me the very same night he went to be with Jesus, and he told me not to tell anybody."

"Well, my goodness," I said. "Was . . . did your daddy, I mean, do you think he knew he was going to, well, go be with Jesus when he gave it to you?" Images of that fearful night when I found Wesley Lloyd slumped over his steering wheel flashed through my mind, the whirling red and blue lights of ambulances and patrol cars, the tubes and black kits with dials and toggles that technicians worked with to revive him, the rough kindness of young deputies trying to comfort an old woman trembling on the porch steps.

"I don't know." Little Lloyd sniffed and wiped tears from his face with the back of his hand. I gave him my napkin. "He didn't feel so good, but he had to leave anyway. My mama wanted to call the doctor, and I think he got mad about that. Me and her stayed in the kitchen while he went to the living room to do something. Then he called me to walk out to the car with him, and that's when he gave it to me. He said for me to keep it and not tell nobody and he'd see me next week." He sniffed wetly. "But he never did."

Wesley Lloyd's last minutes revealed, and they sounded just like him. Calling a doctor because he wasn't feeling well would be admitting to weakness. It didn't surprise me a bit that he'd been too stubborn to take advice. But I was pleased to hear that Hazel Marie had tried.

"So, I guess you figure that if he'd wanted your mother to know about it, he'd've given it to her and not to you?"

He nodded his head. Then he lifted his glasses and rubbed his eyes with his fists.

"You've had a pretty heavy load to carry around." I patted his shoulder. "But listen," I went on, "don't be worried about having a secret from your mother. That's just the way your daddy was. He was treating you like a man, and he didn't think men should get women, even mothers, involved in their business." Wives or girlfriends either, I could've added but didn't.

"Did you know my daddy?" he asked, his voice breaking as he tried not to cry.

I studied him a few minutes, thinking how remiss I'd been in not realizing that this child had lost a father he'd loved, and was still mourning him. Somehow it'd never occurred to me that anybody beside myself could be hurting.

I took a deep breath that caught in my throat and tightened my chest. "Yes, I knew him and I'm sorry that he's gone. I know you miss him, but these things happen, don't you know. We just have to be strong and go on with what we have to do." Platitudes, but that's all I had to offer. I patted his back again.

"Yes'm, I guess so." The paper sack crackled in his lap as he shifted in the chair.

"So," I said, "we still have the problem of what to do with what he gave you. And I think I have the answer. You just pick somebody you trust, tell them what it is, and let them decide what to do. I don't think your daddy meant for you to keep it hidden forever. I think he just meant for you to keep it safe, don't you?"

Worry knotted his forehead, making his glasses slip down on his nose. "You really think he'd want me to tell somebody about it?"

"Yes, now that he's gone, I think he'd want you relieved of the responsibility. But I also think he'd want you to be very careful who you choose to tell. But there're a lot of people you could trust with his secret—Deputy Bates, Lillian, Mr. Sam Murdoch. Your mother, of course. Any of them would be able to help you with it."

He continued to look at the table, avoiding my eyes, his hands resting now on the sack in his lap.

"Would you?" he whispered.

"Me?" I was taken aback. What had I done to deserve his trust? Or put it another way, what had I done to have another burden added to the ones I already carried? "Why, of course," I finally managed to say. "I'll help you if I can, but somebody else might do a better job for you."

"No'm, my mama said you're the best friend anybody could have."

"Well," I said, "I declare."

"It's in here," he said, unrolling the Winn-Dixie sack, and I prepared myself to treat a book about lions with suitable seriousness. To tell the truth, I was beginning to wonder if the boy had good sense, considering how he was agonizing over such a trivial thing.

He pulled the book out of the sack, pushed his coffee cup aside, and laid the book on the table. Very carefully, he leafed through the book and removed a thin, pink envelope.

As he handed it to me, our eyes met, and this time I saw, not Wesley Lloyd, but Little Lloyd himself.

I held the envelope, slowly turned it over, and saw that it was sealed. I was reluctant to open and read what my husband had written to his child in his last hours on this earth. I wasn't sure I wanted to know anything so personal, nor did I feel prepared to comfort his grieving child. A letter from the grave, so to speak, could only open the wounds again. I wished Lillian were there to help me.

"Have you read it?" I asked.

"No'm. I just kept it like he told me to."

"Well," I said, taking a deep breath, "let's see what it says."

I reached behind me to the counter for a bread knife and slit the envelope. I pulled out a flimsy pink page, unfolded it, and silently read the sentence written there in my husband's heavy handwriting, studied his unmistakable signature, and felt my world fall away.

"Little Lloyd," I whispered, "you were right to show this to me. It has to do with your daddy's business. I'll have to study on it a while before deciding just how he'd want it handled. Now, why don't you tiptoe upstairs and get dressed. Or you might want to get a little more sleep, if you can. It's still early, so try not to wake your mother."

"Okay," he said, relief shining on his face. "Now I can get rid of this ole paper sack." He wadded it up and put it in the trash can on his way out of the room. "Thank you for the coffee, Miz Springer."

I watched him leave and listened to his bare feet slither on the polished wood between my Oriental rugs. Then, with an aching heart, I looked back at the sheet of pink stationery that represented my husband's last will and testament.

Chapter 26

The boy trusted me, so that gave me some time. He hadn't read it, probably wouldn't have understood it if he had, so no one on God's green earth knew about it. Except me.

I studied the pink page, taking note of the drawing of pastel flowers at the top, and understood that Wesley Lloyd had used a sheet of Hazel Marie's stationery to cut me off without a dime.

I thought about how it must've happened that night, because that's when the sentence had been written. I didn't doubt that, since the date of the night he died was right there on the page. He must've known something was bad wrong with him, a premonition of some kind, to've made such a sudden and drastic change. Maybe if he'd taken more time to consider his responsibilities, he'd have made some provision for me. Then again, maybe not. Maybe nothing was exactly what he'd thought of me, and exactly what he'd wanted me to have.

I buried my face in my hands, my shoulders shaking with the pain of realizing that in his last hours he'd taken no thought of me at all. I was not included in this, his final testimony to what was important to him. I read the sentence again: "I name my only son, Wesley Lloyd Junior Puckett (Springer), heir and beneficiary of all my worldly goods, and Sam Murdoch as executor of my estate and guardian until the age of majority." Dated at the top and signed at the bottom.

With one sentence, my husband of forty-four years had pauperized me and put me on welfare and food stamps. My home no longer belonged to me, much less any of the other properties that I'd taken such pride in owning. My furniture, my car—everything—it all belonged to a child who should've never been born.

My hands shook with the rage that flowed through me like an electric current. I wanted to crumple the page and tear it to pieces. I wanted to stomp it into the ground. I wanted to tear my hair out and scream my head off. I wanted to hurt Wesley Lloyd like he'd hurt me.

I trembled with the effort of controlling myself, stricken with the power of my anger. I drew a rasping breath and tried to come to terms with my new and impoverished state.

This would certainly relieve Hazel Marie of the concern about supporting herself or about where she and Little Lloyd would live. They could live right here in my house if she wanted it. Lillian could work for her, and probably would for Little Lloyd's sake. Hazel Marie could entertain my friends, go to my Sunday school class, sit in my pew, drive my car, take on my life. She could take my place in everything, just as she'd taken my place in my husband's heart and bed. And on top of losing everything, my pastor and half the town thought I was demented, incompetent, and a danger to every man I met.

I couldn't face it.

I needed time to think about what to do. I folded the page, put it back in its envelope, and slipped it into the pocket of my robe. I lifted my cup of coffee, tasted and swallowed the cold and bitter dregs. Take one thing at a time, I told myself, and this new will was the most pressing problem.

Little Lloyd would assume that I was taking care of his secret; he wouldn't question me. He didn't know it had anything to do with him. Hazel Marie didn't know, thanks to her son's integrity in following Wesley Lloyd's instructions. Sam, involved in executing the older and more appropriate will, didn't know. If I kept quiet, then things would take their course the way they were supposed to. I ground my teeth together as I remembered how important it'd been to Wesley Lloyd to do what was *supposed* to be done. I would only be following his lead, because a wife is *supposed* to benefit from her husband's estate. It was only right.

Besides, I told myself, a case could be made that Wesley Lloyd was not of sound mind that night. Couldn't it? He was sick, even dying, when he set pen to paper. And besides that, he'd not had that will witnessed and notarized. That meant it was invalid, didn't it? I wished I could talk it over with Sam.

Then I thought of something that would make it right, or at least justify me in rearranging Wesley Lloyd's last-minute intentions. I'd set up a fund for Little Lloyd's education. And maybe a monthly allowance for his and Hazel Marie's living expenses. She would be so grateful. She and everybody else would think highly of me for such an act of Christian charity and generosity.

She'd think I was the best friend a person could have.

I covered my face again, sobbing at the position Wesley Lloyd had put me in, and realizing that if Pastor Ledbetter had his way, I wouldn't be able to be generous to anybody.

Then, hearing Lillian walking down the drive, I hurriedly got up and left the kitchen. I couldn't face her this morning. I went upstairs and closed my bedroom door. I couldn't face anybody with the knowledge that my husband had discounted me as unworthy of his care, and I couldn't face anybody with the knowledge that I was considering living a lie for the rest of my natural life.

———

I sat by the window in the floral chintz-upholstered chair that Wesley Lloyd had hated. He'd never liked anything with flowers on it or that was pastel in color, and the wine-dark living and dining rooms reflected his preferences. I'd felt that the bedrooms could be softer, a little more feminine, but he'd put a stop to that when I'd had the chair re-covered. As I sat there, I thought again that it was the only thing in the house that I'd selected. And he'd hated it.

That was a symbol of something.

I rubbed my hand over the arm of the chair, trying to take in what he'd done to me and what he was still doing from the grave. My throat hurt down into my chest as I tried to convince myself that I had every right to destroy his last will and testament. Who could blame me if I did?

No one, I told myself, because no one would ever know.

I sat up straight as Brother Vern came to mind. Did he know? But he couldn't know. Not for sure, anyway. He'd been looking for anything Wesley Lloyd might have left the two Pucketts. He couldn't know there was a new will. Could he? Even if he suspected something, what could he do if it never came to light?

He could accuse me if Little Lloyd ever told anybody that he'd given me a paper from his father. Everybody would suspect what it'd been. I'd be ruined in this town. Hazel Marie might sue me. Little Lloyd would grow up distrusting me, always wondering if I'd stolen what belonged to him.

You could move away, I told myself, just sell this house and move to Florida. Leave this town and its suspicious minds and enjoy your old age in comfort and security.

I declare, I didn't think I could do it. Enjoy it, that is. On the other hand, whatever I decided to do—reveal the new will or destroy it—my feelings about Wesley Lloyd were going to make the rest of my life miserable. Lord forgive me, I prayed, for the bitterness in my heart.

I dressed slowly and carefully, feeling disconnected to the familiar morning routine. Zippers snagged, buttons refused to equal out with buttonholes, hairbrushes fell to the floor, hairpins flew from my hands, yet I overcame each obstacle with deliberate care while my mind whirled on some distant plane.

Dressed at last, I pinned the envelope to the inside of the bodice of my dress. I wasn't about to leave it where someone might find it. As I smoothed my hand across it, the answer came to me. It would be my secret for a few days at least. I'd see if I could live with it staying a secret. Nothing would be lost or gained by delaying a final decision.

Yes, that's what I'd do.

Now, I thought, let's pretend that the page doesn't exist. Let's pretend that everything is just as it was before Little Lloyd turned to me as his trusted friend. And, while we're at it, let's pretend I never laid a hand on Dr. Fred Fowler.

I had too much to do, I told myself, to worry with last-minute, undoubtedly invalid last wills and testaments that probably wouldn't amount to a hill of beans.

I went downstairs, my head high, to confront them all.

———

"What's the matter with you?" Lillian asked as soon as I stepped into the kitchen. "You look downright peaked this morning."

Lord, does it show already?

"I'm fine," I said. "Just not sleeping too well. Too many things on my mind."

"You need to start straightenin' them things out," she told me. "You can't keep hidin' Miss Puckett and that little boy, and you can't keep tellin' stories to the police."

"I know it. And I guess today's the day to do it." I sat down and propped my arms on the table, uncommonly tired and dispirited. "I don't know why I feel like I have to take on the problems of the world. Hazel Marie is a grown woman and capable of caring for herself and her child. There's no reason I should take it on myself to hide them from the police or protect them from their own relatives."

"That don't sound like you." Lillian stood in the middle of the kitchen frowning at me. She wiped her hands with a dish towel and said, "You sure you feelin' all right?"

The pink paper burned against my skin.

"I'm fine," I said again, looking in her direction but over her head. "It's just that I've come to realize that I've taken too much on myself and meddled in business that's no concern of mine. I aim to stop it."

"Hmm," she said, folding the towel and laying it on the counter. "How you figure on doin' that?"

"I don't know yet." I rubbed my forehead, and felt the paper crinkle under my arm. "I've a good mind to move my letter to the Episcopal church, and dare Pastor Ledbetter to slander a member of another church. Then I ought to call Lieutenant Peavey and tell him all about Hazel Marie and Little Lloyd, and let the chips fall."

"You can't do that!"

"Well, I may have to."

"What about that Brother Vern? What if he claims Little Lloyd and gets him away from his mama?"

"He won't. The only reason he wanted the child was because he thought they had some money from Wesley Lloyd. When he learns from Sam and Binkie that neither of them have a nickel, he'll be gone quick enough."

The pink paper seemed to throb with each beat of my heart. It was taking on a life of its own.

"Well, and what about me?" Lillian demanded. "You think the police gonna just forget about what they callin' kidnappin'?"

"They will when they learn the truth, and that's what I'm going to tell them." Except not all of it, not yet.

———

Knowing the risk I was taking, if Pastor Ledbetter was right about my sinful flesh, or rather the danger I was putting him in, I went to see Sam. Walking up onto Sam's broad front porch, I noted the fresh gray paint on the floor at the end of the soft rose-colored old brick of the steps and wide walk. White rocking chairs lined each side of the open front door.

"Julia." Sam stood holding the screen for me. "Saw you coming up the walk. What's wrong?"

"Everything, Sam." I went into the cool hall, and he led me into the living room. Books, stacked neatly on tables and the floor, and newspapers folded on the sofa indicated that Sam truly lived in this room. Unlike mine, which was always cold and polished, ready for company.

"Have a seat, Julia. Want some coffee?"

"I don't want anything but an end to all the mess I've gotten into."

Sam smiled, his eyes crinkling at the corners. "Where do you want to start?"

That was the question. Which secret sin did I most want help with? On the way to his house, I'd thought about showing him Wesley Lloyd's pink paper will and just accepting the fate it decreed for me. Then I'd thought I wouldn't, and by the time I'd gotten there I'd decided to put it off a while longer. To see if I could live with my secret knowledge in the same room as Sam's honesty.

Funny, it never occurred to me that Sam might collude in keeping the new will secret. There was no question that he wouldn't. Some people are honest to the bone. And some aren't.

"Pastor Ledbetter," I said, and told him how Dr. Fowler'd been brought in to have me evaluated. I couldn't bring myself to tell him that they might have reason to conclude I was riddled with sin and out of my mind. "Can they do that?"

Sam leaned back and, if it wasn't completely unlike him, appeared to roll his eyes. "I tell you, Julia, preachers have the least common sense of any group of people I've ever known. Unless it's doctors." He hunched forward in his chair. "Listen now. In this state, it's not difficult to have someone declared incompetent. All they have to do is demonstrate that you lack sufficient capacity to understand the consequences of your actions."

"I understand them, all right. I live with them every minute of the day. But, Sam, there's no telling what they might say about me. You just don't know what they're accusing me of. I need to do something."

"Do like Sophocles and write a play." He was laughing at me now.

"What're you talking about?"

"His son petitioned the court to have him declared incompetent so he could get at his father's estate. The old man asked for a chance to prove himself, and the judges agreed. So he went home and wrote one of the Oedipus plays. When the judges heard a reading of it, they not only acquitted him, they escorted him home. Probably broke open a jug of wine, too. So nothing's new, Julia, that happened back in the fifth century B.C."

"I knew that much," I said, but I wasn't the reader that Sam was. "But if proving the condition of my mind depends on writing a play, I'm in worse trouble than I thought."

Sam laughed. "Ah, Julia, that was just an example." Then he turned serious again. "Look, I don't want to scare you, but I'd better talk to Binkie about this. And, just so you know the process, anybody can make application to have someone declared incompetent. After that, a guardian *ad litem* would be appointed to represent that person's interests at the hearing. If the person's adjudicated incompetent, then a permanent guardian would be named, and that's the end of it."

I thought about it. It would turn me inside out to have to go through such a humiliating experience, but it sounded as if there would be enough safeguards to protect me.

"Well, Sam," I said, "I'd hate it if it comes down to it, but you could be named the guardian *ad litem* and Binkie the permanent guardian. Seems to me that things would go on just the way they are now, except for signing some legal papers and such. Now that you've explained it, it doesn't sound so bad."

Sam shook his head and looked down at the floor. "No, Julia, it's not that simple, but let Binkie and me worry about this. We're not going to let them railroad you, so what you have to do is stand up to them. And I know you can do that. You do it to me all the time."

I managed a smile in spite of the pink paper burning a hole in my skin inside my bodice.

Chapter 27

When I got back to the house, I went through the gate in the back garden and on into the kitchen. I nearly turned back around when Lillian told me that Pastor Ledbetter and Dr. Fowler were waiting in the living room. I grabbed the edge of the counter and prayed for a fainting spell so I wouldn't have to face them. It didn't work.

"I tol' them I didn't know when you be back," Lillian said, as she arranged glasses of lemonade on a tray. "But they say they wait anyway. You better go on in there, 'cause Miss Puckett in the room right above an' she's up tryin' to get herself dressed."

"Little Lloyd with her?" I managed to ask.

"Yessum, I done warned 'em both to stay up there an' stay quiet."

I watched Lillian arrange cheese straws on a silver plate, girding myself for the ordeal to come. I tried to overcome my embarrassment by building up a head of steam to confront those two about their meddling, but it was hard to do. Somehow that pink paper inside my dress was sapping my spirit, and nothing seemed worth the effort anymore.

I took a deep breath and held the door for Lillian as she preceded me into the living room. Both men stood as I entered the room, Pastor Ledbetter's broad smile masking his nefarious intentions.

I nodded a greeting, unwilling to risk a handshake, and took a seat on one of the Victorian chairs by the fireplace. Lillian placed the tray on the coffee table in front of the sofa where both men were seated. She offered the plate of cheese straws and, after an encouraging glance at me, left the room.

I sat and waited for them to begin, ignoring my natural inclination to entertain them with conversation and make them feel welome. This visit was their idea, and since it was so hard on me, I determined not to make it easy for them. I saw them glance at each other over the tops of their glasses of lemonade, then cut their eyes at me while I burned with shame. I couldn't meet Dr. Fowler's eyes, but I held my head up. I couldn't even reach for my glass on the tray, so I just sat there with my hands in my lap, waiting them out.

Finally, Pastor Ledbetter cleared his throat. "Uh, Miss Julia," he began, setting down his glass and patting his mouth with a napkin. "Have you given any thought to what I talked with you about over at the church? We can't let matters drag on forever, you know." He cut his eyes over at Dr. Fowler. To see if he was doing all right, I guess.

"Pastor, all I've thought about is what you said to me in the bridal parlor, and I've come to the conclusion that you were wrong. I've also concluded that you and Dr. Fowler here conspired to put me in a compromising position. I'd like to know how you'd answer that in a court of law, especially when I describe what Dr. Fowler had in his pocket. Well, I don't mean his pocket, but you know what I mean."

"Now, just a minute here," Dr. Fowler said, briefly levitating from my sofa.

Pastor Ledbetter held up his hand, taking charge. "Let me handle this, Fred. Miss Julia, Dr. Fowler has already explained it all to me. What that was, *if* it was anything, was an autonomic nervous system response to unwelcome stimuli, which any man in the world would understand, given the circumstances. It's incumbent on me to advise you not to use that in any way. It would only make you appear even more childlike not to understand these matters.

"Now," he said, hitching himself forward to lean toward me, "here's what I want to talk to you about. None of us wants to take any legal steps against you, but something has to be done. We want to consider your wishes as we decide these matters. Have you thought about what you'd like to do?"

"No, I haven't."

"You should, Miss Julia." He clasped his hands together between his spread legs and looked earnestly at me. "I'll be honest with you, that episode of you taking in that child claiming to be Mr. Springer's son should've been a warning to us that you weren't thinking right. And now"—he spread his hands—"look where it's led us to."

"I don't have an idea in the world what you're talking about, Pastor," I said.

"It's like this," he said, resting his hands on his knees. He gave another look at Dr. Fowler, who was leaning back with his legs crossed, staring at me with those strange eyes of his. "We, that is, the church, the congregation of this church, are your family, the only one you have this town. It's up to us to look after one another. Now, Miss Julia, I come to you not only as your pastor but as a member of that family, to say that we are deeply concerned about you. Besides what I saw with my own eyes, I've had reports that you've exhibited other strange behavior. All of which points to the fact that I've been remiss in not pursuing this matter more vigorously. Now, I know—"

He raised his hand, palm out, to stop any argument to the contrary, but I overrode him. "Tell me about those reports."

"Oh now," he said, smiling and shaking his head, "we don't need to discuss the details. Suffice it to say that several people, people who care about you and want to help you, have noticed a few worrisome things."

"Who?" I demanded.

"Now, don't get upset. We need to talk about this reasonably and come to some decision that'll be best for you."

"Who?"

"Miss Julia," he said, sighing, "this is just the kind of thing I'm talking about. You're not thinking straight. You need to be thinking about what you'll do in the future, not what's happened in the past. That's behind us, and I'm concerned about you right now, and I want you to know that Dr. Fowler here has opened a retirement center, a fine, Christian place, offering the best of care for our senior citizens. It has what's known as lifetime care where you can have a room with your own furniture and personal things, but also have nursing care when you need it. I'll tell you, it's a wonderful place with chapel every morning and evening prayers at night. There're nurses on duty day and night, and a trained dietitian, and therapists of all kinds. Why, they even have a social director who plans outings and all kinds of activities for the residents, things like aerobics and sing-alongs and birthday parties. Why, the days are just filled with wholesome activities, and all your meals are prepared and served in a lovely dining room with white tablecloths and candles at the evening meal."

Some of the old fire flamed up inside of me and I forgot about the pink paper pinned to my bodice. I straightened my back, thankful for all the calcium I'd taken over the years, and looked him in the eye.

"Are you going to tell me *who* has brought reports of my strange behavior to you, or did you break your promise and start the rumors yourself?"

"Now, Miss Julia, you don't want to get upset."

"Upset?" My voice went up alarmingly on the last syllable, and I made an effort to contain myself. "I simply want to know," I went on in a calmer tone, "on whose reports you've made the decision that I need to be in an old-folks home."

"Well," he said, giving another quick glance at the silent Dr. Fowler. Pastor Ledbetter pushed his hair off his forehead and sighed. "Several people have come to me with their concerns. It seems, for one thing, that you're planning to open a kennel right here in your house. And going so far as to buy a number of unlikely medical items for which you have no need at all. Now, you have to admit that that is a little strange and not at all like you. And, for another, people speak to you on the street and they get unusual responses from you, or no response at all, as if you're off in another world. Those are just examples, Miss Julia, and of course, I have not and will not speak of another example if, that is, you get some help. And let's not forget the way you took in that strange child with no idea in the world who he was or what he was after. You're just not yourself, Miss Julia, and we want to see you taken care of. Because we care about you and we're all worried about you."

"Oh, I'm sure Norma Cantrell's just made herself sick with worry over me," I said. "As well as Buck Tatum and Troy Beckworth. Both of them ought to be minding their own business instead of poking their noses in mine. I wouldn't trust either of them as far as I could throw them, since they're the biggest gossips in town. Except for Norma, who you ought to know by now doesn't have a lick of sense."

I swung around in my chair and faced Dr. Fowler. "And what is your interest in this, Doctor, other than befriending lonely old women so you can fill up the rooms in your rest home?"

"I . . ." he began, uncrossing his legs and looking away from me for the first time, "I was asked by Pastor Ledbetter and the session to give my evaluation of your state of mind. For your own good, I might add."

My soul sank inside of me. If my competency rating depended on Dr. Fowler's evaluation, the rest of me was sunk, too. They were giving me the choice of voluntarily committing myself or having a judge do it for me. And either way, it was for my own good.

As I opened and closed my mouth, trying to speak, footsteps sounded on the porch and the doorbell rang.

"Why, Brother Vern," I said, staring at him through the screen door, my mind going a hundred miles a minute, wondering how much he knew or how much he'd guessed, and what he intended to do. I was so shocked I couldn't move, trying to figure out how to get rid of him. And Pastor Ledbetter and Dr. Fowler, too, while I was at it. My mind fluttered here and there, trying to think how to warn Lillian and Hazel Marie.

He took hold of the screen and said, "Miz Springer. May I come in?"

"Why yes," I managed to say. "Yes, come in."

He walked in, nodding to the two men who'd stood as he entered. I saw Pastor Ledbetter take in Brother Vern's brown polyester suit, yellow tie, and white shoes. Short-sleeved shirt, too, since no cuffs showed below his coat sleeves. Brother Vern looked hot, his face red and shiny, his black hair glistening.

I made the introductions and the two ministers of the Gospel looked each other over like two dogs circling. Dr. Fowler might as well not have been there for all the attention they paid him. I could see that Pastor Ledbetter's back was up, since he'd pretty well gotten Brother Vern's number right from the start.

"Reverend Puckett has a television program every week. *Feeding the Flame,* isn't that it?" I said, considerably relieved to steer the conversation in another direction.

"That's it," he said. "I preach to a congregation of some forty to fifty thousand people every week, praise God."

Top that, I thought, as I found myself taking a peculiar satisfaction in setting one against the other. Not that I especially enjoyed it, you understand, but at least they weren't going after me.

"A televangelist," Pastor Ledbetter said, cutting his eyes at Dr. Fowler. "I didn't know you were interested in that kind of ministry, Miss Julia." More fuel for the flame he wanted to set under me.

"I don't expect the Lord is limited to eleven o'clock on Sundays," I said.

"No, indeed," Brother Vern agreed. "In fact, Brother, the Lord is changing a lotta things these days. Have you switched your Sunday night services to Friday nights yet?"

"What?" Pastor Ledbetter looked bewildered, unsure he'd heard right.

"It's the coming thing," Brother Vern went on, coming into his own now that he'd discovered a way to teach a mainline preacher a thing or two. "The Lord has spoken to any number of preachers, evangelicals mostly, and pointed out to them that Sunday afternoons are family times and shouldn't be interrupted for church services. Friday nights do just fine for a substitute, and start the weekends off right. The Lord figures it's a good way to keep people out of bars and dance halls on Friday nights. And," he added with a knowing grin, "country clubs, too."

That was a nice jab.

Pastor Ledbetter drew himself up and said, "There's a clear mandate to honor the Sabbath and keep it holy."

"You certainly know your Bible, Brother," Brother Vern said with a sly gleam in his eye. "And our Jewish friends honor the Sabbath every Saturday that rolls around. But us evangelical Christians honor the Lord every day of the week, don't matter to us what the calendar says."

"Well, but I—"

"Mr. Puckett," I interrupted, "was there something you wanted to see me about? Pastor Ledbetter and Dr. Fowler were just leaving."

Pastor Ledbetter found his voice. "Miss Julia, if you don't mind, we haven't finished with our concerns. Why don't you let Mr. Puckett here state his business, and then we can pick up where we left off."

Pastor Ledbetter wasn't anxious to leave me alone with a preacher who used television to raise money to stay on television. He probably thought I was one of those poor souls who believed a preacher with a Cadillac needed their Social Security checks worse than they did. I noticed Dr. Fowler pulling a little notepad from his jacket pocket.

"Then let's all have a seat," I said. I didn't know how Brother Vern could help my current situation, but he was doing a good job of distracting the other two. And I was happy to note that I wasn't having even a twinge of interest toward him. "Now, Mr. Puckett, what can I help you with?"

He sat across from me in the matching Victorian chair and ignored the other two on the sofa. "You heard about how my precious little great-nephew's been kidnapped?"

Pastor Ledbetter and Dr. Fowler exchanged surprised glances, and Dr. Fowler began jotting notes on his pad.

"I heard," I said. "That is, I heard that a child was missing in Spartanburg. Don't tell me it was the same child! Why, Mr. Puckett, it couldn't be! I mean, you took him to Raleigh! Didn't you? That's what you told me you were going to do." I might've been overplaying it, but he didn't seem to notice.

"Well, now," he said, pulling out a large white handkerchief and wiping the palms of his hands. "We was on our way, but when the Lord leads you to preach, you just have to stop and preach."

"But you took the child on Sunday," I reminded him. "And according to the lieutenant who notified me, the child went missing on Tuesday night. Late Tuesday night, too late for a child of that age to be up. Sounds to me like somebody wasn't taking care of him."

"That boy was gettin' three a day and plenty of sleep," Brother Vern said. "And I was going to take him to his mama, just as soon as I finished my telecast. We was going to drive on down to Raleigh right afterwards." He wiped his face with the handkerchief.

Pastor Ledbetter's eyes bounced from one to the other of us, mentally taking note of what else I was mixed up in. Dr. Fowler was just taking notes.

"Mrs. Springer," Brother Vern went on, a pleading tone in his voice now. "I mightta done wrong by not taking that boy right on down to Raleigh, but my conscience is clear. I did my best by him, and can't nobody help it when some strange black woman comes outta nowhere and snatches him away. Now I've come here to ask your help in gettin' him back. The police're doin' all they can, and it looks like to me that what we need is to offer some reward money." He wiped his forehead and glanced at me with those black eyes. "I've come to appeal to your spirit of Christian charity."

Pastor Ledbetter sat straight up, opening his mouth to protest. I cut him off.

"How much?"

"Why, whatever you find it in your heart to give. Whatever you think best, but it ought to be enough to get people's attention. You know, so if anybody has any information, they'll come forward. Or so that black woman will be tempted. I'll put it out over my *Feeding the Flame* program, and everybody'll be looking for that precious child."

"How much?"

"Miss Julia." Pastor Ledbetter couldn't stand it any longer. "Think about this before you do anything. You need to pray about this. Who knows where that child is? Or who has him? Don't get involved with this until you have more information."

Dr. Fowler's eyes gleamed as his notes began to cover a second page.

I waved off my pastor and kept my attention on Brother Vern.

"How much?"

"Well, I was thinking, maybe, ten thousand?" Brother Vern said.

"Ten thousand," I repeated.

"Five, if that's all you can do."

"I was thinking more along the lines of twenty-five," I said. "For a start."

Brother Vern's face brightened and Pastor Ledbetter buried his in his hands.

"The Lord bless you, Mrs. Springer!" Brother Vern cried. "I'll get that boy back, the Lord be praised!"

"Miss Julia," Pastor Ledbetter said, "you oughtn't do this. You're not yourself, we know it and you know it. Don't make any rash decisions before a guardian can be appointed. I beg you, don't squander Mr. Springer's estate that he worked so hard for. This is just the sort of thing Dr. Fowler and I are trying to forestall by taking care of you."

"Pastor, I don't need taking care of, and Mr. Springer's estate is as safe as it was the day he left this vale of tears." I smiled at him, then at Dr. Fowler and Brother Vern. "If you need more, Brother Vern, just let me know."

"Lord bless you, Mrs. Springer!" Brother Vern leaned back in his chair and gave Pastor Ledbetter a complacent smile.

The door from the kitchen swung open, and Lillian's run-over heels slapped on the floor as she came toward the living room. I started from my chair, my heart pounding.

"I brought y'all some more lemonade," she sang out, balancing a full pitcher on a tray.

Brother Vern sprang from his chair like he'd been shot. "That's her!" He pointed at her, index finger quivering, as he bellowed, "She's the one! Call the sheriff!"

"Jesus Lord, help me!" Lillian shrieked, throwing her hands up as tray, pitcher, and three quarts of lemonade sprayed the room. She turned and ran for the kitchen.

"Citizen's arrest!" Brother Vern cried, running after her. "Stop, woman, you're under arrest!"

"What in the world?" Pastor Ledbetter asked, standing and shaking out his trousers, soaked with Lillian's lemonade. "Has everybody lost their minds?"

Dr. Fowler nodded as he wet a finger and turned a page, then began scribbling even faster.

Chapter 29

I ran from the room, heading for the stairs, as Pastor Ledbetter yelled, "The man's crazy! Call the police!"

"That's what I'm doing," I yelled back, hitting the stairs as fast as I could. No time for the telephone; I had a live-in deputy upstairs.

Brother Vern's voice, loud with outrage and righteous indignation, echoed from the kitchen under Lillian's screams for me to save her.

I got to the top of the stairs, out of breath and terrified, fearing what Brother Vern could do to us all.

"Deputy Bates! Wake up, get up, we need you!" I pounded on his door.

"What is it?" he called, but the door stayed closed.

I pounded harder. "Hurry, hurry! Open up, we need you right now!"

I heard rustling sounds behind the door, almost drowned out by the commotion downstairs. Pastor Ledbetter came to the foot of the stairs, adding his bass rumble to the din.

"Miss Julia!" he called. "If you won't call the police, I will. This is intolerable! We can't have this, we just can't have it!"

I leaned over the banister and said, "Pastor, I'm calling the police as fast as I can. Now, get in the kitchen and keep that fool away from Lillian." A pan banged off the kitchen wall and clattered on the floor.

I pounded at Deputy Bates's door again, screaming, "Get up! We got to save Lillian. Deputy Coleman Bates, get outta that bed, you hear me!"

Behind me, another door banged open and Little Lloyd ran out, eyes big and frightened, his mother right behind him.

"What is it?" she asked. "Is there a fire? Run, Junior, we got to get everybody out!"

"Fire! Fire!" Little Lloyd screamed, jumping around with his skinny arms flying every which way.

"No, no!" I grabbed him and held him close, trying to calm him down. "It's not a fire, it's Lillian. I've got to get Deputy Bates up to help us."

Hazel Marie banged on the door along with me as the racket from the kitchen grew louder. She had on one of my dresses, looking for the first time like she might rejoin the living.

"Deputy Bates!" we both screamed.

The door opened a crack, revealing one of Deputy Bates's eyes, glinting fiercely, and a shock of hair.

"What is it?" He didn't sound pleased at being summoned to duty.

"It's Lillian! And Brother Vern!" I felt Hazel Marie's shock at hearing the name, and thought for a minute that she was going to turn and run. "Get out here and arrest him! I want him in jail before he hurts Lillian!"

Deputy Bates reached down and zipped up his dark blue uniform pants. Then he grabbed a white undershirt and pulled it over his head. "Is he attacking her?"

"That's what I'm trying to tell you! He's attacking her and right here in my own house!"

"Deputy Bates," Little Lloyd cried, "don't let him hurt Miss Lillian!"

"Where'd you come from, Bud?" Deputy Bates stopped, clearly surprised to see Little Lloyd, then he got a good look at Hazel Marie. Her face had healed considerably, but it could still pretty much stop a truck if you weren't prepared for it. Which he wasn't.

"See there," I said, pointing at her. "There's an example of what that man is capable of. He did that, or let it be done. And had my house ransacked, too. Now he's trying to take Little Lloyd away from his mother!" Then I remembered that he didn't know her. "And this is his mother."

"Ma'am," he said, nodding at her. He may have been having trouble absorbing the situation.

A piercing scream from Lillian and men's voices yelling at her or at each other shook the rafters.

"He's killing Miss Lillian!" Little Lloyd screamed, his skinny little legs dancing up and down, his arms flailing like a windmill. "We got to help her!"

"Well, goddamn, I believe it!" Deputy Bates left the door open and ran barefooted to the closet. He reached up and brought down from a shelf his black-holstered police weapon. "Y'all stay up here outta the way."

He swung the door wide as he brushed past us, pulling the gun out and tossing the holster aside as he ran. I had no intention of staying upstairs, but the spectacle in his room stopped me cold.

"Binkie?" I asked, staring at her. I couldn't figure out what she was doing in my upstairs back guest room, rented now to a paying boarder. "Oh," I said, the light dawning as she hurriedly buttoned her blouse.

"Hi, Miss Julia," she said, two spots of red in her cheeks. "Nice to see you again."

She stepped into her shoes and ran her fingers through her hair. It needed a comb and a brush.

Hazel Marie and Little Lloyd stood beside me, unsure of what to do or where to go. I got myself together and made the introductions.

"Pleased, I'm sure," Hazel Marie said with a quick, knowing smile.

There was a sudden break in the action downstairs, and in the quiet of the cease-fire, we heard Deputy Bates say, "Everybody just calm down now, and let's get this straightened out."

It's amazing what the appearance of a man in uniform, even half a uniform, can accomplish, to say nothing of a man with a gun in his hand.

"Well, Binkie," I said, pulling myself together. "It's a good thing you're here. I expect several of us're going to need a lawyer in the next few minutes. We better get on downstairs."

Not too long before, I would've been outraged at the thought of something illegal, illicit, and immoral taking place in one of my bedrooms. However. I had too many other worries to get bent out of shape over Binkie and Deputy Bates jumping the gun, so to speak. Wesley Lloyd would've had a different view, but so would every other hypocrite.

It crossed my mind that Binkie might have a touch of the problem that Pastor Ledbetter accused me of having. But if she did, Deputy Bates didn't seem to mind it very much.

Chapter 30

Deputy Bates had Pastor Ledbetter, Dr. Fowler, Brother Vern, and Lillian all in the living room, seated and separated, by the time the four of us joined them. Deputy Bates stood in front of the fireplace, holding his gun down by his side, looking fully in control of the situation in spite of his state of dress, his bare feet, and what he'd been doing when I interrupted him.

"Oh, Miss Julia," Lillian cried, lifting her face out of her apron. "Don't let 'em put me in jail! You know I didn't go to kidnap that baby!"

Little Lloyd ran to her and put his arms around her. Hazel Marie stood beside her, patting her shoulder. I said, "You're not going to jail, Lillian. Binkie, do something."

"What's the charge, Deputy?" Binkie asked, all business in spite of her blouse being misbuttoned.

"No charges yet on anybody," he said, giving her a quick smile. "Still trying to find out who's done what."

"I can tell you that," I said. But everybody else started talking at the same time.

"That woman," Brother Vern said, pointing at Lillian and drowning out the rest of us, "kidnapped that child." He pointed at Little Lloyd. "And that one," he bellowed, aiming a finger at Hazel Marie, "is a woman totally without morals and unfit for motherhood."

"Miss Julia." Pastor Ledbetter started to rise, the better to pontificate, but Deputy Bates held up his hand. The pastor took his seat again. "Miss Julia, I have to protest. Just what is going on here? Who is that woman? Who is this man, and why are Dr. Fowler and I being held against our will?" He looked from Hazel Marie to Brother Vern, then raised his eyes to the ceiling. Dr. Fowler had filled his notebook and was now searching his pockets for scrap paper so he could keep writing.

"You're not being held—" Deputy Bates started, but Brother Vern popped up out of his chair.

"I demand you arrest that woman for kidnapping! And if you won't do it, I'll make a citizen's arrest right here and now!"

"Just try it, buster," Binkie said, getting right in his face.

"Now, folks," Deputy Bates said. "Let's all calm down."

"I can't calm down," Lillian sobbed. "They gonna put me in jail!"

"No they're not, Miss Lillian!" Little Lloyd cried, throwing his arms around her. "I won't let them put you in jail."

"Stay out of this, boy," Brother Vern said, giving him a cold look. "You'll be in a foster home or juvenile hall. I've had all the trouble outta you I'm gonna take."

"You just shut your trap, Vernon Puckett," Hazel Marie said, pulling Little Lloyd to her and standing closer to Lillian. "We've all had all we're gonna take from you. I've been beat to within an inch of my life on your say-so, and you took my boy from me, and I'm gonna swear out a warrant on you!"

"Listen, listen," Pastor Ledbetter said, unaccustomed to having to struggle to be heard, "this has got to stop. I don't know what's been going on here, but it's evident that somebody's taken leave of their senses." He looked at me. "And no telling what's been allowed to take place upstairs in this very house, what with both these young women up there with this law officer. Looks to me like you've been keeping a disorderly house, Miss Julia, among the other things I know about. Somebody's got to step in and do something."

That was a clear threat if I'd ever heard one, and I shriveled up inside at the thought of him being led to tell everything he knew, or thought he knew. Even if his diagnosis was wrong, even if Dr. Fowler hadn't made a point of his own, so to speak, I didn't want to stand there and be shamed in front of them all.

"It's not what it seems, Pastor. Please, it's just a mix-up." I folded my arms protectively across my chest, bringing to mind the pink paper pinned to the inside of my dress.

"Knock, knock, anybody home?" Sam stuck his head in the door. He looked around the room and said, "Looks like you're busy, Julia. I'll come back later."

He turned to leave, but I called him back. "Don't go, Sam, I need you here." If I had to be relieved of responsibility for myself, I wanted Sam to see that it was done right.

"That'd be a change," he said with a wry smile, but his eyes were traveling around the room taking in the unlikely group gathered there. Hazel Marie he didn't know, and he hadn't met Brother Vern or Dr. Fowler, but I saw him make some quick associations. I wanted to go stand beside him, but I was afraid of what I might do and what Pastor Ledbetter would think of it.

Sam raised his eyebrows as he noticed the gun in Deputy Bates's hand. "Trouble?"

"More noise than anything," Deputy Bates said, laying the gun on the mantel. But he didn't move away from it. "Now, folks. Let's get some things straightened out, and I don't want everybody talking at once. Miss Lillian, you first. Did you kidnap that boy?"

"Nossir, I did not." She sat up straight and smoothed out her apron. She trusted Deputy Bates, knowing he'd hear her out and not jump to conclusions. "That Brother Vern got this baby away from Miss Julia under false pretensions, claiming he'd take him to his mama, but 'stead of that, he taken him off an' put him on teevee, an' then we find out he let Jerome beat up on this pore little thing here." She looked up at Hazel Marie. Then dabbing at her eyes, she went on, "An' knocked out her teef too. That man a menace to decent folk."

"Menace!" Brother Vern shouted, jumping out of his chair again. Deputy Bates tapped his shoulder, and Brother Vern sat back down. But he didn't stop talking. "I'll tell you who's a menace. It's all these women running wild, interfering with the Lord's work! Hazel Marie's been living in sin for lo these many years and borne its fruit, which all I'm trying to do is look after. His daddy would've wanted somebody responsible in charge, an' that ain't her!" The words poured from his mouth like the sweat from his forehead. Brother Vern was mortally exercised.

"And now," he shouted, "here's this woman, a black woman and kitchen help at that, who walked right into my studio while I was *on the air* and put that child right back into this den of iniquity! And that's what this place looks like to me!"

"I couldn't agree more," Pastor Ledbetter said, looking at Brother Vern with something close to approval. "And, Brother, you don't know the half of it."

I grasped the back of a chair to keep from falling. Lord, I prayed, don't let him tell. Please don't let him tell.

"Just a minute, here," Binkie said. "Let's take one thing at a time. It seems to me that the kidnapping charge is moot. Here's the child; there's his mother. Where's the kidnapping?"

"But," Brother Vern said, "she took him from me."

"But you took him from me," I managed to say.

"But he's my child," Hazel Marie chimed in. "And I left him in Miz Springer's care, not his, and he has no right to claim him or raise a fuss when I got him back."

"Kidnapping's not going to stick," Binkie said with all the authority of Wake Forest Law School behind her. "What do you think, Sam?"

"I think you're right. The boy's where he belongs."

"Well. Well," Brother Vern blustered, "well, what about the reward? Miz Springer, you offered a sizable reward and I think I have a claim to it. If it wasn't for me, this child'd still be hid away somewhere."

"I think you have a point, Reverend Puckett," Pastor Ledbetter said, astounding us all. Even Brother Vern was stunned to have such an unlikely defender. "Miss Julia made a rash promise against good advice, and it seems to me she ought to make it good. She's been doing too many rash things lately, and has to accept the consequences of her actions. If, that is, she is able to understand them."

"Just a minute, here," Sam broke in. "Before you go off half-cocked, what reward are you talking about?"

"Yeah," Binkie said.

Pastor Ledbetter silenced Brother Vern with a take-charge look. "Miss Julia offered a twenty-five-thousand-dollar reward for the recovery of this kidnapped child. I was witness to it, and so was Dr. Fowler, just as we were also witnesses to something even more astonishing. I think you have to honor it, Miss Julia."

"But—"

"There was no kidnapping," Binkie said, cutting me off. "No kidnapping, no reward."

"There's something we're all overlooking here," Dr. Fowler said, proving that he could speak as well as write. I braced myself for his contribution. "Now, I realize that I'm an outsider and not familiar with all that's gone on, but it seems to me we need the answer to one important question."

"What's that?" Binkie demanded, squinting her eyes at him.

"Well, my understanding is that the child was taken from somewhere in another town, but now he's found right here. This woman"—he pointed at Lillian—"admits to having him. But the question is, how did she get him? Did she walk? Did she drive? Did she have help?"

Hazel Marie and Little Lloyd looked at me. Lord, where was Dr. Fowler going with this?

"Miss Julia," Lillian wailed.

"That's right," Brother Vern cried. "Somebody was driving that car! Everybody agreed that somebody else drove the car." He turned to me and narrowed his eyes. "Was that somebody you, Miz Springer? Were you a party to kidnapping?"

Binkie said, "Don't answer that."

Sam said, "There was no kidnapping, so it doesn't matter who drove what."

"But there was a *conspiracy* to kidnap," Pastor Ledbetter said. "Then add to that all the aimless driving around the county, plans to turn this fine house into a dog kennel, bizarre answers to common questions, apparent lying to the police, attempting to buy narcotics, getting involved with people she doesn't know and taking them in like members of the family, promising to give away twenty-five thousand dollars to a virtual stranger, and certain intractable behavior that would repulse you all if I told you of it. Well, you can see how it begins to stack up. None of you is doing Miss Julia a favor by ignoring these clear changes in her personality. She needs help, and if it takes a court case to get it for her, then so be it. At least I and her church family care enough to prevent any harm coming to her. We mean to take care of her, since it's abundantly clear she can't take care of herself."

"Clear as a bell," Dr. Fowler said. "As I will so testify."

Chapter 31

My head swiveled from Sam to Binkie, waiting for one of them to say the accusations were ridiculous. Sam frowned, deep in thought, and Binkie chewed her thumbnail.

"Can they do that?" I asked.

"They'd have to prove it," Sam said hesitantly, as if wondering what I'd done that he didn't know about.

"Which they'd have a hard time doing," Binkie added.

"That depends," Dr. Fowler said. "It depends on what they're trying to prove. If it's a criminal charge, yes, it would be hard to prove. But Brother Vern's testimony, added to that of so many others, including mine and her pastor's, could well make a case for diminished capacity."

Binkie turned on him, her hair swinging in her face. "Who *are* you?"

"I'm Dr. Fred Fowler, certified clinical psychologist." He stood a little straighter as he said it. "And I've been retained by the session of the First Presbyterian Church to look into this matter."

"Good grief!" Binkie said, throwing up her hands.

Sam's eyes rolled back in his head worse than I'd ever seen. Hazel Marie tightened her arm around Lillian's shoulders, and Pastor Ledbetter sat back with his hands clasped over his abdomen, composed and content. Brother Vern's black eyes ranged avidly over us all, watching for any other unexpected advantage.

"Now, Mrs. Springer," Dr. Fowler went on, his voice as soft as if he were gentling a wild woman. "We don't want you to be concerned. No one's going to hurt you, I promise. And no one is going to reveal any embarrassing details as long as you allow us to help you. Everything's going to be just fine. All we're concerned about is your welfare. I suggest you let me admit you to my infirmary for a few tests. And you can have a well-deserved rest at the same time."

"Sam?" I said, beginning to realize that they really could have me committed to some linoleum-floored, Lysol-smelling dormitory for the demented, doomed to the droning of game shows and Jenny Jones for the rest of my life.

"You know we'll take care of you, Miss Julia," Pastor Ledbetter said. "I've already begun the process, because I know Mr. Springer would want us to look after you."

"What they talkin' about?" Lillian asked, her eyes big with the fear that was beginning to well up in me.

"Binkie?" I said, turning to her.

"I'm thinking, I'm thinking," she said, pacing back and forth. "The problem is, the *big* problem is . . . Sam, you see what I mean?"

"Yeah, the clerk of court."

"The clerk of court?" I gasped as my soul dropped down to my feet. "You mean *Leonard*? Leonard *Conover*?"

"That's right," Sam said. "Leonard Conover's the one who'd handle this, the one who'd have the final disposition of their application. And the one who'd appoint a guardian. But hang on, Julia, we're not without a few resources of our own."

"Don't be too sure," Pastor Ledbetter said. "You may not be aware of the details of Miss Julia's recent erratic behavior."

I looked at his confident expression and at the gleam in the peculiar eyes of Dr. Fowler, and I knew they were prepared to ruin my life forever. I pictured a line of my friends and neighbors testifying in open court about the changes they'd seen in me. I pictured Dr. Fowler describing that episode in the bridal parlor, and I pictured Leonard Conover, who thought the sun rose and set on Pastor Ledbetter, deciding my fate. I felt a tremor run through my body. Men, religious men, had been making decisions for me all my life, telling me not to worry, do what I tell you, I know what's best for you, what you want is not important. And I'd let them, always assuming that they were right, that they knew more than I did, that it was my place to agree and go along, even as the icy knife of resentment cut wider and deeper into my heart. While I smiled and kept on smiling. Only since Wesley Lloyd's passing had I felt like a real person. So, yes, Pastor Ledbetter was right; I had changed. I was different from what I'd always been. Now I said what I was thinking instead of packing it down inside. Now I did what I wanted to do instead of what I was told to do. Now I followed my own inclinations instead of waiting for instructions. I'd discovered that I was neither a child nor a half-wit, and I'd refused to be treated as either. I was a grown woman.

No wonder they thought I was crazy.

Yet I also knew that without Wesley Lloyd's money, there wouldn't be this concern for my welfare, even if I threw myself at every man in town. If I'd been as broke as Hazel Marie, they might bring me a few casseroles and a box of dusting powder at Christmas, but they wouldn't be trying to put me in a two-hundred-dollar-a-day nursing home. That money had given me a freedom I'd never known, and now it was about to bind me up worse than Wesley Lloyd ever had.

My hands shook as I reached up and began to unbutton the bodice of my dress.

Brother Vern drew in a sibilant breath, while Dr. Fowler and Pastor Ledbetter began to back away. Pastor Ledbetter's face paled, his mouth dropping open, as if he feared I'd choose him as my next victim.

"Don't," he gasped. "Fred, do something."

But Fred ducked his head and sidled toward the door. He wasn't about to tangle with me again.

I unbuttoned the second button. Sam and Binkie looked shocked, but no more than Lillian and Deputy Bates.

Hazel Marie was the only one who moved. She walked over and stood in front of me, shielding me from them. She placed both her hands on mine.

"Oh, honey," she said, so softly I could barely hear her. "Don't do this. Let's me and you go upstairs."

My bones went weak on me as her poor, battered face swam out of focus through the tears that flooded my eyes. I'd never before in my life been called a sweet name by somebody who really meant it.

"It's all right," I whispered to her. "It's really all right."

We looked at each other a long second, then she nodded and took her hands from mine. But she stayed in front of me while I continued to unbutton my bodice. I reached inside and unpinned the pink paper. When I had it out, Hazel Marie rebuttoned my dress for me and stepped to my side.

"Here, Sam," I said, holding the paper out to him. "This should go to you. I expect it'll change a few things."

Sam walked over and took the paper from me. He unfolded it, read it, and looked at me with what might've been a gleam of admiration in his eyes. It might've been pity, though, I couldn't tell which. Everybody watched as Sam looked down and read it again, shaking his head and pursing his mouth in thought. Hazel Marie slid her arm around my waist, and I was grateful for the support since I was feeling a bit wobbly. Everybody in the room was aware that the flimsy piece of pink paper was of great import. Only Sam and I knew how great.

Binkie said, "What is it?"

"It's a holographic will," Sam said.

"A holy what?" Hazel Marie asked.

"A handwritten will." He held it out to Binkie to read. "Wesley Lloyd Springer wrote it the night he died, according to the date. And it does change things. A good many things."

"What do it say?" Lillian asked, picking up on the charged atmosphere and misinterpreting it. "What time Mr. Springer write that thing, befo' he passed or after?"

"Before, Miss Lillian," Binkie assured her, "before. Probably sometime that day."

"Read it out loud, Binkie," I said, "so everybody'll know."

"Here, Sam," she said, handing the paper to him. "It's your place to read it." She went over and stood by Deputy Bates.

"What it says," Sam began, "is that Mr. Springer left his entire estate to his son, Little Lloyd here."

Dead silence as everyone looked at the boy. Except me, who was still trying to control the trembling as I waited to feel their pity directed my way.

"What!" Pastor Ledbetter was the first to find his voice. "Why, that can't be! Can he do that? Is that thing legal?"

"As legal as it can get," Sam said. "I can attest to the signature."

"I don't believe it! Miss Julia, I . . . you, we have to do something, fight it, take it to court, something!"

"Forget it, Pastor," Binkie said, standing under Deputy Bates's arm, which was stretched out across the mantel. "That will's as solid as a rock, much to Miss Julia's sorrow, I'm sure."

As Pastor Ledbetter looked for help from Dr. Fowler, who had none to offer, Brother Vern approached Sam. "Spell that out for me if you will, Brother."

"It simply means that the boy inherits his father's estate when he reaches maturity."

"Everything?"

"That's what it says."

"The Lord be praised! Child," he said, turning a benevolent face toward Little Lloyd, "you have been blessed beyond belief and, undoubtedly, your family with you. Hazel Marie, you gonna need help raisin' this boy. It's a great responsibility, but I'm here to help every step of the way."

Hazel Marie had not moved from my side. She looked from Sam to Brother Vern, and back to Sam again.

"You mean," she said, "Wesley Lloyd left everything to Junior when he gets grown?"

"Yes," Sam said, "but it also means that he, and you, will be taken care of financially from now on."

Hazel Marie was trembling worse than I was by this time. She put her hand up to cover her mouth. "I don't understand," she said.

"It means, Hazel Marie," I said, "that you won't have to crack a lick at a snake ever again."

She crumpled against me, both hands covering her face as she sobbed. "Oh, Miz Springer, that's just not right."

"Of course it's right," I told her, patting her back. "Sam wouldn't make such a mistake."

"No, I mean it's not fair. You were his legal wife, can he do this?"

"Mama?" Little Lloyd came to us, his face wrinkled with worry to see his mother crying. "What's the matter, Mama? What's going to happen to us?"

"Not a thing, Little Lloyd," I said. "All your troubles are over, and your mama is crying from happiness. You don't have to worry where you're going to live or what you're going to do from now on. In fact, you can live right here, if you want to." I patted Hazel Marie's back with one hand and put my other arm around Little Lloyd's shoulders, trying to comfort them in their joy.

"Right here?" Little Lloyd's face glowed at the thought. "With you? And Miss Lillian? Mama, hear that? Miz Springer wants us to live here with her."

"Oh, child." I sighed, thinking my heart might break.

I glanced at Lillian, who had thrown her head back against her chair. Her eyes were closed and her mouth moved in what I hoped was fervent prayer for us all. Me, especially, because I was the one who needed it.

"Miss Julia," Pastor Ledbetter said, "I am so sorry." He dropped into a chair and leaned his elbows on his knees. Then he wiped his face with both hands, frowning and slowly shaking his head. "Nobody could've foreseen such an outcome. You don't suppose," he said, looking hopefully at Dr. Fowler, "that we could help Miss Julia break this new will?"

"Unlikely," he snapped, as if he were fed up with the whole situation, "if it's as authentic as it appears to be. Besides, if we supported her in breaking it, how would it appear to the court if you then made application to have her declared incompetent?"

"Good point," Binkie said.

"Well," Pastor Ledbetter said, "I don't suppose anybody will believe this, but I am truly concerned for Miss Julia. What will she do, in her condition, if this will has made her destitute? Sam, what can the church do to help?"

"Maybe the best thing," Sam told him quietly, "is to give Julia a chance to absorb this. It comes as a shock, you know. There are a few options she can consider, so why don't you and the good doctor, or whatever he is, give her some time. Then if she needs the church's help, she'll let you know."

"Yes, that's good advice." He rose to his full height and came over to me. "I am so sorry about all of this, Miss Julia. Maybe I was wrong to proceed as I did, but I want you to know it was from the best of intentions."

"I know, Pastor, and I appreciate those good intentions. And I'd appreciate it even more if you'd call off Leonard before he does some major damage."

He nodded, murmuring something about the Lord issuing a call to a new ministry. We're told to forgive those who trespass against us, but I declare it was a bitter pill to swallow to keep my mouth shut about his current ministry.

After Pastor Ledbetter and Dr. Fowler took their leave, Brother Vern seemed to expand to fill the space. "Let me add my deep concern to theirs for your misfortune, Miz Springer," he said, hardly able to suppress the smile that pulled at the corners of his mouth. "Now, Hazel Marie, pull yourself together, girl, and let's let these lawyers tell us about this child's inheritance. Maybe we ought to decide right quick how it'll be managed; you can't get slack on these matters, you know."

Hazel Marie took her tear-stained face from my shoulder and looked around. "Brother Vern, there's no *we* involved in this. Deputy Bates, I want to swear out a peace warrant on this man. Can you do that for me?"

"Yes, ma'am," he said. "We'll have to go to the magistrate's office, but for now, Brother Vern, I'd advise you to keep your distance from these people. Are you understanding me?"

"Why, Hazel Marie, I'm your own kin, and your nearest male relative," Brother Vern implored. "Nearest that's grown, I mean. But if that don't mean nothing to you, remember that I can have you declared an unfit mother and have myself appointed the boy's guardian. I don't want to do that, 'cause it'll be a long, drawn-out mess, but I will if you push me to it."

Sam said, "Maybe you better look this over before you make any plans to go to court." He held the will out so Brother Vern could read it, but he didn't let go of it.

Brother Vern took enough time to read it two or three times, his face growing longer and sadder as he read. "Hazel Marie's not the guardian?" he finally asked.

"No," Sam said. "I am."

Hazel Marie's body vibrated with tension at this new turn of events. "Does he mean," she asked me, "that he wants to take my boy, too?"

"No, that's not what it means," Sam assured her. "All the will specifies is that I am the executor of the will and the boy's financial guardian. The court will assign me to oversee the boy's general welfare, his education, and to manage his affairs until he's old enough to do it himself. You are his mother and primary caregiver, and it'll be up to me to see that you both live comfortably. And," he said firmly to Brother Vern, "having Miss Puckett declared unfit will not change my responsibility to the estate in any way and it would not benefit any other member of the boy's family. On top of that, my opinion of Miss Puckett's fitness will weigh heavily in any court in the land and, from what I've seen, she's doing a fine job with this boy."

Brother Vern's face darkened as Sam laid it out for him. He didn't linger after that, leaving with an ill grace and a show of bad manners, like letting the screen door slam behind him. You can always tell when somebody's not been raised right.

"I still can't believe all this," Hazel Marie said, tears threatening again. "And I still don't think it's right. Miz Springer, what does all this mean for you?"

"Well," I said, taking a deep breath and trying to accept my fate more gracefully than Brother Vern. "It means that I'm destitute. It means that Wesley Lloyd didn't care whether I had a roof over my head or not."

"I care, Miz Springer!" Little Lloyd cried. "You can live with us, can't she, Mama?"

"She sure can." Hazel Marie smiled her closed-mouth smile. I hoped the first thing she did with Wesley Lloyd's money was to get her teeth fixed. And the second thing, a pair of glasses for his son that fit. "Why don't you do that, Miz Springer? I'd really like you to."

"No, it wouldn't do at all. I can't accept charity, though I thank you for offering. No, what I have to do is submit to the Lord's will, or to Wesley Lloyd's, whichever is responsible for this. The Lord giveth, and the Lord taketh away," I added, striving for a piety I was neither familiar with nor presently feeling.

"Wel-l-l," Sam said, eyes twinkling as he smiled broadly. "He hasn't quite taken everything away."

Binkie laughed out loud and snuggled up against Deputy Bates, right there in my living room. Except it wasn't mine any longer, so I didn't care if she did snuggle.

"I don't see a thing funny about an old woman with no place to lay her head and with nothing to eat," I told them. "It seems to me that you two would have a little more sympathy, or at least wait to laugh at me when I'm gone."

"Don't you worry, Miz Springer," Hazel Marie said. "You'll never be without as long as I have a nickel to my name."

Binkie and Sam couldn't control their laughter, both of them sputtering and carrying on until my feelings were hurting so bad I wanted to bawl out loud.

"Tell her, Sam," Binkie said, finally coming up for air.

"Julia, Julia, Julia," Sam said. "Sorry to carry on this way, but I think we've put over a big one on all those who wanted to get a hand in your pocket. Fact of the matter is," he said, coming over beside me, "in this state, a spouse always has a share in an estate. No matter what Wesley Lloyd intended, and he may well have known this, as his widow you are entitled to half of his estate. And half of the Springer estate is not to be sneezed at. We'll have to file a dissent to the will, but that'll be pretty cut and dried."

I had to sit down. Then I had to get my breath back. And I didn't want Sam too close to me, not knowing what I'd do in my weakened state. I had a powerful urge to throw my arms around him.

"That mean," Lillian asked, "that bof' Miss Julia and this baby gets Mr. Springer's financials?"

"Yep," Sam said, still grinning. "That's what it means."

"Thank you, Jesus!"

"And thank the state of North Carolina," I said, giving credit where it was due. Then, squinching my eyes at both of them, I said, "Sam, did you and Binkie know this all along?"

"Sure we did," Binkie said. "But I was afraid Dr. Fowler or somebody else might've known it, too."

"Well, this beats all," Deputy Bates said, his arm firmly around Binkie by now. He seemed almost as happy as I was beginning to feel.

"But, Julia," Sam said, "you weren't really concerned about anything, were you? You could always come live with me, you know."

"I know no such thing." And he wouldn't offer such a thing if he'd known my suspected condition.

"Aw, you know I'd take care of you."

"Sam Murdoch, let me tell you something right now. I don't need you or any other man to take care of me. I can do that well enough by myself. And I can do it even better with the help of Little Lloyd and Hazel Marie, if they're willing. I think this house is big enough for the three of us. And Deputy Bates, and Binkie, too, if she wants."

"An' me, too," Lillian said.

"Yes, you, too, Miss Lillian," Little Lloyd said, so happy I was afraid he was going to start flailing those skinny arms around again.

"Praise God," Hazel Marie said, smiling so wide that the two-toothed gap was open for viewing.

We'd have to get that fixed, along with several other things before too long. One of the first things, in case Pastor Ledbetter'd been halfway right, would have to be getting myself straightened out. Even if it meant going to Switzerland or Sweden or wherever they have those quick-change clinics. I'd make a list of all we needed to do, and Hazel Marie and I could spend some time spending Wesley Lloyd's money. He'd always thought he'd take it with him, but it was ours now and I knew we'd put it to better use than he ever had. And enjoy it more, too.

———

Spending his money and enjoying it is mostly what we've been doing for some time now. Lillian still comes by the day, and Binkie's in and out, although Deputy Bates spends a lot of time at her place. They ought to be thinking about making it legal, and I aim to tell them so if they don't soon come to it themselves.

We haven't heard from Brother Vern, but he's still feeding the flame on television. I sent him twenty dollars a few weeks ago, and got back a book he'd written about the end of the world. I couldn't fathom it, since it was all about the Book of Daniel and Russia and Revelation and blowing hot and cold.

Pastor Ledbetter doesn't visit much. His time's mostly taken up with his retirement-home ministry now, and he's over there most days ministering to the sick, the demented, and the dying, none of which applies to me. He's very solicitous of me, though, greeting me mournfully each and every Sunday, like he understands how hard I'm having it. He's still leery of Hazel Marie, as she is of him. Or rather of the Presbyterian way of worshiping. She's not used to our sedate ways, but she goes with me and holds her head up high.

LuAnne Conover still can't get over our living arrangements. She told me that she could never bring herself to be friends with a woman Leonard took up with. I thought to myself it was unlikely that any woman would ever take up with Leonard, but I didn't say anything. She's visiting a little more now since Hazel Marie showed her how to backcomb her hair.

I've adjusted to living with a house full of people better than you might think. I moved my bedroom downstairs to what used to be Wesley Lloyd's study, and gave what used to be our bedroom to Hazel Marie. I threw out the bed I'd shared with him, and bought new ones for her and for myself. I'm cutting off as many untoward associations as I can.

This house is big enough to have privacy when we want it, and when Deputy Bates moves on we'll fix up that area as a sitting room for Hazel Marie and Little Lloyd. With the back staircase, she can entertain privately if she wants to. So far, she's shown no inclination toward entertaining anyone, in spite of one or two widowers in the church casting their eyes in her direction. I think she's like me, once burned, twice shy—especially since it was a man like Wesley Lloyd Springer doing the burning.

But for now, she's good company to me, and I'm learning a lot from her. She's going to do my colors as soon as the scarves come.

Sam is Sam, and I like him that way, which is all I'm going to say on that subject.

On second thought, I might as well say one more thing. Sam asked me not long ago if there was anything I wanted to tell him.

"Like what?" I asked, wondering if he'd guessed or heard something about my awful secret. I thought I had my problem pretty much under control, if I had a problem at all, since with all the men I'd been around recently, not one had created any inner disturbances.

Well, to be honest, I'd felt the condition stir around a little whenever Sam smiled at me.

"Ledbetter kept hinting that something was wrong with you. Are you sick, Julia?" He put both hands on my arms and said, "If anything's wrong, I want to know about it."

I shook my head, feeling the tears well up at his concern. "No, you don't," I whispered. "It's too awful."

"Tell me. And let me help you with it."

"It's incurable, Sam, at least that's what the pastor said." All the secrets and shame that I'd locked up inside seemed to rush out on his shoulder as I leaned against him. "He said it's a sin I have to guard against all the time, and I don't know whether he was right about it or not. And, Sam, I'm so tired of praying about it, I don't know what to do."

"I can't imagine you having a sin that bad, sweetheart." He put his arms around me and pulled me close, not realizing what danger he might be in.

"You better turn me loose, Sam," I said, unable to leave him under my own steam. "Pastor Ledbetter and Dr. Fowler said I'm suffering from"—I lowered my voice, hardly daring to say the word but wanting to protect Sam from the consequences—"*nymphomania*."

"Wha-at?" He started laughing and he laughed so hard, I tried to pull away from him so I could run hide in a dark corner somewhere. "Oh, Julia, why didn't you tell me you were suffering from this condition?" He ran a finger down the side of my face and said, "Don't you know I've got the cure for that?"

And he does, and that's really all I'm going to say on the subject.

The rest of us have been getting along fine together, too. Little Lloyd has filled out some and he's taken on more of his mother's looks and, Lillian tells me, some of my ways. Which will undoubtedly be of help to him in the future. Sam opened a small checking account for him, and I'm teaching him to write checks and reconcile his bank statement. I must say, he's taken to it right smartly and does it well. You're never too young to learn to handle your money. Or too old, either, as I'm living proof of.

I've learned a lot through all these ups and downs, and the greatest of these is not to live a lie. Wesley Lloyd did, and look what it got him: a heart attack brought on by the stress of it and two women who hardly ever give him a thought. I was tempted to live a lie, almost did it, and look what not doing it got me: a real, though unrelated, family and a conscience that's as clear as a bell. I declare, that's worth half of Wesley Lloyd's estate any day of the week.

Miss Julia Takes Over

Acknowledgments

Many thanks to special agent Chris Smith of the North Carolina State Bureau of Investigation for being generous with his time and expertise, as well as for an afternoon of cop tales that curled my hair. My thanks, too, to Steve Barkdohl, general manager of Andy Petree Racing, Inc. for a tour of the shop and a hauler. Special thanks also to Larry Parmalee, former NASCAR driver, now an instructor of beginning race-car drivers; and to John Lampley, a longtime sports-car driver whose favorite track is the North Carolina Speedway. All of these racing professionals revealed the nuts and bolts of a sport of which I knew little, and made, in the process, another racing fan. My thanks also to Greg Rummans, who listened to my ideas and laughed when he was supposed to.

For Delin

Chapter 1

I declare, if it's not one thing, it's two more. Or, in my case, a half-a-dozen. Seems like everytime I turn around, there's something else to worry me half to death.

Feeling too antsy to sit still, I closed my checkbook and put it in the desk drawer. Who can balance a bank statement with troubles whipping around like the cold wind outside? March, I thought, with a shiver. We could do without it, if you ask me, yet the whole unpredictable month was still ahead of us.

I walked to the window and looked out at the gray morning, noticing the one, lone crocus poking up through the ice that lined the hedge along the side yard. If I'd had a poetic turn of mind, I might've seen it as a symbol of hope or of a brighter day coming or of some other such uplifting thought. But all I could do was wonder how the voles had missed it when they ate the rest of them.

I walked back to the fireplace and adjusted the flame in the gas logs that I'd had the good sense to put in after the last time we lost power in an ice storm. Be prepared, I always say, but nobody could be prepared for all the troubles and worries and problems that were piling up everywhere I looked. If we'd had a real fire, I'd've kicked a log.

Lillian stuck her head around the swinging door and called through the dining room. "You goin' to see Mr. Sam 'fore you eat, or after? I need to know 'fore I set lunch on the table."

"I can't be worried with him now. Lillian, I can't stand this. Where is she?" I threw up my hands, just about at the end of my rope. "And I don't want anything to eat."

"Uh-huh, I hear you, but I already got it fixed." She propped her hands on her hips and announced in that bossy way of hers, "An' I don't know anymore'n you do about where she is, but somebody better be doin' something about it."

I knew who that somebody was. Me. Lillian'd been pushing me to do something ever since she'd come to work at seven this morning, while I kept hoping Hazel Marie would show up with a decent explanation for her overnight absence. I declare, it's a burden when everybody stands around, waiting for me to make everything right. Lillian, though, had been with me for so long that she didn't mind telling me what to do and when to do it. Half of what she said usually went in one ear and out the other. But not today, because I was either going to have to do something or pull my hair out, one.

But she wasn't through giving me instructions. "Go on over to Mr. Sam's an' see what he say. He countin' on seein' you, anyway."

"What can he do, laid up like he is with a cast up to his you-know-what? Serves him right, is all I can say, out there in a trout stream in the dead of winter."

"What's done is done," she said, "an' no use rantin' around about it. Now, come on in here an' get your coat."

With a click of my tongue, I followed her into the kitchen. "Well, he deserves to suffer the consequences, and I don't mind seeing that he does."

"Mr. Sam, he just want your help to see 'bout that home nurse the doctor say he have to have. It won't hurt you to go over there an' be sure she know what she doin', since he can't hardly do a thing for hisself with that leg hiked up all the time. He need you to lighten him up a little."

She moved a pan off the stove, while I stood there, feeling pushed and pulled a dozen different ways. I didn't have time to be entertaining Sam Murdoch, frittering away my day when I had so much to contend with right where I was, what with LuAnne Conover pestering me to death, moaning about Leonard and the state of their marriage, which as far as I could tell, had never been a model of conjugal bliss in the first place. And there was Brother Vernon Puckett, Hazel Marie's uncle—the sorry thing—calling on Pastor Ledbetter, as I'd seen with my own eyes that very morning when his low-slung, maroon and white Cadillac pulled into the church parking lot right across the street from my house. Now, I ask you, what could a self-proclaimed preacher of the airwaves have in common with a seminary-trained Presbyterian minister like Larry Ledbetter? Well, that had an easy answer. They'd both give their eyeteeth for a way to get their hands on the estate left by my lately deceased husband, Wesley Lloyd Springer. But, thanks to Sam and the State of North Carolina, Little Lloyd and I had it safely in hand.

But, worse than any of those worries, Hazel Marie Puckett, Little Lloyd's mother, had turned up among the missing, and I was about to jump out of my skin, not knowing which way to turn. I'd called every hospital in three counties, asking if an attractive, forty-year-old woman with professionally dyed blonde hair and a full charm bracelet on her arm had been recently admitted. The calls had told me where she wasn't, which was some comfort, but they hadn't told me where she was.

Lillian said, "You better quit standin' there, bitin' yo' lip like that. Go on over to Mr. Sam's an' see 'bout that home nurse woman, an' ask him what we ought to be doin' to find Miss Hazel Marie."

"Lord, Lillian, I'm of two minds about that. Sam always has good advice, but the doctor said not to worry him with anything. Make sure he gets his rest and don't agitate him."

I tapped my foot, thinking of how everytime I needed Sam Murdoch, he'd go and do something unforeseen and, in my eyes, just plain reckless. Take the time Wesley Lloyd passed so unexpectedly, and I was left with wills and bills and so-called financial advisers and grasping preachers and, as if that hadn't been enough, Wesley Lloyd's bastard to boot.

And where was Sam? Retired, that's where. And right when I'd needed his legal expertise the most. And here, history was repeating itself, since I'd have to bite my tongue about my current problems and be *pleasant,* of all things.

Well, give Sam credit, I thought, though at the moment I hated to. He'd come through for me, straightening out Wesley Lloyd's two wills so that neither Little Lloyd nor I had been stranded without a nickel to our names. Far from it, in fact.

And, to give Sam more credit, he'd handed me over to Binkie Enloe, as good a lawyer as any hoary-headed regular-type lawyer in town, and better than most. I can't help it if she carries on with Deputy Coleman Bates with no legalization of the situation anywhere in sight. I've gotten where I don't let things like that bother me. As long as she does my taxes right and gives me advice I can live with, I'm just not going to say anything about her private life. Although I do mention it, on occasion.

"Lillian," I said, as I reached for my coat, "I've tried my level best not to worry about what Hazel Marie's doing. I know, I know," I held up my hand to stop what I knew she was going to say. "You think it's none of my business. But it is. As long as she's living in my house, out of the kindness of my heart, I might add, I feel responsible for her. I think I have a right to know where she is, especially when she stays out all night long.

"Now, I don't think she'd do anything wrong, well, I mean, criminal. Well, I don't know what I mean." I stopped, remembering that

Hazel Marie had lived in sin with my husband for ever so long, and it might've been a crime as well, for all I knew.

"The thing about it is," I went on, "Pastor Ledbetter's been instructing her in the catechism, since she wants to be a Presbyterian instead of a foot-washing Baptist or whatever she was, and now she stays out all night long with a man whose family nobody knows. Word will get around, Lillian, and that bunch of old men on the church session may refuse to write for her letter. It won't matter that she's never done anything like this before, or that she's doing it with a church employee, if that's what you can call Wilson T. Hodge." I sniffed at the thought.

Nothing would do but Pastor Ledbetter had to bring in an out-of-town fund-raiser to rouse the congregation into a pledging frenzy, since he couldn't raise any funds from me. And for what? Why, to get that family activities center built, that's what. You know, the one the pastor recommended I underwrite out of Wesley Lloyd's estate, seeing, as he'd said, that I needed some Christian financial guidance? Well, I'd put a lid on that as soon as he brought it up, not three days after the funeral, since I knew exactly where he'd guide it to. I didn't have any need for a gymnasium or a running track or a basketball court, nor did anybody else when all they had to do was join the YMCA. I ask you, how many times would I go over there and dribble a ball or lift weights?

"Lillian," I went on, with a sinking heart, "what am I going to tell that child when he gets home from school?"

"Well, I been wonderin' 'bout that, too," Lillian said, coming to the counter and leaning on it, "I thought his mama'd be in 'fore this or least, call an' say when she be here. It's gettin' on toward middle of the day, an' not word one from her. I thought maybe they be jumpin' the gun a little, havin' a early honeymoon like some folks do. But I don't know, Miss Julia, look like she have enough of it by now." Lillian looked up at the clock on the wall.

"You would think so. How long does it take to have dinner and see a show, even if they did drive to Asheville to do it? They've had more than enough time for decent people to do what they need to do. And I don't mean what you're thinking. They've been gone all night and half the morning, and I know something's bad wrong. We both know it's not like Hazel Marie to go off and stay gone, with neither hide nor hair of Wilson T. Hodge to be found, either. I've called his apartment so many times I'm sick of doing it, and he's not at the church, either, where he's supposed to be working."

"Yessum, an' that little chile just gonna be sick about it when he come home, an' she not be here. He know she don't have no sick friend like you tole him this mornin'."

"Well, what was I to do? You know how hard it is for me to out-and-out lie, and it was the only thing I could think of at the time. Should I've told him his mother was out all night without benefit of matrimony? She did that long enough with the child's father, which he doesn't need to know at this tender age.

"Oh, me, Lillian," I stopped and leaned my head against the door, overwhelmed with disappointment. I'd risked my name and reputation to take in my husband's paramour and the then nine-year-old result of their secret relations, and just look what had come of it. Two full years of my close supervision and exemplary influence didn't seem to've made a dent. "I declare, I thought Hazel Marie had given up such loose ways. I thought I'd shown her a more decent way of living and now, she's fallen right back into the gutter."

"You don't know that for a fact. Maybe they have a flat tire."

"Even I know it doesn't take this long to fix a flat, much less make a phone call." I straightened up, confirmed again in my first, unim-pressed impression of Wilson T. Hodge, the man Hazel Marie'd cho-sen to have her first legitimate happiness with. I declare, I couldn't say much for her taste in men, and that included Wesley Lloyd Springer, too. But, if Wilson T. Hodge was her choice, I was trying to be happy for her. Even though I'd had my doubts about him from the first time he'd put a foot in my living room, smiling and standing too close and flattering me with compliments on my house, my furnishings and my own gracious self, as he smoothed that smudge of a mustache with a ring-laden finger. I don't trust people like that as far as I can throw them. He had thin lips, too.

I wouldn't've trusted him even if I hadn't known the line of work he was in. Lord, I didn't think it was right to pay somebody good money to raise more money. Something's wrong with the whole sys-tem when Christians have to be begged and pleaded with and finan-gled into pledging more than they can afford in order to build something they don't need in the first place. That'd been the reason I'd voted against hiring him, sight unseen, but they'd done it anyway.

"Maybe they have a wreck," Lillian said. "That car might be in the middle of Briar Creek, and nobody found 'em yet."

"Lillian! Don't say that! Besides, I've already put the Highway Pa-trol on alert and, besides that, Briar Creek is so shallow, you couldn't hide a go-cart in it, much less a full-size car. No, it's something else that's holding them up; I just don't know what it could be."

Hearing a gust of wind rattle the windows, I wrapped a wool scarf around my neck, readying myself for the icy blasts.

"I'd better go, if I'm going, but I won't be long," I said, picking up my purse and car keys. "If Hazel Marie comes in, give me a call, will you? But don't say anything to her."

"You don't have to tell me that. Not none of my business to say anything to that sweet woman." She turned away, folding the dishrag and hanging it on the faucet. " 'Sides, you do enough for both of us, and she don't need to hear it twicet."

I rolled my eyes and opened the door. Stepping out on the side stoop, I wrapped my coat close against the wind and scrunched up in it. As I walked the few steps to the garage, I glanced out at the street and across to the church parking lot. With a start, I stopped, gasped and tried to catch my breath which had been snatched away at the sight.

Hurrying back to the door, I slammed it open and called, "Lillian! Do you know what he's done?"

"What? Who you talkin' about?"

"That preacher! That idiot preacher! Have you seen it? Come out here and look."

She came around the counter to the door, her run-over shoes flapping on her heels. "What in the world goin' on out there?"

Following me out, she squinched her eyes as I pointed to the church parking lot. There, directly across the street from my front porch, was a huge rectangle outlined by stakes and string. Little orange flags fluttered from each stake.

"You see it?" I demanded. "You see what he's doing?"

"I see it," Lillian said, "but I don't know what it mean."

"It means he's going to build that blamed building that's been on his mind ever since Wesley Lloyd passed, that's what it means. And look, Lillian," I said, grabbing her arm and pulling her along with me, "he's got it laid out right along the sidewalk over there. Do you know what that means?"

"No, I don't know what it mean, an' I'm freezin' out here."

"Well, just look! If he puts a wall along that string, what do you think we'll look out on from every window in the front of the house? A brick wall, that's what!"

"Yessum, but you have the street in between."

"I don't care about the street! He's putting that brick wall right in front of my eyes! It's vengeance, Lillian, that's what it is! I wouldn't build that building for him, so he's getting back at me by putting a wall right out in front, blocking my view, isolating me from my church." I was so mad, I could've wrung the preacher's neck if he'd been standing there. "I'm not going to have it! I tell you, I'm not. I'll have that vindictive man's head on a platter, along with the session's and every member of the congregation, see if I don't!"

"Well, jus' 'member you one of them members, so how you gonna do that?"

I jerked around and headed for the garage. "I'll think of something or, even simpler, I'll stop being a member. I'm going to see Sam, and I'm not going with nice, pleasant things to say to him, either. I don't care what the doctor ordered."

Chapter 2

I parked in front of Sam's large, white house with the floor-to-ceiling windows, bordered by Charleston green shutters. Then I stomped up the brick walkway, fuming at the nefarious ways of our pastor, and ready to demand that Sam do something about him.

"Mister Sam in the living room," James said, greeting me at the door as I crossed Sam's broad front porch.

That was plainly evident, since I heard laughter coming from the large room opening off the hall where we were standing. One deep rumble from Sam, and another lighter, almost infectious laugh from a woman. From the sound of it, Sam had taken a sudden turn for the better.

"That nurse," I said to James, "she's here already?"

"Yessum, she been here a while. She workin' on Mister Sam real good."

"I can tell," I said with a sniff, climbing off one high horse and getting ready to mount another one. I handed him my coat and scarf. "No need to hang them up. I won't be staying long."

I walked to the large arch that opened into Sam's living room and stopped in my tracks. All the worries that burdened my soul flew out of my mind as I saw what was going on. A fire blazed in the fireplace, warming the high-ceilinged room, filled with bookshelves and leather furniture. Sam sat in the big chair by the fire, his cast-laden leg stretched out on an ottoman. Everything was as it should be, except for the fact that he was bent over, half-naked and some curly-headed young woman was leaning over his back doing I couldn't determine what to him.

"Julia!" Sam called, looking up from what had to be a most uncomfortable position, though it didn't seem to be bothering him. "Come on in here. I want you to meet this angel of mercy. This is Miss Etta Mae Wiggins. Miss Wiggins, meet Mrs. Julia Springer."

"Pleased, I'm sure," Miss Wiggins said, continuing whatever ministrations she was conducting on Sam's back. Bright, cupid face framed with blond curls smiled at me. A face that would've been considerably improved with several layers of paint stripped from it. She wore one of those white pantsuits that nurses have so unprofessionally taken to, which do so little for most of them. This young woman, however, filled it admirably, if you admired tight fits.

"Miss Wiggins," I said with a formal nod of my head. I wanted it understood that I hadn't come to join in the kind of merriment they were obviously enjoying. "Don't let me interrupt whatever treatment the two of you are involved in. Sam, you asked me to come over and help you evaluate the need for a representative of the Handy Home Helpers, but it looks as if you've already made up your mind."

"So I have, Julia. But come on in and sit by me." He reached out his hand, which under other circumstances I would've taken. Sam was the kind of man that makes you feel comforted when you're close to him. Probably because he's a big man, full-chested and white-haired. Distinguished looking, I'd say, until you noticed his sparkling blue eyes that saw the humor in everything. That was the only thing I could hold against him, since I'm a woman of serious demeanor and intent.

"I'm glad to see you," he went on. "Miss Wiggins, here, is giving me a backrub to end all backrubs. Sit down, Julia, sit down."

I did, perching on the edge of the sofa near Sam's chair, but considerably ill-at-ease at the close proximity to his unclothed state.

Wiggins, I thought, watching her slather her hands with a floral-smelling lotion, nothing medicinal about it, and continue to massage Sam's back. I knew some Wiggenses. Knew *of,* that is, as did every resident of Abbot County. That family was known for as many less than stellar accomplishments as the Puckett family, of which Hazel Marie was a notable exception.

Miss Wiggins leaned over and whispered something in Sam's ear, making him shake with laughter. That was just so rude, to whisper in front of someone else. And Sam was as much at fault as she was, laughing without including me.

I stood up. "Well, I see you're busy with your therapy, so I'll be getting back. I do wish you'd called me, Sam, and saved me a trip in this weather."

"Don't go, Julia. You just got here. I want you to get to know Etta Mae. She's just what the doctor ordered, and has already done me a world of good."

That just put my back up. Obviously, all my help and care and concern since he'd gotten home from the hospital were not worth mentioning, since this little twit had come in for thirty minutes and canceled out everybody else. And *Etta Mae?* Since when had nurses allowed their patients such easy familiarity? This wasn't like Sam at all, who was as formal in his dealings with women of all ages as any well-bred Southern gentleman ought to be.

What had the young woman done to him? Just came into his home and within an hour had him laughing and chuckling and half-naked, rubbing her hands all over his back and around and under his arms and whispering things in his ear. It was the most unseemly kind of nursing I'd ever seen.

"Miss Wiggins," I said, as I stood up, "what is the condition of Sam's broken bone? Is the cast too tight? What about the itching that's driving him up a wall? What do you plan to do to make him more comfortable at night? He's hardly able to sleep with that heavy thing on him."

"Oh, don't worry about any of that; we're taking care of it," she said. Then, with a knowing smile, she went on, "Mr. Sam's not going to have any trouble sleeping tonight. Not after I get through with him." She ran her hands up around his neck, massaging the muscles with an indelicate kind of touching and rubbing. "You're gonna sleep good tonight, aren't you, you ole sweet thing, you."

My mouth dropped open. I expected Sam to put her in her place with that devastatingly polite way he had of cutting people down to size. But no, all he did was grin up at me, like, See, Julia?

I turned on my heel, having had enough of the spectacle. If that was the kind of service a home health care professional provided, then I wanted no part of it. And I was fuming because Sam couldn't see straight through her the way I could.

It was a settled fact that he had neither the time nor the interest to listen to my problems.

"If you need anything after Miss Wiggins leaves, you can have James call me," I said, heading across the room. "Although I doubt there's anything I can do for you."

"Julia," Sam said, straightening up and reaching for his shirt. Miss Wiggins helped him get into it, coming around in front to button it for him. A chore that he could've easily managed for himself. It was his *leg* that was broken. "Julia, don't go, we've hardly had time to visit."

"I'll come back when you're not so busy. How often do you plan to come, Miss Wiggins?"

"Anytime Mr. Sam wants me, I'll be here," she said, breezily. "All he has to do is whistle."

I could've smacked her. And Sam too, because he laughed with her, his eyes sparkling, as the brazen little snip took a brush to his hair.

"I'm gonna have you lookin' so handsome and feelin' so good that all the ladies in town're gonna be ringin' your bell," she said, leaning over him so that her bosom was practically in his face.

It was more than I could stand. "Sounds like you're going to be here all the time," I said, letting my feelings put an edge to my words. I couldn't help myself. "Maybe you should just move in."

"Why, I'd do it in a minute if he'd have me," she said, and part of what made me so mad was the fact that everything she said to me was really addressed to Sam. And he was eating it up. She reached down and smoothed his eyebrows. Then she had the nerve to say, "Any woman with any sense would grab this good-lookin' man and hold on to him as hard as she could."

Sam did have the grace to blush, but he liked it. Men just don't have any sense at all. Here was this little flirt, young enough to be his youngest daughter if he'd had one, flattering him without a lick of shame and he couldn't or wouldn't see through it. If this was what nursing had come to, it was time to reconsider the value of the whole profession.

If Sam needed flattery, which comes down to just plain lying, then I could do it just as well, and probably better. And it wouldn't cost him a dime. But you won't see me lowering myself to such a degree.

"Julia," Sam said, settling back in his chair after Miss Wiggins had buttoned his sweater and put an afghan over his knees. "Come on back here and talk to me a minute. I know you have something on your mind, and I want to hear it."

"Oh, it's nothing that won't wait until you have more time." I could be just as breezy as Miss Wiggins. "Just a few small matters like Pastor Ledbetter getting ready to build something in my front yard and Brother Vern sticking his nose in where it doesn't belong and LuAnne Conover about to leave Leonard after forty-something years and Hazel Marie off gallivanting all night long and nobody knowing where she is. Nothing at all to worry you with, since you're too sick to give a thought to what other people might be going through."

"Hazel Marie Puckett?" Miss Wiggins said. I gave her a glance that should've frozen her, but didn't. Most people know better than to enter a conversation that has nothing to do with them. But that didn't stop her. "I know Hazel Marie, and that girl's just had the hardest time. I heard she was living with you, her and that sweet little boy of hers. How's she doin' these days?"

Not wishing to discuss the hard time Hazel Marie'd had, especially since she'd had it with my husband, I pursed my lips and considered just ignoring her. But I was not one of those people who could be intentionally rude. "I don't know how she's doing right this minute since, as I said, she hasn't come home yet. Other than that, I guess she's doing fine. Sam," I said, turning to the one I wanted to talk to, "I don't know what to do. She went off with that Wilson T. Hodge, and you know what I think of him."

"Well, Julia, she's a grown woman, so I don't know that there's anything you can do."

"I'm worried about her. She's never done this before, and I don't care if she is thinking of marrying him. She ought not to be spending the night with him or anybody else. She has that child to consider."

Miss Wiggins looked from one to the other of us, her eyes as wide as the blue paint on them would allow. "That doesn't sound like Hazel Marie," she said. "That little boy's her whole life."

"Don't encourage Julia in her worries, Etta Mae," Sam said, as if I had to be calmed down and patted on the head. "Julia, Hazel Marie knows that Little Lloyd is in good hands with you. She's not going to be worried about him. For all we know, she and Wilson T. have eloped. They probably didn't want to go through that elaborate wedding you've been planning. I'd just not worry about it, if I were you."

"Well, you're not me. And don't start putting it off on me, either, implying that the plans I had for their wedding were not appreciated. I don't care if they elope or walk down the aisle of the First Presbyterian church with sixteen attendants, all I want to know is, where is she now."

"Give her a little more time, she'll be home. Now, Etta Mae, where's that special treat you promised me?"

"Right in the kitchen. It's some of my Granny's tea, and believe me it's just the ticket to young you up by about twenty years. Not that a fine man like you needs it, though. Miss Julia, would you like some? I've got plenty."

"No, I would not, thank you all the same. I have things to do." Better things, I wanted to say, but it's not my way to be sarcastic.

"I wish you'd stay," Sam said, but his eyes were on Miss Wiggins as she swished herself out of the room.

"You'll have to do more than wish," I said, half under my breath, as I headed into the hall, got my coat and left.

The temperature had dropped, although the wind had begun to slack off by the time I stood on his porch, wrapping my scarf around my neck and trying to get myself together. All I could think of was how history was repeating itself. First, Wesley Lloyd had cast an eye, as well as other things, toward a younger woman, now Sam was doing the same thing. Was it in every man's nature to discard a decent, upright and loyal woman in favor of any little twit who threw herself at him? I shook myself, not wanting to open up old wounds having to do with Hazel Marie who was now in different circumstances, thanks to my efforts. But it was hard, having just been a witness to how easily a man could be taken in. Even someone like Sam, who was as level-headed as you could ask for. If he couldn't see past the makeup and the bouncing and jiggling and the flattery, then there wasn't a hope for any man alive.

Well, it was a settled fact that, like Wesley Lloyd, Sam couldn't be trusted. Better to know now, I told myself, than to find it out after the whole town was laughing behind my back.

A sudden gust of wind blew across the porch, making me shiver as I pulled my coat closer. But as cold as it was, I was steaming inside, knowing how close I'd come to making a fool of myself for the second time in my life.

And knowing that I was left to do everything by myself. As usual.

"She jus' called, jus' this minute." Lillian had the side door open, waiting for me, as I hurried in from the garage.

"She still on the line?" I pulled off my gloves, throwing them on the table, as I headed for the phone by the refrigerator.

"No'm, she hung up 'fore you could get in here." Lillian was wringing her hands, so I immediately thought the worst.

"What'd she say? Is she all right? She's not hurt, is she?"

"No'm, yessum, I mean I don't know. Miss Julia, she jus' hang up in the middle. Well, not even in the middle, she jus' start in to talk, then she jus' quit. Of a sudden, she jus' quit an' the dial tone come buzzin' on."

"Well, what did she say? Exactly. Tell me exactly what she said." I glared at the telephone, willing it to ring again and tell us something.

Lillian sank down onto one of the chairs at the breakfast table. Taking a corner of her apron, she dabbed at her eyes.

"Lillian, I'm sorry. I didn't mean to jump on you. It's just, well, I guess I'm more worried than I thought I was."

"It ain't you," she said, leaning an elbow on the table. "You don't bother me none. I jus' scared to death for Miss Hazel Marie 'cause she sound so scared."

I took a deep breath to settle my nerves, and pulled up a chair beside her, slipping out of my coat. "Tell me," I said. "Just take it slow and tell me everything she said."

"Lemme see here." Lillian looked off into the distance, her hands folding and pleating her apron. "The phone ring. I pick it up an' say, 'Miz Springer's residence,' an' Miss Hazel Marie, she say, 'Lillian, let me speak to Miss Julia, please, an' hurry. Please hurry.' She say it jus' like that, 'hurry. Please hurry.' "

"Oh, Lord," I said.

"Yessum, an' I say, 'She ain't here. She over to Mr. Sam's.' An' I try to say, 'She be back pretty soon,' or 'You can call her over there,' or some such, but she don't give me a chance. She cut in an' say, 'Tell her I need help. Tell her I'm at the big,' an' then that when it sound like she drop the phone an' that dial tone come on."

"She said she needed help? You're sure about that?"

"Sure as I'm settin' here. 'Tell her I need help,' that what she say. An' 'I'm at the big.' What you reckon she mean by that?"

"I don't have an idea in the world. But, I'll tell you this, Lillian, we were right to be concerned about her. She's in trouble of some kind, and it's that Wilson T. Hodge who's gotten her into it. I said from the first time I met him that he wore his shorts too tight. Nobody can be that upright and pious without trouble going on underneath."

"Bad trouble, sound like to me. These days, you don't never know what gonna happen ever' time you step out the door. Them UFOs is circlin' 'round all the time, first this way, then that, an' don't nobody know when they snatch somebody up."

"Lillian, for goodness sakes, Hazel Marie has not been snatched up in a UFO. Be practical." I jumped up and started pacing the kitchen floor. "We've got to do something. We can't just ignore a cry for help. And that's what it was." I whirled around and said, "Tell me again. She said she was at 'the big'? You're sure of that?"

"Sure as I can be. Ain't nothin' wrong with my hearing, and that what she said. 'Tell her I'm at the big.' But I don't know what 'big' she talkin' about, 'less it's that big ballfield at the high school where a UFO could swoop in an' swoop out 'fore anybody know it."

"Lillian," I sighed, "think of something else." I walked to the sink and gazed out the window, noting a few snow flurries swirling around the yard. "I need your help in figuring this out. What could 'the big' mean? That big movie house over in Asheville? No, no, forget that. They wouldn't still be at the picture show. Somebody's big house? A big store? That big intersection right outside of town? Wait, wait, let's back up. She had to be inside somewhere; that's where telephones usually are. Unless she was using an outside one. Do you know of any public phones on the side of the road anywhere? Did you hear any traffic sounds? Any background noises of any kind?"

"No'm, not nothing like that. It so quiet I hear her charm bracelet jingle one time. Miss Julia, I jus' think of somethin'. She kinda whisperin', like. Not so low I couldn't hear her, but not real normal, neither. An' she talkin' real fast, so I don't have time to tell her anything or ast her anything."

"Well, that settles it. I'm going to see Deputy Bates right now, and make him start looking for her."

I slung on my coat, which I'd barely had off, and grabbed my keys. "He's working days now, isn't he?"

"Yessum, Miss Binkie real glad about it, too, since he be home at night."

"Home," I grunted. "The man's home is supposed to be right up these back stairs, where he's paying good money to rent a room from me. But, I don't have time to think about that. I'm going to the sheriff's office and put this in their hands. With my supervision, of course."

"What about yo' lunch? You ain't had a bite since breakfast."

"I can't eat now, Lillian, I'm too upset. You go ahead, though, and I'll get something when I get back. Stay close to the phone in case she calls back. Grab it as quick as you can, as soon as it rings."

"Don't you worry. I'm gonna get me a plate and set right here beside it."

I was out the door and into the garage without stopping to see if Pastor Ledbetter had done any more stake-stringing. One thing at a time, I told myself, as I backed out into the street. I would take on the preacher when I had Hazel Marie well in hand.

There wasn't a parking place for citizens in trouble anywhere near the sheriff's office, so I pulled into one marked DEPARTMENT USE ONLY. I could make a case for my taking it, since I certainly intended to use the department.

The wind whipped my coat around my lower limbs, as I tackled the steps at the back of the courthouse. I held on to the metal railing, fearful of ice that might have accumulated on the worn concrete steps. It was one time I wished for fur-lined boots, instead of the slick leather-soled Red Cross oxfords I had on.

Closing the door firmly behind me, since I wasn't raised in a barn, I hurried over to a sliding glass window in the wall where a pony-tailed woman in a uniform was busy at a console of blinking lights. She had one of those wrap-around telephone sets on her head, leaving her hands free to do other things.

"I want to see Deputy Coleman Bates, please. Tell him Mrs. Julia Springer needs to see him right away."

She looked up at me, gave me a brief, I've-been-trained-to-meet-the-public smile and said, "He's out on a call right now. He should be back in about an hour. Can someone else help you?"

"No, I need to see him." My foot was tapping on the floor. The idea of him being out on a call tightened my nerves until I could feel them strumming. "Could you call him? Just tell him I'm here, and that it's urgent."

"Ma'am, I'm sorry, but he's answering a fairly urgent call already.

You're welcome to wait, though, and I'll tell him you're here just as soon as I can get through to him."

I didn't want to be rude, that gets you nowhere, but I wanted to shake her. Instead, I turned and paced the waiting room or whatever the tiny space reserved for the public was. I'll tell you this, we needed better facilities for our law enforcement people and the public they were supposed to serve and protect. There wasn't a magazine or newspaper anywhere, not that I could've read anything, but it just didn't look good to have nothing available. Three metal chairs were against one wall, and one of them was bent. I walked back and forth, knowing that if Deputy Bates knew what was going on, he'd drop whatever he was doing and come zipping in to help me.

"Have you heard from him yet?" I was back at the window, drumming my fingers on the wooden ledge.

"No, ma'am, they're real busy with that call."

"You don't think you could just let him know I'm here?"

"No, ma'am, not on a call like this. You sure nobody else can help you?"

"Yes, I'm sure. No, wait. Maybe they can." I took a deep breath and my life in my hands. "What about Lieutenant Peavey? Is he available?"

"Well, he's monitoring the call Deputy Bates is on, but he's in the building. I don't know. . . ."

"Ask him. Please, just ask him if he'll see me. Mrs. Julia Springer, he knows me. Remind him about that kidnapping last year. No, maybe you better not. Just tell him I really need to speak to him before something awful happens."

She looked at me with a frown on her face, and began working some buttons and toggles, but not before sliding the glass closed so I couldn't hear her.

I guess Lieutenant Peavey did remember me, because it wasn't but a minute before a deputy came out and motioned me to follow him. We walked through a narrow hall into the inner workings of the sheriff's department. Deputies, male and female, passed in and out of the offices on each side, most of them nodding in a friendly, but distracted, way.

My guide knocked once on a closed door, then opened it for me. I walked in to face the man I'd lied to last year when Lillian, Hazel Marie and I had rescued Little Lloyd from Brother Vern's sticky grasp. And I'd lied with a straight face and without a qualm on my conscience. It had been necessary at the time, and I had no regrets now. I just hoped he hadn't figured out my part in the mess.

I declare, the day was dark and dreary, the wind blowing in snow flurries, and the temperature hovering in the low thirties, and there that man sat with his mirrored sunglasses on. Maybe he had an eye problem. I didn't know, but seeing myself reflected in those double mirrors put me off something awful. I almost forgot what I needed to say. Especially since I'd also almost forgotten how big he was, how silent and, well, suspicious his manner was. If you were a criminal, you wouldn't've wanted Lieutenant Peavey turning that big head in your direction while he waited for a confession that you couldn't wait to give him.

"Lieutenant Peavey," I said, edging near the front of his desk. "I'm Mrs. . . ."

"I know who you are." No change of expression, no welcoming smile, no nothing but that blank face and what I assumed were hard eyes behind his glasses. "What can I do for you?"

"Well, my friend, Hazel Marie Puckett, is in trouble and I don't know what kind or where she is or how to help her or anything."

"Puckett." Just like that. *Puckett,* as if that said it all.

"You need to understand," I said quickly before he could jump to conclusions, "that, even though she's a Puckett, she's not really one. I mean, she lives with me, her and her little boy, you remember him? He was the one that his great-uncle, Vernon Puckett, kidnapped? And you were looking for him, but he showed up at my house and, well, the two of them have been there ever since. Except for now, when she went out last night with Wilson T. Hodge, that fund-raiser from Charlotte who's been running all over town trying to drum up, . . . well, you're not a Presbyterian, so maybe . . . Anyway, she hasn't come home and it's been way too long and . . ."

"I remember a number of things about that episode last year."

"Well, but that's over and done with. And it worked out just fine, I wish you wouldn't bring it up, because this is something entirely different. Please, Lieutenant Peavey, I really need some help here."

"Have a seat."

I sank gratefully into a wooden chair that needed a cushion or padding of some kind. Lieutenant Peavey reached behind him to an open bookshelf, taking out a preprinted form and placing it before him on the desk.

"You have a missing person?"

"Yes," I said with great relief, "that's exactly what I have, or don't have. I mean she's missing and I don't have her."

"Let's hear the particulars. Name, age, date of birth, most recent address, Social Security number, where she was going, when you last saw her."

I started in telling him everything I knew about Hazel Marie which, as it turned out, was somewhat lacking in particulars.

"I'll get all that for you, Lieutenant, it's just that I was so worried about her that I didn't think to get her vital statistics before I left. I wanted the sheriff's department to start looking for her right away. I know she's in trouble; she said so herself."

"She said so?" Those mirrors aimed themselves at me, as he stopped writing. "When did you talk to her?"

"I didn't. Lillian did. You remember Lillian, she works for me? Hazel Marie called, well, barely thirty minutes ago, wanted to speak to me but I wasn't there. I was over at, well, that doesn't matter. Anyway, she told Lillian that she needed me to help her and that she was at 'the big.' But we don't know what 'the big' is or where it is. That's what I need you to find out."

He folded the paper he'd been writing on. "Mrs. Springer, if you heard from her thirty minutes ago, she can't be classified as missing. Twenty-four hours before we can step in, unless there's evidence of a crime being committed, and it doesn't sound as if one has been."

I stared at him with my mouth open. Then I said, "You mean to tell me that you can't, or won't, do anything? Lieutenant, the woman's in trouble! She wouldn't've called, whispering and getting cut off, if she wasn't in desperate straits!"

"She's not hurt; she's not involved in a crime. . . ."

"You don't know that! I mean, she's not, I'm positive, but she could be the victim of a crime. Lieutenant Peavey, what does it take to get some help from this department?"

He stared at me for a good two seconds. At least, I guessed that's what he was doing; he may have been gazing over the top of my head for all I knew. "There are certain guidelines we have to follow, and this situation doesn't appear to meet them. You can let us know if something else occurs that would warrant our stepping in or when it's been twenty-four hours since you've heard from her but, for now, I'd advise you to wait it out. Nine times out of ten, a so-called missing person shows up sooner or later, and usually sooner. Now, why don't you go on home and see if I'm not right. Let me know if I can be of further help."

And with that, he rose to his full height, which was considerable, and indicated that the interview was over.

"But she needs help now!" I almost wailed. "How can I just go home and wait, while she's in peril or something?"

222 · ANN B. ROSS

"Well," he said, with the hint of a smile at one corner of his mouth, which just about blew my fuse, "you can always hire a private investigator."

I got myself to my feet, and gave him a stare as blank as the ones he'd been giving me. "That's exactly what I'll do. When I'm paying somebody directly, without going through the tax commissioner, I guess I'll get my money's worth. Thank you for your time, Lieutenant, meager though it was. I'll just take care of this problem myself."

And I stomped out, my head held so high that I took a wrong turn and had to ask for help to get out of the place.

Chapter 4

"Has she called again?" A gust of wind practically blew me into the kitchen, but I hardly noticed. Slamming the door, I came out of my coat and hung it on a peg. "Have you heard from her?"

Lillian was sitting in the chair right under the wall phone, staying close to it as I'd asked her to. "No'm, it ain't rung since you been gone, an' I b'lieve I'll get up from here now, since you can help get to it if it do." She got to her feet and went to the stove. "Set down and tell me what them deputies doin' while I fix you something to eat."

"Just some soup, Lillian, if you have it. I'm not even sure I can eat that. And as far as what they're doing, it's absolutely nothing. Not one thing. They can't go against their guidelines, and Hazel Marie doesn't meet them. I declare, Lillian, I'm so undone I don't know what to do."

She turned, holding a pot in one hand and a Campbell's Soup can in the other. "You mean to tell me they not doin' nothin' to find that pore woman? I can't b'lieve Deputy Bates do any sucha thing."

"He's not. He was answering a call and unavailable to the likes of me. I saw Lieutenant Peavey. Does that tell you anything?"

"You mean Lieutenant Peavey what was ready to lock us up that time?"

"That's exactly who I mean, and he wasn't any more friendly or sympathetic today than he was then. Lillian, I didn't get a smidgen of satisfaction out of that man. Nothing we can do, he said. Then he suggested hiring a private investigator, which is what I'm just before doing."

"Why don't you then?"

"Well, I would, if I knew one to hire. I mean, it's not like going to Wal-Mart and picking out one of a dozen or so. Where are they located, I'd like to know. How do I get in touch with one, and how do I know he'll do a good job?"

"Oh, he do a good job, if you watch him like a hawk which I know you gonna do. I bet Deputy Bates know who you can get. Set down at that table, now, an' rest. You got yo'self all upheaved and nervous, an' you not gonna be doin' Miss Hazel Marie any good atall if you do yo'self in with all that worryin'. This soup be ready in a minute."

"Right. You're right. I've got to get myself under control here. But, I'll tell you, Lillian, it just makes me a crazy woman to need help and have everybody and his brother telling me there's nothing to worry about."

"That's not what I'm tellin' you. I tellin' you to get yo' ducks in a row, then do whatever it take to get done what you want done."

"Lillian, that's the best advice I've had all day. While you're fixing my plate, I'm going to put in some calls to Deputy Bates. He's not going to be able to turn around without somebody telling him to call Mrs. Julia Springer. If he ever gets away from whatever he's doing that's so important."

I called Binkie at her office, left my message for Coleman in case she saw him and cut her off when she started telling me that Hazel Marie would be home any minute. "Maybe so, Binkie," I told her. "But, in the meantime and in case she's not, I want to put some things in motion."

Then, I called Binkie's house, in case Deputy Bates got there before she did—he had his own key, I happened to know—and left a message on her machine. As much as I hate those impersonal things. Then, to be on the safe side, I called the sheriff's department again and left word for Deputy Bates to call me as soon as he came in. Surely the message would reach him at one place or the other.

After that, there wasn't anything to do except try to eat the soup Lillian had put before me, and worry myself sick with wondering how and what I was going to tell Little Lloyd. School would soon be out, and he'd be coming in here asking for his mother, and what in the world was I going to tell the child?

I put down my spoon and stood up. "Lillian, I can't just sit here, doing nothing. I'm about to jump out of my skin. I think I'll go on and pick Little Lloyd up at school. It's too cold for him to be walking anyway."

"It still a little early."

"Well, I may just get him out early. I want him home where we know he's safe. I declare, Lillian, I can't stand my family, such as it is, being spread all over creation." Of course, neither Hazel Marie nor Little Lloyd were my family in the strictest sense of the word, but they'd come to me in need and they'd repaid my efforts tenfold.

"What I gonna say if somebody calls?"

"If she calls, break right in and ask her where she is. We're at a loss until we know that. And if Coleman calls, tell him to come right over.

Don't go into anything on the phone, because we don't want to tie up the line. I ought to be back here in fifteen or twenty minutes."

Braving the cold again, I left to pick up Little Lloyd. As I drove to Abbotsville Middle School, my mind was in a turmoil. Everybody— Sam, Lieutenant Peavey, Binkie—thought I ought to let things run their course. Not one person so far had felt the same urgency that I was feeling. Except Lillian. She and I knew Hazel Marie better than anybody else, and we knew she was in trouble.

Since I got there so early, I was able to park up close to the main door of the school, without having a line of cars in front me. I decided to wait for the bell to ring and not risk scaring the child to death by getting him out early. So I just sat there, keeping the motor running so I wouldn't freeze, and so it'd be warm for Little Lloyd. Just sat there, thinking and stewing over what and how much to tell him, and over the fact that nobody was as exercised over the situation as they should've been. The more I thought about it, the more frustrated I felt. That's what happens when you have to delegate duties to other people and then have to sit and worry about them getting done. I squinched up my eyes and tapped the steering wheel. One thing was for sure, though. When you do it yourself, you *know* it'll get done.

As children began streaming out of the school building, I decided that I'd give Deputy Bates a chance to swing into action on my behalf, or rather on Hazel Marie's behalf. And if he failed me, I'd put a private investigator on my payroll and hound him till we had Hazel Marie back where she belonged.

Seeing Little Lloyd hurry out with a crowd of children, I leaned over and opened the door for him so he could crawl in, that heavy bookbag swinging from his arm. I declare, he looked so thin and pale that my heart clutched up in my chest. He was a worrier worse than I was.

The first words out of his mouth were, "Has my mama come home?"

"Let me get out of this traffic," I said, as the line started to move with young mothers manhandling those clumsy-looking sports vehicles which, if you happened to be behind one, you couldn't see through, around or over. "We need to talk, Little Lloyd, and I can't do it with all this going on around me."

His glasses started to fog up in the heat of the car. When he took them off to clean them, his little face looked so pinched and peaked that I reached over and patted him, though I'm not a demonstrative woman by any stretch of the imagination. When the traffic thinned out as cars peeled away in several directions, I took a deep breath and began.

"I've never tried to shield you from things that directly affect you, Little Lloyd, and I'm not going to start now." I told him of my and Lillian's concern, the lack of help I was getting every time I turned around, and his mother's phone call. In detail, because he was a sharp little thing and, if anybody could figure out *the big,* he could.

"What do you think?" I asked.

His lip trembled as he gazed straight ahead through the windshield. "Maybe she's gone to Raleigh."

"Raleigh?" That surprised me, but then I recalled that Raleigh was where she'd said she was going that day last year when she'd shown up at my door to drop off Wesley Lloyd's illegitimate child while she went to beauty school to learn the manicure business. First time I'd ever heard of either her or the child, so you can imagine the state my mind had been in. I was over that by now, considerably aided by the thought of Wesley Lloyd spinning in his grave at my taking them in like they were my own. Giving hardly a thought to the gossip in the town and in the church that my act of Christian charity generated, I'd been comforted by the fact that the gossip had been about him, and not me.

But now, I understood that in the child's mind, Raleigh was the place mothers go when they leave their children. "No, I think we can forget about that. Nobody but a politician would want to go there anyway. Besides, her call was a local. At least, there's no indication that it wasn't. If she had time to say 'the big,' she had time to say 'Raleigh,' so I think we can pretty well figure she's around here somewhere."

"Here we are," I said, pulling into the driveway at home. "Let's get in. Maybe Lillian's heard from her again, and maybe Deputy Bates has some word for us."

We hurried inside where Lillian met us at the door, her face sorrowful enough to tell me there was no news. She wrapped Little Lloyd in her ample arms and crooned to him as he buried his face in her apron.

"Come on now," I said, "let's have a snack and get ourselves organized. Little Lloyd, take off your coat and have a seat at the table. Lillian, something hot for this child, and for me and you, too. I'm going to try Deputy Bates again, there's just no sense in this sitting and waiting."

I couldn't believe it. When I called 911, because to my mind we certainly had an emergency, I was told to call the regular number. On top of that, when I did, I was told that Deputy Bates was still on that urgent call that was taking up his entire workday and then some, and he wasn't expected back for several more hours. I started to argue, but it was no use.

I hung up and turned to see Little Lloyd's peaked little face, blotched with worry and those unfortunate freckles he'd inherited from his father. His thin shoulders hunched over the table, as he waited for me to do something.

"Push up your glasses, Little Lloyd," I said, trying to make things as normal as I could. "And drink your hot cocoa. We have to keep up our strength, because I'm not about to throw in the towel yet. Not by a long shot."

He leaned over and took a quick sip from the cup without picking it up, a habit I thought I'd broken him of, but I didn't want to correct him under these worrisome circumstances.

"Miss Julia," he said, his magnified eyes gazing at me like I was his last hope. "Maybe we ought to go look for my mama, ourselves. I know we could do it, because you always say if you want something done, you have to do it yourself."

Well, that just put a spark to my logs. The child took to heart everything I ever said, which made all my efforts on his behalf more than worthwhile. He thought I could do anything I set my mind to, and I determined, then and there, not to let him down.

"You never said a truer word, Little Lloyd, and I thank you for reminding me of it."

I turned and dialed the same number again. "Let me speak to Lieutenant Peavey, please. Tell him it's Mrs. Julia Springer, and remind him that he said to let him know if he could do anything for me. And he can."

It took a while, but he came to the phone, sounding as if he hated doing it. "Lieutenant Peavey," he said and waited.

"This is . . ."

"I know who it is."

"Well, I need to know the name of a private investigator you'd recommend. Then I won't bother you anymore, you may be sure."

The line hummed for a few seconds, then he said, "If that's what you want, I'd recommend J. D. Pickens. He's got an office in south Asheville, not sure where. You can look him up in the phone book."

"I'll do that and, Lieutenant Peavey, I'm putting a lot of trust in your recommendation, and I expect you to stand behind it. Is this man the one you'd hire, if you were hiring?"

"No. I wouldn't be hiring one in the first place, but he's the choice if you are."

"I guess you're in a position where you don't have to go outside of normal channels when you need help," I said. "Seeing as how you have the whole sheriff's department at your beck and call. Some people, however, are not so fortunate. Thank you for your time."

He grunted and I hung up.

When I told Lillian and Little Lloyd that Deputy Bates was out of the picture, at least for the foreseeable future, the boy hung his head so low it was practically on the table. I watched as his little shoulders began to quiver with the strain he was under and the tears began to flow.

Lillian went to him, hugging him close and telling him he needed to be loved on and she was the one to do it. I don't know if that helped, but maybe it did. Temporarily, at least. What the child really needed was his mama back safe and sound.

"Lillian, where's the Asheville phone book?"

"If it not in the drawer under there, I don't know where it is."

"Well, I can't find it," I said, pushing through the accumulated odds and ends in the catchall drawer. "Just one more thing to try my patience; nothing's ever where I need it, when I need it. I was counting on Coleman. I mean, if you know somebody on a personal basis in law enforcement, you'd think you'd get some personal consideration. Wouldn't you?"

"I think I know what he doin'," Lillian said, handing Little Lloyd a napkin to wipe his face.

I straightened up. "What? How do you know?"

"I know 'cause I called Willet who clean down at the sheriff's. He hear all they doin', though he ain't supposed to talk about it. I get this outta him 'cause I got something on him he want me to keep quiet about. Them deputies on a big raid down 'round Jessup Mountain. They been plannin' it an' studyin' on it, an' checkin' on it ever since somebody broke in that racing man's place down east somewhere. It was in the paper the other day. An' today the day they goin' after somebody up here they think did it. So that's what Deputy Bates doin', an' why he can't come he'p us out."

"Well, thay Lord," I said. "What kind of raid? Did Willet say?"

"No'm, he don't say. He only hear so much, you know, when he sweepin' round their feet."

So that's how Lillian knew so much of what went on in town. The people who swept and mopped and emptied trash cans in the shops and offices all over town heard and saw what the shakers and movers were doing. I smiled at the thought.

Giving up on finding the Asheville book, I flipped through the yellow pages of our thin directory, surprised to find a listing for private investigators. And sure enough, there was The Pickens Agency, J. D. Pickens, P.I., as big as life.

I glanced over at Little Lloyd, who had his hands clasped between his knees. He was a nervous child even under the best of circumstances, what with biting his nails and blinking his eyes and just being jittery by nature. His nerves acted up on him a lot, in spite of all my efforts to calm him down and teach him to take life as it comes, the way I did.

His face was pale and drawn, those freckles standing out like new pennies. "Sit up straight, Little Lloyd, and take heart. I'm going to get us some help and get something done about this situation. I declare," I went on, "it's a shame when you have to do everything yourself."

As I reached for the phone, it rang under my hand. Hoping it'd be Hazel Marie again, we all looked at each other before I snatched it up and answered it.

"Julia," Sam said, "how about you and Little Lloyd coming over and having supper with me? James has made a roast that I'll be eating on all week if you two don't help me put a dent in it tonight."

I bit my lip to keep from making a sharp remark about that woman who'd been all over him earlier. Instead, I glanced over at Little Lloyd's miserable face and said, "I'm afraid I can't make it, Sam, since I still have a number of things to do. But Little Lloyd could use some cheering up. Why don't I send him on, and I'll pick him up after you've had supper?"

"I'll miss you, Julia. I have a lot to talk to you about."

Uh-huh, I thought, and I don't want to hear it. But I didn't say it, just thanked him and hung up.

"Little Lloyd," I said, feeling the need to reassure him and give him some hope. "Sam wants you to come over and have an early supper with him. So run on over and I'll pick you up a little later. Now before you start worrying again, I want to put your mind at rest. I'm going to call this private investigator and we're going to find your mother. You can count on it."

The boy started up out of his chair, obedient as always, trying on a pitiful-looking smile as he rubbed his eyes. "I knew you'd think of something, Miss Julia. You always do what you say you will."

Lord, when a child puts his trust in you, it can scare you to death. Or at least, it ought to.

After getting Little Lloyd off, with instructions to go straight to Sam's and wait for me to pick him up, I dialed the number of the private investigator. A man answered, taking me aback since I thought I'd have to go through a secretary or two.

"Mr. J. D. Pickens, please."

"You got him."

"Oh. Well, this is Mrs. Julia Springer, over in Abbotsville? And I'd like to employ you to find a missing person, and don't tell me she's not missing just because she called this afternoon to tell us she needed help."

"Whoa, back up there a minute. You got a missing person who called to say she's in trouble?"

"That's right. And Lieutenant Peavey, he's the one who recommended you, won't do anything, and Deputy Bates is too busy, and we are quite understandably at the end of our rope, here."

"Well, you've come to the right man. Let me look at my appointment book."

"No, I don't want an appointment," I said quickly, fearful of being put off for days. "I need to see you right away, today."

"You're in luck, then. I'm between cases right now, but it's pretty late in the day. How 'bout first thing in the morning?"

"That won't do, Mr. Pickens. How am I and Hazel Marie's little boy, to say nothing of Lillian, going to sleep one more night without something being done? What about right now? I could be at your office in thirty or forty minutes."

"Can't do it that quick."

I thought I might break down as Little Lloyd had done and start some crying myself. It is just so frustrating to have to push people to do what you want them to do.

"Tell you what," Mr. Pickens said. "How about meeting me halfway? Say in a couple of hours, about six or so? I've got some things to do here, then I'm going to La Casa Roja for supper. You know where it is? Right off the interstate at the Delmont exit?"

Relief flooded my soul. "I'll find it. Now, Mr. Pickens, I need to know one thing before we go any further. Just how good are you at your job?"

There was a moment of silence, then I heard what sounded like a strangled cough. "Mrs. Springer, I'm like the Canadian Mounties; I always get my man. Or woman, as the case may be. You won't find a better P.I. in the area."

Well, that wasn't saying a whole lot, considering the area, but I let it go with some throat-clearing of my own.

"Then I'll see you about six, and I thank you, Mr. Pickens."

"Thank *you*, Mrs. Springer."

It was like a burden rolling off my shoulders to know that we now had somebody who was going to find Hazel Marie. The fact that I'd detected a note of relief in Mr. Pickens's voice hardly registered at the time. Maybe he needed the work.

"We've got us some help," I said with a lightened heart, as I hung up the phone and turned to Lillian who'd been following my side of the conversation with nods of her head. "We're meeting Mr. Pickens at a Mexican restaurant at six o'clock tonight, although I'd just as soon have regular food here before we go. I don't think my system can take that spicy stuff, nor Little Lloyd's either. At least he'll have a decent meal in him before we get there."

"That man say he gonna find Miss Hazel Marie?" Lillian asked.

"He said he always finds whatever he's looking for, which I hope is not a blatant overstatement. But I'll be there making sure he works at it. Now, Lillian, we need to get together everything we know about Hazel Marie. Lieutenant Peavey asked me questions I couldn't answer, so I want to be ready for Mr. Pickens. I'll need her birth date, well, I know that but I don't know the year. I'll need a picture of her; there ought to be several good ones in Little Lloyd's album, and anything else you can think of."

Trying to think of all we needed to do, I sank into a chair and put my head in my hands. "Lillian, I hope to goodness this works. Now . . . ," I stopped as the front door bell interrupted me. "Who in the world is that?"

"I'll get it," Lillian said, heaving herself up. "But I know it not Deputy Bates. He always come in back here."

"No, keep your seat, Lillian. I'll see who it is and get rid of them. I don't have time for drop-in company today."

When I got to the door, I wished I'd pretended not to be home. LuAnne Conover stood there looking as pitiful as she could be, a Kleenex wadded up in her hand and her eyes red and overflowing.

"Oh, Julia," she wailed as I opened the door and before I could say a word. "I'm at my wit's end. I don't know what I'm going to do. I just can't stand it anymore."

I sighed and opened the storm door. "Come on in, LuAnne, before you freeze. Come sit by the fire a minute before you go home. Sorry I can't visit with you, but I have to be somewhere in a little while."

Instead of taking the hint, she took off her coat, dropped it on the sofa and plopped down in one of the Victorian chairs by the fire. She opened her purse and took out a handful of fresh Kleenex, and I knew I was in for another long session.

As I took the chair opposite her, she blew her nose and said, "Julia, I don't know what I'd do without you. If I didn't have you to talk to, I think I'd go crazy."

"What about Pastor Ledbetter? Aren't you talking to him?" The pastor had recently taken a course in pastoral counseling and, since he was now an expert with a framed diploma on the wall to prove it, he'd make an appointment at the drop of a hat. I'd had to caution him on several occasions about mixing psychology in with the catechism sessions he'd been having with Hazel Marie.

"Well, of course. I've just come from the church but, Julia, you're a woman and you know what I'm going through and another man, even if he is a preacher, just can't understand this kind of misery. Oh, Julia, I don't know where I've failed. I've tried my best, you know I have."

I sighed and did a little eye rolling since she was wiping her own and didn't see me. "LuAnne, it seems to me that Leonard needs some counseling too. I mean, he's part of the problem, or maybe the whole problem. Get him over at that church, either by himself or the two of you together."

"You don't understand!"

"You just said I did."

LuAnne's little birdlike hands ripped that Kleenex to shreds. "I mean I haven't told you everything. See, Julia, it's like this." She stopped, took a shuddering breath, wiped her eyes again and went on, "I don't know if I can tell you."

"That's all right," I said, beginning to rise from my chair in the hope that she would too. "We can talk when you feel more like it, and when I . . ."

"But I've got to tell you. I have to tell somebody; it's driving me crazy." And I had to wait out another sobbing fit, checking my watch as she kept on.

"It's Leonard," she wailed.

"I know that," I said with as much sympathy as I could muster. I mean, she'd been complaining about Leonard for the last six months and, if he'd been my husband, I'd've been complaining about him long before that. But he'd been her choice, not mine. "What's he done now?"

"It's not just *now*." Her voice rose, and I wondered if she was going to get hysterical on me. Frankly, I didn't think Leonard deserved that kind of emotion. "This has *been* going on. And on and on, till I can't stand it any longer."

"Well, LuAnne, I know it's hard to have a retired man underfoot all day, every day, but there ought to be something he could do that'd get him out of the house and give you some time to yourself."

"That's not it!" She put her head on her knees, crumpling up on herself as she gave way to gulping sobs. I thought to myself that all I'd heard for these many months was how Leonard made every step she made, tagging along on her heels like a puppy. She couldn't go to Velma's to get her hair done without Leonard going along too, much less to the Winn-Dixie where he questioned everything she put in her grocery cart.

"Well what is it then? I declare, LuAnne, I can only go on what you tell me, and that's what you've complained about ever since he retired. Now, if it's something else, let's hear it or at least, tell the preacher. If you're inclined that way." Though I wouldn't be.

"Oh, Julia, I *have* told him." She sat up, her face streaked with tears. "In so many words. And he says it's up to me to get Leonard over it, and I've tried everything I know to try, and nothing does any good."

"What in the world is wrong with Leonard?" Other than having no life, I wanted to add, but didn't. Leonard was as dull as dishwater, having been a civil servant all his life, which tells you everything you need to know.

"Oh, LuAnne," I said with sudden understanding of her distress, "don't tell me Leonard's got some terrible disease."

"That's exactly what I'm telling you, and I don't think I can handle it any longer. I've *suffered,* Julia, you just don't know."

I hated to hear it, but I couldn't help but wonder why she was the one doing the suffering and not the one who was afflicted.

"I'm so sorry," I said, and I was. I'd never thought much of Leonard, nor had Wesley Lloyd, but I felt for LuAnne. "What does he have?"

"Oh, Julia, he has . . ." She stopped, looked around and back over her shoulder to be sure we were alone. Then she leaned forward, took a breath and whispered, *". . . e.d."*

Chapter 6

"E.d.?"

"*Yes,*" she whispered fiercely, "and it's a terrible affliction. It affects the wife just as much as the man. No, even more than the man, take my word for it. Julia, I've tried everything I know to try, read those books the pastor gave me, which didn't even *mention* this problem since they're Christian books and, besides, I need more than prayer in this case. I've been on my knees a million times, and nothing works. But the worst thing is that Leonard is not the least concerned about it, says he's too old and set in his ways to try anything new, in spite of the fact that I spent a fortune at Victoria's Secret."

"E.d.?" I knew that every new disease or condition got shortened to its initials these days, but this was a new one on me. I tried to figure it out. Esophageal displacement? Eating disorder? Environmental disease? Educational deficit?

"Yes, and I can't live with it any longer. Julia, I've made up my mind. I have to divorce him and find a life for myself."

Well, I couldn't blame her, but it seemed to me a little late to be looking for a life. I mean, she'd put up with Leonard for more than half of the one she'd had, why get fed up now?

She dabbed at her eyes again and went on, "Pastor Ledbetter said that was the worst thing I could do and he couldn't recommend it, because it's a sin. But, either way, Julia, I'm running into sin. If I stay, I can't get Leonard to do anything and the pastor says that's my fault, too."

"I don't understand. How can this e.d. disease be your fault? You didn't give it to him, did you?"

"Of course not!" She glared at me, outraged at the question.

"Then how'd he get it?"

"Well, I don't know! But it's certainly not my fault, I don't care what the pastor says."

"LuAnne, I hate to admit this since you think I know what e.d. is, but I don't."

She jumped up from the chair and, tiny as she was, towered over me. "You don't know what it is! How can you give me advice when you don't know what you're talking about? I declare, Julia, I thought you were a better friend than that."

"Don't jump on me, LuAnne Conover." I stood up too, and did a little glaring of my own. After all, I hadn't been the one demanding help and advice. "I don't happen to keep up with the latest medical news, not being interested in it myself. In spite of having it crammed down my throat every evening by Peter Jennings and the like. Now, sit down and tell me what it is."

The air seemed to go out of her, and she sank back into the chair. She covered her face with her hands and whispered, "Leonard is experiencing, well, I've got to be brave and just say it." She drew a long, shuddering breath and said, "*erectile* dysfunction. Just like Bob Dole, but without his courage to do something about it."

I stared at her, while unwonted mental pictures of Leonard's problem and LuAnne's efforts to solve it flashed in my mind, along with images of what I'd seen in Hazel Marie's Victoria's Secret catalog that came by mail, which I made sure Little Lloyd never got his hands on.

As these unseemly pictures revolved in my mind, I was beginning to get about half mad at the nerve of her, telling me more than I ever wanted to know about things better left unsaid. All I could think of for a minute was the certainty that Pastor Ledbetter would have had the same pictures in his mind. No telling what kind of sermon we'd be getting, come Sunday, but I knew he'd be stirred to a rouser.

"LuAnne," I said, with my hands on my hips, determined to draw the line. "I don't want to hear any more about it. I'm your friend, but there are some things that friends shouldn't be privy to, and this is one of them."

"Julia, you've got to help me."

"What in the world can *I* do?"

"I don't know," she wailed, throwing her head back against the chair. "I just know that I can't go on like this! He follows me around all the time, crowding me and getting in my way, wanting to know where I am every minute of the day, but, Julia, he never *touches* me! He gets in the bed and turns over, and that's it!"

I covered my ears and turned away. "Don't tell me any more. I don't want to hear it."

"Well," she said, drawing herself up straight, "Looks like you don't have the time of day for me, but I guess I shouldn't've expected any help from you, what with having so much going on in your own house." She cut her eyes at me, looking to see how I'd take this bolt from the blue. "People talk, you know and, if I were you, I'd put a stop to what's causing it."

Before I could get into it with her and find out what rumors were currently making the rounds, Lillian stuck her head around the kitchen door, and I was never so glad to see anybody in my life. "Miss Julia," she said, "I sorry to innerrup', but you got that meetin' an' you gonna be late, you don't get started pretty soon."

"Thank you, Lillian," I said with some relief. "LuAnne, I'm sorry, but I have to be somewhere. Look, why don't you give this some thought before you do anything you'll regret. And I'll think about it too, then we'll talk. I hate that I have to hurry you out, but this is just not a good time for me."

I held her coat, giving it a little shake to get her moving, and finally she did. "I really expected more from you than this, Julia. But if you can't spare the time." She sniffed.

Lord, I couldn't tell you the amount of time I'd already spared for that woman, listening to her and sympathizing with her, and all that time she'd kept me in the dark as to the real problem. And after hearing the real problem, I wished I was still in the dark.

"I'll talk to you later, tomorrow maybe," I told her with a pat on her back as I opened the door. "We'll come up with something, don't worry."

I closed the door behind her and leaned against it. Here I was telling somebody not to worry, when that's what everybody'd been telling me. Lot of help that was, and I knew it. But when you can't or, in some cases, won't offer any help, what else can you say? And what in the world had she meant about something going on in my house and people talking, telling me such a thing when I'd been the prime subject of gossip for years on end?

Well, LuAnne was going to have to take second, maybe third, place on my list of worries. I had an appointment with J. D. Pickens, P.I, and more important things on my mind than Leonard Conover's husbandly duties. Or lack of same.

"You better come on in here and eat something 'fore you take off to see that private man," Lillian said, holding open the kitchen door.

I followed her and, glancing at the clock, said, "I don't have time to eat. I declare, Lillian, some people have problems I didn't even know existed."

"Ain't that the truth. But we got enough of our own. Now, eat this sam'ich I fixed for you or yore stomick gonna be growlin' so you won't hear what that Mr. Pickens got to say."

I knew it was the truth, so I began to eat, not even taking the time to sit at the table. I still had to go by Sam's and pick up Little Lloyd, since I wanted him with me to watch the exit signs while I watched the traffic. I didn't like driving at night, not being accustomed to it and, regardless of how much of it I'd had to do lately, I still got nervous when I had to do more of it.

"I think I better go with you," Lillian said. "I don't like you an' that chile out toolin' round by yo'self at night."

"We'll be all right," I said, though I wasn't as sure as I sounded. "Besides, Hazel Marie might call again, and I'd feel better if you were by the phone. Do you mind staying late, and I'll run you home when we get back?"

She frowned, but then nodded in agreement. As I reached for my coat, the front doorbell rang. We both looked at each other, wondering who else was interrupting our evening plans.

"I'll see who it is," I said, slipping into my coat. "Whoever it is will see I'm on my way out and won't stay long."

"It good an' dark out there," Lillian said, "an' it ain't no time for people to be ringin' no doorbells." She stopped and looked at me with her eyes getting bigger. "Maybe it some word on Miss Hazel Marie. I'll go with you."

So we both went to the door, Lillian hanging back behind me. We both gasped out loud when I opened the door and saw a sheriff's deputy standing there with his hands full of thick papers.

Hazel Marie, I thought, and I hung on to the door, as Lillian reached for my arm. Bad news always comes in a dark blue uniform, and this one was topped by a round face with a sandy fuzz above his lip, looking more like a high schooler selling magazines than an officer with news of our worst fears.

"Yes?" I quavered, not even able to ask him in as I'd ordinarily have done.

"I need to see a . . . ," he glanced at the papers, "Hazel Marie Puckett. Is she here?"

It took me a minute to realize that if he was looking for her, he couldn't be there to tell us what we didn't want to hear. "Ah, no, not at the moment," I said, my mind working overtime, trying to figure out why he was looking for her and why he didn't know she was missing. I straightened up and got myself back together. No need giving anything away until I knew just what was what.

"No, officer," I went on, "she's not here at the moment. May I help you?"

He shifted his feet, then said, "Well, ma'am, maybe so. I have to serve these papers on her."

"Papers! What *kind* of papers?" I squinched up my eyes at him and demanded, "Is Lieutenant Peavey behind this?"

"Ah, no, ma'am," he said, giving me a look like he thought I'd lost my mind, "I don't believe he had anything to do with this. It's usually a neighbor or a relative with an interest in the child who comes in and files a complaint."

"You're telling me that somebody has filed a complaint against Hazel Marie? Why? Who would do that when she's done nothing wrong? I never heard of such a thing in my life! You ought to be ashamed of yourself!"

"Ma'am," he said, taking a step backward, "this is pursuant to, ah, let me see, chapter seven of the Codified Juvenile Code of the North Carolina General Statutes. It doesn't always mean anything's wrong; the law says that anybody who's concerned about a child's welfare can ask the court to look into it. But, see, that's what the summons is for, so the complainee can come in and state their case. Then there'll be a hearing and a judgment handed down. That's the law, ma'am, and, well, that's all I know, except I'm supposed to pick up a . . . ," he studied the papers again, "minor child, Wesley Lloyd Puckett. Is? . . ."

"What are you talking about!"

"Ma'am, I've got instructions to take this child into protective custody. See, it's right here." He opened up an official-looking document and held it in front of my face. "It's called a snatch-and-grab order, and I'll need to take him with me."

My mouth dropped open, and so did Lillian's. I couldn't believe what I was hearing.

"Young man," I said. "What is your name?"

"Uh, Jim," he said. Then, as his face turned red, he corrected himself, "I mean, Deputy Daly."

"Well, Deputy Daly," I said, pushing the document away, "that child is not here and neither is his mother. And if you think you're going to be doing any snatching and grabbing around here, you can just think again. Now you just take those papers right back where you got them and tell them they have a nerve to be serving papers on an old woman. And after dark, too!"

"Well, ma'am," he said, shuffling his feet, "we know this is their legal residence and, if they're not home, I'll have to ask you to accept the summons. Hazel Marie Puckett will have to appear within ten days and, I'm sorry to upset you, but I'll have to take the child as soon as I can, since the complaint has to do with his welfare. Judge's orders, straight from the clerk of court. When will he be home?"

Lord, my mind was in a whirl, trying to think what to do and what to say. And what not to. Lillian's hand gripped my arm tighter and tighter, and I was glad of the support.

While I tried to think of something to put him off, Lillian chimed in. "That chile spendin' the night with a frien'. We don't know who it is, 'cause his mama, she know, but she ain't here. I 'speck she be home 'bout midnight, she out on a date with Mr. Wilson T. Hodge. You know, that man what works for the Presbyterium church over there."

"Oh, well, okay," Deputy Daly said, and I could've hugged Lillian for coming up with some church-related credentials for Hazel Marie. And not even lying too much about it, either. "Well, I'll just leave these papers with you, ma'am, and ask you to see that she gets them. Somebody'll be back for the boy first thing in the morning."

"He goin' straight to school from his frien's house," Lillian said, with a straight face, "so he won't be here then. It be 'bout three o'clock tomorrow 'fore he be home."

"Okay, if we don't get him from school, we'll be back then. Sorry to disturb you so late, but these papers just came through and we have to serve them." He held out the documents, which I took because I didn't know what else to do.

As soon as I closed the door behind him, I leaned against it and said, "What in the world is going on?"

Lillian said, "Look at them papers an' see if they tell us anything."

I did, and they did. "Brother Vern!" I yelled. "Lillian! It's that money-grubbing, television-preaching country fool, Vernon Puckett, Hazel Marie's uncle, who's behind this! Can you believe it! He's signed a complaint against Hazel Marie, claiming that it's in the best interests of the child that he be granted custody."

"How can he do such a thing?"

"It's easy!" I shrieked, ready to pull my hair out at the thought of gullible judges and magistrates and clerks of court. "Didn't you hear that deputy standing there, quoting chapter and verse? Anybody with an ax to grind can do it! Looks like, in this state, all anybody has to do is walk in and swear up, down and sideways that a child is in peril, and they'll snatch up the child and issue a summons for the parent to appear and answer the complaint."

"Well, but she can't answer no complaint if she not here."

"I know that! But *see*," I shrieked, unfolding the document with a flip of my wrist, "it says right here that the child's circumstances require the sheriff to place him in protective custody! That makes me so mad I could spit. The child's in better circumstances than he's ever been in his life, and it's the circumstances that *I've* provided that's in question!" I stopped to catch my breath, then nearly sunk to my knees.

"Good Lord, Lillian, this is absolutely the worst time in the world for this to happen. Do you reckon? . . ." I stopped again, my eyes narrowing as things began to fall into place. I grabbed Lillian's arm. "Listen, Brother Vern was over at the church to see Pastor Ledbetter this very morning. I *knew* I should've gone over there to see what was going on. You know what it could mean, don't you?"

"No'm, 'less them two up to something."

"That's it, exactly. Though I can't imagine Brother Vern and my pastor in cahoots about anything. Unless, *unless,* Pastor Ledbetter knows Hazel Marie's missing, and Brother Vern knows it, too. But how could they? It doesn't make sense, but I know that man would take any advantage he could to jump in and try to get Little Lloyd and his inheritance away from us. But whatever he knows or doesn't know, he's pulling the same stunt he tried last year, only this time he's using the law to do it. And Pastor Ledbetter," I went on, squinching up my eyes till I could hardly see through them, "he'd help the devil himself to get that blasted building built. It's a conspiracy, that's what it is. Lillian, what are we going to do?"

"Better call Mr. Sam and Miss Binkie, first thing. Then worry 'bout the next thing."

"Yes. No. Wait a minute, let me think. All these papers are official, no mistake about that, signed and sealed and everything." I shuffled through the papers again, hoping to spot a technicality, though I'm not sure I'd've recognized one. "Binkie's an officer of the court, or some such thing, so she'll have to do what the court tells her to do. And, as for Sam, I don't know what he is now that he's retired, but you know him. He wouldn't go against the law for anything." I stopped and thought for a minute. "If he knew he was going against it, that is, but he's got his mind on other things, so I'm not going to bother him. I'll handle this myself."

"What you thinkin' 'bout doin'?"

"I'm thinking two things," I said, looking off in the distance as I got my mind together. "First, I have to meet with Mr. Pickens and get him started on finding Hazel Marie. She's got to get back here to answer this complaint. And second, I'm thinking that we have to keep Little Lloyd out of sight of any and all sheriff's deputies. And that includes Coleman, too. I declare, Lillian, I'm surrounded by people who won't do anything but follow the law to the letter."

" 'Cept me."

We smiled at each other, knowing that it was up to us to keep Little Lloyd out of the clutches of Brother Vernon Puckett. Which meant hiding him from the Law, as well.

"I'm going to Sam's and pick up Little Lloyd," I said, heading for the kitchen to get my purse and keys. "Then we'll go meet Mr. Pickens and get him started looking for Hazel Marie. In the meantime, let's be thinking what we can do with Little Lloyd to keep him out of sight till his mother gets home. Then, we'll get Binkie on it to answer that fool's complaint with a complaint of our own."

"What kinda complaint you gonna make on him?"

"I don't know. Something, harrassment or fraud or maybe for trying to get at Little Lloyd's inheritance under false pretenses. There ought to be something we can get him on. But I'm not going to worry about that right now. Lillian, the thing is, well, just think, you and I have no legal claim on that child and, if his mother's not here to make her appearance, the court'll grant custody to the next of kin. Which means . . ."

"I know what it mean," Lillian said. "It mean we got to find Miss Hazel Marie and we got to hide Little Lloyd so good, not nobody find him till we want him found. I can hide him at my house."

I stopped the pacing I'd been doing, thinking she'd hit on the perfect solution. But then I reconsidered. "No, it stands to reason they'd come looking there, since everybody who knows us knows how much that child means to you. Besides, it'd be hard to keep him hid, since he's likely to stand out a little. We'll have to think of something else— maybe LuAnne would keep him. No, that won't work; she's got her own problems and it wouldn't do to put a child in that situation." I did some more hand-wringing, then pulled myself together. "But right now I have to get out of here or Mr. Pickens'll think I'm not coming. At least, Little Lloyd'll be safe for a little while."

"I be thinkin' what to do with him while you gone, maybe something'll pop up. But, Miss Julia, he got to go to school. How we gonna manage that?"

"I'm not going to worry about it. He can miss school without it doing any damage. He's so far ahead of the others, his absence'll give them time to catch up. Besides, what good will one day of school do, when it'd just mean being taken out by a bunch of deputies? I declare, I never heard of sending the sheriff to pick up a child who's never done a wrong thing in his life. I say, snatch and grab! I'll tell you one thing, if we ever get all this straightened out, I'm going to do a little snatching and grabbing of my own. And Brother Vern's going to be first in line."

I pulled on my gloves and turned my collar up. "I've got to go, Lillian, before somebody else rings the doorbell with more bad news. We shouldn't be but an hour or so."

"You watch that weather out there," she said. "It feelin' like the North Pole with that wind scurryin' around."

I waved and headed for the car.

————

When I pulled in at Sam's, I determined not to give him much more than the time of day. Even though I'd've given anything for his help, I just couldn't trust him. If Sam knew that Little Lloyd was being sought by the sheriff, he'd try to talk me into doing the right thing. According to his lights. But I knew better. And on top of that, I was still mad at him for the spectacle he'd made of himself with that Wiggins woman. Perky, was what she was and, believe me, perkiness can get old in a hurry.

But if Sam thought it'd bothered me, I aimed to put his mind to rest. There's nothing like an old fool, and he was welcome to his foolishness, as far as I was concerned.

When James opened the door, I spoke and hurried on into Sam's living room where a table had been pulled up over his cast-laden leg. He and Little Lloyd were hunched over it, putting a puzzle together.

"Julia!" Sam said, smiling with what at any other time I would've taken as pleasure at seeing me. "Come on in here. We need help with this puzzle, and you're just the one we need."

"I don't have time for puzzles, Sam. I've got enough of my own to deal with. Get your coat, Little Lloyd, we have to get on home."

"What about . . . ?" he started, but I cut him off.

"All taken care of. Now come on, you still have some homework to do."

He began to shake his head, both of us knowing his homework had been done at school, but at my squinch-eyed look, he subsided and went for his coat. He always got my unspoken messages, since our minds worked so much alike.

"What's your hurry, Julia?" Sam said, as if he thought I had nothing better to do than entertain him. "Looks like you could spare a minute to cheer up an ailing man. Have a seat over here by me."

"Ailing man, my foot," I said. "I had some pity for you up until I saw how that so-called nurse cheered you up without half trying."

"Why, Julia," Sam said, his eyes twinkling like he'd just discovered a secret. Except I didn't have one, so there wasn't a thing he could discover. Then he laughed a little and held out his hand to me. "Come on over here. You know I like a mature woman, one who understands me like you do."

"*Mature* just means old, and I don't understand a thing about you, Sam Murdoch, so don't be trying to flatter me. I'm not in the mood for it."

"Well then, what *are* you in the mood for?"

"Not a thing you have to offer. And you needn't smirk at me like that. I have to get this child in bed, so we'll be going." I started out to the hall, but felt bad leaving on that note. Turning around, I said, "I have a lot on my mind today, Sam, which I'd like to share with you. But I don't have time tonight."

He didn't like it, but I was too busy worrying about the long arm of the Law to linger in his house. Besides, it wouldn't hurt him to have a few of the feelings I'd had that morning.

Little Lloyd was quiet as we got in the car, and so was I as I drove through town watching for patrol cars. Who knew but what the sheriff had roadblocks out for us? But probably not, because nobody but Lillian knew we were going anywhere.

Little Lloyd suddenly sat up and looked out the window. "Where're we going, Miss Julia? We've already passed our house."

"Yes, you and I have an appointment with Mr. J. D. Pickens, P.I. at a Mexican restaurant, of all places. If we like his looks and his manner, we're going to hire him to find your mother."

"Tonight? Right now?" The child swung his head toward me, his face lit up in the glow of the dash lights.

"We certainly are. So let's just hope he's up to the job. And, there's another thing you need to know, but first I want you to help me watch where we're going."

He sat up in his seat as far as the seat belt would let him, eager now that I'd put some things in motion. I hated to tell him the latest in the Brother Vern saga, but I had to. He needed to know what the scoundrel was up to, so I told the child how we had to keep him out of sight so he wouldn't be snatched and grabbed.

"Now, just remember," I cautioned as I finished the sorry tale, "nobody knows this but you and me and Lillian. Well, the sheriff does, and all his deputies, which means Coleman, too. That's why I didn't want to say too much to Sam, because he'd probably feel obligated to obey the Law and turn you over to them. Anyway, all we have to do is keep you out of sight until we locate your mother. Then we'll call Binkie and put that great-uncle of yours in his place."

"I don't know why Brother Vern would want to do something like this," Little Lloyd said, his shoulders hunched over with worry. "He never has acted much like he wanted me around."

I heard the fear and confusion in his voice, and took a chance at releasing one hand from the wheel to pat his arm. "Who knows what that man is thinking," I said, although I well knew what was on his mind. He was thinking dollar signs, now that Wesley Lloyd's estate had been probated or whatever it was that had to be done to it. "But you'll be safe with Lillian and me, because we're going to take care of you. Now, put your mind on this Mr. Pickens and help me decide if he has what it takes to locate your mother. But let me caution you, Little Lloyd, let's not say anything to him about Brother Vern and his complaints and summonses. The fewer who know we're hiding from the Law, the better. Don't you think?"

"Yessum," he said, slumping back in his seat. "It'd be better not to confuse him, so he'll keep his mind on finding my mama."

"First things first, right?" Then in an effort to cheer him up, I added, "And when she's home, we're going to cook Brother Vern's goose."

"I sure hope so," he said with a sickly smile. Then, proving he'd learned something in Sunday school, he added, "He's been a thorn in our flesh long enough."

"Watch for the Delmont exit," I reminded him, squinching my eyes against the glare of headlights as we merged onto I-26. "I know about where it is, but everything looks different at night, so give me plenty of warning before I have to come off this thing." The interstate was as busy as it ever was in the daytime. Big trucks, little trucks, loud trucks and every kind of automobile whizzed past us, but I stayed right under the speed limit, not wanting to be the cause of an accident.

Little Lloyd navigated as well as he did everything else, being the steady and reliable child that he was. I often thought he resembled me in many of his attributes, even though we weren't a lick of kin. Environment plays a heavy role, don't you know.

"That's it, right over there," Little Lloyd said, pointing at a former steak house at the end of an exit ramp on our right. The place was lit up with neon signs and red, blue and green Christmas lights strung across the front and in the trees along the side of the parking lot. As soon as I parked and shut off the motor, I could hear Mexican music being piped outside. No telling what it'd be like inside.

"I hope he's already here," I said. "I'm in no mood to sit and listen to that squalling while we wait for him."

We walked across the parking lot along with several other patrons, most of whom had arrived in pickups and blacked-out vans. Not quite the clientele of the Abbotsville Country Club, but most of them had children with them, so I took some comfort in that. In spite of the fact that I heard talking in Spanish and English and some combination of the two, making me feel like a foreigner in my own county.

"I don't have an idea in the world what Mr. Pickens looks like," I said to Little Lloyd as we waited in line for one of those smiling Mexican men who worked there to seat us.

"Why don't we just ask for him?" the boy said, showing again that he was smart as a whip. "I'll bet he's left word at the desk for us."

That proved to be so. The man at the desk knew just who we meant when I mentioned Mr. Pickens's name and, even though I didn't understand a word he said on the way, he led us to a booth along the back wall. A man, neither young nor old, but about the right age to've had a little experience in the world looked up at us with eyes as black as sin. He had a head full of black hair and what looked to be an equal amount under his nose. I took his measure when he stood as we walked up. I appreciate any courtesy I can get from a man, and gave him a preliminary gold star for making the effort.

Mr. Pickens was one of those men who don't look as tall as they actually are because of their thick chests and wide shoulders. Lots of black hair on his arms, which I couldn't help but notice because the sleeves of his white shirt were rolled up. A quick association flashed through my mind, as I wondered about the likelihood of his chest being similiarly arrayed.

I flushed, furious again at LuAnne because of the thoughts she'd put in my head. I don't ordinarily entertain such intimate matters. I mean, at my age you'd think my mind would've long put such thoughts to rest. But Mr. Pickens was one of those few and far between men who generated some sort of male hormone into the air around him, which was mixing in with Old Spice, of all things. Considering the trouble that aromatic mixture had gotten me into one time before, I determined to keep my distance.

"Glad to meet you," Mr. Pickens said, as I introduced myself and Little Lloyd, and received a firm handshake and a gleam of white teeth from under that bristly brush. "Slide on in." He motioned to the booth.

Little Lloyd scooted in opposite Mr. Pickens and I followed him on the torn plastic. Looking into Mr. Pickens's black eyes, I tried to determine just what kind of man he was and whether he possessed the qualities to help us. I didn't want any fly-by-nighter who would take my money and do nothing.

Saying that he'd just ordered, he handed us a menu that had been propped against a napkin holder.

"We've eaten," I said, waving it away, "but you go right ahead. Mr. Pickens, I want to know one thing right off."

"Let's have it."

"What are your qualifications for this job?"

He leaned across his forearms as they rested on the table and looked me straight in the eye with the most serious expression on his face. "Listen, hon," he said, "I'm the most qualified man you'll ever meet. I know this business backward and forward, inside and out. I was with the Charlotte-Mecklenburg Police Department for ten years and the Atlanta PD for four before that. I've worked vice, missing persons, crimes against property, homicide, you name it. Had my own agency for going on eight years now, and what you're looking at is the most experienced and the dead-level best private eye in the business. Bar none."

I appreciate a high degree of self-confidence as much as the next person, but it's been my practice to withhold judgment until I see some results. So, I discounted the bragging he was doing without letting it irritate me as much as it ordinarily would've. I was still hung up on that "hon" he'd thrown at me.

Before I could straighten him out on the proper term of address when speaking to me, the waitress sat a huge platter of strange-looking food before him. Then she put down a frosted glass and a full pitcher.

My back stiffened at the sight. "Mr. Pickens, would that pitcher contain an alcoholic beverage?"

"It sure would." Glancing up at the waitress, he said, "How about another glass, darlin'?"

"No." I held up my hand. "No, thank you. I don't care to partake." And I didn't care for him partaking either, if the truth be known. If he was a bad drinker, then Lord help us, but I was at my wit's end and had to use what was available. But I didn't like it. Nor did I like the undue familiarity he was exhibiting to every woman within earshot.

"Do you good," he said, winking at Little Lloyd as he poured the frothy stuff into the glass. "Put hair on your chest, too."

I reared back in the booth, dismayed at how he'd picked up on some of my earlier unwelcome thoughts. "Mr. Pickens," I said, "we're not here to discuss masculine hair patterns, and I'd appreciate it if you wouldn't mention such matters in front of this child."

"Sorry," he said, with another wink at Little Lloyd. Then he started in on that conglomeration of cheese, beans and I-don't-know-what-all on his plate. "Why don't you go ahead and give me a run-down on your case."

So I did, although I'd've hardly called Hazel Marie a case. I handed him her birth certificate, Social Security card and a picture. He gave considerable attention to the last-named item, while I told him all the details of our concern. During my recital, he ate and shot occasional sharp glances at me from those black eyes of his. Almost putting me off worse than the way he was steadily emptying that pitcher.

Chapter 8

After he finished his meal and paid the check, he ushered us out of the booth. The tip he left for the waitress indicated a generous, but somewhat profligate, nature. I'd have to watch that, too.

When we walked out of the restaurant, I pulled Little Lloyd's cap down over his ears. The temperature had dropped considerably while we'd been inside, and both of us huddled in our coats as we stepped out onto the porch. Mr. Pickens didn't seem bothered by the cold, braving it with only a black and white tweed sport jacket. His hand on my back as we negotiated the few steps to the parking lot felt like a heating pad through my coat.

"Where're you parked?" he asked.

"Right over there." He walked us to the car, earning another gold star in my mind.

Before opening the car door, he stood for a minute studying Hazel Marie's picture in the glow of the Christmas lights. It was one of those so-called glamour shots that she'd had done at Wilson T.'s insistence. I'd gone with her to the studio in the mall and watched while they gave her a makeover, undressing and draping and back-lighting and airbrushing her like she was a model or something.

The picture didn't give a hint of the shape she'd been in the time she'd come to my door, all bruised and battered and bleeding. She'd had a hard life all the way around and had needed a firm hand, which I'd given her. That hair, for instance, had been bleached to within an inch of its life. I'd taken her to Velma, who'd conditioned it and put on a softer color than the brassy yellow it had been. And I'd introduced her to a better make of clothes than she'd been able to afford with the pittance Wesley Lloyd had made available to her. She still wore her dresses way too short to my mind, but that seemed to be the style, so I hadn't said too much about it.

Hazel Marie was a pretty little thing, even though she didn't much think so herself, and was remarkably improved since I'd had those two lost teeth replaced for her. Skinny, like Little Lloyd, with thin arms and legs. But uncommonly large in the chest area. You know the type. She'd taken the eye of every widower and single man and, I'm sorry to report, several of the married ones in the Presbyterian church and, I'll tell you the truth, it'd been something of a relief to me when Wilson T. came along and took her out of the running, so to speak. Even though I wouldn't've given two cents for him or the kind of work he was engaged in.

"Nice," Mr. Pickens said, giving the picture an uncommonly long study. Then, smiling at Little Lloyd, said, "I see where you get your good looks, sport."

Little Lloyd ducked his head, smiling at the compliment, but I began to wonder if Mr. Pickens knew the truth from a hole in the ground.

"Regardless of how she looks," I said, anxious to keep his mind on the subject, "can you find her for us?"

"Oh, yeah," he said, as he finally slid the picture back into its envelope. "I'll need to keep this awhile. First thing in the morning I'll run a credit check, see if she's used a credit card anywhere. Then I'll run down this 'big,' whatever it is. We need a starting point, and that looks to be the obvious one. Unless," he said, looking up with one of those sharp glances, "you know what movie they were going to see?"

"I don't have a clue, neither knowing nor caring what those Hollywood types do. Little Lloyd, did she say what they were going to see?"

"No'm, she just said they were going to Asheville to eat and see a movie." He stopped, thought for a minute, then said, "She doesn't like action movies much. But Mr. Hodge does, so I don't guess that helps, does it?"

"You never know," Mr. Pickens said. "Tell you what I'll do. It's about the same time now that they would've gone to the movies last night, so the same people ought to be working tonight. I think I'll make the rounds, show 'em this picture, and see if anybody remembers seeing her."

My heart lifted at his willingness to get right to work, and I felt some better about my choice of private investigator, in spite of his drinking habit. I'd have to watch that and nip it in the bud as soon as I had him on my payroll. At least, though, he hadn't given me a song and dance about waiting around, doing nothing, until Hazel Marie showed up on her own.

"Excuse us a minute," I said, turning Little Lloyd by the shoulder and walking a few steps away.

Leaning down to the boy, I whispered, "What do you think? Should we hire him or not?"

Little Lloyd craned his neck around me, giving Mr. Pickens a thorough going-over. Then he nodded and said, "Yessum, I guess we better. But he sure does like that beer."

The child and I thought so much alike, it lifted my heart. I smiled and gave him a pat. "We'll just have to keep an eye on him, and him away from it."

Walking back to where Mr. Pickens was waiting, I said, "I take it, then, that you're willing to take the case?"

"You bet. Shouldn't take more than a day or so to find somebody that looks like this." He waved the picture-holding envelope. "She's the type that sticks in your mind."

I wasn't sure of the healthiness of his motive in looking for Hazel Marie, but at that point I figured I'd take what I could get.

"Now," he went on, "we need to settle the matter of my fee. It'll be sixty dollars an hour, plus expenses, with a three-hundred-dollar retainer."

"My word."

Little Lloyd looked up at me with a worried frown on his face. He knew how careful I was with my money, and I expect he figured I wouldn't stand to be soaked for that much. It gave me pleasure to reassure him.

"You're awfully expensive, Mr. Pickens," I said, not wanting the man to think I threw money around any which way. "But," I said, with a long sigh, "if that's what it takes to get this boy's mama back, I guess I'll have to put up with it. Unless you want to give us special rates, seeing as how Hazel Marie's looks will make it so easy for you."

He threw his head back and laughed out loud. Then he gave my arm a squeeze. "I like your style, hon. I'll have to watch what I say around you, won't I?" Then he got all businesslike. "But no, no special rates, other than the fact that you're getting the best in the business for just your average cost."

"I'll believe it when I see it. Or rather, when I see Hazel Marie safe and sound. In the meantime," I said, opening my pocketbook, "I want you on the job. So I'll give you your retainer right now so you can get started."

I thought it'd hurt to write a three-hundred-dollar check made out to a perfect stranger but, when it came down to it, I went ahead and wrote it for five hundred.

"This is to ensure that you'll be working just for us. I don't want you frittering away your time with any other clients," I said, handing him the check. "I want results, Mr. Pickens and, if you're as good as you say and you find Hazel Marie before this money runs out, I'll expect a refund."

I think his eyes twinkled in the red and green glow of the Christmas lights, but I couldn't be sure. I was sure that his eyebrows went up when he saw the amount on the check.

"She's as good as home right now," he said. "Count on it." He folded the check and put it in a billfold that was curved from being sat on. "I'll check in with you every day but, if something breaks, I'll let you know right away."

"That won't do," I said. "You can't expect us to just sit home twiddling our thumbs, waiting for word from you and never knowing what you're doing. We're going with you and, when this boy has to be in school or otherwise occupied," I said, thinking of how I had to keep him hid, "*I'll* be with you."

"Uh-uh," he said, shaking his head. "That's not the way it works."

"That's the way it'll have to work, if you work for me, Mr. Pickens. I know how people are. They take your money and when it suits them, they might get around to doing the job they're hired to do. Well, I'm not having that. I want to know what, when and how you're conducting my business, and I want Hazel Marie home before something awful happens to her." I saw, or maybe felt, Little Lloyd take a deep breath at what I'd said, and I felt bad about scaring him. But it had to be said in no uncertain terms so Mr. Pickens would see that I meant business.

"Look, hon," Mr. Pickens said, as he put his hand on my arm, rubbing my sleeve up and down. "I know you're upset, but what I do is not something either of you ought to be involved in. Investigative technique is a specialized subject, and I can do a better job by myself. That's why I left the Charlotte PD and Atlanta before that, too many people looking over my shoulder. Trust me. I can do the job."

Well, I've never trusted anybody who felt it necessary to say "trust me," so I was even more determined to keep my eye on him. I stepped back out of rubbing distance from his hand and said, "Mr. Pickens, the matter is not up for argument. I've hired you and you've taken my money, so accept the terms. We're going with you."

"No," he said, having the nerve to point a finger in my face, "you're not."

"Yes, we are."

"Uh-uh."

"How does a bonus sound?"

He studied me for a minute, undoubtedly adding up figures in his mind. "What're we talking about here?"

"I'm talking about a sizable one, say, a forty-hour week's worth if you find Hazel Marie within twenty-four hours. It'll go down for every day after that, but I won't expect a refund from the retainer."

"You drive a hard bargain."

"Not as hard as I'm going to drive you."

He turned those dark eyes on me, considering the proposition for several seconds. Then he said, "You'll slow me down."

When they start to give, you know you've won. "Not for a minute, Mr. Pickens. We'll be a help to you, you'll see. I want you to earn that bonus, and you'll feel good about yourself when you do. Now, we've still got a couple of hours before Little Lloyd's bedtime, so where do we go first?"

He looked off into the distance and shifted his feet. Then shaking his head, he said, "I still don't like it. It won't work and, if you're right, and she's in danger, where does that put you and the boy?"

"Right behind you, Mr. Pickens. If you're as good as you say, I'm sure you'll protect us." I sighed then, realizing what he was up to. "I'm disappointed in you, Mr. Pickens. You're just trying to soak a poor widow woman but, if that's what it takes, so be it. I'll double the bonus."

He did a double take. "Double? Well, why didn't you say so. Hon, for two weeks' income for a day's work, I'll take you, the boy and anybody else you want to drag along."

That told me all I needed to know about J. D. Pickens, P.I., right there. He wanted money, or needed it, one, and when I saw the dented and rusted car he was driving, I knew he was in bad financial shape. I smiled at the sight, figuring I had his number and sure that he'd do things my way. I was in the catbird seat, which was where I intended to stay until Hazel Marie was safe in her own home. Well, my home, but what difference did that make?

"We'll take my car next time," I said, trying my best to find a comfortable position on the rump-sprung bucket seat. I wasn't even sure the door was closed tight, which was one reason I was hanging on to the armrest.

Mr. Pickens just grunted and stomped down on the gas pedal. The outside of the car might've looked like a bent-up tin can, but there was nothing wrong with the motor.

Little Lloyd, belted in the backseat, said, "I like this car, Miss Julia. It's a Firebird."

"Well, whatever it is, it needs some body work."

Mr. Pickens ignored our discussion of his vehicle, keeping his mind on the highway and weaving in and out of the traffic, as we headed for Asheville and the four most likely movie houses. I'd wanted to follow him in my car, but he'd said no. That wasn't all he'd said, following it up with the comment that if I was bound and determined to go with him, I could just do it, because he couldn't be bothered with having another car trailing him. Which, he'd added, couldn't keep up with him, anyway. I believed him, having now been witness to and passenger in a tire-squealing, oil-burning, nerve-racking, high-speed car ride.

"Are we speeding, Mr. Pickens?"

He glanced at me in the light of the dashboard and oncoming cars, one hand on the wheel and the other on the gear shift. "Make you nervous?"

"Certainly not." I made a conscious effort and released the armrest. "I'm just worried about Little Lloyd. I wouldn't want him to be in a wreck."

"I'm okay, Miss Julia," Little Lloyd said. "I like to go fast."

I immediately took that as a critical comment on my own careful driving, but decided to let it pass with only a sniff. Mr. Pickens's mouth twitched as he swerved to pass another car that was poking along at the speed limit.

"We'll start with this one," Mr. Pickens said, turning into a south Asheville mall with a double movie house at the far end. He slowed down enough to avoid arrest as he maneuvered through the parked cars.

Parking the car in the fire zone right in front of the ticket booth, he got out of the car without a "be back in a minute," or a "kiss my foot" or anything else.

"Wait, we're coming, too," I said, but I don't think he heard me as he slammed his door and walked off. "Come on, Little Lloyd."

We followed as quickly as we could, coming up behind Mr. Pickens as he shoved Hazel Marie's picture through the opening in the glass booth. A thin, washed-out-looking young man wearing a white shirt, black bow tie and a maroon vest gazed at Mr. Pickens like he couldn't understand a simple question. Pimples dotted the young man's face, as did patches of beard that his razor had missed.

"Huh?" he said.

"Have you seen this woman?" Mr. Pickens said again. "She was here last night about this time. The man she was with probably bought the ticket, but you might've noticed her."

"Well," I chimed in, wanting to get the facts straight. "We're not sure she was at this picture show, but she could've been."

The ticket seller swung his eyes from Mr. Pickens to me and back again. "Uh-uh, I ain't seen her."

Mr. Pickens glared at me, jerked the picture back and grabbed my arm. Pulling me away from the booth, he leaned right down in my face and said, "Look, when you're questioning somebody, you don't give them an out. Which is exactly what you just did. He hardly looked at the picture, much less gave it any thought before you let him off the hook."

"Well, I'm sorry."

"Sorry won't cut it. Now get back in the car and stay there." He punctuated the order with a pointed finger in my face. Then he headed for the double doors leading inside the movie.

"Hey!" the ticket seller yelled, leaning down to call through the slot. "Hey, mister, you got to buy a ticket."

Mr. Pickens swung back and leaned down himself. "I'm not going in to see the movie. I'm going to see if anybody working inside has seen this woman."

"It don't matter," the ticket seller said. "Anybody goes through the doors has to have a ticket. That's the policy."

Quick as a flash, Mr. Pickens's hand went to his inside coat pocket and came out with a wallet. Flipping it open and flapping the badge pinned on it in the ticket seller's face, he said, "Police business."

As the doors closed behind Mr. Pickens, I shivered in a gust of wind that scattered popcorn boxes across the sidewalk.

"I guess we better get back in the car, Little Lloyd," I said, my hand on his back. In spite of the cold and the dressing down Mr. Pickens had given me, I was beginning to feel somewhat pleased with myself, all things considered.

"Little Lloyd," I went on, as we settled in our seats, "I think we've made a good decision by hiring Mr. Pickens. I tried my best to get some official help through official channels and couldn't get to first base. But, without even knowing it, we've gone and hired our very own private policeman. You saw that badge, didn't you?"

Little Lloyd looked over the seat at me, frowning and twisting his mouth. "I'm not sure he's a policeman, Miss Julia. I don't think policemen have their own businesses."

"Well, I'm not going to worry about the details. He seems to know what he's doing and, what's more, he has the wherewithal to do it. Bundle up back there; I don't want you catching cold."

By the time Mr. Pickens came out of the warm theater, the car felt like the inside of a refrigerator. We should've gone in with him, whether he liked it or not.

"Did anybody recognize her?" I asked as he swung into the driver's seat.

"No. I'll try another one."

After pulling out onto the city street and turning toward downtown, gearing down with a roar at each stop light, he finally turned to me and said, "Let's get something straight. *I'm* the one doing the questioning." And he had the unmitigated gall to take his hand off the gear shift and point that finger at me again. "Remember that."

"Mr. Pickens," I said, drawing myself up to face him down, "you point that finger at me one more time, and you'll draw back a nub."

He cut his eyes at me, then started laughing. At *me*. I took immediate offense, as anybody would've who'd been both reprimanded and laughed at but, with an admirable act of will, I decided to let it go. At least, he now knew where I stood when it came to being on the receiving end of orders. Lightheartedness in a man, especially in a man who's supposed to be working, didn't ordinarily inspire a great deal of confidence from me, but then, active hostility between us wasn't going to be of much use in finding Hazel Marie. So I relented enough to manage a smile to let him know there were no hard feelings.

But he had to learn who was in charge. When we got to the Northside Cinema, I told Little Lloyd to stay in the car while I marched my-self in right behind Mr. Pickens. In spite of the fact that he stopped dead, put his hands on his hips and glared at me.

"I just want to learn how it's done, Mr. Pickens," I said, as pleas-antly as I could. "From an expert, so to speak."

He rolled his eyes, then turned without a word. I trailed behind him and watched while he showed Hazel Marie's picture to the ticket seller—this one was a bald man who was sweating inside his glass booth—then followed him inside.

"Don't say a word," Mr. Pickens said in a low, commanding tone as we went into the lobby.

The smell of popcorn filled the carpeted area, and had drawn sev-eral patrons from their seats. Mr. Pickens waited while the young girl behind the counter sold buttered and nonbuttered, Cokes and candy. When the last lanky teenager turned toward the curtained doorway, sucking on his drink as he went, Mr. Pickens went to the counter. I stood back, as ordered, and observed. I learned a lot but I wasn't ex-actly sure what it was.

"How you doin'?" he began, leaning one hand on the counter and smiling like the ponytailed, earringed girl before him was a good friend instead of someone he'd never seen before. "I wonder if you could help me out, and I just bet you can."

She smiled, but it was a little on the tentative side, I thought. "Well, I'll try."

Mr. Pickens didn't say anything for a minute, just stood there smil-ing at her, taking her in with his eyes. And the more he did, the broader her smile became. I didn't know what he was communicating to her, but she liked whatever it was. "I bet you see a lot of people come through here," he said. "They probably all run together and you don't remember any of them."

"Well," she said, raising her arm to twirl the ponytail and, Mr. Pick-ens couldn't help but notice, to pull her sweater tighter. "Some of 'em kinda stand out in your mind. But mostly, it's just 'I want this,' 'I want that.' Why?"

"Reason I asked, I'm a private investigator and . . ."

"You are? Cool."

"Yeah, and I'm looking for a woman. . . ."

"Oh, yeah?" She laughed and leaned across the counter toward him. "You better watch yourself with that line, you might get one."

Mr. Pickens laughed, too, and slipped Hazel Marie's picture out of his pocket. "Looks like I'd be in luck, if I wasn't working. Too bad, but I might get back this way sometime soon and see if I can find me one. Unfortunately, I have to look for this one tonight." He held the picture in front of her, and it took a few seconds for the little twit to look away from him and give it some attention. "Maybe you saw her here last night?"

"Uh-uh. I don't think I seen her."

"Think hard," he urged as she continued to shake her head.

"I might reco'nize her if I seen her again but, like I say, it's mostly 'Gimme this,' 'Gimme that' around here and I don't have time to look at faces. Well, you know, unless it's somebody like you that comes up to talk. I prob'bly won't forget you."

"I won't forget you, either," he said, putting away the picture and handing her a card. "Here's my phone number. If you see her or happen to remember anything from last night, will you call me?"

"I sure will. I might even call if I don't remember."

Giving her a last throb of the heart, he grinned at her and whispered something that made her blush. The whole thing put me in mind of Sam's unseemly behavior with the Wiggins woman. Disgusting, if you want to know the truth.

Before I could say anything, he turned and breezed past me, on his way outside. With me tagging along behind him.

In the car again, I said, "Well, that was certainly instructive. I can see why you wouldn't want anybody around to witness a display of your investigative technique."

"Honey gets more flies than vinegar, or haven't you noticed?"

The car took off with a jerk and we were speeding down the street before I could answer. When I caught my breath, I said, "You were certainly spreading enough of it around in there."

He glanced over at me and, with a lopsided smile, said, "Keep watchin', hon. You might learn something."

I turned my head and looked out the side window, biting my lip to keep from teaching him a thing or two.

We made stops at two more large cineplexes, as they call those places these days, with me learning little more from Mr. Pickens's techniques than he'd already demonstrated.

"Let's try one last place," he said, throwing the car in gear and taking off so fast that the seatbelt tightened up on me.

The car careened down the streets, as he headed it right downtown, then brought it to a screeching halt in front of a dilapidated marquee with half its lights out, announcing that we were at the Adult Art Cinema.

"Where are we?" I asked, looking around at the empty sidewalk and dark store windows, several of them boarded up. It wasn't a part of town I was familiar with and, from the looks of it, I didn't want to know it any better.

"You don't want to go in this one," Mr. Pickens said as he opened his door. "Trust me."

"I've seen picture shows before, Mr. Pickens," I said, determined to show him that I was up for whatever it took. Opening my door to follow him, I told Little Lloyd to stay in and lock the doors.

I was right behind Mr. Pickens as he approached the ticket seller, an unhealthy-looking man who hardly listened to the questions, for staring so hard at me. I guessed he wasn't used to seeing a lady in that part of town. As Mr. Pickens went through his questioning ritual, I took note of the posters and nearly lost my breath.

I plucked at Mr. Pickens's coat to get his attention, and whispered, "Mr. Pickens, do you know what kind of shows they put on here? Hazel Marie would never come to something like this."

"You never know," he said, turning to me with a know-it-all grin that made me want to smack him. "I told you to stay in the car."

And he headed into the lobby, with me right behind him. Well, what else could I do?

I stood right inside the doors, fearful of taking another step, while Mr. Pickens went up to an usher who was looking through one of the magazines he had for sale. I wouldn't for the world mention what all was on the covers of those magazines but, believe me, they were a poor substitute for popcorn and Milk Duds.

"How you doin', Harry?" Mr. Pickens said, as he pulled Hazel Marie's picture from his pocket. I started to snatch it out of his hand, not wanting anything about her associated with what I was seeing.

But before I could do anything, it hit me that Mr. Pickens was showing an unnerving amount of familiarity with this Harry person, smiling and joking with him. What kind of man would patronize such a place? And drink beer, too? I backed up against the door and clutched my pocketbook with both hands, wondering what I'd gotten Little Lloyd and myself into. All I could do was pray that Mr. Pickens would hurry up and finish so we could get out of there.

"Ready?" he said, grabbing my arm and pulling me along with him as he hurried outside.

"More than," I said, trotting to keep up with him, anxious to shake the dust of that wicked place from my feet.

Chapter 10

By the time Mr. Pickens took us back to the Mexican restaurant where my car was parked, I couldn't say much for my first private investigative experience. And said as much to him.

"That's part of it," he told me as he parked beside my car, "and I warned you before we started. Knocking on doors, asking questions, stakeouts where you just sit and watch, going over and over the same things until something breaks, that's what an investigation is. When I was with the Charlotte-Mecklenberg PD, I cleared more cases than any other detective because I've got the patience for it."

He cocked an eye at me, as if to say I didn't.

"Give me your address," he went on, without a "please" or "do you mind" or anything else. He certainly liked to give orders, I'll say that for him. "I'll be over first thing in the morning to take a look at her room, see if there's anything that'll tell us where she might've gone. In the meantime, I want you to be writing down everything you can think of about this Hodge she went off with. Any ideas about him?"

"You don't want to hear the ideas I have about him," I said with a twist of my mouth. "I've never trusted a man with a mustache. . . ." I stopped, staring at the bushy thing under Mr. Pickens's nose, and corrected myself, ". . . with a *thin* mustache. The first place to start, though, would be with Pastor Ledbetter, who thinks the sun rises and sets in him, and knows him better than anybody. Leave that little matter to me, Mr. Pickens. I'll handle the pastor."

"Okay, but I'll need Hodge's full name and date of birth so I can track his credit card usage. I may want to interview your preacher, too."

"Feel free anytime you want to tackle him. But I warn you right now, the man'll likely hit you up for a donation to his building fund if you give him half a chance."

"Huh," he said, echoing my sentiments exactly.

I shook my head then, thinking of the time I'd wasted that day worrying myself sick instead of doing something. "I declare, Mr. Pickens,

I should've started making some inroads on Wilson T. before this, learning as much about his background as I could. All I can tell you is that he's been missing all day, too, if unanswered phone calls are any indication. He has a temporary apartment in Abbotsville while he's working for our church, although his permanent address is in Charlotte, I believe. I don't have that address or phone number, but I've called his local number a dozen times today, and he's not there. He hasn't been at the church, either. I'm convinced that he's the reason Hazel Marie is missing, but I don't want you considering any romantic eloping nonsense. She wouldn't do that to Little Lloyd and me, and she wouldn't be gone these twenty-four hours without letting us know something." I stopped, then told him what I really thought. "I might as well admit it. I've had my suspicions of Wilson T. Hodge from the first time I laid eyes on him."

"What's your problem with him?" Mr. Pickens asked, his eyebrows raised.

"He's a church fund-raiser. Does that answer your question?"

He nodded. "Oh, yeah."

His quick grasp of the situation gratified me, and I decided Mr. Pickens ought to have a little more background on Hazel Marie. Turning toward the back seat, I said, "Little Lloyd, jump on out and get in our car. I want a word with Mr. Pickens before we go."

When Little Lloyd had crawled out from behind my seat, I pulled the door to and told my new employee about my husband and Hazel Marie, their dozen or so years of illicit communion that I'd known nothing about although the whole town had and the result of that communion who'd been riding in his back seat. I told him how it'd just about killed me when I'd learned what Wesley Lloyd had been up to all those years at the same time he'd been an elder in the church and a dominating force at home and in his business.

"Everybody was amazed when I asked Hazel Marie and Little Lloyd to live with me, but I wanted to show the town that I could rise above the common crowd. And by that time we'd been through so much together, getting Wesley Lloyd's two wills straightened out and rescuing Little Lloyd from Brother Vern and nursing Hazel Marie back to health that, well, I'd just gotten used to having them around. Besides, that child needed a firm hand and a decent home, which I've been happy to provide." I stopped and thought for a minute. "Maybe another reason I took them in was to get back at Wesley Lloyd. His reputation meant everything to him, and I guess I wanted everybody to know what he really was. I'm not proud of that reason, Mr. Pickens, but I'm an honest woman."

I waited for him to say something but, when he didn't, I went on. "I can't say I blame Hazel Marie for taking up such a life and bearing a child out of wedlock. Well, maybe I did at first a little, but she was young and impressionable, and, well, you had to've known Wesley Lloyd to understand the situation."

"Good-looking man?"

"Oh, no. No, I can't say much for his looks. He was a man of will, I guess you'd say. Able to make people do what he wanted them to. Maybe that's why Hazel Marie and I took to each other so well; we'd both put up with him longer than we should've. Anyway, he's out of the picture now, and I hardly ever think of her and him together anymore."

He was impressed or, maybe, stunned at my Christian forbearance and said as much. Well, what he said was, "I hadn't figured you for the forgiving type, Mrs. Springer."

"I can't take much credit," I told him, "since it was easy enough with Wesley Lloyd in the ground. If I'd learned what he'd been up to while he was still around, it would've been a different story, let me tell you.

"Now you know the background," I went on, "but don't let the fact that she and the boy are not my blood kin slow you down. I've invested a lot in those two, my reputation in town, for one thing, since everybody thought I'd lost my mind by taking them in. I intend to prove them wrong. So, if Hazel Marie has gotten herself into head-line-making trouble—since I don't trust Wilson T. Hodge as far as I can throw him—I want to get her out before anybody knows about it." I stopped, mortally tempted to tell him about Brother Vern's latest effort to disrupt our lives, and how I had to hide Little Lloyd from the sheriff. Then I decided that the better part of discretion was to find out a little more about Mr. Pickens's views on law and order before trusting him to circumvent them.

"I'll find her," he said, giving me one of those smouldering looks again. "Count on it."

"That's what I'm doing, Mr. Pickens." And after hesitating a moment longer, tempted again to tell him everything, I bade him good night and got in my car. With my lips still sealed.

———

Little Lloyd and I didn't make much conversation on the way home. Night driving usually takes up most of my concentration, and he seemed tired and subdued. I tried to interest him in making a list of all we knew about his future stepfather, but I couldn't get much out of him. And the more I thought about it, the more I realized that we didn't know a whole lot about the man. He was from Charlotte, the so-called Queen City of the South, and he was part of a fund-raising organization that sent its employees all over the country when pastors needed outside help to pry money out of their congregations. He was what I called a typical salesman: an overly polite arm-twister and instigator of guilt. Wilson T. was selling Pastor Ledbetter's dream of a church complex that he could point to and say, "Look what I built." The pastor wanted the entire block filled with buildings, monuments to family values, family recreation and family fun.

Well, whoever heard of church being fun? That wasn't why I went but, if it had been, I certainly wouldn't've gone to the First Presbyterian Church of Abbotsville to find it.

As we came into town, my nerves began acting up on me again. All I needed was to see a patrol car, and I'd've probably gone through the roof. I glanced over at Little Lloyd as we crossed Main. He had his head leaning against the door and, at first, I thought he'd drifted off. I turned down Polk and slowed considerably, peering at the few cars parked along the street. If the sheriff had my house staked out, I wanted to know it before I drove in. Lord, I'd gotten nowhere in coming up with a safe place for Little Lloyd, what with going to one picture show after another with absolutely nothing to show for the effort, so all I could do was take him home again.

As I inched the car along, looking right and left for cars with light bars on top, he straightened up with a long sigh.

"Tired?"

"Yessum, a little." He slumped back in the seat and said, "I sure wish my mama was home. I'm getting real nervous about her."

"I am, too. But maybe Lillian's heard from her while we've been gone." I hated to give the child false hope, but I had to keep us both going. "Here we are."

As I turned into the driveway, relieved that no blue lights were flashing my way, I noticed lights on in the pastor's suite of offices over at the church. Another Building Fund Committee meeting, I supposed. Then, with a sudden flash, it occurred to me that it was a good time to check again on the whereabouts of Wilson T. Hodge. Maybe the pastor had heard from him or knew where he was.

Lights were on in the back of my house where I knew Lillian was holding down the fort and waiting for the phone to ring.

"Let's get inside, Little Lloyd," I said, stepping out of the car. "It's cold enough out here to freeze."

"Y'all find her?" Lillian had the back door open before we got up the steps.

"No'm, we went to all the movie houses, but nobody's seen her," Little Lloyd said with enough despair to wring my heart, as I followed him inside. "Has she called again?"

"No, honey, but y'all come on in here an' tell me about that private eye man."

"Little Lloyd," I said, smoothing down his hair that was full of electricity from the cold. "You tell Lillian about Mr. Pickens and how he goes about his investigating." Giving him a pat, I looked up over his head. "Lillian, they're having a meeting at the church, so I'm going over there to see if anybody's heard from Mr. Hodge. Now, while I'm gone, I want you to get this child in bed, but do it without turning on the lights in his room. I don't want anybody knowing he's home. Wait a minute, though. I just thought of something." I thought it through for a minute, then said, "We never know when Coleman'll show up to spend the night in his room, so maybe Little Lloyd's ought to stay empty. If Coleman takes a mind to look in on him, we don't want him to find anything. What do you think, Little Lloyd?"

He started wringing his hands in that nervous way of his, so I took one of them in mine. "I think," he said, "that I don't know where I'm going to sleep."

"Why, with me, of course. You don't mind, do you?"

"No'm, I guess not."

"Well, see, I know it's not the best solution, but Coleman would never open the door to my bedroom. He's too much of a gentleman, even though he is a deputy. Nobody but me and Lillian will go in there, so you'll be safe till I can figure something better or till your mother gets home. Which Mr. Pickens has assured us will be very soon. Lillian'll get you in bed, and I'll be back in a minute or two."

He started taking off his coat, then turning to me, he said, "I don't want you to get in trouble because of me."

"Lord, child, don't you worry about that. If the sheriff wants to put an old woman in the Atlanta Pen for taking care of her own, well, just let him try. We'll put him on *60 Minutes* and he couldn't get elected dogcatcher after that."

He gave me a quick smile, making me want to grab him and hold him close. Instead, I gave his arm a little squeeze and hurried outside.

I wrapped my coat around me against the cold and headed across the street. Just as I approached the back door of the church, several men walked out, some lighting cigarettes and others talking together as they went to their cars. Most of them nodded at me and all of them looked surprised to see me going into the church at that late hour. Gallivanting around after dark was not a customary practice for me. I hurried inside, not wanting to engage in conversation in which I knew my reasons for being abroad would be questioned. It was none of their business.

Heading for the pastor's office, I could hear the rumble of his voice as he spoke to a few stragglers from the committee. When he saw me, I saw the surprise on his face.

"Miss Julia, what're you doing out this time of night? Is anything wrong?" He came over to me, and I was pleased to note some evidence of concern over my welfare. The pastor had generally avoided my path ever since that episode last year when he'd tried to have me declared mentally incompetent, with the intent of getting himself appointed my financial guardian. Don't you just hate it when somebody thinks they know what's good for you better than you do, yourself? I hadn't had much use for him ever since.

"I need a few minutes of your time, pastor. I won't keep you long; I know you want to get home."

"Come on in here, then," he said, leading me into his dark paneled office as he said his last good-byes to those who were leaving. "Have a seat, Miss Julia, and tell me what I can do for you."

"I'm not going to stay that long," I said, refusing the chair he pointed to. "I need to know one thing. Was Wilson T. Hodge at your meeting tonight? It was the Building Committee, wasn't it?"

"Yes, it was. Now, Miss Julia, I know that you haven't yet come around to supporting our efforts for the Lord, but I hope you'll give it a lot of prayer and reconsider your position. The Lord has blessed you with considerable gifts, and it is our privilege to return those gifts to him. Whatever you give will come back to you sevenfold."

"That may be, pastor, but I don't need any more than I already have. So getting back more than I give is not an argument that cuts any ice with me. But I'm not here to discuss your athletic building or whatever it is, nor the means by which you plan to erect it, nor *where* you plan to erect it which is practically in my front yard. I'll take that up with you at another time. Right now, all I want to know is, was Wilson T. Hodge present tonight?"

"He's in Charlotte for a few days so, no, he wasn't here. But if you want to discuss your Building Fund pledge with him, I'll be glad to make an appointment for you and he'll see you as soon as he gets back."

The man had a one-track mind, and I didn't have the time or the energy to derail him, so I said, "When do you expect him back?"

"Sunday, at the latest. But the fund-raising drive continues apace even when he's not here. I'll tell you, Miss Julia, the committee is highly enthusiastic, though I know you and a few others were against our decision to bring him in. But professionals can do so much more than we can on our own. And Mr. Hodge is a true professional, just gets us all so spirit-filled and eager to erect that building for the glory of the Lord. It'll be a witness to everybody in the community."

"I'm sure it will be, pastor," I said, but refrained from mentioning just what it would be a witness to. "But to get back to the subject I'm interested in, when did you last speak with Mr. Hodge?"

"Why, just this morning, early. He called from his car phone to say he was needed for a few days at his Charlotte office. He assured me he'll be back by the Sunday morning worship service. You can speak to him then, if you want."

"He called you this morning?" So, where was Hazel Marie while he was doing this calling?

"Yes, he always lets me know when he has to leave town. Why? Is there a problem I can help you with?"

I glanced around his office, suitable for any business executive but hardly appropriate for the pastor of a church that couldn't support itself without holding auctions, bake sales and car raffles, wondering how much I should confide in him. He had not proved to be a solid rock on which I could stand in the past, but I could see no harm in planting a seed of worry in his mind. Especially since I knew Brother Vern had visited him that morning, and two more unlikely conspirators you'd never find anywhere.

"My problem is this, Pastor. Wilson T. Hodge and Hazel Marie left to go to Asheville yesterday evening for dinner and a movie. At least, that's what he said. Hazel Marie still hasn't come home, and it's been more than twenty-four hours and we don't know where she is. Now you tell me that Wilson T.'s gone to Charlotte, and that he called without saying one word to you, me or anybody about where *she* is. I want to know what he's done with her. That's my problem, and I want some help from you in tracking him down."

He lost his soothing, ministerial manner then, and began making excuses. "I, well, surely, you're mistaken. Wilson T. is as fine a man as I've ever known. He wouldn't just . . . Maybe he brought her home and she went off with somebody else before coming in?"

I had to lean against his desk, in an effort to keep myself collected as he began to lay blame on Hazel Marie. "That's the most foolish thing I've ever heard. Now, let me tell you another thing, Pastor," I went on with renewed vigor. "I know that Hazel Marie's uncle was over here today, because I saw his car, which can't be mistaken for anybody else's. And after that visit with you, the fool apparently went crazy and instituted legal proceedings that require Hazel Marie's presence. So I need an explanation from you as to what's going on between you and Brother Vernon Puckett, and I need an explanation from Wilson T. as to what he's done with Hazel Marie. And if I don't get them, I'm going to raise a hue and cry in this town the likes of which it's never seen."

"Well," he said, consternation spreading over his face as the possiblity of rumors and gossip floating around about his Christian fundraiser, as well as about his connection to Brother Vern, occurred to him. "Well, well, I'll be upfront with you, Miss Julia. I asked the Reverend Puckett to come by. Ecumenism is a big thing now, you know, and I thought, since he's had so much experience raising funds, that he could give me some pointers. I've been worried that some few of our members, like you for instance, haven't responded to our building fund drive as I'd hoped. And that means, of course, that the total hasn't, well, *isn't* where I expected it to be. In fact," he stopped, fingered the Bible on his desk, looking somewhat pensive, "it's way off. But the Lord always provides, so I know it'll work out."

"Let us hope so," I said, although I never minded giving the Lord a hand now and then. "But what I want Him to provide right now is Hazel Marie's whereabouts."

The pastor drew himself up and went on. "Well, as far as Ms. Puckett is concerned, I expect you misunderstood the situation. I mean, are you sure she went out with Wilson T.? He didn't mention her when he called. I don't want to distress you, but from the talk that's unhappily come to my attention, I understand that she's quite popular around town."

"*Talk?* What talk?"

"Now, Miss Julia, you understand," he said in the patronizing way he had that just burned me to a crisp, "that as a man of God, I don't engage in gossip or the passing on of rumors. It is my duty, and her uncle feels the same way, to issue a caution when certain actions of certain people give rise to untoward talk."

"I don't have an idea in the world of what you're talking about." And if he'd had an idea of the head of steam I was building up, he'd've backed off right then. But no, not him.

"I'm just saying that our church members have to be like Caesar's wife. And Ms. Puckett even more so, given her past history which you, of all people, know so well. Understand me, now, I'm not saying anything against her; it's been my privilege to instruct her in Presbyterian theology and she's been an apt pupil. But, Miss Julia, you know that where there's smoke, you're likely to find some fire. The Reverend Puckett said as much just this morning and he knows her better than anybody. He's deeply concerned about some of her more recent activities that've given rise to rumors and gossip."

"Stop right there," I said, holding up my hand. "I'm not about to let you or that unprincipled uncle of hers slur Hazel Marie's name. I don't know who else you've been listening to, but you ought to know by now that Brother Vernon Puckett would do and say anything to get his hands on Little Lloyd and the funds Wesley Lloyd left him, and I'll tell you right now that's not going to happen. I'll have you know that Hazel Marie's conducted herself better than Caesar's wife ever hoped to do. Although I don't know what a dead Roman has to do with it. She hasn't gone out with anybody but Wilson T. Hodge since she's been in my house, so if you need to caution anybody I'd recommend a word to him." I took a deep breath and barreled on. "And, I will remind you that the only reason she went out with him in the first place was because he was said to be a church-going man and a committed Christian. By *you,* Pastor. So you can take comfort in the fact that at least one person in your congregation listens to you, and believes what you say. Now look what's come of it."

"Okay, okay. I'll tell you what I'll do," he said, quickly backpedaling from throwing off on Hazel Marie when I brought up Wilson T. again. "I'll call his Charlotte office first thing tomorrow. I was planning to do that anyway, since there's this other little matter concerning the fund's balance I need to talk with him about. Nothing for you to worry about, but at least we'll know something."

"No, we won't. All we'll know is whether he's in Charlotte or not. And I'll tell you one thing, he better *not* be there, going about his business like nothing's wrong. If Hazel Marie's in trouble, he better be in the same trouble. The idea of a man taking her out and leaving her somewhere! One thing you need to know, Pastor, I intend to track him down and get some answers. And to that end, I want his Charlotte address and his date of birth. Social Security number, too, and anything else that's on his job application form."

"What? Why? I can't give out that information."

"You can either give it to me," I informed him, "or you can give it to Lieutenant Peavey or the private investigator I've hired."

Consternation wasn't the word this time. Pastor Ledbetter's face went white at the thought of a police search for and an investigation into the man he'd backed, pushed, praised and recommended to his congregation. If Hazel Marie was suffering from town gossip, without a reason in the world for it other than Brother Vern trying to besmirch her any way he could, then just wait till word got around about Wilson T. Hodge and his shifty ways.

"Miss Julia, please," he said, his hand raised to ward me off, "let's not do anything rash."

"Oh, Pastor, you know me. I never take a step without knowing where my foot's coming down."

The pastor gave me the information I wanted, albeit reluctantly, and I left him in a discomfited state of mind and went home. I was quite pleased that my investigative technique had gotten some results, contrary to some other techniques I'd recently observed. Which I fully intended to mention to Mr. Pickens.

Chapter 11

I hurried back across the parking lot, watching out for the pastor's stakes and strings so I wouldn't break my neck, and thinking to myself that it was past time for him to get a call to another church. It'd been my experience that the Lord never called a preacher to a smaller, less affluent congregation than the one he was in, it being plain that the Lord believes in progress and upward mobility as much as any American. But would you ever get a preacher to admit to such a thing? No, you wouldn't. I've heard preacher after preacher in my day get up in the pulpit and with a long face and sadness dripping from his words announce that the Lord had called him elsewhere. He acts as if it's a matter of great regret to him, as if he's making a huge sacrifice to obey the Lord's leading and accept a call to a larger church and a bigger salary. Have you ever noticed that?

I decided then and there that if Pastor Ledbetter kept on at me to contribute to a monument to his pastorate and if he didn't relocate same from in front of my house and if he said one more word against Hazel Marie, I was going to see if I couldn't arrange a call from the Lord. I knew some Presbyterians in a large church down in South Carolina who were looking for a preacher. A note to the effect that Pastor Ledbetter might be open to a move should do the trick. I might even be open to contributing to the salary they were offering, just to get him away from here. If I could get away with it.

When I opened the kitchen door, Lillian started up from her chair with a face as long and mournful as the ones I'd been thinking about.

" 'Bout time you got yo'self back here," she said. "I been worriet sick."

"What's going on? Have you heard from her?" I took off my coat and hung it up. "Little Lloyd gone to bed?"

"Yessum, he already down, an' I hope don't no deputies an' the like try to come an' get him. An', no'm, I ain't heard from Miss Hazel Marie, but I heard from somebody else."

Tears welled up in her eyes, and my heart skipped a beat. "Who? What's happened, Lillian?"

"Deputy Bates, he come by not long after you left. An' he say he know you been lookin' for him, an' I tell him Miss Hazel Marie missin' an' that's what you want with him. He say he already heard that an' he got somethin' important to talk to you 'bout, an' him an' that Lieutenat Peavey want to see you down at the sheriff's at eight o'clock in the morning an' it have to do with Miss Hazel Marie."

"Oh, dear Lord." I took hold of the counter and hung on to it. "What in the world does that mean? Did he say?"

"No'm, well, kinda, but he say he have to talk to you. I mean, he real businesslike, come to the front do' an' all, an' he jes' say it serious."

"Wait a minute, let me get this straight. Was Deputy Bates looking for Little Lloyd like Deputy Daly was?"

"That's what I thought, an' I was gettin' scared, 'cause I don't know I can tell Deputy Bates a bareface lie. But he didn't ast, an' I didn't bring it up. He say he need to talk to you 'bout Miss Hazel Marie."

"Oh," I gasped, patting my breast, "what could he want to talk about? What if she's in jail somewhere? And Brother Vern found out about it and that's why he filed for custody? But no, how would he know something before the sheriff, and Lieutenant Peavey didn't know a thing this afternoon." I grabbed a dish towel and started wringing it worse than Lillian ever had, my heart pounding. "But I'll bet you money that Brother Vern knows Hazel Marie can't answer that summons. Why else would he pounce right at this time?" I stopped as a chilling possibility filled my mind. "Oh, Lillian! We could lose that child just like we've lost his mother. He could end up in an orphanage or living in that Cadillac of Brother Vern's, being carted around from one revival to the next." I felt the blood drain from my head as I clutched at the counter again to keep from falling into a dead faint.

"You jes' stop that," Lillian said, grabbing my arm. "This ain't no time to be weakin' down on us. Don't matter what Brother Vern knows or don't know, what we got to do is keep Little Lloyd safe somewheres. Then we can find out the rest of it." She gave my arm a shake. "You hear me, now."

"Yes, you're right. I'm all right now." And I was, knowing that it was entirely up to me, and I determined to be entirely up to it. I took a deep breath. "What I have to do is brace myself for whatever Lieutenant Peavey and Coleman have to tell me, and figure out what kind of story to tell them if they straight out ask me where Little Lloyd is."

"If they got something bad to tell you 'bout Miss Hazel Marie, you gonna be so done in you not be able to tell 'em anything."

"Well, that's true," I said, with some relief that I wouldn't be put on the spot with maintaining a lie. Then I sank down in a chair. "Oh, my word, Lillian, I don't want to get out of it that way. No, no, I'm not even going to plan for that. I'm going to get my story straight and stick to it." I straightened up with a new thought. "I know! I'll tell them Little Lloyd went with Wilson T. and his mother to the movies, and he's been missing as long as they have. That'll do it."

"Then they gonna ast you why you didn't say so when you reported his mama missin'."

"Oh. Well, I'll think of something. Which brings me to the problem of thinking of something, or some*where*, to really hide him. We can't keep him here, with me planning to be gone all tomorrow with Mr. Pickens. Who knows, Brother Vern could get a search warrant and snatch him out of here." I rubbed my forehead as all kinds of dire possibilities roiled around behind it. "Lillian, I'm beginning to get an idea."

"What kind you gettin'?"

"I'm getting an idea of putting that child where nobody'll think to look, and if I can manage it, Lillian, I'm going to lie through my teeth about it. Although I don't think this kind of thing is really a lie, do you? I mean, when you're doing it for somebody else's good?"

"I don't know 'bout that, but it don't worry me none. Where you gonna put him?"

"I better not tell you. I don't want you to be in a situation where you have to lie, too. The less you know, the better."

"You don't think I can lie as good as you?" She glared at me like I'd insulted her. Maybe I had.

"That's not it. I just thought you'd rather not have to lie about it. I mean, Lillian, when that Lieutenant Peavey looks at you through those dark glasses of his, well, it makes you want to beg him to let you confess."

"Well, you right 'bout that. I tell you what, don't tell me now, but if I ast you again, you go ahead an' tell me."

"Count on it, as Mr. Pickens says. And that reminds me, he'll be over here early tomorrow morning to go through Hazel Marie's things, just when I have to be in Lieutenant Peavey's office. Give him this information on Wilson T. that I just finagled out of the pastor," I said, handing her a sheet of paper where I'd copied down Wilson T.'s personal statistics. "And let Mr. Pickens look wherever he wants except in my room, where I want you to keep Little Lloyd, and don't let Mr. Pickens leave till I get back."

"How I gonna keep a grown man around if he want to go?"

"Tell him the truth, Lillian, which is always the best policy." She frowned at me. "You know what I mean, it's the best policy except in cases where it's better not to. He'll need to know whatever I find out, though, since it has to do with Hazel Marie, and she's the one he's looking for. Just don't say anything to him about Little Lloyd's problem."

"You want me to hide Little Lloyd from him?"

"Yes, pretend he's in school. It shouldn't even come up, if you don't say anything. Let him assume the child's not around."

"Look like you don't trust him too good."

"Oh, I do. It's just that I don't know how *legal* he feels he has to be. I'm sure not going to keep a secret from Sam and Binkie and Coleman, and then tell a perfect stranger who might turn right around and hand Little Lloyd over to the sheriff. I've got to feel Mr. Pickens out first. If he's like me and you, he'll keep a secret no matter how illegal it is. But if he's not, well, we'll keep him in the dark, and do what we have to do by ourselves."

"Well, I hope you figure out what it is we have to do by ourselves. And do it before mornin' comes which, if you ast me, ain't too long in comin'."

"You're right. You are staying over, aren't you?"

"I'm not about to leave with all this goin' on. I already got that cot made up in the spare bedroom."

"Lillian, for pity's sake, use the bed. You don't need to be pulling your back out, sleeping on a cot. Now let's turn these lights off and go on up."

After I made sure Lillian would sleep in the bed by taking the covers off the cot, I went into my room. I looked down on Little Lloyd, all scrunched up on the far side of my bed, and felt the anger well up in me at the idea of Brother Vern getting his greedy hands on the child. He didn't want him for any other reason than the money Wesley Lloyd had left, and I didn't see how in the world any judge wouldn't see that right off the bat.

I tucked the covers up around Little Lloyd more tightly and smoothed his hair down where it stuck up in the back. He moaned a little in his sleep, dreaming, I guessed, of all the troubles piled on top of him.

I stood by the side of the bed and silently promised him that nobody was going to take him away from his mother or, if she couldn't be found—which made my heart sink—from me. I'd take the both of them to Canada or even to Timbuktu if that's what it came down to.

Chapter 12

I declare, I didn't think I'd be able to sleep with another person in bed with me. I'd gotten so used to sleeping alone since Wesley Lloyd had been put to rest in the Good Shepherd Memorial Cemetery, that I doubted I'd get any rest at all. Having the bed all to myself made getting into it something to look forward to. Not having the covers jerked off or being kicked during somebody else's nightmare or made to suffer through hours of ear-splitting snores seemed to me to be one of the blessings of widowhood. I'd said as much to a more recent widow of my acquaintance, trying to show her the bright side of her situation, and she'd said none of that had ever bothered her because the cuddling she got more than made up for it.

I wasn't able to judge one way or the other, since Wesley Lloyd had never been the cuddling type.

I crawled into bed beside Little Lloyd, and he hardly stirred. I lay there for a while, fuming over Brother Vern and Pastor Ledbetter and worrying about Hazel Marie. And then switched to wondering what Lieutenant Peavey and Coleman were going to pile on me the next morning, and trying to get all my stories straight in my mind. Laying part of the burden before the Lord, I told him that he was just going to have to look out for Hazel Marie by himself, while I made sure of Little Lloyd's safety. When that was taken care of, I'd be happy to take up Hazel Marie again.

To that effect, I began going over what we needed to do to keep the child occupied while Mr. Pickens, or whoever else dropped by, was in the house. Schoolbooks, I thought, and sat bolt upright in the bed. Lord, his schoolbooks were in his room, which if anybody noticed, especially that sharp-eyed Mr. Pickens or Lieutenant Peavey, or Coleman for that matter, they'd know the boy was neither in school nor had he spent the night with a friend.

I got up and put on my robe and slippers, shivering in the cold since the furnace automatically cooled down during the night hours, and slipped across the hall to Little Lloyd's room. I dared not turn on a light, for fear that Deputy Daly or somebody was watching, but there was enough glow from the church's safety lights and the street lamp for me to make my way to his desk. I gathered up his books and notebook and backpack, and tiptoed back across the hall. I slid them all under my bed and had my robe halfway off when I thought of something else.

I hurried as quietly as I could past the room where Lillian slept, and crept down the stairs. Feeling my way into the kitchen, I took the boy's coat and toboggan cap off the hook by the door, and carried them with me back up the stairs.

Back in my room with the door shut, I hung them in my closet, then sat down for a minute to decide if there was anything else out in plain view that would give away his whereabouts.

There was. I went back across the hall to his bathroom and got his toothbrush, comb and a washcloth that was still damp, and took them with me. And while I was at it, got a change of clothes for him for the next day. Lord, when you set out to lie, you have to think of every little thing.

When I finally crawled back into bed, I didn't think I'd sleep a wink, what with having traipsed all over the house in the dark and having Little Lloyd mumbling and moaning in his sleep and having so many worries on my own mind.

But I did. In fact, I got a good night's sleep, which just goes to show that your conscience won't bother you if you know you're in the right.

————

I was ready to leave for my meeting with Lieutenant Peavey and Deputy Bates by seven-thirty the next morning. Lillain fussed at me for not eating any breakfast but, I declare, I was too nervous to risk putting anything on my stomach. Coffee was all I could stand, and even that was sloshing around in a threatening sort of way.

"Now, Lillian," I said, smoothing on my gloves. I'd dressed with extra care that morning, wearing a fox fur hat and one of my Sunday woolens under my new winter-white cashmere coat with a fox fur collar. It was the kind of ensemble that LuAnne called a CCC—country club, church and cemetery outfit. One that was suitable for all the ceremonies of life, and I figured that being summoned to a conference at the sheriff's department qualified for ceremonial attire. Besides, I wanted Lieutenant Peavey to know I was somebody he shouldn't be messing with, although not much had stopped him in the past. "Be sure and see that Little Lloyd stays behind closed doors. And don't let anybody in the house but Mr. Pickens. I don't care who comes to the door."

"How I gonna know who he is?" She was spooning grits onto a plate for Little Lloyd. A tray with a glass of milk and a plate of biscuits waited on the counter.

"You won't have any trouble recognizing him," I said, as I pinned my hat on more firmly. "Just look for a big, black mustache and he'll be behind it. Besides, Lillian, he'll have identification, and he drives a beat-up black two-door car with a loud motor. You can't miss him. He's one of those men who take up a lot more space than their size justifies. Although he's big enough to begin with."

She grunted, frowning at my description, then wiped her hands on a dish towel and came over to the counter where I was standing. "What you reckon that lieutenant and Coleman gonna tell you 'bout Miss Hazel Marie? I'm jes' so worriet, I can't hardly think what kinda news they got. An' after I get so roiled up 'bout that, I start worryin' 'bout them wantin' to take Little Lloyd."

"I know what you mean, and I'm sick about it too. But I can't put off facing them any longer. At least we'll know what we have to contend with." I took a deep breath and headed for the door. "We have to depend on each other, Lillian, and I'm depending on you to keep Little Lloyd hidden and to keep Mr. Pickens here till I get back. Be sure and give him that information I got from the pastor, so he can start tracing Wilson T. Well, I'm going now. Wish me luck."

"Yessum, and me too. We both gonna need it."

———

Coleman came out to the pitiful waiting room at the sheriff's department to meet me. He touched me on the arm to draw me aside before we headed for Lieutenant Peavey's office, and said, "Lillian told me last night about Hazel Marie. Have you heard anything from her yet?"

"Not one word. Oh, Coleman, I am so worried."

He frowned, glanced down the hall and apologized for not being able to meet with me the day before, saying he'd been on a raid. Then he said, "Things're getting messy, Miss Julia. I wasn't here when Brother Vern came in yesterday, but I heard about it. Everybody's talking about how he went to the clerk of court's office, demanding immediate action, saying that Hazel Marie's not caring for the boy and that Lloyd needed to be in protective custody. Then he came over here to see that we served the papers right away." He stopped and looked straight at me. "Then I heard that you'd come in yesterday to report Hazel Marie missing. That was not good news, Miss Julia, because it gave Brother Vern's claims credibility. At least, a judge might see it that way. I hate to tell you this, but you'll have to give up the boy temporarily. At least until his mother gets back to answer the complaint and prove her fitness as a parent, which we can all testify to. Where is Lloyd, anyway?"

"He spent the night with somebody," I said. Which was as true a statement as I'd ever made.

"We'll be picking him up this morning. I'm just as sorry as I can be about it, but we're required by law to do it when a complaint like this is made. Now, Miss Julia, don't get upset. Once Hazel Marie appears before the judge, the whole thing won't amount to a hill of beans. She's just got to get back here for the hearing. And, ah, that may present a problem, which is what Lieutenant Peavey wants to talk to you about."

Lord, I'd never seen Coleman so serious in my life. What was coming through to me was that, without Hazel Marie, Brother Vern could have Little Lloyd impounded in his care. All I could do at the time was clutch my pocketbook to my bosom and try to temper my pulse as the blood pounded in my head. I nodded at Coleman, unable to get a word out, and followed him on down the hall.

Knocking once on Lieutenant Peavey's office door, Coleman opened it and waited for me to precede him. I did, to be greeted by the lieutenant who, to my surprise, stood and welcomed me. He gestured to the chair in front of his desk and asked me to be seated. I did, as Coleman took a chair at the side of the desk.

The three of us sat for a few moments waiting, it seemed to me, for somebody to open the show. I certainly wasn't going to do it, since I'd been the one summoned and, besides, I'd come of my own accord the day before and gotten nowhere for my trouble. Not to mention the fact that Lieutenant Peavey's unexpected courtesy was scaring me to death.

"Mrs. Springer," Lieutenant Peavey began, "you reported a Hazel Marie Puckett missing yesterday."

It wasn't a question, but I answered it anyway. "I did."

"Have you heard from her?"

"Not since the telephone call I told you about and which you said indicated she wasn't missing."

He squirmed just a little in his chair. "Well, just to refresh my memory, you reported that she went off with a," he paused to consult a folder in front of him, "Wilson T. Hodge on Wednesday night and, other than the phone call, you've not seen or heard from her since. Correct?"

"Why? Have you found her?" My heart began to thud, as I waited to be told that she'd been found in a condition I didn't want to think about. Then, just as I thought I was beginning to hyperventilate, I reassured myself that Coleman wouldn't've let me learn of it this way. He'd have come to the house and stayed until I got there. He'd have been there to comfort Little Lloyd and me. Or certainly he'd've prepared me for the worst out in the hall. No, I told myself, they haven't found her; this little meeting had to be about something else.

"No, we haven't found her," Lieutenant Peavey said, scanning the papers in the folder again. "A coupla questions, Mrs. Springer, before we get to her whereabouts. First off, when was the last time you saw her?"

"Night before last. She left to go to dinner and a movie with Wilson T. Hodge." I thought I'd already told him that.

He wrote something on his paper, then, without looking up, asked, "She a race fan?"

"What?"

"Does she go to the races? NASCAR races? Make a little bet now and again?"

"I should say not!" If I could've sat up any straighter, I would have. "Hazel Marie's a fine, Christian woman who neither races nor gambles. What in the world makes you ask such a question?"

He and Coleman exchanged glances, then he said, "Deputy Bates, here, has something to show you. Deputy?"

Coleman took a small plastic bag from the side of the desk, opened it, and spilled a tiny gold something or other out on the desk in front of me. "You recognize this, Miss Julia?"

I bent down to look at the thing, glanced up at the worried frown on Coleman's face and wondered if mine was giving anything away. "What is it?" I asked, playing for time.

"Looks like a charm from a bracelet," Coleman said, "or maybe a pendant from a necklace. Could it be Hazel Marie's?"

I wasn't ready to commit myself, not knowing where they'd found it nor what its presence in their possession meant to Hazel Marie's welfare. I wished Mr. Pickens or Binkie or Sam was there to advise me but, as usual, I was left to take care of everything myself.

"I'm not sure," I said, reaching out to touch the little thing with my finger, turning it right side up. Yes, there was the opal on the top of the miniature baby shoe. "Where did you find it?"

Lieutenant Peavey shifted in his chair. I gasped with a sudden thought. "You didn't find it in a wreck, did you? Oh, Lord, Coleman, it didn't come from some poor woman so mashed up in a wreck that you couldn't recognize her?"

"No, no, Miss Julia," Coleman said, reaching out to hold my hand. "Don't think that. It didn't come from a wreck, and it wasn't taken from a body. It was found in a warehouse that we raided yesterday, along with some incriminating evidence of a crime that was committed in another jurisdiction. We're just trying to trace the owner of this, hoping for a lead."

"Well," I said, keeping my expression as neutral as possible and pretending that the thought of Hazel Marie being in the midst of incriminating evidence had not shaken me to my core. It was a settled fact that I'd never admit recognizing the charm as the one I'd given Hazel Marie to commemorate Little Lloyd's birthday last October. She loved the clash and jangle of the charm bracelet I'd started for her soon after the two of them moved in with me. "You're on the wrong track then. Hazel Marie's not the criminal type, but I know a few who are. What kind of evidence are you talking about, and who does it incriminate?"

"Whoever owns this." Lieutenant Peavey was bad for giving short answers. He stared at me through those dark glasses like he could see right into my mind and read the thoughts that I was trying to keep from him. "All we need to know now is, do you recognize it as belonging to the person you reported missing?"

"I didn't exactly *report* her missing," I corrected him. "I *told* you she was missing, but you refused to make a report."

"Look," he said, hunching those huge shoulders over the desk. "I need some straight answers. This thing," he poked it with a finger twice as wide as the charm, "was found in a warehouse at Jessup Mountain in the southern part of this county, along with some pieces of computer disks that were stolen a few days ago from a well-known NASCAR driver down in Rockingham. Now, the Rockingham deputies notified us that they'd found a monogrammed baseball cap at the scene of the crime that was apparently left by one of the thieves. That cap points directly to the race team who had their shop set up in the warehouse here, which means somebody in our jurisdiction was involved in, or knows something about, the Rockingham theft. Namely, the owner of this trinket."

"Wait," I said, acting confused and trying to put him in the same condition. "Are you saying that this," I pointed at the charm, "was stolen in Rockingham? Or found in Rockingham? Or that Hazel Marie lost a cap? Why, she doesn't even own a baseball cap."

"No, that's not what I'm saying." Lieutenant Peavey looked peeved. He hiked himself up in his chair and spoke slowly and deliberately. "Look, Mrs. Springer, we're dealing with two racing teams." He counted on his fingers, so I'd be sure to follow him. "One is a big, famous operation in Rockingham, and that's the one that was robbed. The other team has two shops, one in Rockingham and one here at the Jessup Mountain warehouse. We found this thing," he pointed to the charm, "in the warehouse *here,* along with some broken computer disks that'd been stolen from the first shop *there.* The Rockingham sheriff found a cap in the shop that was robbed, and that cap had the logo of the team located here. You following me? They're connected in some way, is what I'm saying."

I tried to look addled, which wasn't hard considering my state of mind. Lieutenant Peavey frowned, then carried on. "Whoever owns this trinket," he said, "may know something that will lead to an arrest and the recovery of the other stolen goods. You reported a woman missing during the very time the warehouse was being raided and, if you can identify this as hers, it'll give us a direction to go in."

I was stunned, to say the least. I looked at Coleman, hoping for a little help and he responded.

"Miss Julia, you need to understand," he said, in a calming sort of way. "This is big. The disks and some other valuable stuff was stolen from Jerry Johnson. You ever heard of him?" I shook my head, unable to speak. "Well, he's a big-name NASCAR race driver, and he's got friends all over. The media's giving it a big play, especially since something we *didn't* recover is important to his career."

Things were taking a turn that I didn't at all like. I couldn't understand why the loss of this Jerry Johnson's material goods was getting more concern than my loss of Hazel Marie, nor how her charm had turned up where crooks had hung out. I needed to get home and place it all in the hands of my own investigator.

"If this thing," Lieutenant Peavey said, poking the charm again, "belongs to the woman you reported missing, then she's a suspect and we need her in here for questioning."

"A *suspect?*" I shrieked, jumping up from my chair. "Now see here, Lieutenant, I'm not going to sit here and have you accuse a woman who's not here to defend herself of a crime. The woman's in trouble, and all you can do is try to connect her to some criminal activity, when all she's done is not come home when she should've. Through no fault of her own, I am convinced."

"Miss Julia," Coleman said, standing with me and putting an arm around my shoulders. "That's not what we're doing. I'm concerned about Hazel Marie too, and all we want to know is whether she might've been at a place where evidence of a crime was found. She could've been there weeks ago and lost it then. She's not being accused of anything. We just want to question her and try to find some answers."

I stepped away and pulled myself together. "Well, that may well be, but I can't go so far as to definitely identify the charm as hers. The fact of the matter is, half the women in town own jewelry of this nature."

Lieutenant Peavey sighed like he was tired of fooling with me, and said, "We know that, Mrs. Springer, but half the women in town haven't been reported missing. Do you know of any reason this Hazel Marie Puckett would've been at the Jessup Mountain warehouse?"

"I do not." That was one question I could answer with assurance. "It's not hers, if that's all you have to go on. She was with Wilson T. Hodge when she left my house, and a man like that wouldn't be caught dead in a place where he might get his hands dirty."

I stopped and bit my lip again. "You didn't find him dead, did you?"

"We didn't find anybody, dead or otherwise," the lieutenant said, as if he hated to admit it. In fact, it looked as if it was all he could do to keep from grinding his teeth.

"Well, Wilson T. Hodge's the one you ought to be looking for. Find him and you'll find Hazel Marie. Although, I don't know what she could tell you about this." I waved my hand toward the charm, as if it didn't start my heart pounding every time I looked at it.

"Well, we're going to get to the bottom of it," he snapped. And this time I heard his teeth scrape together. "One way or the other. Now tell me more about this Hodge. Where can we locate him?"

"I wish I knew. According to Pastor Ledbetter of the First Presbyterian Church, Mr. Hodge is in Charlotte but, as far as I'm concerned, he better not be. But the pastor can tell you more about Wilson T. Hodge than I can, and I know he'd be happy to assist you."

It couldn't hurt to spread the lieutenant's attention around a little. I sank back into my chair and leaned my head in my hand. "This is so upsetting," I said. "I'm sorry I'm not being much help to you, but so much worry . . . I'm not as young as I once was and I'm not handling all this too well." I sniffed, and rummaged in my pocketbook for a Kleenex.

Coleman was immediately solicitous, leaning over me and telling me not to worry. Lieutenant Peavey, when I peeked at him, didn't seem impressed.

Chapter 13

"I think I'd better go home now," I quavered, holding on to Coleman and rising to my feet. "I have these weak spells, don't you know. The medication helps a little."

The only medication I was on was an aspirin every now and again, and a dose of Metamucil when I needed it, but they didn't need to know that. Especially since Coleman was worried enough to offer to drive me home. I hated pulling the wool over his eyes, but I had to get out of there before Lieutenant Peavey asked any more questions. I didn't quite make it.

"Mrs. Springer," Lieutenant Peavey said, standing to his full height. "Sorry you're not feeling well, but there's one more thing. Ms. Puckett's son, where is he?"

I stopped and leaned against Coleman, afraid to turn around and face the man. "Right at this minute, I don't know, Lieutenant," I whispered shakily. "But I'm sure I can put my hands on him later today. Let's hope so, anyway."

I felt Coleman stiffen. "Is Lloyd missing too? Why didn't you tell me?"

Lord, I hated to lie to him, and I tried my best not to. "I kept trying to reach you yesterday. I wanted to talk to you, and oh, Coleman, you just don't know."

Lieutenant Peavey frowned. "You didn't say anything about a missing child yesterday."

"You didn't give me a chance," I snapped. Then, afraid I'd given myself away, I wiped my eyes and whispered, "I wasn't sure. I assumed he was in school, but . . . Oh, Coleman, I don't know how I can bear up under this strain." I cried as best as I could manage.

Lieutenant Peavey frowned some more and when he finally spoke, I detected some concern in his voice. "You know we have a court order to remove the child." He thought for a little, then went on, "Maybe that's why they're both missing."

"I don't think so, Lieutenant," Coleman said. "Miss Julia reported Ms. Puckett missing before her uncle filed the complaint."

"You're right, Coleman," I said before the lieutenant could respond. "She went missing Wednesday night, and Deputy Daly showed up at my house with his papers late yesterday. According to him, the complaint had just been made, so she couldn't've known about it. And, Coleman, that deputy said he was there to snatch and grab Little Lloyd. Can he do that? Are you going to let him do that?"

I heard Lieutenant Peavey make some kind of irritated noise down in his throat. "That's a term that shouldn't've been used. Deputy Daly is new on the force, so just ignore what he said. But a complaint's been filed, so we're obligated to pick up the child. He'll be held in protective custody until his mother appears to present her side. Then a judgment'll be rendered."

A hot flame surged through me at the idea of North Carolina laws that let a conniving you-know-what like Brother Vern make unfounded claims and tear up all our lives. I made an effort to control myself so Coleman, who was still letting me lean against him, wouldn't notice. "Lieutenant Peavey," I said, as pitifully as I could, "how's his mother going to answer anything if she can't be found?"

Lieutenant Peavey wouldn't let go of anything, in spite of my weakened condition. He shrugged just enough to make me want to smack him. "That's a problem, from her viewpoint, but we're responsible to the court. He'll be picked up as soon as he's located, with or without his mother."

Coleman nodded, but I could tell he wasn't happy about it. He knew how much Little Lloyd meant to me and Lillian, to say nothing of his mother. I scrunched up my shoulders and headed for the door, wanting out of there before I heard any more distressing news.

"Mrs. Springer," the lieutenant said, stopping me again just as I thought I was on my way. "What about the private investigator you asked me about?"

I didn't know what to tell him, so deep in lies by that time that I didn't know which end was up. So I hedged. "I have an appointment with him this morning." Which was the absolute truth.

"You don't need to do that, Miss Julia," Coleman said. "Let us take care of it. We'll find them both, and quicker than any private agency can."

"Well, if you think you can," I said, letting him think whatever he wanted to. "I just know that Lieutenant Peavey recommended a Mr. Pickens, and I know Lieutenant Peavey wouldn't steer me wrong. I was just doing what the lieutenant seemed to think was the best thing to do, but if he's changed his mind, I'll talk to Mr. Pickens this morning."

With that, I finally got out of the office and headed toward the front door. Coleman followed me, offering a ride, concerned about my condition, telling me they'd do everything they could, and that I didn't need to worry myself.

Hah, was all I could think, but didn't say. Coleman had a good heart, but he was a signed and sworn deputy sheriff and, as such, limited by the law. I was neither.

Thanking him, I assured him my car was near and that I could make it home all right, and that I had complete trust in the Abbot County Sheriff's Department.

Alone in my car at last, all I could think about was whether Mr. Pickens was waiting for me at the house. I needed him worse than I had at anytime before.

————

I hurried into the house through the kitchen door, having left my car half off the driveway in my agitation. Lillian was setting a plate of hot cinnamon rolls before Mr. Pickens, who was sitting at the table with a cup of coffee in front of him. They both turned to me as I entered.

"Mr. Pickens," I cried. "I'm so glad you're here. I've got news, and you need to do something about it right away."

I hung up my coat and went on before either of them could speak. "Lillian, pour some more of that coffee and sit down with us."

I pulled out a chair and plopped down, wondering where to start. Mr. Pickens just waited, watching me from under his black eyebrows.

While I tried to get my breath, he reached across and patted my hand. "Take it easy, hon. Don't get yourself in a tizzie; just tell me what you found out."

To my mind, I had enough reason to get into two or three tizzies, but I let it go and told them about the charm that the police had found.

Mr. Pickens frowned, and Lillian asked, "Was it Miss Hazel Marie's?"

"Of course it was. Don't you remember, I had it custom made with Little Lloyd's birthstone. They found it at that warehouse they raided, which turned out to be a place of racing criminals, so I didn't let on that I recognized it. And, Mr. Pickens, it was *broken*. I mean, the little gold link that held it to her bracelet was pulled apart." I grasped the edge of the table, wanting him to reassure me. "That doesn't mean what I think it does, does it?"

"Let's don't jump to conclusions," he said, sounding too calm to suit me. "It could mean that it'd been loose and just dropped off there.

It could mean that she snagged it on something and it fell off by itself. It could mean a lot of things but, if you're sure it's hers, it does mean that she was there at some time, but not necessarily in the past few days."

"No, she was there recently, I just know it. Because, if she'd lost it before this, she'd've said something about it. She loved that charm. She'd've turned the house upside down, crying and looking for it, wouldn't she, Lillian? So, no, Mr. Pickens, she had to've lost it sometime since she's been gone. The problem is, I can't for the life of me figure out what she'd've been doing with a racing team down in the southern wilds of the county. I mean, there's nothing down there but woods and thickets and dirt roads. And hunters and marijuana patches. Oh, Lord," I moaned, thinking of men with rifles and machetes, and I didn't know what all.

"Thay Lord," Lillian said, sinking into a chair. "What that pore woman doin' down there with them mean folks?"

Mr. Pickens hunched over the table, twirling a spoon while he thought about it. At least I hoped he was giving it some thought. He glanced up at me, and said, "No reason at all for her to be down there? She's not into racing?"

"I should say not. Lieutenant Peavey asked the same thing. I don't know what she could've been doing in such a place. In fact, I don't know what *anybody* would be doing there."

"Peavey didn't tell you anything else? Why the cops raided the Jessup Mountain shop in the first place?"

"Well, now that you mention it, he did. Not that I understood it all, but he said there'd been a theft from some big-time race-car driver in Rockingham, and one of the thieves lost his cap. In a hurry to get away, I guess. But some way or another, that cap pointed to the Jessup Mountain racing team, which is why the Rockingham deputies told our deputies to raid the place. All of which culminated in finding Hazel Marie's charm, along with some broken computer disks that'd been stolen, too. And from that little coincidence, Lieutenant Peavey called Hazel Marie a suspect and wants to question her. Can you believe that?"

"Jessup Mountain," Lillian said, slowly rising from her chair. "I jes' think of something." She walked over to the counter by the refrigerator and picked up the morning paper. "Look at this here," she said, holding out the front page.

And there it was, making headlines: DEPUTIES RAID RACE SHOP, with a grainy picture of a large low-slung building with a sign over the door that I couldn't make out. Lillian spread the paper out on the table so Mr. Pickens could read it with me. I skimmed the article, leaned back in my chair and said, "Well, I never."

But Mr. Pickens read every word, the frown on his face growing deeper and more solemn. "Jerry Johnson," he said, almost to himself. "How 'bout that."

"Yes, they mentioned that name. He's the one the thieves stole the disks from, although why anybody'd go to the trouble of breaking in for those things, I wouldn't know. Hazel Marie certainly wouldn't, I can tell you that. Some other things were stolen from him, too, but they didn't say what."

"Says here," Mr. Pickens said, as he ran his finger down the article, "there was some heavy-duty vandalism, and a lot of tools and equipment were taken. Those disks you're talking about had chassis set-up data on them."

"What that mean?" Lillian asked.

"Well, see, all the NASCAR speedways have different lengths, degrees of banking and so on. You have to know what they are so you can calibrate the amount of rpm's, horsepower and torque in your engines to conform to each track. Like, for instance, you'd need high horsepower and low torque for the Atlanta Speedway, but high torque and low horsepower for Bristol."

Lillian and I looked at him like he was speaking in tongues.

I shook my head, not a bit interested in mechanical engineering. "That's all well and good, but it doesn't have a thing to do with Hazel Marie. I mean, I'm sorry this Jerry Johnson, whoever he is, had his disks stolen. But he can buy more where they came from, whereas she can't ever be replaced. I can't understand why everybody's so exercised over his problem, putting it in the newspaper and all, and not even raising an eyebrow about Hazel Marie being missing."

"Look here," Mr. Pickens said, pointing to a paragraph. "Jerry's quoted as saying the theft and vandalism were done to cover up something else, but he doesn't say what. Listen to this, 'When I come in and found what they'd done, I knew the sorry rascals wanted to knock me out of the points race. But I know my fans're behind me, and they can count on my Number 17 truck being in Phoenix, come next weekend.' " Mr. Pickens shook his head and said, "Poor ole Jerry. He'll be climbing the walls over this. But I'll say this, Lieutenant Peavey's right. There is a connection between your lady and what happened to him. Got to be, if her charm and his disks were found at the same place."

"I don't like the sound of that," I said. "Mr. Pickens, Hazel Marie wouldn't steal a thing if her life depended on it. Would she, Lillian?"

"No'm, she wouldn't. But Mr. Pickens got a head start on them deputies, 'cause he know that charm belong to Miss Hazel Marie, an' they don't. Lieutenant Peavey, the only reason he ax you questions about her is 'cause you tole him she been missin', an' I 'spect he axin' 'bout everybody else missin' in town, too."

"I hope you're right, Lillian," I said, knowing there couldn't be that many more people missing from Abbotsville. There were a gracious plenty of thieves, though, so Lieutenant Peavey had his work cut out for him. I hoped it'd keep him busy enough to forget about Hazel Marie. "Mr. Pickens," I said, leaning toward him, "do you know this Jerry Johnson person?"

"Yeah, I know Jerry." Mr. Pickens gave me a crooked smile. "Have for years, ever since I did a little dirt-track racing back in my younger days. He's a good man, and other teams'll help him get ready for the next race. I'd like to help him, too, and maybe I can. We've got a missing woman and he's had a theft, and we know they're tied together."

"That's fine, if they are," I told him, somewhat troubled by his admitting to having been a racer himself. I didn't see that as exactly a high-class recommendation, but I didn't say anything. "Just as long as you don't get your priorities mixed up. Your first concern, Mr. Pickens, is Hazel Marie, and I don't want you to forget it."

"I'm not likely to," he said, with a wry twist of his mouth. "But it won't hurt us to do what we can for Jerry. He's special to a lot of people, including the governor and some state senators. Wouldn't surprise me if he decided to run for office one of these days."

"Well, that's real interesting," I said, having heard as much as I cared to about Jerry Johnson. "But I can't see what any of it has to do with Hazel Marie. Especially this NASCAR thing everybody seems to be mentioning. What is that anyway?"

"Winston Cup?" he said, raising his eyebrows. "Busch Grand National?"

"Sorry." I shook my head. "I neither smoke nor drink."

He flashed me a quick grin, shaking his head. "Your education is sadly lacking, Miss Julia. You don't mind me calling you that, do you, hon?"

"I don't care what you call me, but now is not the time for niceties. Let's get serious here." I realized with a pang how quickly time was passing, and I'd still not done one thing about hiding Little Lloyd. I stared hard at Lillian and lifted my eyes to the ceiling, trying to ask her how he was doing. She frowned at me and mouthed, "What? What?"

I gave up, and said to Mr. Pickens, "I think it's time for you to be doing something."

"Don't rush me. I'm thinking. Which means I'm doing something." He ignored my skeptical look. "I've not been able to track them, since neither of them has used a credit card in the past twenty-four hours. And there's nothing in her room that tells me anything, no ticket stubs, no match covers, no letters, no diary or notes of any kind."

"I could've told you that. What's next?"

"I'll get in touch with Jerry, get some details on what happened to him. Then I'll run another credit check on her and Hodge to see if there've been any charges for gas or hotels since I last checked. And I want to feel out some contacts I have in the local law enforcement, as well as the SBI. The paper says the state boys were in on the raid, too."

"Oh, my goodness, that's right. Lord, if the state is looking for Hazel Marie, she's really in trouble. Lillian, I don't think I can stand this."

"Me, neither. But that jes' mean we got to get her outta their way. I don't want them puttin' her down in that Raleigh jailhouse no more'n you do."

"Don't even think it! Mr. Pickens, I assure you, Hazel Marie is not a criminal, and she doesn't know how to race. If she is mixed up in this NASCAR outfit, it wasn't her own doing." I stopped, thinking of all the possibilities. "It had to be Wilson T. Hodge who's got her involved. If she is, which I don't believe for a minute."

"Okay," Mr. Pickens said, "don't ruffle your feathers. I'll find her. Then we'll see what her legal situation is."

"That's exactly what I want to hear. Let's find her and get her out of the situation, legal or otherwise. And do it before the sheriff or those state boys you know can do it. We're counting on you, and it's time you got started on it."

"You want some more coffee?" Lillian asked him, as she reached for the coffee pot.

"No, he doesn't," I said. "Mr. Pickens, you need to get a move on. The time for sitting around thinking is over."

I stood up, reaching for my coat, ready to accompany him on his search for Hazel Marie. He opened his mouth, probably to say I couldn't go, but he didn't get a chance. The front doorbell stopped us all in our tracks.

Lillian and I stared at each other, both of us thinking of the endangered child upstairs.

As the bell sounded again, Mr. Pickens looked from one to the other of us. "You gonna get that?"

"Look and see who it is, Lillian," I said. "But don't let them see you." She headed for the dining room to peek out the window, wringing her hands as she went.

While we waited, I noticed Mr. Pickens's raised eyebrows at our strange behavior, so I said, "I have a friend who drops by and pesters me with her problems. I just don't have time for her this morning. If it's her, we'll just sneak on out."

Lillian pushed back through the swinging door, the whites of her eyes showing. "It's that Lieutenant Peavey and Deputy Daly standin' out there, big as you please. What we gonna do?"

I needed something to hold on to. I clasped the back of the chair, my knuckles white with the strain. Deputy Daly had called in the big guns to help him pick up a sweet, innocent child. I declare, it didn't seem fair.

"Good," Mr. Pickens said, getting to his feet. "I'll talk to Peavey, see what else they have. And let him know I'm working the case, too."

"Sit down, Mr. Pickens," I managed to say. "I have a proposition for you."

"Mr. Pickens," I went on, gripping the back of the chair hard enough to snap the thing in two, "I don't have time for arguments or explanations. I want you to go on ahead and take Little Lloyd with you. Lillian, run up the back stairs and bring Little Lloyd down that way. Bundle him up good, but hurry and don't make any noise."

She took off, moving faster than I'd given her credit for being able to do.

Mr. Pickens's black eyes followed her, then he turned them on me. "What's going on?"

"I'll explain later. You just take the child to your office and wait for me there." I started out of the kitchen, wanting to smash the bell and whoever's finger was mashing it so hard. "But don't leave until I get those two out there in the living room, so they won't see you. And be quiet about it."

"Wait just a damn minute," Mr. Pickens said, stopping me as I reached the swinging door. "You're not sending that boy with me. I've got things to do."

I heard Lillian's shoes flopping on her heels in the hall upstairs, and knew she was herding Little Lloyd down to the kitchen.

"Watch your language, Mr. Pickens," I said. "The deputies're here to pick up that child, and I'm not going to let them. And you're going to help me and, if you can't see your way clear to protecting a poor, innocent child, well, let it be on your head. Now I want you to sneak Little Lloyd out to your car, and keep his head down till you're out of town."

"Hold on," Mr. Pickens said, holding up his hand like he was stopping traffic. "I need more than that. Just what're you getting me into?"

Little Lloyd entered from the back stairs, Lillian right behind him, both of their faces showing the strain. Little Lloyd had one arm through his coat sleeve, with Lillian trying to get the other one on him.

"Little Lloyd," I said, ignoring Mr. Pickens for the moment, "you're going with Mr. Pickens. He'll look after you till I can get there. Hurry now." I crossed the room to the back door and eased it open, looking out to see if any other deputies were sneaking around, while the doorbell kept on ringing. "Lillian, go let them in, but keep them in the living room."

"What I gonna tell 'em?"

"Tell them anything. No, wait, tell them I'm indisposed, but you'll go upstairs and see if I'm able to get out of bed. But take your time doing it. That'll give Mr. Pickens time to get Little Lloyd out of here and into his car."

She shuffled off toward the front of the house, calling, "I'm comin', I'm comin'."

Mr. Pickens was still shaking his head, standing there acting as stubborn as a mule. "Taking care of a child is not in my job description. I want to know what's going on."

Well, he just made me so mad. When you employ someone, you expect them to do as they're told. "Truancy, Mr. Pickens," I snapped, saying the first thing that popped in my head. "That's what's going on. The boy's not in school as you can plainly see, and the reason is, he's worried sick about his mother. And instead of looking for her as they ought to be doing, those deputies out there are piddling away their time on such as this. Now, help us out here or return my check."

We glared at each other, with the sound of Lillian opening the front door trickling back to us, and I wondered if I'd gone too far. I didn't want my check back; I wanted Mr. Pickens to do what he was told.

"Look," I said, trying a different tack in spite of the urgency of the moment. "If the boy's cited for truancy, his mother'll have to answer for it. And as you've noticed, she's not here to do any answering. So I'll have to do it for her, and that'll take up time I need to help you find her."

"That's not a bad idea," he said. "Because I'm telling you right now, I'll do what you hired me to do but I'm not going to have you and the boy tagging after me every step of the way. Are we clear on that?"

I steamed for a minute, then decided that it'd be better to let him think he was winning a round. "Very clear, Mr. Pickens. But do this one thing, and I'll come get him as soon as they leave. Then we'll let you find Hazel Marie."

"I'm holding you to that," he said, pointing a finger at me, which made me want to wring it off. But then he turned to Little Lloyd. "Come on then and let's go. Miss Julia, I hope you know what you're doing. I don't want to lose my license for aiding and abetting."

He winked at Little Lloyd, who'd been standing there trying to follow what was going on. I didn't think it necessary to explain to the child the story I'd given Mr. Pickens. He knew why the deputies were looking for him, and I gave him credit for understanding why we didn't need to tell Mr. Pickens what he didn't need to know.

Just as I was shooing them out, Little Lloyd glanced at the newspaper on the table, then stopped on a dime. He reached for it and, pointing at the picture, said, "I know where that is. Mr. Hodge took me and my mama down there one time. Left us in the car while he went in to talk to his cousin. My word, Miss Julia," he went on, sounding more like me than I did myself at times. "It says it was raided."

"Cousin?" I said.

Mr. Pickens leaned over the boy's shoulder to look again at the picture. "Hodge's cousin owns it?"

"Yessir, and I wanted to go in to see the race trucks, but Mr. Hodge said kids weren't allowed. I know it's the same one 'cause, see, you can just make out THE BIGELOW MOTORSPORTS CENTER right there on the sign, and that's where we went."

Mr. Pickens and I looked at each other, both of us saying "The *big,*" at the same time.

"That's it, Mr. Pickens," I said, relieved and agitated at the same time. "That's what Hazel Marie was trying to tell us. Now you've got something to get your teeth into. So get on out of here and do it."

"It's a start, anyway," he said, still studying the picture.

Voices from the living room drifted back to us, reminding me of our current crisis. I was about to jump out of my skin by that time, so anxious to light a fire under Mr. Pickens that it was all I could do to keep from smacking him out the door.

"You've got to go, Mr. Pickens," I said. "I'll meet you at your office as soon as I've handled the situation here, and we can figure out what to do next."

To my great relief, Mr. Pickens put a hand on Little Lloyd's back and moved toward the door. "My car's on the side street, so we'll go 'round the back of the house. But I hope you understand that I can't do any work if I have to babysit."

"Oh, for goodness sake. Little Lloyd's not going to hold you up. It's you who's doing that. Now, go on so I can take care of those two out yonder."

I closed the door behind them and hurried up the back stairs, grateful that I'd changed my mind about giving my room to Hazel Marie. I'd fixed up a bedroom for her downstairs, since it wasn't appropriate for her to be on the same floor as Coleman even though he had eyes only for Binkie and spent most of his time with her. You can't be too careful these days, and I'd not wanted to give anybody cause for talk.

By the time I got to my bedroom, I could hear Lillian calling me as she came up the front stairs. I didn't know what to do, whether to undress and get in bed or just sling a robe over my clothes.

"Miss Julia," Lillian whispered, as she poked her head around my door, her eyes wide with apprehension, "they say they got to look through the house, see if Little Lloyd be here. And they got a warranty that say they can do it."

"A search warrant?" I couldn't believe they'd go that far, which plainly meant that Lieutenant Peavey had not believed me when I'd let him think Little Lloyd was missing too. The idea!

"Oh, Lord, Lillian, quick, look around and see if there's anything that'll give us away."

"His pajamas," she said, pointing to them on my bed.

Footsteps sounded on the stairs, and we gaped at each other. The nerve of them, just taking over my house like it belonged to a common criminal.

"Go," I told her. "Go stop them. Hold them up as long as you can. Tell them I'm sick and they can't come in here."

She left, while I grabbed the pajamas and threw them in the hamper. Looking around the room, I could see no other evidence of Little Lloyd's night there. Then, fearing they'd do more than glance around, I stooped and pulled out the child's books and backpack from under the bed. Taking them with me, I went into the bathroom and put all of Little Lloyd's things in the linen closet, stacking my Charisma Supima cotton sheets over and around them. Then I locked the bathroom door. From inside.

I put the lid down on the commode and sat on it, my hands shaking and my heart racing. I can't stand to hang a gown and robe in full view on the back of a door, but this was one time I wished that's where mine were. I could've undressed with time to spare, but mine were in the clothes closet where I couldn't get to them.

I sat there scared to death, wondering if they'd break down the door and come into a woman's most private place. I could follow their voices and heavy footsteps as Lillian led them across the hall to Little Lloyd's room, then down the hall to Coleman's room. Which he hardly ever used since he'd taken up with Binkie. In fact, it seemed the only time he used it was when he was so starved for a decent meal that he'd show up at my house. Binkie couldn't boil water.

I heard the deep voices and heavy footsteps come toward my room, with Lillian's lighter voice warning them that I was sick as a dog and might be catching. I closed my eyes and held my breath, going over in my mind the things in my room that might draw their attention. Thank goodness, neither Lillian nor I had had time to make my bed. That should prove I was sick.

As I heard them enter the bedroom, I held on to the toilet seat with both hands.

Lillian tapped on the bathroom door. "Miss Julia? You have some gentlemans to see you."

Lord, Lillian, I thought, no gentleman would insist on visiting a woman while she was on the toilet.

I took a deep breath and, in a pitiful-sounding voice, said, "Who is it?"

"Lieutenant Peavey," Lieutenant Peavey said, standing right outside the door. "Sorry to disturb you, Mrs. Springer, but we have a warrant to search the house for the Puckett child."

"Well," I quavered, "he's not in here."

There was a moment of silence, and I wondered what was going on in Lieutenant Peavey's mind. He'd already proven to be the suspicious type.

"Lieutenant?" I called weakly.

"Ma'am?"

"I'm sorry I'm not able to help you. I wasn't feeling well when I left your office, and now it looks like I've picked up that intestinal flu that's been going around. Lillian's just getting over it, but it's gone through both of us like Sherman through Georgia. I hope you don't get it from us."

"Uh, well," he said, as I heard him back away from the door, "I guess we'll have to take that chance. I'll give you a minute, but we have to inspect that room."

I moaned softly, like I was being ravaged by an internal spasm, and said, "Step out in the hall, lieutenant, and I'll do my best to get off this thing."

When I heard them move out of the bedroom, I flushed the commode and dashed for the bed, dress, sweater, shoes and all. Pulling the covers up to my neck, I weakly called them to come back in.

Lieutenant Peavey strode in, glanced at me with a muttered "sorry to bother you," and went into the bathroom. In which he found absolutely nothing that wasn't supposed to be there, even behind the shower curtain. Deputy Daly watched from the hall, clearly uncomfortable at this invasion of a sick woman's privacy. I could tell he'd been raised better than Lieutenant Peavey, who had no such qualms. Or manners, either.

On his way out of the bedroom, Lieutenant Peavey said, "We'll try the school. But if the boy shows up here, you're required to turn him over immediately."

"Yessir," I mumbled, shivering under the covers. "If I'm able."

Then I closed my eyes in relief, as they turned and went down the stairs. When I heard the front door close behind them, I got up and straightened my clothes.

Chapter 15

I met Lillian on the stairs as I was going down and she was on her way up.

She took my arm and said, "Let me he'p you on down."

"Lillian, for goodness sake, I'm not sick."

"Well, you sho' sounded like it. Didn't sound like no playactin' to me."

"Good. Maybe it convinced them too. You're sure they're gone?"

"Yessum, I watched 'em till their car went right on outta sight towards Main Street."

"Good," I said again, relieved that we'd slid past that problem. Now I could turn my attention to Hazel Marie. "Lillian, I'm going on over to Mr. Pickens's office. Thank goodness he's located in south Asheville and out of the sheriff's jurisdiction. I'll just keep Little Lloyd with me all day, and he'll be out of their sight. And their minds, too. I hope."

"What you gonna do with him when you have to come home?"

"I'll worry about that when the time comes. Or maybe," I said, stopping to think through an earlier thought I'd had, "maybe he can stay with Mr. Pickens. Yes, that might do it."

"That Mr. Pickens, he don't act too happy 'bout takin' care of him."

"Making Mr. Pickens happy is not high up on my list. Anyway, I better get on over there, so we can figure out where Hazel Marie is."

As soon as we reached the kitchen, I didn't stop, just headed straight for my coat, ready to get on the road.

Lillian said, "What I gonna tell them deputies, if they come back again? You s'posed to be sick in the bed."

"Tell them I've gone to the Emergency Room. Nobody could find anybody in that place. Lillian, I'm gone. I'll let you know if we learn anything."

I was halfway out the door when the phone rang. I stopped, fearing it was more bad news but hoping it was Hazel Marie again. Lillian hurried to it, jerking the receiver off before it could ring again.

"Miz Springer's residence," she said, then stopped, listening as the frown on her face deepened. Then her face brightened, and she jumped with excitement, "Yessum, we will. We sho' will."

I hurried over to her, as she thrust the phone at me. "Hello? Hello?" Nothing but static on the line. "Who is this? Hello?"

Then I heard a recorded voice telling me to hang up the phone. I jiggled the receiver, but it did nothing but get me that loud, annoying noise that means a phone is off the hook.

"Lillian, who was it? There wasn't a soul on the line."

"It was Miss Hazel Marie callin', least that's what the operator say. She say, do we accep' a collect call from Hazel Marie, and I say we will, then you take the phone and that's all I hear."

"Oh, Lord, why can't she stay on the line long enough to tell us anything?" I sank down in a chair, just about undone with how close we'd come to learning where she was. "Lillian, was there any hint of where she was calling from?"

"No'm, I done tol' you everything I hear."

"Then I know what to do," I said, picking up the phone again. "I saw this on *The Rockford Files* a long time ago, but it ought to still work." But it didn't. The operator could not be wheedled, cajoled or threatened into telling me anything about where the collect call had originated. I'd get it on my bill at the end of the month, if, she said, the call was actually connected.

"That just beats all," I said, slamming down the phone. "Well, this is where Mr. Pickens can start earning his money."

I dialed his office number, hoping he'd had time to get there but ended up having to leave my message on a recording, which I mortally hate dealing with. I told the machine to tell him to get busy and trace the call we'd received, using whatever special methods he had to get the information, and that I was on my way and would expect some results by the time I got there.

Complaining half under my breath about people who slow-poked around and weren't where they were supposed to be, I finally got on my way to Mr. Pickens's office.

It took me thirty minutes to get to south Asheville and almost another thirty to find his office, which was located in a strip mall between a beauty supply house and an insurance office. A covered sidewalk ran the length of the several shops and offices that faced the highway. When I pulled in and parked, I was relieved to see Mr. Pickens's semblance of a car nearby. I didn't care how much Little Lloyd admired it, it was one step above a rattletrap to my mind and I hoped I'd never have to set foot in it again.

To that end, an idea occurred to me, one that would kill two birds with one stone—keep me from having to ride in it and put Mr. Pickens in my car with us. I wasn't sure how to do it, but Jim Rockford had done it plenty of times so it couldn't be too hard.

Locking my car, I surveyed the area, taking special note of the lack of pedestrian traffic and how close together the cars were parked in front of the shops and offices. Then I slipped between the cars and stooped down beside a front tire of Mr. Pickens's car. Using a ballpoint pen from my pocketbook, I began letting the air out of the tire. Deciding that method would take forever before any evidence showed up, I found my nail file and used a rock to hammer it in between the treads. By the time I got it done, my lower limbs were so stiff I could hardly get back up.

But I did, holding my head high so no one who might be watching would dream that a woman of my caliber could do what I'd just done. Turning toward Mr. Pickens's office, I noted the large window that faced the arcade and the chipped black and gold paint on it that spelled out THE PICKENS AGENCY. Underneath in smaller letters, I read PRIVATE INVESTIGATIONS & DISCREET INQUIRIES.

The only thing that could be said for the looks of the place was that at least he didn't operate out of the trunk of his car. As I opened the door and stepped into the unlit reception area, I stood and took it all in. Furnishings can tell you so much about the person who chooses them, but I didn't much like what these were telling me. The whole place was paneled in dark wood, so the first thing I did was reach over and open the blinds. Then sneezed from the dust. One of those nubby-fabric upholstered sofas and a matching chair—you know, the kind with wide wooden arms—took up most of the space. An end table with a brass lamp that I'd seen advertised in a Kmart ad, an artificial tree that looked like nothing that'd ever grown in nature over in the corner, and a magazine rack with gun and car periodicals in it made up the rest of the furnishings. With a decor like that, it was no wonder no one was waiting to see him.

Following the narrow hall off the waiting room, I stopped in the door of a small office in the back. Glancing in, I was pleased to see that it, at least, looked as if some work at some time had been done in it. A large wooden desk, which Mr. Pickens sat behind, just about filled the room. File cabinets were lined up along one wall, and a narrow table extended the desk to hold a computer and various books. Another table near the door where I stood held a coffee maker, mugs, a bag of sugar and an empty Krispy Kreme doughnut box. Various plaques, pictures, diplomas and framed official-looking certificates and citations hung wherever there was space on the wall. In contrast to the piles of paper, folders and other odds and ends on all the surfaces in the room, the material on the wall was perfectly aligned and carefully hung. Mr. Pickens had obviously taken a great deal of care to document the progress of his career.

A radio on top of a file cabinet played something that passed for music and, just as I stuck my head in, Little Lloyd asked Mr. Pickens when he thought I'd get there.

"I'm here now," I said, walking into the office, "and I'm glad to see the two of you here too. I tried to get you earlier, Mr. Pickens, when I thought you'd had plenty of time to get here." Mr. Pickens frowned from behind his desk. I'd already figured out that he didn't take criticism too well, even when it was meant for his own good.

"We stopped for a Hardee's biscuit, Miss Julia," Little Lloyd said, his face alive with excitement, "And guess what, we got your message about Mama calling you, and Mr. Pickens used his police contacts and a telephone operator who's a friend of his, and now we know where my mama is!"

I put a hand on the door to steady myself. "Where?"

"Have a seat," Mr. Pickens said, waving at the only unoccupied one in the crowded space. "I traced that collect call to a truck stop off I-85 just east of Gastonia."

"My word," I said, collapsing into the chair. "What could she be doing at a truck stop? And in Gastonia, of all places? That's the murder capital of the state. Is she still there? Did anybody see her?"

"Hold your horses," he said, infuriating me. "I've talked to some of the people working there, and one of the waitresses may've seen her about an hour ago. But don't get your hopes up; she'll be long gone by now."

"Did they say who was with her? She couldn't've been by herself. Whoever's with her won't let her complete a phone call. Mr. Pickens, I declare, we've got to do more than just sit here discussing the matter."

"I've been doing plenty, don't you worry."

"He has, Miss Julia," Little Lloyd confirmed, twisting in his chair as he excitedly defended Mr. Pickens. "He just talked to Jerry Johnson, you know, *the* Jerry Johnson. They're real good friends, and Mr. Pickens put him on the speaker phone so I could hear him, too. And we were right, it was somebody from Bigelow Racing who lost his cap when they broke in. BMC was what was on the cap that the thieves dropped. BMC, Bigelow Motorsports Center, Miss Julia, and Jerry said that was the only race team with those initials, plus my mama said "the big," so we know it's them."

Mr. Pickens reared back in his patched executive chair and propped a foot on an open drawer. "Yeah, that's the way it's shaping up. Jerry and Bigelow've been rivals in the Craftsman Truck Series for years. Not that Bigelow drives; he's an owner, but he's put one driver after the other in his trucks, and none of 'em ever comes close. So Jerry's convinced that Bigelow's behind it to keep him out of the Chevy Trucks 150 at Phoenix that's coming up next weekend. Then right after that is the California Truck Stop 250 at Mesa Marin. If Bigelow can keep Jerry out of both of them, he'll be so far behind in points, he'll never catch up."

"Jerry, Jerry, Jerry," I said, pursing my lips. "I've heard all I want to hear on that subject. Besides, this Bigelow's gone to a lot of trouble for very little return, it seems to me. You've already said that other teams'll help Jerry out, and he said he'd be ready to race anyway, so what has Bigelow accomplished?"

"There's something else going on that Jerry doesn't want publicizied. It'll ground him, for sure, so he's pretty broken up over it."

I rolled my eyes. I had just about lost all sympathy for this Jerry Johnson, whose problems were taking first place in everybody's mind, except mine. "Back to Hazel Marie, Mr. Pickens. What's the agenda? From what we now know, she's with this Bigelow crowd against her will or she wouldn't be calling for help, which makes sense since Wilson T. has a kin connection there. So we can figure that *he* got her involved with Bigelow, right? And now she's called from Gastonia, so where're Bigelow and Wilson T. taking her, and where is she now? That's the question."

Mr. Pickens sat up suddenly, his foot coming down on the floor and the springs of his chair squeaking. "That *is* the question. Jerry, if you'll pardon the mention, said Bigelow has another place outside of Rockingham. Near Jerry's, in fact. I'm figuring Bigelow was using the shop in Abbot County to get his trucks ready for Phoenix, because he didn't want to hang around Rockingham after stealing Jerry blind. But when he found out about that cap one of his team dropped, he'd know the sheriff'd show up, so he had to pull out fast, taking whoever happened to be there with him. Looks like Hazel Marie might've stepped in at the wrong time."

"Huh," I said. "I don't buy that. It was Wilson T. who put her in it."

"Probably." He nodded, agreeing with me for a change. "Hazel Marie's call came from Gastonia, which is on the way to Rockingham, so he's headed back that way. I don't know why, though, since he's well known around there. I'm wondering why he didn't just go on to Phoenix, even if he'd be a few days early for the race."

"Maybe his trucks aren't ready," Little Lloyd said. "Maybe he has to have some equipment that's in Rockingham."

"Could be," Mr. Pickens said. "Now, the question is, do I head for Gastonia and Rockingham to look for them, or do I fly to Phoenix and wait for them."

"That's no question, Mr. Pickens," I said, not at all liking the way his mind was working. "You'll go to Gastonia and on to wherever they went after that. There's not going to be any flying and sitting around waiting for them to show up. We don't know what indignities Hazel Marie's suffering, so I want you right on her heels every step of the way."

"Okay, I was just waiting for you to get here so I could leave. Now, I want you to take this boy home, and wait till you hear from me."

"No sir, that's not what we're going to do. We're going with you."

"No, you're not. I need room to operate, and . . ."

I held up my hand and rode right over him. "Don't give me any excuses or reasons why not. Little Lloyd and I can't just go home and wait, now that we definitely know she's in with a bunch of thieves. How can you expect us to do that?"

"I don't care how you do it. You're not going."

"We'll just see about that. Come on, Little Lloyd." And taking his hand, I sailed out of the office and got us in our car. Cranked it and sat there waiting for Mr. Pickens. If we couldn't go with him, we'd go behind him. He'd be glad to see us when his tire started wobbling. If, that is, I could keep up with him.

Mr. Pickens came storming out of the office, his face as dark as a thundercloud, and didn't even look at us. He got to his car, the keys dangling from his hand, and stopped as if he'd run into a clothesline. He stared at his front tire like he couldn't believe what he was seeing, then he squatted down to get a closer look. He stayed that way an inordinately long time, his head bowed over.

"What's wrong with him?" Little Lloyd asked. "I'll go see if he needs anything." He reached for the door handle.

"Stay in the car, Little Lloyd," I told him. "Mr. Pickens is learning that pride goeth before a fall, and we'll be right here when he's ready to be helped up."

As I revved my motor, pretending not to notice Mr. Pickens's plight, he stood up and glared at me across the hood of his crippled car, his mouth as tight as a zipper. Breathing hot and heavy, he barreled over to my car and jerked my door open.

"I'm driving," he said, in a tone I didn't want to argue with. "Get in the back."

"Little Lloyd . . ."

Mr. Pickens pointed at Little Lloyd. "Sit still." Then he pointed at me. "You. In the back, and no back talk."

I got out, pushed up the seat and crawled into the back, telling myself that the owner of a car ought to know how it rides from behind the driver.

I gathered my coat around me and buckled the seat belt. Little Lloyd glanced back at me from between the two front seats wondering, I was sure, why I'd let Mr. Pickens take the wheel without a word of protest.

"Push up your glasses, Little Lloyd," I said, as Mr. Pickens backed the car out with a jerk. My head snapped back, and I opened my mouth to tell him to watch what he was doing.

I closed it again upon seeing his fierce glance in the rearview mirror.

Deciding not to comment on his driving, I took refuge in pleasantries. "Something wrong with your car, Mr. Pickens?"

Chapter 16

We got to Gastonia in something under two hours, taking back roads and overtaking every vehicle on the road. I'd bitten my tongue a hundred times to keep from saying anything. My restraint had little visible effect on Mr. Pickens, however, because he drove like one of those NASCAR racers he'd been talking about. My little car had never had a hand like Mr. Pickens's on it, but it didn't seem to mind. We zoomed down the highway like we were the only ones on it, and it was all I could do to keep from mentioning highway safety tips to him. I refrained, though, because he didn't seem to be in the mood for conversation. Little Lloyd took his cue from me and, other than a few glances my way and some at our silent driver, didn't open his mouth the whole way.

So I held my peace and the armrest, nervously telling myself that we were on a mission of mercy. Sometime soon after we'd started, Mr. Pickens had adjusted the front seat, sliding it back and cramping me up something awful. I didn't even say anything about that, figuring that was one way I could give him room to operate.

I'd seen truck stops from the highway as I'd passed by, but I'd never been in one. When Mr. Pickens took an exit ramp and pulled into Smiley's, it was like going into a new world. Well, not exactly new, but different. We threaded through parked tractor-trailers, some just sitting there rumbling and emitting diesel smoke, others way over to the side, empty and still, while several were hooked to gas pumps or air hoses. Cars and pickups were parked closer to the restaurant that advertised real good home cooking. Somehow I doubted it.

Mr. Pickens parked with a jerk and opened his door. "Stay in the car," he said and, slamming the door, headed toward the restaurant.

"Well," I said to Little Lloyd, "I don't know about you, but I've about had enough of taking orders and being treated like I'm in the way. Don't you need to use the rest room, Little Lloyd?"

"Yessum, I do. But he told us to stay here, so he might not like it if we get out."

"The man can't be that insensitive. And we might not have another chance anytime soon. Let's go."

I'd never seen a restaurant quite like it. As soon as we walked in the door, passing several men on the way out with toothpicks in their mouths, I just stopped and looked around. A long bar faced us with men on stools, their wide shoulders hunched over their plates, and along each side of the door there were booths filled with a few women and a lot of men. I didn't know who'd raised the majority of the men in the room, but somebody hadn't taught them to take off their caps when they came inside.

The din of deep voices ordering the meatloaf, the loud laughter of half a dozen waitresses, and the clatter of forks, knives, pots and pans filled the long room. Over it all some cowboy singer on the jukebox was wailing away about blowing smoke rings in the dark, which is a good way to kill yourself.

"There's a coupla empties at the counter, hon," one of the waitresses said as she passed with plates in her hands and stacked along her arms. "Better grab 'em quick."

She didn't wait for a reply, which was just as well. I'd never eaten perched up on a stool, and I didn't intend to start.

Looking around, I noticed Mr. Pickens leaning over the end of the counter to our right, talking with a frowzy blonde waitress at the cash register. She was smiling and leaning right back at him. Another incidence of the professional investigative technique he was so proud of.

I touched Little Lloyd's shoulder and nodded toward the left where the room took an angle. A large sign indicated that rest rooms, showers and beds were in that direction. Lord, I thought, I didn't want to eat there, much less sleep in the place.

About that time, Mr. Pickens turned and saw us. He straightened up, scowling something awful. I pointed toward the rest room sign and, not giving him the chance to stop us, proceeded toward it. But not before I saw the waitress touch his hand to bring his attention back to her. Which he was quick to do. The man was a caution when it came to women.

We walked the narrow aisle between the counter and the booths, dodging waitresses with pencils stuck in their hair, and cowboy boots stuck in the aisles. We passed between shelves of toiletries, snacks and truck magazines, and racks of postcards and keychains. In a nook off the room we found the rest rooms, the doors to the men's and the women's facing each other.

"Go on in," I said to Little Lloyd. "I'll wait by the door till you come out. But don't sit down."

"No'm, I won't. I don't have to."

I waited by the door to the men's room, ready and willing to go in after him if something untoward happened. While I waited, I noticed two telephones for public use hanging on the wall between the rest rooms. Hurrying over, I knew from Mr. Pickens's call tracing that Hazel Marie must've been in that very spot, using one of them. We were close to her, I could feel it, and I began to read all the numbers and notes that were written on the wall. Some of the writing was just doodles, while some lonesome somebody had left a string of phone numbers, but more than you might imagine was most unsuitable for reading. And in a public place, too.

Little Lloyd came out and walked over beside me. I hoped he wasn't tall enough to see some of the worst. He studied the phones and said, "She might've called from here."

"I think she did, and I've been reading the wall, thinking she might've left a message. But I don't see a thing she could've written. You don't need to look, I've checked them all.

"Now, you wait right here while I go to the ladies'. Don't go anywhere and don't talk to anyone. I'll be right out."

It didn't take me long, because I never liked to leave Little Lloyd alone in a strange place and because the room wasn't fit for lingering. I adjusted my hat in the mirror, then went out drying my hands on a Kleenex, since all they'd had in there was one of those hot air devices that never dried anything.

"Miss Julia, look," the boy said, his eyes sparkling behind his glasses. He held out his hand for me to see. "I found it and it's Mama's. I know it is."

I leaned down for a closer look, and he was right. It was another tiny charm from Hazel Marie's bracelet, a thin gold disk with her initials on it, plain as day.

"Oh, my goodness. Where'd you find it?"

"In that phone." He pointed to one. "I checked the coin return on both of them, and found this just laying in one."

"Then she was certainly here, and not long ago or somebody would've already found it. And, Little Lloyd, *she* put it there herself. It couldn't've fallen off or been torn off, and end up where you found it."

"We've got to tell Mr. Pickens." And the boy hurried off, with me close behind to find our expert investigator who hadn't wanted us along.

We turned the corner at the end of the counter, and I wanted to cover my ears from the caterwauling on the jukebox. I mean, whoever heard of anybody thinking such as that about a tractor?

Then I stopped in my tracks. Mr. Pickens was nowhere to be seen.

"Oh, Lord," I said, clutching Little Lloyd's shoulder, "he's gone off and left us."

"He's right over yonder," the boy said, pointing toward the last booth.

I could've sagged with relief. Believe me, you don't want to be stranded at a truck stop with a ladies' room in the state that one was in.

Marching toward Mr. Pickens, I could see him sitting with that same waitress he'd been all over before. The woman's hard life was plain as day on her face, but that hadn't stopped her from pretending otherwise. I declare, if I'd lived that hard I wouldn't've drawn attention to the fact by dying my hair, painting my face and wearing my pink uniform half unbuttoned. She leaned across the table, eating Mr. Pickens up with smiles and eyelash fluttering, and he was encouraging her for all he was worth.

I hadn't yet figured out whether playing up to every woman he met was a calculated method of investigation or whether he just couldn't help himself.

I came to a halt beside the booth. "Mr. Pickens, Little Lloyd found . . . are you *eating*?" I couldn't believe it. Here, the boy and I had been finding clues, while the one being paid to do so was idling away his time with a hot roast beef sandwich and a truck stop strumpet.

"This lady thinks she saw Hazel Marie. And I couldn't refuse a hot meal on the house while this sweet thing tries to remember who was with her. You and the boy'd better get something too. To go, because I'm not waiting on you." And he had the nerve to dangle my keys in front of me, then turn his attention back to the woman.

I turned my back on him, but not before hearing her ask if I was his mother. That just burned me up. For one thing, I didn't like such an uncalled-for assumption of my age and, for another, I hoped she didn't think I'd've raised such an out-and-out womanizer as Mr. Pickens was turning out to be.

Placing a rush order at the counter for two grilled cheese sandwiches and two chocolate milk shakes, I was too mad at Mr. Pickens to feel ill-at-ease as I stood next to a driver on a stool, who was spooning up chili practically in my face.

"Miss Julia," Little Lloyd said, "aren't we going to tell him what I found?"

"He's too busy for us right now. We'll get our lunch and go on out to the car. He doesn't know it, but I have an emergency key in my purse. If he's still hanging on that woman when we're ready to go, we'll just leave him."

Little Lloyd frowned, making his glasses slide down his nose. "I don't think we ought to do that."

I sighed. "Well, he's about stretched my patience to the breaking point."

When our lunch came, I took the bag and swung past Mr. Pickens's booth, Little Lloyd right behind me. I shook the bag in front of him and said, "We've *paid* for our lunch and we're ready to go. And you might be interested to know that we've found a clue. So whenever you're ready . . ." Hoping he'd pick up on my subtle hints about his behavior, I left before he had time to open his mouth.

I had a good mind to sit in the front seat and put Little Lloyd in the back, but decided I wasn't ready for an all-out confrontation. As we unwrapped our sandwiches, Mr. Pickens came out and took his seat under the wheel. Just like it was his own car.

"So what's the clue you found?"

"This." Little Lloyd held out his hand, showing him the charm. "I found it in one of the telephones by the restrooms."

Mr. Pickens picked it up and held it, examining both sides. "These her initials?"

"Yessir."

"Okay, hold on to it." He handed it back to the boy. "It confirms what we already know. That waitress thinks the woman she saw was with a man, tall, well dressed in an overcoat, not your run-of-the-mill truck stop patron."

"That had to be Wilson T.! What else did she say?"

"She thinks there were several other men with them, but she's not sure. They didn't all come in together, just one or two at a time. But she got the impression that they knew each other. Now, we're going on to Charlotte, and if it doesn't suit you," he said, angling the rearview mirror to look at me, "that's too bad."

"I thought you said we were going to Rockingham, wherever that is. Although we're not exactly prepared to go anywhere for any length of time." Thoughts of no toothbrush or change of underclothes, and Lillian worrying about us were getting all mixed up with some relief that Little Lloyd'd be safe from police custody for a few more hours. "I just want to know what we'll do in Charlotte."

"You mean, what will *I* do in Charlotte. What you'll do is sit in the car and wait for me."

Mr. Pickens cranked the car and pulled back out on the interstate, edging and twisting and scooting in and out among those long-haul trucks, barreling toward the Queen City.

I intended to change Mr. Pickens's plans about who would do what. But not before he got us off that eighty-mile-an-hour highway.

Chapter 17

We passed the airport on our right, with me ducking as a huge plane took off over the highway. Mr. Pickens swerved off the interstate onto a ramp that led to a broad avenue into the city. At every traffic light, he studied a piece of paper, then checked the street signs.

"Is that a computer map?" Little Lloyd asked.

"Yeah. Got it before we left."

"I can call out the directions for you, if you want me to."

"Okay." He handed the map to the boy. "Don't get us lost."

Since Mr. Pickens was sounding a little more amenable to friendly intercourse, I decided to join in. "Little Lloyd's a good navigator, you don't have to worry about him. I expect, though, that we'd both like to know where we're going."

I didn't think he was going to answer, then he said, "To Wilson T. Hodge's house. I got the address while we were waiting on you this morning. Gastonia's too close to Charlotte to pass up a chance to check it out, and it's on the way to Rockingham."

"Well I declare, Mr. Pickens. I commend you for thinking ahead."

"That's what I'm paid to do."

I subsided, since the man couldn't even graciously accept a compliment. Besides, we were entering an area of the city where large, well-kept houses took my eye and attention. Beautiful homes and tree-lined avenues gave off a sense of ordered lives, causing me to reflect on my own confused and agitated state during the last several days.

At least, though, I comforted myself, Mr. Pickens was obeying the speed limits and Little Lloyd's directions. We turned into an area bounded by a tall brick wall, passing through an open iron gate onto curving lanes between rows of two-story townhouses.

"Real good security," Mr. Pickens noted, as we passed an unguarded guardhouse. "But fine for us."

I was pleased to note his use of the plural pronoun, including his passengers for a change. Mr. Pickens drove slowly in and out the maze of similar-looking houses with neat, well-kept miniature yards, looking left and right for a house number. The place looked empty to me, with few cars on the street and garages tightly closed.

"Does anybody live here?" I asked, wondering at the lack of children in the yards and pedestrians on the broad sidewalks.

"Oh, yeah. It's got the look of hard-hitting go-getters who're all at work. I hope."

"There it is," Little Lloyd said, pointing to one that looked no different from any of the others, except for the number over the door.

Mr. Pickens parked two doors away from the townhouse that Little Lloyd had indicated, then he turned in his seat to look at me. "Stay in the car, and I mean *stay in the car.* I don't care what kind of reason you think you have, I don't want to see either of you put a foot outside this car. Are we clear on that?"

"Well, of course. You don't have to use that tone of voice; a pleasant suggestion's all that's needed."

He rolled his eyes, then got out. We watched him walk back down the sidewalk and up the several steps to the door of number 218. Interested in learning more of his investigative technique, I carefully watched him, seeing nothing more unusual than a man ringing a doorbell.

"What do you reckon, Little Lloyd?" I asked the boy, who was also craning his neck to watch. "You think Mr. Hodge is in there, and'll just open the door and tell him everything we want to know?"

"No'm, I don't think he's home."

"Then this was a wasted trip. Seems to me that Mr. Pickens could've accomplished the same thing with a telephone call. Now we've wasted all this time when we could be halfway to Rockingham."

"Look! He's going in. Somebody must be home. Oh, I hope my mama's there. I'm going to see."

He had his hand on the door handle. "Wait. Don't get out yet. Let's wait till Mr. Pickens calls us. I don't want to upset him any more than he already is."

The fact of the matter was, I didn't know what would be found in the house and I didn't want Little Lloyd to be the one finding it.

"Look, Miss Julia!"

I did, and Mr. Pickens was crossing the yard toward us, not running, but moving with purpose. He opened Little Lloyd's door and said, "Both of you, out. Hurry, but don't run. No telling who's watching. We're going in for a visit, so act like it."

I started to ask if Mr. Hodge was in there, but a broad hand on my back didn't give me a chance. Mr. Pickens urged us up the steps and into a showplace of a living room. And when I say showplace, that's what I mean. It looked as if it'd been copied from a magazine, lots of chrome and glass and leather, with shiny, waxed floors and little indication that anyone had actually lived in it.

Mr. Pickens closed the front door and walked up so close to me that I could feel the heat he generated. His metabolism must've been working overtime. "Now, listen to me. This is important unless you want to spend the night in jail."

I gasped, and Little Lloyd whimpered. "What's wrong?" he asked. "Is my mama here?"

"No, nobody's here, but there will be in about two minutes. The house has a security system that I set off when I jimmied the door. It's a silent alarm, so the police or some guards'll be coming to check it out. I want you two to look like you're here legitimately. Tell 'em you're visiting Hodge from out of town, and you didn't know how to turn off the alarm. Tell 'em, well, tell 'em anything. Wing it, but calm 'em down so they won't look upstairs."

"Where're you going?" I asked, happy to be of service in his investigation. He'd just proven again that he lacked moral qualms when the circumstances, such as a locked door, dictated. I mentally congratulated myself again for hiring him, although he was certainly hard to get along with.

"Up there somewhere." He pointed to the stairs. "Just make 'em think you're supposed to be here, and get rid of them."

He took the stairs two at a time, leaving us standing there looking at each other.

"Quick, Little Lloyd," I said. "Take off your coat and let's find the kitchen."

Throwing my coat on a chair, I hurried to the kitchen, hoping I could find a prop or two, and Little Lloyd followed me.

"See what's in the refrigerator," I said, opening cabinets and finding a glass and a cup and saucer.

"Not much in here," he said, his head stuck in a Sub-Zero. "Here's a Coke."

"Take this glass, then, and pour some in it. Wait, pour some in this cup, too. Now hurry back to the living room and make yourself at home." I filled what looked to be a brand new kettle with water and put it on the stove, turning the eye on low. Then finding a tea bag in a cannister, I bobbed it in the soda pop in my cup, squeezed it out and left it on the saucer—a practice that I don't ordinarily condone. The dark liquid wouldn't've fooled anybody, so I diluted it with water until it looked vaguely tea-colored.

By the time I got back to the living room, I saw a car with a large decal on the door pull up at the curb and two guards in gray uniforms get out.

"Find a magazine, Little Lloyd, and be looking at it."

I put my cup and saucer on a small glass and chrome table beside a chair, then noticed the pilot light on under the logs in the fireplace. I leaned down and turned it on. A nice fire sprang up, and I thought we'd set the stage as well as we could, given the circumstances.

The doorbell rang and, with a concerned glance at Little Lloyd, I started to answer it before they took it in their heads to break the door down. "Little Lloyd, you're my grandson, and Wilson T. is your uncle, okay? He knew we were coming to visit and gave us a key."

"What if they ask you for it?"

"I won't be able to find it. Trust me, people expect the elderly to be absentminded."

I opened the door to a thin uniformed man with slumping shoulders and a protruding abdomen. He had a thin mustache, stained teeth and a squinty-eyed look.

"How do you do?" I said, as friendly as I could be. "If you're selling something, we don't want it."

"You the owner?" He said it like he was expecting trouble, harsh and suspicious sounding.

"No sir, I'm not. Mr. Wilson T. Hodge is, but he's not here right now. Still at work, I suppose. Why, what's the trouble?"

"The alarm went off here, which means that somebody's in here who's not supposed to be. Mind if I look around?" And he pushed past me, just as his partner, a heavier, younger version, came around the corner of the house.

"Oh, well, it's just us. Wilson T.'s my sister's son, and my grandson and I have come from up in the mountains for a visit. He didn't tell us about an alarm system, just gave us a key. Oh, you mean that thing on the wall that keeps on blinking and beeping? I declare, I wondered what that was. We don't have such things up where I come from, don't even need them."

The both of them stood looking around, noticing Little Lloyd sitting on the leather couch with a magazine in his lap and a Coca-Cola in his hand. The fire added a nice, homey touch. The younger one kept hiking his right hand to his hip, like he wished there was a gun and holster there instead of a ring of keys. I don't know what they'd've done if they'd found a real crook in the house. Yelled for help, maybe.

"Could I offer you some refreshments, officers? There's some soft drinks and tea, if you'd care for anything."

"No, ma'am," the younger one answered, shifting his eyes to his partner to see what he wanted to do next. His partner was shifting his eyes around the room, looking for clues, I guessed. "Mind if we look around? Just to be sure everything's okay?" He moved toward the kitchen without waiting for my permission. The older one went toward another downstairs room that I had yet to visit.

"Why, go right ahead. Little Lloyd and I just got here and, I declare, that bus trip was enough to do me in for a week. We're just waiting for Wilson T. to get here so we can go back to the bus station for our bags."

Little Lloyd gave me a worried look as we heard them opening and closing closet doors and wandering through the house. He cocked his head toward the second floor, frowning, as we both wondered how well Mr. Pickens was hidden.

"Everything looks okay," the older guard said, as he came back through the living room. "You say you had a key? And the door was locked, no evidence that somebody had come in before you?"

"That's right. Locked tighter than Job's hat band. You just wait till I get my hands on Wilson T. for not telling us about that alarm. I'm just so sorry to've bothered you, making you come out here for nothing. But I'll also tell him how good you are at your job. I declare, it makes me feel as safe here in the big city as I am in my own home. I commend you both," I said, as the younger one came in just in time to be included in what I was laying on thick. "I wouldn't be surprised if Wilson T. doesn't write a letter of commendation, recommending a bonus or a raise in pay. He'll be so pleased when I tell him how pleasant and efficient you've both been."

There was a noticeable easing of tension between the two of them as I buttered them up good.

"Well, we'd appreciate that," the older one said. "And looks like everything's under control here, so we'll be on our way."

The younger one cocked his head and raised his eyebrows toward the stairs, so I quickly reached for my pocketbook. "Could I interest you gentlemen in a little something for your time, since I know you don't have it to be wasting on an old woman who didn't know any better than to interrupt your regular work?"

I held out two twenty-dollar bills. They looked at each other, each waiting for the other to reach for them. I wouldn't've dared do it if they'd been real officers. I know a bribe when I see one. But they didn't, or didn't care if they did.

I saw them off, each twenty dollars richer and pleased with themselves for conducting such a rewarding investigation.

I closed the door and leaned against it, marveling again at how easy private investigation was turning out to be.

Chapter 18

"Mr. Pickens?" I called from the bottom of the stairs. "You can come down now. They're gone."

"Hold your horses," he called back. "I'll be through here in a minute."

The man was enough to make a preacher cuss. I wanted out of there before those guards decided to take another look. Besides, it was plain that Hazel Marie was not in the house, and searching for her was our first order of business.

"Let's straighten this place up," I said to Little Lloyd, "and be ready to go when he is."

I stuck the things we'd used in the dishwasher, hoping they'd give Wilson T. a turn when he saw them, and turned off the stove and the gas logs. We put on our coats and sat down to wait.

"Miss Julia," Little Lloyd said, "I don't see a Bible anywhere. Reckon he's even got one?"

I glanced around at the coffee table where a large display book lay, and at a set of chrome bookcases where a pitifully few books were arranged with some awful-looking knickknacks. I'd never been able to understand the taste of some people.

"Maybe it's by his bed. But you'd think a man in his business would have more than one, wouldn't you?"

"Yessum, that's what I was thinking."

Mr. Pickens appeared in the door, having come down the stairs without making a sound. "Let's go." And he headed for the front door.

We scrambled after him, with me getting more and more put out with him. He could've at least told us what he'd been doing upstairs and what he planned to do next. But no, he had that car cranked before I could squeeze into the back seat. You'd think he'd've had the courtesy to commend us for fooling those guards, but he didn't have a kind word for us.

"It does beat all, doesn't it, Little Lloyd," I said, as Mr. Pickens drove out of the area and back onto a broad street, heading away from the way we'd come. "I mean, here we were, unwanted and ignored, yet wasn't it a good thing that we were around to save somebody's bacon when that somebody needed us?"

Little Lloyd peeked around his seat, a smile on his face, and nodded. Mr. Pickens had the child too intimidated to speak his own mind and agree with me. Then I looked up and saw the hint of a smile at the corner of Mr. Pickens's mouth. His mustache might've been tickling him, though, for all he let on.

"Little Lloyd," I went on, "would you be so good as to ask Mr. Pickens where we're going now?"

"Mr. Pickens . . . ," Little Lloyd started.

"We're going to Jerry's."

"My Lord, why?" I asked, leaning forward as far as the seat belt would let me. "It's getting dark and no time to be visiting old friends. We need to find Bigelow's place."

"Look," Mr. Pickens said in that tone of voice he used when he wanted no argument, and which I was getting real tired of hearing. "You two take a nap or something, and let me think this through."

"Think what through?"

"What I found in Hodge's home office."

"What'd you find?"

"Mrs. Springer," he said, sounding tired and put upon. "Give it a rest."

"Well," I said, sitting back and huffing to myself.

By this time we were leaving the city, getting out where the traffic was thinner and the strip malls were interspersed with small, brick residences waiting to be bought out. I put my head back against the seat, determined not to speak to Mr. Pickens again. Let him see how he liked my silence when it came time to be paid.

He picked up speed when he got on a highway headed east. Then he reached over and turned on the radio, twisting the dial until a country music station came on loud and clear. I rolled my eyes, which I was sorry he couldn't see, and resigned myself to listening to that squalling for I-don't-know-how-many miles. I'd just stay quiet and let him alone, and I managed to do that for a good long while. Then I thought he needed reminding that he had passengers to consider.

"I guess if you take it in your head to drive all the way to the Atlantic Ocean, you'd let us know, wouldn't you?"

Mr. Pickens's shoulders slumped. "I knew it. I just bet myself that you couldn't stay quiet for ten miles."

"That being the case, why don't you just tell us what you're thinking about, and maybe we can be thinking about it too? If I had something to engage my mind, I wouldn't feel the need to interfere with your mental processes." Whatever they are, I thought to myself.

"Hush a minute," Mr. Pickens said, reaching for the radio dial.

Before I could let my displeasure be known at being hushed, he turned up the sound and we heard a plaintive, country voice fill the car. "This is Jerry Johnson speakin' to all my fans out there and askin' for your help. You all know about the damage done to our shop and how it's put us behind for Phoenix. But we're gonna make it, I promise each and every one of you. It sure would help us out, though, if y'all would help the police track down that sorry bunch and get back what all they stole from me. We just got a few more days before the Chevy Trucks 150, so I'm askin' if anybody knows anything, you'll call your local law enforcement or call me direct at 1-800-Go-Jerry. I'm offerin' a reward that'll knock your socks off, pit passes for the rest of the season and no questions asked. He'p me out here, all you racin' fans. I 'preciate anything anybody can do, an' you won't regret it."

Mr. Pickens turned the radio down, shaking his head. "Poor ole Jerry. He's got a real problem."

"Poor ole Jerry, my foot. Keep your mind on Hazel Marie, Mr. Pickens, and forget about Jerry Johnson's problem. Now, tell us what you're thinking about."

"All right. All right." Mr. Pickens reached into his breast pocket and brought out some folded papers. He handed them back to me. "It's all tied in together, like I thought. That's the motive, right there."

I unfolded the papers and studied them for some time. "I can't make head nor tails out of this stuff. Looks like a list of races, for one thing."

"Right. A list of possible entries in the Bud Pole next weekend, too."

"That doesn't mean a thing in the world to me."

"Qualifying laps for the race the next day."

I rolled my eyes, sick to death of hearing about the racing world. I now knew more about it than I'd ever wanted to know, and didn't understand the half of it.

"Well, where's that motive you mentioned?" I shuffled through the papers, picking up ticket stubs and a small, black notebook as they fell to my lap.

"Right there in your hand," Mr. Pickens said, as he swerved the car into the fast lane and kicked it into overdrive. I'd done more gasping since he'd been behind the wheel than I'd ever done in my life. And the day wasn't over.

"These things?" I managed to say, holding up the stubs. "What are they?"

"Betting stubs," he answered. "And from the looks of 'em, your Wilson T. Hodge hasn't had much luck betting on Bigelow's drivers."

"Betting?" Little Lloyd asked, his eyes wide behind his glasses. "Mr. Hodge bets on races? Why, he works for the church; he's not supposed to be placing bets."

"You got that right," Mr. Pickens said, although I detected a hint of sarcasm in his voice. "But from the looks of that little notebook, he's expecting his luck to change at Phoenix."

I flipped through the notebook, glancing at such unintelligible notations as NAPA 250, Powerstroke 200 and Ram Tough 200. What was intelligible, however, was the dollar sign on a number of breathtaking figures beside each notation. "My word," I said. "Does this mean what I think it does?"

"Probably, but it's hard for me to know what you're thinking." Mr. Pickens had a smart mouth on him, and I glared at the back of his head. "Check out the Phoenix entry."

"I don't see Phoenix."

"Look at Chevy Trucks NASCAR 150," he said. It was a mystery to me how he got Phoenix out of that, but I found it and nearly lost my breath.

"Ten thousand dollars! Has that idiot bet ten thousand dollars on a *race*!"

"Looks like it. See the check mark beside it? Probably means called in and placed."

Little Lloyd's mind was way ahead of mine. He said, "I bet that's 'cause he figures Jerry won't be there, don't you, Mr. Pickens?"

"Right." Mr. Pickens nodded. "So I figure Hodge knew they were going to put a crimp in Jerry's chances."

"Don't bet, Little Lloyd," I admonished him, anxious to curb any bad habits before they took root. "And I agree that it looks like Wilson T. has been in on it from the start. That sorry thing. What I want to know, though, is where did Wilson T. get this kind of money. Working for a church is not one of your better-known high-paying jobs."

"He may be placing bets for Bigelow," Mr. Pickens said. "NASCAR officials keep too close a watch on the teams for them to risk it themselves. Then again, Hodge may have money of his own."

"Shoo," I said, waving that thought away. "Wilson T. Hodge doesn't have a pot to . . . Oh, my goodness, Pastor Ledbetter! Oh, my goodness!" I started patting my chest with my hand, unable to put the awful thought into words.

"What is it, Miss Julia?" Little Lloyd turned in his seat, his face a picture of worry. "Are you all right?"

"I just remembered something. The pastor said something last night. Something about the building fund not being as full as it ought to be. Oh, Mr. Pickens, you don't reckon Wilson T.'s embezzled church funds, do you? And Hazel Marie's involved with him. Oh, Lord, I knew it, I knew that man was as crooked as a snake."

"No, you didn't, Miss Julia," Little Lloyd said. "You liked him at first."

"That was just good manners, Little Lloyd." I leaned up and tapped Mr. Pickens on the shoulder. "We've got to hurry, Mr. Pickens, this is getting worse by the minute."

"I'm doing the best I can. It's rush hour, and every damn fool in the city's on the streets."

I pursed my lips at his language, but I was too busy studying the implications for Hazel Marie to reprimand him.

"I'm gonna stop up here in a little," he went on, "and find a phone. I need to put Jerry in the picture, so if you two need a rest stop, you'll have ten minutes."

"I could use a stop, and I expect Little Lloyd could too. Though I hate to take the time for it. We might think about getting some supper pretty soon, too. It's getting dark, Mr. Pickens, and we're a long way from home."

"Nothing would do but you had to come along, so don't complain to me."

"I'm not complaining, I'm just reminding."

I think he growled, so in an effort to make him feel better, I said, "If you need to use a phone, why don't you use the one in the car?"

The car swerved as he jerked his head around toward me. "You have a car phone? Why didn't you tell me?"

"You didn't ask."

He said an ugly word under his breath that nearly raised the hair off my head. Then, "Well, where is it?"

"I don't like that kind of talk, Mr. Pickens, and I'm not going to warn you again. Look in the console."

But by that time Little Lloyd had gotten it out for him. "I should've told you, Mr. Pickens; I just didn't think."

"Let me have it first, Little Lloyd," I said, reaching between the seats. "I need to call Lillian, and Mr. Pickens shouldn't talk on the thing while he's driving, anyway."

That got me a rearview mirror glare that I pretended not to see. "Hurry up, then. I need it."

Little Lloyd showed me how to turn the power on, and I dialed home. When Lillian answered, I could hardly get a word in edgewise as she castigated me for being out of touch so long.

"Where you been? Where're you now? Why don't you let me know something? I been settin' here, worryin' myself sick all day. Have you found her? When you be home?"

"Lillian, Lillian, wait, let me catch up here. We're on the highway, outside of Charlotte on our way to see Jerry Johnson . . . Well, I don't know, but Mr. Pickens seems to think Mr. Johnson can help, although it's hard to tell what Mr. Pickens thinks half the time." And I did a little glaring of my own at the back of that black head in front of me.

Then Lillian told me something that gave me a start. "Deputy Coleman Bates come by this afternoon, an' he set an' talk for a long time. He say he figure you done take Little Lloyd off somewheres, though that Lieutenant Peavey don't 'spect nothin' like that yet. An' he say it be better if you bring that boy on home an' face the music, an' it got to be done real soon. Time runnin' out, but he say he don't think no judge gonna grant custody to anybody but his mama, but runnin' from the Law ain't no way to handle it." She took a deep breath. "I think I got all he say. But, Miss Julia, he worriet 'bout you an' the trouble you lettin' yo'self in for, an' he want to help but he say his hands're tied up, long as you don't show up with Little Lloyd like you 'sposed to."

I turned away from the front and lowered my voice, not wanting Mr. Pickens to hear this line of discussion. "Doesn't Coleman know we're looking for the child's mother?"

Mr. Pickens looked up in that mirror he was so fond of and said, "Don't stay on the phone forever. I need to use it."

"Have patience, Mr. Pickens," I said, then whispered into the phone, "Now, Lillian, we're not exactly running from the Law, even though it might look like we are. We're dealing with two separate things here, and Coleman needs to understand that."

"I don't think he do," Lillian said. "They all mashed together in his mind, seem like. Anyway, Mr. Sam been callin' off and on all day long, an' he get that home nurse to bring him over here, too."

That got my back up in a hurry. "What! Why'd he do a thing like that?"

"He jus' see if I doin' all right by myself, an' see have I heard from you. He real upset, not knowin' where you are an' what you doin'."

"Well, just let him be upset. The idea, bringing that woman into my house." I gripped the phone as if my life depended on it, trying to hold on to my temper. That Sam, out running around with a tempting woman who'd stop at nothing. I knew her type, and Sam was doing nothing to put a stop to it. You can't trust anybody these days, especially a man you find yourself thinking about too much.

Lillian broke into my thoughts. "You still there?"

"Just thinking. Lillian, call him tomorrow and tell him I don't need his worry or his concern. Tell him I hope he's enjoying himself."

"I'll do no sucha thing. All he want to do is help us out, an' the least you can do is be nice to him."

Mr. Pickens chimed in again, "Hurry up back there; you'll use up all the power."

"Oh, hold your horses. Not you, Lillian. Mr. Pickens thinks everybody ought to jump on his say-so." I turned even further into the upholstery and whispered, "Now, listen, don't tell Sam about Little Lloyd's trouble. Since he's taken up with that woman, no telling what he's likely to do, and remember to let Lieutenant Peavey think that the child's with his mother, and that I'm sick, and remember not to tell Coleman too much."

"I don't know can I keep all them stories straight, but one more thing. Miz Conover, she come over all upset an' cryin' this mornin', an' I hope you know what her trouble is, 'cause it don't make no sense to me."

"To me, either," I said, thinking that I was glad to've missed that visit. "Call her, if you don't mind, and tell her I'll be in touch as soon as we get back. You didn't tell her what we're doing, did you?"

"No'm, but she get mad when I told her you not here. She don't ax no questions, jus' say it a fine time to be out of town when yo' friends need you."

I sighed. LuAnne couldn't allow anybody but herself to have trouble on their hands. "I'll make it up to her when we get home. Anything else?"

"Yessum, yo' preacher, he come over an' he don't want to say too much. But he go all the way 'round Robin Hood's barn tryin' to find out if I know anything about that Mr. Hodge. He worriet about that man, I could tell, an' yo' church, too. He pale as a sheet, eyes flittin' about everywhere, mumblin' 'bout Miss Hazel Marie, an' when she be home, an' church financials, an' I don't know what all. Then he kinda come to hisself an' say he sure Mr. Hodge be in Charlotte doin' the Lord's work, an' he worriet that you might be slanderin' him."

"Slandering who? Him or Mr. Hodge?"

"Mr. Hodge, I think he mean."

"I'll tell you this, Lillian, I'm going to do more than slander Wilson

T. Hodge if we ever find him. I have to hang up now; Mr. Pickens is having a fit, and him driving, too."

"Well, one more thing happen you not gonna like."

"Thay Lord, what else?"

"Somebody call on the telephone, wantin' to speak to Little Lloyd. When I say he not here, that somebody say real mad like, 'Well, where is he?' He say that boy 'sposed to be here an' he say Miss Hazel Marie, she messin' with fire, leadin' the Lord's anointed into sin an' he ain't gonna set by an' do nothin' an' he have a good mind to sue somebody. He don't say who he is but, Miss Julia, I think it be that Brother Vern. He hang up 'fore I get it outta him."

"My Lord." I sat there, running up the phone bill, trying to make sense of it all. "What in the world was the man talking about? Wilson T.'s nothing but a hired fund-raiser, and how anybody could call him the Lord's anointed is beyond me. And, for his information, Hazel Marie's not leading anybody into sin; it's the other way around. I declare, Lillian, the man's crazy as a loon." I started to say that's what happens when you get so wrapped up in the Gospel that you start judging everybody but yourself, but I didn't, since once I got started on that subject, I wouldn't be able to quit.

"I'll straighten him out when we get home. Lillian, it sounds like you're holding things down real well, and I thank you for it. Just keep on like you're doing, and I'll let you know if, I mean when, we find Hazel Marie. I'd put Little Lloyd on, but I'm afraid Mr. Pickens would cut a flip. We'll see you soon."

I punched the off button and said, as pleasantly as I could, as I handed the phone over the seat, "Here you go, Mr. Pickens. Your turn now."

He took it out of my hand, without a word, and turned the car into the parking lot of a McDonald's, which I would've bypassed if it'd been up to me. But I figured by that time I'd better keep my preferences to myself.

"You two go on in," he said. "And don't linger."

As we got out of the car, he began dialing without telling us another word about what his plans were. I was about fed up with his behavior, and hoped Little Lloyd wasn't taking any lessons in unacceptable conduct from him.

I stuck my head back in the car, thinking that I'd show him I could be nice, even if he couldn't. "You want us to bring you something?"

"No, I do not."

"Well, no need to be rude, Mr. Pickens. It's most unattractive. Come on, Little Lloyd, let's leave him to sulk by himself."

Chapter 19

By the time we got back to the car, Mr. Pickens was just finishing with his telephone call, but did he tell us what he'd learned? No, he did not. But I'd brought him the biggest Big Mac on the menu, thinking he'd be in a better mood if he had something on his stomach.

He unwrapped the thing with a nod of thanks, which was certainly insufficient, and set his coffee in the cupholder. Then he cranked the car, backed out and steered us out on the highway, all with one hand.

"Where're we going now?" I ventured to ask.

"I told you. We're going to Jerry's."

"You just talked to him, didn't you? Going to see him'll just delay us that much longer. It's Hazel Marie we need to be looking for, I don't care how much sympathy you have for your friend."

"Give me some credit here," Mr. Pickens said, wadding up his hamburger wrapping like he wanted to do the same to somebody. "Jerry knows Bigelow, knows where he lives, knows where he hangs out, knows what we need to know. That's why we're going to see him. I hope that meets with your approval."

I studied on that for a minute, wondering why Mr. Pickens had such a prickly temperament. Poor upbringing, probably. All I was trying to do was keep his mind where it was supposed to be. As I looked out the window at the darkening streets, the car lights and street lights coming on, it seemed to me that his mind was working out what to do with the passengers he hadn't wanted along in the first place. I wouldn't've put it past him to be planning to dump us off for the night while he went off on his own. And if that's what he was thinking, he was going to have another think coming because I didn't plan to let him out of my sight.

"Maybe Jerry Johnson can help us, Miss Julia," Little Lloyd said. "He's real famous and knows a lot of people." Then turning to Mr. Pickens, he asked, "Do you think he'd let me see his racing truck?"

"You bet, sport," Mr. Pickens answered. "You can see his shop, meet his team, sit in the truck, whatever you want."

Huh, I thought, sounds like Mr. Pickens is planning to stay awhile. Which meant we'd be staying, too.

"If you're not going to look for Hazel Marie tonight, Mr. Pickens, I'd as soon stay at a Holiday Inn."

He ignored me.

"I can't wait." Little Lloyd bounced in his seat, as the two of them continued to discuss a matter foreign to me. "He won at Homestead-Miami last year. I saw it on ESPN. Did you see that, Mr. Pickens? Did you see it when he made contact with the wall and spun out? He came out of it and poured on the power, fish-tailed around the turn and took the lead again."

"Yeah, and he's right on up there this year."

"How many points does he have so far?"

"Beats me. I used to keep up with him, but I've lost track here lately."

I'd had enough of being left out. "What're we talking about?"

"Jerry Johnson's run for the championship, Miss Julia," Little Lloyd said, craning his head around the front seat. "You know, his standing in points."

"Well, no, I don't know, but I'll take your word for it. And at the risk of repeating myself, I'd prefer to go to a motel, unless Mr. Pickens plans to drive home tonight. Which I don't think he ought to do since he's been on the go all day long, and ought to be tired. Besides, I think we ought to find Bigelow's place and see if Hazel Marie's there or not."

Mr. Pickens said, "Give it a rest, hon. I'm working on it." Which had to suffice because that's all I could get out of him.

It'd been dark for a good while by this time, although it wasn't that late, and we'd quickly driven through and out of the little town of Rockingham. All I could see was flat country, farmland, sandhills and pine trees that were typical of that area of the state. As far as I could tell we were going south on a straight, two-lane road, with nothing between us and South Carolina but more of the same. It made me nervous.

"Mr. Pickens," I said, "I need to know exactly what you have in mind. May I remind you that you're in my employ, and I'm requesting an accounting from you."

He glanced in the rearview mirror. "Got you worried?"

"Why, no. I generally enjoy tooling around in strange places after dark with somebody I hardly know at the wheel."

He may have smiled, but who could tell since he did it so infrequently. "Jerry knows the area, and he knows the racing circuit. If this

Bigelow has a place to hole up, Jerry'll know it. And he can give us some background on him."

"Well, that makes sense then. I declare, Mr. Pickens, you have a good mind for your business and, if you'd just tell me what you're doing, we'd get along so much better. That's just my opinion, though."

"I figure you'd have something to say regardless of what I come up with, and I'd as soon not have to put up with your arguments until I have to."

"Why, Mr. Pickens, when have I argued with you?"

"When have you not?"

"Well, don't expect one now. You're doing just fine, and as long as you don't expect me to get in something that goes around in circles on a racetrack, I'll put up with whatever you decide on."

"We'll see," he said, giving Little Lloyd another sideways grin.

"Miss Julia," Little Lloyd said, "I wish you and Mr. Pickens wouldn't fuss at each other so much."

"Don't let us worry you," I said, reaching up to pat him. "Mr. Pickens doesn't pay attention to me anyway. Everything I say just rolls off his back, although he'd do well to listen to me on occasion."

Mr. Pickens grunted, which I decided to take as agreement. Then he said to Little Lloyd, "Watch for a turnoff up here pretty soon. It's a state road, so there ought to be a sign."

When we came to it, Mr. Pickens turned left onto an asphalt road that led between nubby pines crowding up on each side of the road. Weeds grew in the ditches and, in the dark with only our headlights to see by, it seemed as if we were traveling through a tunnel. There wasn't a streetlight or a glow from a house or any other indication of human habitation. I couldn't for the life of me figure what a race-car, or race-truck, driver would be doing so far off the beaten path. It gave me an awful lonesome feeling, especially at the thought of Hazel Marie in some similar place without a friendly face around her. At least I had Little Lloyd and, I guess, Mr. Pickens, who could be as friendly as you please as long as he was getting his way.

Soon, though, after several twists and turns in the road, a bright glow ahead lit up the countryside. Mr. Pickens turned through a gate in a chain-link fence onto a large paved area. Pole lights made the place clear as day, and I could see a huge low-slung building in the center with a sign that read JERRY JOHNSON RACING on it. Several cars were parked in front and on the side of the building, and I caught a glimpse of a huge tractor-trailer in the back.

"End of the line," Mr. Pickens said, as he parked close to the front door of what looked like an office entrance. "Everybody out."

Before we got to the door, it swung open and a skinny backwoods-looking man with a head of straw-colored hair and a matching bushy mustache bounded out, grinning to beat the band.

"J. D.!" he yelled. "Where the hell you been, son? Man, you showed up just in time. Get on in here an' let me look at you."

Lord, the man was loud, making me want to step back out of range of what was coming out of his mouth. He was a picture, too, wearing blue jeans so tight that I wondered if he'd given a thought to the damage they could do. A wide belt with an engraved buckle rode low on his thin hips, and a bright blue silk shirt made in the Western manner was tucked neatly into his pants. Cowboy boots, a large gold watch on his wrist, and several gold chains around his neck rounded out his outfit. I don't ordinarily trust men who wear necklaces but, if he was willing to give us some help, I'd be willing to make an exception. Although when I caught sight of a tiny gold ring in his ear, I nearly reconsidered.

His lined and weathered face creased in a wide grin as he led us through a narrow hall with an office on either side, then through another door into a cavernous space littered with parts and carcasses of pickup trucks, tools, rolling carts and various pieces of machinery.

"Look at this, would you?" he bellowed, giving Mr. Pickens a whack on the back. "Man, we oughta been smokin' with the new sponsors we got, JR Landscaping's handin' out money right and left, there wasn't nothin' too good for us. But take a gander at it now. It's just a flat mess; they musta took a ballpeen hammer to everything in here." His voice caught in his throat at the outrage he was feeling.

I couldn't see it, myself. The place looked pretty much like every other garage I'd ever seen, although bigger and considerably cleaner. I'd give them that.

"Hey, boys," Mr. Johnson yelled. "Look who's here! Got us some real help now."

Several men in white coveralls disengaged from under hoods and axles and came over, smiling and wiping greasy hands on the cleanest rags I'd ever seen. They swarmed around Mr. Pickens, grinning and smacking him on the back. That seemed to be the normal method of greeting, and I determined to keep my distance from all of them, not wanting to be pounded half to death.

Little Lloyd and I hung back while Mr. Pickens shook hands all around, asking how everybody was and, in general, enjoying the welcome he was getting.

I heard one of them say, "What you been up to, J. D.? Drinkin' the whole state dry?" I figured right then that Mr. Pickens's dissolute character was well known to them.

Mr. Pickens finally turned to us, saying, "Jerry, I want you to meet Mrs. Julia Springer, and this is Lloyd Puckett." He gestured toward us, just as I was wondering when he was going to take notice of the one who was footing the bill.

Jerry Johnson whirled around and came bounding over to us, his hand outstretched. "Glad to have you," he bellowed, "real glad to have you folks. Hey! I know a Southern gal when I see one. Bet they call you Miss Julia, don't they?"

I gave him my hand in greeting and almost had it wrung off. "Some do," I said. "Mr. Johnson . . ."

"Jerry! Call me Jerry! Hell, 'scuse me, ma'am, last time I got called Mr. Johnson, it was a judge doin' the callin'!" Then he offered his hand to Little Lloyd, who shook it just like I'd trained him to do. "How do? You like racin'? Look around all you want, Floyd, there's lots to see."

"Lloyd," Little Lloyd corrected him, but he seemed dazed to be in the presence of this loud-talking, seemingly famous personage. I don't think he cared what name he was called.

"We got a lounge over yonder," Mr. Johnson yelled, making me wonder if he thought we were all deaf as posts. "Come on and take a load off. We'll lift a few and get ourselves caught up. J. D., I got trouble you won't believe, son, and I hope you can help us out here. Come on, Miss Julia, honey, you look like you could use a little."

He swung an arm around Mr. Pickens's shoulders and motioned for me to come with them. I followed, but kept my distance, not wanting to lose my hearing and not sure of what he was offering. Coffee sounded good, since it looked as if our bedtime was nowhere near. He led us to a corner room with couches, easy chairs, a television set and racing magazines open on the tables.

I glanced back at Little Lloyd, but he'd been taken in hand by the mechanics and seemed intently interested in what they were showing him under the hood of one of the garishly painted, though dismantled, trucks.

As I made my way to a chair, Mr. Johnson pulled out three bottles of beer from a refrigerator, handing one to Mr. Pickens and setting another one in front of me. That just did me in. Did I look like somebody who'd drink that stuff?

"I don't care for it," I said. "Thank you all the same."

"Oh, you want a glass?" Mr. Johnson was instantly solicitous. 'Scuse me, I wasn't thinkin'. I'll get you a glass."

328 · ANN B. ROSS

"No, thank you. A glass won't change the contents, though I appreciate the offer. I'm a Presbyterian, Mr. Johnson."

"That a fact? Well, I'm a Baptist myself, but lemme get you a soft drink. Don't want you to break no rules or nothin'." And he laughed in a good-natured, but ear-shattering, way.

Mr. Pickens was having nothing to say, just sitting there with a self-satisfied smile on his face with that brown bottle in his hand. It seemed to me that he'd follow my lead and turn his back on temptation, but before I knew it the both of them were opening two more bottles. I sat stiffly, registering my disapproval as best as I could, but it didn't seem to affect them one way or the other.

Just as I nudged Mr. Pickens to get down to business and engage Mr. Johnson's interest in our problem, Mr. Johnson began to regale us with his own.

"J. D.," he blared, "I swear to God, you couldn't of showed up at a better time. Man, I need some help real bad."

"Nothing's changed since we talked?"

"Not a blamed thing." Mr. Johnson bowed his head and, I won't swear to it since that's not my way, but his eyes seemed to get wet and glittery. My heart went out to him, knowing as I did, what it was like to suffer a loss.

"Don't look like I'm ever gonna get it back," Mr. Johnson went on, shaking his head in sorrow. "Might as well hang it up, as far's my driving's concerned. I guess I'll go ahead and send the crew on to Phoenix, then we'll light out for Mesa Marin, but it'll just be goin' through the motions. We had to buy more power tools, and then we begged and borrowed some setup disks. You know, I got the best fabricator and engine man in the business, and they was able to get a truck halfway ready to run, but I'm gonna have to put a young driver in it. Won't be me, that's for sure, even though everybody's countin' on me. I swear, J. D., I won't hardly be able to hold my head up anymore, settin' on the sidelines watchin' my Number 17 JR Landscapin' GMC truck come trailin' in like a cow's tail."

"Hey, don't be giving up so quick," Mr. Pickens said with a great deal more concern than he'd been showing me. "You've still got a few days before the Phoenix race and, now that I'm here, we'll track down Bigelow and get you set."

That deserved a comment from me, if anything ever did. "Mr. Pickens has a lot of self-confidence, Mr. Johnson. You may have noticed that."

"I sure do need some from somebody," Mr. Johnson said, hanging his head low and modulating his voice to a normal level. Clearly, he was powerfully moved. "Any kind of confidence I ever had is flat gone. I tell you, J. D., I've had bad dreams about even climbing in that truck. I hate to admit it, never thought I'd get so dependent on anything in my life. I'm thinkin' I ought to just pull on out now. All I can see is my Number 17 truck comin' in dead last, embarrassing myself and my whole crew. Or something even worse. No way in the world I'm not gonna go down in points, and that's just gonna kill me. Here I got a world-class pit crew and a A-number one sponsor, and not a lick of luck to go with 'em."

"Jerry," Mr. Pickens said, leaning toward him, "I know you put a lot of stock in that lucky charm of yours, but that's not what makes you win races."

Lucky charm? I thought, frowning. It beat all I'd ever heard to listen to two grown men talking about lucky charms.

"I know it don't make no sense," Mr. Johnson said. "But like I told you on the phone, once something like that gets in your head, all you can do is go with it. If you got it, which I don't since that's what Bigelow was after all along. Everything else he did was just to cover up."

Mr. Pickens frowned, commiserating with his friend, while I wondered how a grown man could be so superstitious as to be undone over a charm like the ones Hazel Marie had been dropping like bread crumbs along her trail. But, of course, you could never tell about a man who wore as much jewelry as Mr. Johnson did. Some people I knew had lucky coins or four-leaf clovers that they thought brought them good luck, and most of them churchgoing people too. I even knew one man who carried a buckeye in his pocket every day of his life. Not that it'd done him any good, since his place of business burned down and he was arrested for arson.

I tried my best to be patient and sympathetic to Mr. Johnson's plight but, let's face it, Hazel Marie was more important than finding a piece of jewelry or an Indian-head nickel or whatever it was. Even if it meant losing a race or two, which I couldn't bring myself to believe would happen in the first place. I'd always believed that luck was a matter of grit and determination, to say nothing of your basic character traits and willingness to work for what you wanted. But I didn't share my thoughts, being a visitor and all.

I did get concerned, though, that Mr. Pickens would let himself be sidetracked and would put his mind on Mr. Johnson's minor problem to the detriment of what he was hired to do. I began to tap my foot, impatient to get to our business.

Even though I was agitated enough to jump out of my skin, Mr. Pickens went right ahead and promised again to help Mr. Johnson find his lucky charm. Then, to my great relief, he said, "But I've got Miss Julia's case to wrap up first. Although one might well wrap up the other. Here's how I see it."

And Mr. Pickens began to tell Mr. Johnson how he'd put together my missing person with Mr. Johnson's missing trinket. He told him what the Abbot County deputies had found in Bigelow's shop, which didn't include any people to rescue or crooks to arrest. Then he told him about our stops in Gastonia and Charlotte.

"Looks like they headed back this way," Mr. Pickens said. "I'm figuring that from the Gastonia connection, as well as what I found in Hodge's townhouse. Show him, Miss Julia."

I dug the notebook, papers and ticket stubs from my pocketbook and handed them over.

"Well, I be dog," Mr. Johnson said, as he shuffled through them. "I knew Bigelow had a hand in stealin' my lucky charm from the cap somebody lost. But I thought it was just to put me outta the runnin', seein' as how he's always wanted to beat me. I can't stand him an' his underhanded ways, an' he can't stand me. But I sure didn't know he was up to his neck in gambling. This here's big money, son."

"We still don't know if he's in it," Mr. Pickens said. "Those bets may just be Hodge's doing." Then he went on to tell Mr. Johnson about Hazel Marie and her connection to Wilson T., as well as about the charms we'd been following, and how we needed to know whatever Mr. Johnson could tell us about Bigelow and where he might be.

Mr. Johnson kept quiet, listening and tipping up his bottle and nodding his head. When Mr. Pickens wound down, Mr. Johnson nodded again and leaned forward in his chair, his arms resting on his knees.

"Ole Bob Bigelow used to be big in street stocks. Did a lot of drivin' when he was a young man. Daddy knew him. Never liked him much, though. He was mixed up in all kinda stuff on both sides of the Law, so they say. But whatever you're lookin' into now, he ain't in it. Kicked the bucket 'bout ten year ago. He left a bunch of kinfolk, though, an' all of 'em into racin' of some kind. Coupla of 'em drive on the monster truck circuit, some in the Daytona Dash, an' this, that, an' the other, all tryin' to work up to the Busch and Winston Cup Series. On my back, too. An' you might be interested in this. Hodge is the name of one side of the family, but the worst of the whole lot is Bobby Bigelow, Jr., who took up where the ole man left off, and that's who you're lookin' for. I'll tell you one thing, he's meaner'n a snake.

Puts on a good front for NASCAR officials, but he'll do whatever it takes to win. And what he's done to me is a good example of it."

"Yeah, well, now we know how far outside the Law he's willing to go," Mr. Pickens said, emptying his second bottle and getting up to help himself to another one. I frowned at him but he didn't notice. "It looks like they want to take you down and make some money on it, too. Hodge is one of them, maybe the one assigned to place the bets even if he didn't take part in the break-in. I found phone numbers and addresses for both Bigelow shops in his house, and some other stuff that puts him right in with Bigelow. But," he went on, nodding his head at me, "my main concern is finding the woman 'cause it sure looks like she wants to be found."

"It do, don't it? Dropping all them clues like she done. I hate to say this," Mr. Johnson said, in what for him was a subdued kind of way as he looked at me, "but they's some rough folks back in these parts. So I'd like to he'p you, and maybe find my lucky charm too. Besides," he went on in a normal tone, which for him was just below a bellow, "I don't like the idea of them tryin' to fix NASCAR races. Us drivers have a reputation to uphold with the fans. That kinda stuff puts us all in a bad light."

"We don't like what they're doing to NASCAR, either," I said, although I'd never lose a wink of sleep over it. But I was determined to nip in the bud any further display of self-pity about his loss. First things first, I always say. "And that little boy out yonder is just worried sick about his mother, to say nothing of myself. I'd be so grateful for any help you could give us in finding Hazel Marie."

"Okay, here's the scoop. Bigelow's place's about twelve miles west of here if you got wings, twice that on wheels." And he began telling us how you go so many miles and take a right at Junior's Stop and Shop, then a left at old man Whitaker's place, then you take a right on a dirt road that was easy to miss if you didn't know what you were looking for. He stopped and took a deep breath. "I might better go with you. You don't want to tangle with him by yourself."

"Let's go, then," I said, gathering my coat and purse and thinking it was about time we did something besides talk.

Mr. Pickens and Mr. Johnson looked at each other, nodded in unspoken agreement, then Mr. Pickens said, "Not tonight. I want to check in with the local sheriff, see what they've come up with, and be sure we won't be stepping on an operation they've already got in place. First thing in the morning, okay?"

"Yeah," Mr. Johnson agreed, "it'd be better to go on to my house for the night. If Bigelow's Abbot County crew cleared out up there like you say, they'll be joining up with the team at his shop here. We'll probably need a little help to handle 'em. And I'm like J. D., I don't wanta mess with anything the sheriff's got goin'."

I didn't like it, but far be it from me to interfere with the Law.

"Mr. Pickens," I said, fastening my seatbelt as we prepared to follow Mr. Johnson to his house. In spite of the fact that I'd made my sleeping preferences so clearly known. "Why does that gentleman talk in such a loud manner? Does he think we're all deaf?"

"No, but he is." Mr. Pickens switched on the headlights and pulled out behind Mr. Johnson's fancy red car that Little Lloyd was so taken with. "Or all but. He's been around racing all his life, driving, and testing and building engines. The noise is something else. You ought to go to a race sometime and see for yourself."

That was a suggestion that didn't warrant an answer, so I turned to another subject. "Well, tell me this. What in the world would a race-car driver be doing with a lucky charm? I mean, I know men have taken to wearing earrings and necklaces and such, but a charm bracelet? I'm surprised a man would admit to such a thing."

"It's not that kind of charm," Mr. Pickens said. "Tell the truth, not many people know what it is since he keeps it pretty close to his chest." That seemed to tickle him, but he didn't share the joke with us. "I know a little about it, but I'm not at liberty to tell anybody. Client confidentiality, you know," he said, with a glance in the rearview mirror. "But it's not unusual for drivers to have something they consider lucky, like a special pair of driving shoes or something. I know one driver who has to have a pat on the back from his crew chief right before he starts his engine. He can't stand it if the chief forgets. But Jerry, well, he really believes his charm not only helps him win, but it keeps him safe. He doesn't want anybody to know how much he depends on it, and the fact that he admitted as much to us, shows how it tears him up to be without it."

"Well, I never," I said.

"How'd whatever it is get to be lucky?" Little Lloyd asked, while I hoped he wouldn't be influenced by hearing so much about such superstitious beliefs. Pastor Ledbetter would say it was all of the devil, but I couldn't help being somewhat interested in the answer, myself.

"All I know is that Jerry had it with him when he was running in the Pronto Auto Parts 400 a few years ago. Somebody made contact as they were coming off turn two going wide open, bounced Jerry off the wall and flipped him three or four times. Threw the engine two hundred feet one way and the transmission into the infield. About all that was left was the bent-up frame with Jerry still strapped in. Worst thing I ever saw, but he came out of it like a, well," he stopped and grinned, "like a charm. Banged up pretty good, but it's a wonder it didn't kill him. Ever since, he's been convinced that something his wife gave him that morning was what kept him alive." Mr. Pickens stopped again, giving us time to absorb what he'd said. " 'Course," he went on, "the wife's long gone, but he's still got that lucky charm. Or did, up until now."

"What a remarkable story," I said, unable to comprehend such dependence on a material item. "Pitiful, though."

Mr. Pickens didn't answer, so I sat back in the corner of the back seat, contemplating our next moves.

"Mr. Pickens?"

"What?"

"If Mr. Johnson's lucky charm is such a big secret, how would anybody know what to steal?"

"That's the kicker," Mr. Pickens said. "Bobby Bigelow, according to Jerry, is one of the few who knows what it is. Saw Jerry putting it on under his Nomex one time, that's a driving suit to you. That's one reason he kept it under lock and key from then on."

I thought about this for a while, feeling the car sway through the turns on the back road. And wondering where Hazel Marie was and what she was doing.

"Mr. Pickens?"

"What now?"

"Well, we now know where this Bigelow garage is, but what're we going to do about it? I mean, it's possible that Hazel Marie is there, isn't it? Or that somebody there knows where she is? I still think we ought to go right out there and do some investigating."

"We are. First thing in the morning."

That didn't make sense to me. The best time to sneak around and see what somebody was up to was in the dead of night, and I said as much to him. And Little Lloyd agreed with me, which should've decided it once and for all. But it didn't.

"Look," Mr. Pickens said, and I prepared myself for another lecture on investigative techniques. "I know what I'm doing, so just let me do it."

"Well, it seems to me that going to some stranger's house and spending the night is not doing much of anything. And I hope you're not going to let yourself get diverted by Mr. Johnson's loss. I mean, I sympathize and all that, but who knows what Hazel Marie's going through right this minute? I say let's go on and try to find her."

"I do, too," Little Lloyd said. "They might take her somewhere else by morning. My stomach gets all knotted up, just thinking about it."

"Both of you, listen to me," Mr. Pickens said, as he turned into the yard of a house with four large pillars along a front porch. I had Hazel Marie so much on my mind that I couldn't give the place the attention it deserved, but it crossed my mind that the racing business must pay real well. Mr. Pickens parked the car on the horseshoe drive and turned in his seat to face me. "I need to make some phone calls, check in with the local sheriff and the Abbotsville Sheriff's Department, then talk to some of my buddies on the Charlotte-Mecklenburg force. See what else I can come up with on this Hodge character. I don't want to go out there blind, not knowing how many's out there or what I'll find. I'm going to get your lady back for you, but I don't want to put her in danger when I do. And Jerry's gonna be a help, not a hindrance. Now does that explain anything to you?" Then turning to Little Lloyd, he said, "What about you, sport? You all right with this?"

"Yessir, I just want to find my mama. My nerves're getting real bad, I'm so worried."

"I know you are, but you get a good night's sleep and we'll find her tomorrow."

It seemed I'd heard that promise before. Still, his reasons for delaying made sense, so I contented myself with following him out of the car and into Mr. Johnson's house.

It was a sight. I didn't know who his decorator had been, but whoever it was ought to've been ashamed of herself. I'd never seen such a conglomeration of styles in the furnishings, lots of cowhide and leather and animal heads, along with crocheted pillows and afghans. Embroidered samplers and Bible verses were framed and hanging on the walls in between racks of guns. There were braided rugs on the floor and a huge stone fireplace taking up most of one wall. A lot of money had been spent to so little effect, other than to unsettle a woman of taste like me. Still, Mr. Johnson was a gracious host, offering food and more drink, which Mr. Pickens was foolish enough to accept, and showing Little Lloyd and me to our rooms off a hall that overlooked the two-story living room.

Lying in bed sometime later, unable to close my eyes, I could hear Mr. Pickens and Mr. Johnson talking, especially Mr. Johnson. But the house was so large that I only heard bits and pieces. As best as I could make out, they were making phone calls and working at Mr. Johnson's computer, whose programs and Internet access Mr. Pickens had been pleased to discover.

I turned over for the dozenth time, wishing for daylight and wondering how Little Lloyd was resting in the next room. Knowing I wouldn't sleep a wink with Hazel Marie weighing so heavy on my mind, I dropped off before I knew it.

———

I got up the next morning to a cold, overcast day from the dreary looks of Mr. Johnson's yard from my window. And from the looks of my face and hair in the bathroom mirror, I needed a croker sack over my head. It just doesn't do to go off without hygienic aids and clean step-ins. Thank goodness, I had a comb and face powder in my pocketbook.

I hated to face the day feeling and looking frowzy and disheveled, but you do what you have to do. This was the day we were going to find Hazel Marie or, barring that, at least make a raid of our own on another Bigelow warehouse or shop or garage, or whatever it was. To that end, I was eager to get started and wondered why I wasn't hearing Mr. Johnson's braying voice downstairs.

It struck me that the both of them had imbibed so much the previous night that they were still laid up in bed, sleeping it off. "If that's the case," I mumbled to myself, "I'm going to take a broom to both of them."

I went next door and got Little Lloyd moving, telling him to do the best he could with his teeth and urging him to hurry.

As I went downstairs to find out the plan of action for the day, the silence in the big house put me on edge. I wandered through the downstairs rooms, noting the empty bottles just left out to smell up the place. And the more I wandered the madder I got. There wasn't much I could do to straighten out Mr. Johnson; he wouldn't be under my influence long enough. But Mr. Pickens was another story, and I was determined to let him have some choice words on the matter of drinking on the job.

Although the truth of the matter was, he didn't need to be indulging at any time. That stuff just eats up your stomach.

By the time Little Lloyd came downstairs, looking a good deal worse for the wear as I did myself, I was getting more and more agitated. I took my comb to his hair, which was sticking up every which way, not that it did much good.

"Run back upstairs, Little Lloyd," I told him. "See if you can find

Mr. Pickens and Mr. Johnson and get them up. Tell them we're ready to go."

By that time I'd taken to wringing my hands, trying to calm my nerves and not let on to Little Lloyd how upset I was. The house had an empty feel to it, and I was beginning to suspect that the boy and I were the only ones in it.

My suspicion was confirmed when Little Lloyd came back down, his formerly sleep-glazed eyes now wide with worry, and said that they weren't in any of the beds. I knew what'd happened as soon as I opened the front door and found my car sitting where we'd left it and Mr. Johnson's car missing in action.

"They've gone, Little Lloyd! They've gone to look for your mother and just left us here." I stomped back inside, so outdone I could've wrung Mr. Pickens's neck if I'd had my hands on him. "I can't believe this! He knew we wanted to go, knew I wanted to get my hands on Wilson T. and that Bigelow, too. And what has he done? Waited till we were asleep and snuck off just to keep us from going. I've a good mind to get in our car and go home without him! Just strand him like he's stranded us. That'd show him!"

Little Lloyd was watching me rant and rave, his face screwed up with worry. "Let's don't do that, Miss Julia. We have to wait for him. If he finds my mama at Bigelow's, he'll bring her back here."

Well, of course the child was right. But that didn't make me feel better about any of it. Mr. Pickens had me where he wanted me—out of his hair and stuck where I was. I didn't like it one little bit.

"How long have they been gone, I wonder? Did you hear them leave? I didn't either. I didn't hear a thing, just slept like a log while Mr. Pickens—I know it was him—planned this sneaky, underhanded and totally unwarranted maneuver to keep us from going. Just had to do it himself, that's all it was. I'll tell you, Little Lloyd, egotism is a terrible affliction and I hope you take a lesson from this."

"Yessum, I will." The child was wringing his hands by this time, and I realized that I wasn't being much help in easing any of his worries.

"Are you hungry?"

"No'm, not much."

"Let's go to the kitchen anyway. Mr. Johnson can just treat us to some coffee."

We headed for the kitchen, a huge tiled room with every labor-saving device known to man. Which didn't do me a bit of good, since I didn't know how to work most of them.

When I got the coffee going, I turned to the boy with a sudden thought. "I know what we can do."

"I don't think we ought to, Miss Julia. We ought to stay right here and not go off anywhere. They may be on their way back right now, and have my mama with them." Little Lloyd had begun to pick at a hangnail, a sure sign of his distress. I took his hand and put it in his lap.

"No, I wasn't thinking about going off anywhere. We have to stay here, as Mr. Pickens well knew, because he was careful not to discuss his plans in my presence. No, I was thinking of calling Lillian again. You didn't get to talk to her yesterday, and maybe it'll keep us from worrying about what Mr. Pickens is up to."

He brightened at that, and looked around for a phone. "Will Mr. Johnson mind?"

"I don't care if he does. Well, on the other hand, maybe you ought to call collect. You know how to do it?"

"Yessum, I think so." He headed for the telephone on a far counter, while I poured coffee for both of us. While he spoke to an operator, I rummaged through the cabinets and refrigerator, looking for some little something to eat.

As soon as Little Lloyd got through to Lillian, I heard her shriek all the way across the room. Little Lloyd jumped off the stool he was sitting on, his face white and drawn, as he held the phone out to me.

"Something's happened, Miss Julia! She wants to talk to you." I snatched up the phone. "What? What is it? Lillian, slow down and tell me."

I listened, my hand clutching Little Lloyd's shoulder as he bit at his fingernail. We were both trembling, frightened at what couldn't be anything but more bad news, considering the run of bad luck we'd been having. I put my arm around the child and hugged him close, as much for my own comfort as his.

"What!" I jerked upright at Lillian's news. "Is that all she said? Tell me again, Lillian, tell me exactly what she said."

Lillian took a deep breath, ending with a quiver in it. "She say he takin' her to Phoenix, I think is what she say, an' she don't wanta go nowheres but home."

"Phoenix! Why?" But I knew why. It had to be for that blasted race next weekend.

"Miss Julia, I don't know an' I don't get a chance to ast her 'cause I break in an' say 'Where you at now?' an' she say she locked up in a RV goin' all over creation, an' now she parked in a field somewhere I never heard of."

"In a *field*! Where?" Lord, if we'd finally gotten the specifics but couldn't understand them, we'd be no better off than having no word at all.

"I don't know, Miss Julia, I jus' tellin' you what she say an' she talkin' real fast, sayin' she parked at the, let me see, I wrote it down, at the North Carolina Speedway an' they leavin' for Phoenix soon's they do some kind of practicin', so you got to hurry."

"Lillian, none of that helps me at all. The North Carolina Speedway could be anywhere in the state, and we can't search everywhere. Did she say anything else?"

"No'm, she kinda screeched then an' I hear some awful fumblin' an' mumblin' on the line an' the phone get hung up real hard. I jus' been worryin' something awful, 'cause I didn't know how to call you, so it a good thing you call me."

I nearly sagged with the thought that I'd only thought to call her to give Little Lloyd something to do besides jiggle around from one foot to the other. And with the thought that if we'd gone with Mr. Pickens, we wouldn't've called at all. Some things do work for good, even those you don't expect to.

"Hold on, Lillian. Little Lloyd, you have any idea where the North Carolina Speedway is?"

He put a finger to his lips, frowned in concentration and said, "No'm, but I know how to find out."

He ran out of the kitchen, and I quickly told Lillian we were hot on the trail and would be back in touch. Following Little Lloyd, I found him hunched in front of Mr. Johnson's computer. The thing was dinging and changing pictures, and I marveled at what they were teaching children in school these days.

I watched over his shoulder and whispered, "What're you doing?" Afraid to disrupt what was going on on the screen.

"Going online," he said, which didn't help. "Hold on a minute. Mr. Johnson's got NASCAR in his bookmarks. There it is. Now I'll just hit tracks and scroll . . . got it! Now, click on North Carolina Speedway and check the directions to it. Miss Julia! Look, look! We're practically at it. Ten miles from Rockingham. See that, on Highway One, ten miles from town. We can be there in no time."

Well, modern conveniences are wonderful, and that is a fact. Of course, you have to have somebody who knows how to make them work, and Little Lloyd knew more than I ever would.

But even with this new information, I began to wring my hands again. "That Mr. Pickens! Gone, just when we need him! Should we wait here for him or go look for her ourselves?"

Little Lloyd turned off the computer and swiveled around in the chair. He squinched up his eyes as he thought about our dilemma. "No two ways about it, Miss Julia, we've got to go. They've been moving all over the place and, if we wait, they may take her off somewhere else." He shivered. "Like Phoenix."

"You're right. Get your coat and let's go." Then I thought of another problem. "We can find Highway One, I have no doubt, but will there be signs to that speedway? How will we find it?"

"It's pretty big, Miss Julia. I don't think we can miss it. If you're willing to try, I'm willing to help."

The child's confidence was a comfort to me and I told him so. "Little Lloyd, you are a wonder, and I don't know what I'd do without you." Which brought to mind the danger waiting at home for him, and my redoubled determination not to have to do without him. "Let's go get your mama."

Well, the change in that child was nothing short of a miracle. Life came back to his eyes and color to his cheeks. And the jiggling turned into jumping, which I had to caution him against. Although I felt somewhat like doing it myself.

"Oh," he said, gloom settling on him again. "What if she's gone again by the time we get there?"

"One thing at a time, Little Lloyd. Let's just get there, then we'll see what else we have to worry about." It ran through my mind that here I was, doing everything myself. Again. And even with a private investigator on the job. But then, that's the burden an industrious person such as myself has to bear.

We scurried around, getting our coats and my pocketbook, and pinning on my hat with my heart pounding at the thought that they might take Hazel Marie across the country before we could get there. Lord, I didn't know the way to Phoenix and didn't want to learn.

But as anxious as I was to leave, I took the time to write Mr. Pickens a note, thinking as I did that it'd serve him right if we just left without telling him a thing, just as he'd done to us. But I'm a considerate person, and didn't want to put that kind of worry on him. Still, he needed to be taught a lesson.

So I wrote:

Gone to NC Speedway, 10 miles north of R., which is where H.M. is, parked in a field in somebody's RV and not at Bigelow's place as you have now ascertained for yourself. Will call you as soon as we find her. If you're back from wherever you went. Hope Mr. Johnson can get you somewhere to meet us before we go on to Abbotsville, since he's so willing to take you places. My kind regards to him for putting us up for the night.

There, I thought as I signed my name, that'll fix him. Maybe Mr. Pickens would think twice the next time he decided to leave us behind.

Thank goodness for the extra car key I kept in my purse, just as the manual recommended, for Mr. Pickens had known better than to leave the one he had. As if that was going to stop me.

But I had to admit to a few qualms about going off without him, even as I was pulling out of the driveway. I'd never liked doing unto others what they'd done unto me, although given the circumstances I had no choice in the matter. Hazel Marie needed us, and there was no telling when Mr. Pickens would get back. We surely couldn't be expected to sit around waiting on him while she was in danger.

"Let's hope we can find the place without spending all morning looking for it," I said, shivering in the cold car. "This weather's looking worse all the time."

Little Lloyd stopped biting his fingernail and put his mind to the directions he'd written out.

"Turn right when this road dead-ends, go back to Rockingham and look for Highway One. I don't think it'll be hard to find; it runs right into town." I declare, the child was smart as a whip, working computers, reading maps and doing all the things I didn't have time for. He wiggled in his seat, glanced at the speedometer, and revealed a bent for tact. "We might ought to hurry. What if she goes off again before we get there?"

"It won't be her doing, if she does. I tell you, Little Lloyd, that Wilson T. has a lot to answer for."

He nodded. "Bigelow, too," he said, biting his lip, because the thought of his mother being under somebody's thumb wasn't at all a comforting thought. It wasn't to me, either. But I strengthened my resolve by picturing Wilson T. and Bigelow and everybody with them at the mercy of Mr. Pickens. No, in the hands of Lieutenant Peavey made a more satisfying picture. That'd fix them, if they survived what I planned to do to them.

I grasped the steering wheel with both hands, seeing from the corner of my eye Little Lloyd wringing his, and knew that worry nagged at him, as well. I pushed on toward Rockingham, noticing with a sinking heart that a little rain was spitting against the windshield. I put the wipers on intermittent sweeps, and hoped the rain wouldn't get worse.

Neither of us had much to say, exchanging frowning glances as we entered the small town and started looking for highway signs. I continued to be concerned about the weather, what with the heavy clouds and freezing temperature. There was little chance of the rain turning to snow this far south but, up around Abbotsville, it'd be a different story.

"Those clouds look threatening, Little Lloyd. I just hope this rain doesn't freeze on the streets. But let's worry about one thing at a time. Once we have your mother with us, we'll manage whatever else comes our way."

"I wouldn't be so nervous if I knew she'd still be there. What if she's gone off again? You reckon she has?" Before I had to express my own worry on that score, he sat up and pointed to a sign. "There it is. Turn there, Miss Julia. Now it's just ten more miles."

I nodded, drove through the town as fast as I safely could and headed north toward Hazel Marie. Lord, I was beginning to wish Mr. Pickens was with us. And I was also about to worry myself sick over just how we'd get her away from people who didn't want to let her go. As much as Mr. Pickens could outrage me, I could've used some of his high-handedness in facing a bunch of thieves and crooks. But, as you've noticed, he was off on a wild goose chase while we were solving the case.

"Look!" Little Lloyd pointed ahead to our right. "There's the speedway!"

I gasped at the size of the thing. "My stars, it looks like a stadium."

"It kinda is, Miss Julia. Oh, I hope it's open. It's not a race day, so what if we can't get in? Look, there's a road. Turn right there."

I headed the car toward the huge structure, entering a parking area the likes of which I'd never seen except around a Wal-Mart. But this one was a sandy field with paved access roads running through it, and it was all but empty, with just a few cars and pickups inside a fence up near the stadium where the back of the bleachers rose up to a monstrous height. From the expanse of the parking area, racing must've been a popular spectator sport. Or else the owners were the optimistic type. A gate stood open, I was glad to see, and I drove right through it.

"I had no idea the thing would be this big. How in the world are we going to find her?"

"Go on around, Miss Julia. Maybe the parking lot is the field she was talking about."

But it wasn't. We went all through that sandy parking lot and there wasn't a recreational vehicle to be seen. And not much else, if the truth be known.

"Miss Julia!" Little Lloyd yelled, making me jump.

"What!"

"It's the *in*field! That's what she was talking about. It's got to be, or else they're gone. Oh, please, Miss Julia, let's try the infield."

"Well, I'm perfectly willing if I knew where it was."

"It's inside the track, you know, where pit row is."

Not knowing a pit row from a corn row, I said, "Just tell me how to get there."

"Keep going around," he said, leaning toward the dashboard to see better. "There ought to be a tunnel somewhere that'll take us under the grandstand and the track."

"Tunnel," I said, not at all liking the sound of that.

"There it is! Look, right down there. Drive in, Miss Julia, and we'll come out in the infield."

I hesitated at the mouth of one of the tunnels, reassured by the lights inside. Then I looked up at the back of the seats that towered over us, and lost my reassurance.

"You sure?"

"Yessum. This is the way all the transports and the fans' RVs go to get inside. Go ahead, Miss Julia, let's take it."

As I gingerly nosed the car into the passageway, Little Lloyd suddenly cried out, "Wait, wait, we're going in the out!"

"Too late," I said, thoroughly committed with no room to turn around. And I certainly wasn't going to back out. "I'll toot my horn."

I'd always thought tunnels were dark and narrow, but this one was plenty wide enough for my car. I caught my breath, though, when the tunnel took a downward slant and I realized what all was on top of us. But then, we were on an upward ramp and daylight, such as it was on a cloudy, threatening day, showed us the way out. I stopped as soon as we emerged, taking in the several acres of a grassy oval with paved drives threaded through it and several low block buildings scattered around. I looked up and around, marveling at the racetrack that curved and banked around us and the rows of bleachers stretching above our heads.

"You think we ought to be in here?" I whispered, awed by the immensity of the place.

"Look!" he shouted, pointing toward the buildings on the oval inside the track, "there's some people down there around that tractor-trailer. I bet they've been doing some practice runs."

I saw several men in coveralls closing up the back of the trailer, then I caught a glimpse of a beige recreational vehicle on the far side of it.

"There's one of those things she said she was in," I said. "You see it? I'm going to drive on up there, if I can manage it."

"Drive on the apron, Miss Julia. That's the level area at the bottom of the track. See it? Oh, I hope my mama's in that Winnebago."

"You watch for her, while I maneuver this thing." I eased the car onto what Little Lloyd had called the apron, which would be a surprise to Lillian, and drove sedately toward the tractor-trailer and the RV. As we drew closer, the men stopped what they were doing and watched us. I smiled and gave them a little wave, like we were tourists just passing by. Or the queen out for a drive.

I followed the curve of the infield, leaving the men still staring behind us. We drove around to the far side of the oval, with Little Lloyd twisting around to keep the RV in sight.

"How should we do this, Little Lloyd? If we knew for sure that she's in that Winne-whatever, we could drive right up to it and knock on the door. But if she's been moved to one of those buildings, we'd've given ourselves away."

"I know what we can do, Miss Julia," he said, bouncing up in his seat. "Hit the panic button and, wherever Mama is, she'll hear us."

"Hit the what?"

"This," he said and reached over to smack the large, red button in the middle of the dashboard. Then his little hands flashed here, there and yonder, twisting and turning knobs, and flipping switches all around and on the steering wheel. Well, that car kicked up a fit like it was in mortal agony, lights flashing and horn blaring and windshield wipers flapping, carrying on the likes of which I'd never seen nor heard.

"Thay Lord!" I said, coming to a halt, so unnerved I didn't know what to do.

"Don't stop! Keep going, but slow so she'll see us."

The child seemed to know what he was doing, so I followed directions and drove slowly on around the apron, drawing about opposite to where the RV was parked in the infield. The coveralled men had come around the tractor-trailer, trying to see what was wrong with us. Well, a lot of car horns get stuck, so I just looked straight ahead and pretended I didn't notice the racket we were making.

"There she is!" Little Lloyd screamed, jabbing his arm in front of my face and pointing to the infield. He unbuckled his seat belt, and

crawled between me and the steering wheel so he could lower my window and scream, "Mama! Mama!"

Thank goodness I was going slow or we'd've wrecked right there. I was finally able to get the child off me so I could see where I was going. Quick-thinking as always, Little Lloyd reached up and slid open the sunroof. Then he climbed onto the console and stood there, his head and shoulders sticking out of the top of the car, waving his arms and yelling to his mama. And here came Hazel Marie running across the grass, no coat, hat or gloves to her name. The RV door stood open behind her, and Wilson T. Hodge was bounding down the steps after her.

Hazel Marie screamed, "Miss Julia! Lloyd! Wait, I'm coming!" She ran for all she was worth, but Wilson T. was closing fast. The men on the far side of the field watched, then a few trotted off to join the chase.

"Hold on, Little Lloyd," I said, jerking the wheel and giving it the gas. We bounced onto the grassy field, the back wheels sliding a little before they grabbed and held.

I headed for Hazel Marie, lights still flashing and horn blaring loud enough to wake the dead. She ran toward us, screaming, her hair tangling in the wind and cold sprinkles of rain, and the dress she'd left home in three days ago flipping up around her you-know-what. Wilson T. looked beyond her and saw us coming. He put on a burst of speed and almost caught her. She swerved, then turned and swatted at him with her fist. As he grabbed at her again, she reared back and landed a kick that slowed but didn't stop him.

"Oh, hurry, hurry!" Little Lloyd screamed.

I was doing the best I could, trying to decide what to do first, get Hazel Marie or run Wilson T. down. As I swung the car between the two of them and skidded to a stop, Hazel Marie made the decision for me. She grabbed the door handle on my side and flung the door open.

"Miss Julia!" she screamed and leapt into the car, across the steering wheel and my lap, reaching for Little Lloyd as he tumbled back down into the car.

As Wilson T. stretched out his hand for the passenger door, I stomped on the gas, in spite of the fact that I couldn't see anything but Hazel Marie's bottom. She was wedged between me and the steering wheel, with her legs dangling out the open door.

"Get in!" I yelled, trying to drive by feel. The car bounced and swerved and skidded on the field, with Wilson T., first dodging, then chasing us. "Lordamercy, Hazel Marie, I can't see!"

She wiggled on across just as the car hit the pavement of the racetrack and we bounced back onto the oval. Crying and gasping and screaming, she ended up on top of Little Lloyd, while I slowed enough to get my door closed.

"Get us out of here!" Hazel Marie yelled. "Hurry, Miss Julia, hurry."

"Oh, Lord," I said, as I saw the RV trundling across the field toward us, and Wilson T. running alongside it until he could grab on and swing up inside. "They're after us. How do we get out of this place, Little Lloyd?"

"The tunnel! Find the tunnel."

I didn't have time to look, for the RV was coming fast. There was nowhere to go but around the track, so that's where I went. I didn't know those big, lumbering vehicles could go so fast but, before I knew it, the RV was right on our bumper.

"Speed up! Speed up!" Hazel Marie yelled, looking back at the thing filling our rear window. "It's Bigelow and he'll run us down!"

Well, I wasn't going to have my little car smashed to smithereens by the likes of him, not after having survived Mr. Pickens's driving. I mashed down on the gas pedal, feeling the car gather itself, then shift into a heretofore unused gear. It took off like a rocket and, before I could get a deep breath, we were zooming down the straightaway with that RV close behind and the first curve coming up fast.

"Go low, Miss Julia!" Little Lloyd screamed, trying to see the track from over his mother's shoulder. "Go low into the turn!"

That's what I was trying to do, aiming for the flat apron that we'd cruised so sedately only a few minutes before at—my Lord!—sixty-five miles an hour! I felt the car tilt as we went into the turn. Then we were slung up on the banked track, like we'd been snapped out of a slingshot. The next thing I knew we were whipping up on the bank, headed for the wall.

Hazel Marie shrieked. Little Lloyd screamed bloody murder.

"Turn it, oh, turn it!" Little Lloyd yelled.

Well, I'd been driving on crooked mountain roads for most of my life and, when you've seen one hairpin curve, you've seen them all. Although not ordinarily at this speed. I gave it some gas as we flew up into the turn, nudged the wheel just a little as the tires dug into the curve, and that little car whizzed by the wall with room to spare. Not much, I admit, but a miss is as good as a mile.

Then we were zooming down the opposite straightaway, edging toward eighty, and I risked a glance in the rearview mirror. The RV was coming on, but it'd lost ground on the turn, which didn't surprise me at all. Those things are top-heavy, don't you know. I managed the next two turns pretty much the same way, but the wall on that end seemed a whole lot closer.

"Look!" Hazel Marie yelled, pointing across the infield. "Oh, no, they're pulling the tractor-trailer across the track!"

"Find the tunnel!" Little Lloyd yelled, flailing the arm that wasn't pinned under his mother.

"One more of these turns and I'm heading for the field. Look for the tunnel so I'll know where to go."

The RV had pulled right back on our rear bumper as we headed into the next turn, and I didn't think I could go any faster. Not, and keep the car from flying off into the grandstand.

Holding on to the wheel for dear life and feeling the car swing up on the banked curve, we heard the most awful banging and scraping and sliding and skittering.

"They're shooting at us!" Little Lloyd screamed. "Oh, Lord!" I screamed.

"No, they've wrecked!" Hazel Marie yelled, craning her neck to look back. "Look! They blew a tire and slammed into the wall!"

I slowed somewhat and looked back. The RV was on its side, sliding along the bank with its top scraping the upper retaining wall. Smoke billowed up around the tires, and pieces of chrome and glass were flying along the track. The back end began to slue toward the apron, still sliding along the track.

"Oh, my Lord," I said, and poured on the power to get us out of the way. The thing was coming after us on its side about as fast as it had when it was upright. Then I looked ahead to see the tractor-trailer pulling across the straightaway. "Hold on!"

I was too close to the monster to stop, so I twitched the car into the remaining space between the truck grill and the wall, getting a glimpse of the driver's open mouth as we whizzed through. Hazel Marie and Little Lloyd screamed their heads off.

"Look for the tunnel!" I yelled, turning off the track and skidding onto the field. "I'm all turned around; help me find the thing!"

"There it is!" Hazel Marie screamed, her partially denuded charm bracelet jangling on her arm as she pointed ahead of us. "Right down there!"

I saw it then, and headed for it with hardly any let up in the speed. As we dashed across the field toward the tunnel, I caught a glimpse of Wilson T. and Bigelow climbing out of the RV. It had come to rest on the apron, lying on its side with wheels still spinning and smoke roiling around it. Bits and pieces of metal and tire treads were strewn in its wake on the track.

I aimed for the opening of the tunnel and hit the down ramp hard. The car leveled out at the bottom, then bounced up on the up ramp, popping out of that place like a piece of toast from a toaster. Lord, I was glad to see something besides a paved oval in front of me.

I headed for the highway as fast as I could, having had my fill of racetrack driving. There wasn't much traffic, which was both a good and a bad thing. Good, because we could make better time, and bad, because those idiots behind could overtake us. But not in the RV, I thought, with some satisfaction and a great deal of relief.

"Close that hole in the roof, Little Lloyd," I said, as I punched the button to run my window up. "It's freezing in here."

He did, then reached around his mother and stopped the racket the panic button had started. The quiet was a welcome relief from the spectacle we'd been making of ourselves. I wiped a hand on my coat, marveling that I was able to break the grip I'd had on the steering wheel. As I slowed to normal speed on the highway, I noticed that ice had begun to collect on the sides of the windshield where the wipers had swept it.

"This stuff's freezing," I said, as my blood pressure jumped a notch. I'd just run a road race that hadn't worried me half as much as the thought of driving home on icy roads. "You'd think the weather'd know it's March, and not January, wouldn't you?"

But Hazel Marie and Little Lloyd weren't paying attention to my problems. They were busy carrying on over each other.

"Lloyd! Baby, oh, sweetheart!" Hazel Marie cried, as the two of them wrapped themselves around each other, crying and squeezing and laughing all at the same time. "Where'd you come from? How'd you find me? Oh, my goodness, I'm so glad to see you!"

Then as they untangled themselves and Little Lloyd climbed between the seats to get in the back, Hazel Marie turned to me. "Oh, Miss Julia, I've never been so glad to see anybody in my life. How'd you know to come out there? I called Lillian but she didn't know how to get you. It was like a miracle when I looked out the window of that RV and saw your car. I couldn't believe it. Seemed like I'd just managed to slip and call Lillian on Wilson T.'s cell phone."

So I told her how we'd followed the trail of gold charms she'd laid out along her way, and that we'd been at a certain Jerry Johnson's place, at which time Little Lloyd interrupted to tell her that it was *the* Jerry Johnson of some little racing fame. Before she got too impressed, I went on to tell her how the same Jerry Johnson had helped Mr. Pickens sneak off and leave us in order to rescue her from Bigelow's local garage where, as it was plain to see, she had not been.

Instead of immediately putting to rest our fears about her safety the past few days, she said, "Who is Mr. Pickens?"

"Mr. J. D. Pickens, the private investigator I hired to find you."

"You hired a private investigator? Oh, Miss Julia." Tears welled up in her eyes and, before I knew it, she leaned over the console and hugged me. An intimacy I'd never much cared for and had avoided whenever I was able to. Especially when I was trying to drive.

"I can't believe you'd do that for me," she said, her voice breaking as she wiped her eyes.

"And why not, I'd like to know? You think I'd just let you go off and never hear from you again, with this child mourning you the way he's done? To say nothing of Lillian and, well, me? Nosirree, that's not the way I operate."

"Look!" Little Lloyd yelled. I nearly had a heart attack, thinking Bigelow and Wilson T. had confiscated one of those pickups we'd seen and come after us. But Little Lloyd was waving and flapping his hands out the side window. "It's Jerry and Mr. Pickens!"

I caught the flash of Mr. Johnson's red sportscar as it whizzed past us, headed for the speedway. So they'd found my note and were riding to the rescue. Somewhat late, I might add.

"Look at that!" Little Lloyd was kneeling on the back seat, looking out the rear window. "He's doing a one-eighty!"

I glanced in the rearview mirror in time to see Mr. Johnson's car skid into a turn that slung him around in the opposite direction. Then he was coming up fast behind us.

Just as the red car filled the rear window, Mr. Johnson swung out beside us, cruising at our speed. Mr. Pickens rolled down his window and had the nerve to point his finger at me, then at a gas station up ahead. I pursed my mouth at being given orders again, especially since we'd been doing so well without them.

As Mr. Johnson spurted on ahead and pulled in at the gas station, I decided that the better part of wisdom was to do what I was told. So I turned in and stopped beside them. It wouldn't hurt to have their help, since I doubted Bigelow and Wilson T. were through with us.

Mr. Pickens got out, leaving Mr. Johnson in the car with his arm crooked on the rolled-down window, watching us. The motor of his car rumbled, as he waited beside the road. The storm clouds on Mr. Pickens's face, as he approached us, were worse than what was overhead. He came to my side of the car and, as I lowered the window, he put his hands on his hips and said, "What the hell you think you're doing?"

"Your job, Mr. Pickens, and watch your language. This is Hazel

Marie Puckett who, as you can see, is no longer in the clutches of criminals."

He leaned down to glare across at her, and did it a good long time. She gave him a sweet smile. "Glad to meet you."

He grunted, took another long look, then said to me, "Get in the back. I'm driving."

"I'll have you know . . ." I started.

"The roads're icing up." He cut me off, opened my door and waggled his hand for me to get a move on. I did, crawling into the back seat with Little Lloyd, fuming at Mr. Pickens's reassumption of the driving responsibilities. I don't know why all the men on the face of the earth think they're the only ones who know how to drive.

"Look!" Little Lloyd screamed in my ear. "It's them! They're following us."

Sure enough, a white pickup truck slowed as it came abreast of the filling station. Three men in the cab looked us over, taking in my car and Mr. Johnson's, then spurted on out of sight.

"Oh no," Hazel Marie said, sliding down in the seat. "The one in the middle was Wilson T. He's still after me. What're we going to do?"

"Don't worry, Mama," Little Lloyd said, with more confidence that I had. "Mr. Pickens and Jerry will take care of us."

Mr. Pickens gave the child a quick smile. "Hold on a minute," he said, and went over to consult with Mr. Johnson.

When he came back, he slid behind the wheel without a word as to what they'd concluded. He just reached over and turned on the defroster, which I'd forgotten about in all the excitement, glanced at Hazel Marie in her Wednesday night date dress, and said, "Cold?" Then he jacked up the heater and pulled out behind Mr. Johnson's car.

As I sat steaming in the back seat, I began thinking of how much catching up we needed to do with Hazel Marie. Questions flooded my mind, but the atmosphere in the car wasn't conducive to detailed interrogation. At a stoplight in Rockingham, Mr. Pickens came out of his coat and handed it to Hazel Marie. She was shivering, even though the car was warm. I'd had my mind on too many other things to've noticed her miserable state. I declare, Mr. Pickens could make me mad enough to spit, then do something so nice that I had to somewhat reevaluate my opinion of him. Although he undid me again because he kept flicking his eyes in Hazel Marie's direction, instead of keeping his mind on his business.

Of course, I was familiar with Hazel Marie's effect on men in general and, by now, familiar with Mr. Pickens's propensity for women in general. Hazel Marie would have to be cautioned about him, although you'd think she'd've learned her lesson by now. I leaned my head back for a minute, feeling worn out from keeping him in line, to say nothing of all the perils to life and limb we'd so recently been subjected to and that I'd had to overcome on my own.

Then I straightened up. "Where're we going, Mr. Pickens?"

"Back to Jerry's."

"Do you think that's wise? Don't you think those men in the truck recognized Mr. Johnson and that souped-up red car of his? And Wilson T.'d certainly know my car. He can put two and two together as well as the next person. Besides, Hazel Marie needs to get home, and that's where I think we should go."

He gave me a quick look in the rearview mirror from those hot black eyes and said, "I know what I'm doing, so let me do it."

I sighed, because here we were, going at each other again. The man just would not brook a question, much less a more than reasonable suggestion.

Then I thought of something else. "If you think we're going to fiddle around here while you help Mr. Johnson find his lucky charm, I remind you that your job for me isn't over till we get Hazel Marie home." Hazel Marie glanced back at me, then at Mr. Pickens, wondering, I was sure, at my forbearance of his intolerable behavior. Little Lloyd kept reaching up to touch her, making sure she was safe.

"Have you noticed the weather?" Mr. Pickens asked, with an unattractive touch of sarcasm. "It's worse to the west of us."

I gave up and concentrated on his driving. The streets through Rockingham were getting slushy, and we passed a wreck in which the two drivers were standing out in the freezing stuff while they examined the damage.

"Be careful, Mr. Pickens," I said, as I felt our wheels slip when we pulled away from a stop sign.

"You want to drive?"

"Well, no, I don't believe I do."

"Then let me do it."

"I'm happy for you to. I'm just pointing out the road conditions."

He reached a hand back and, to my surprise, patted my knee. "Don't get yourself in an uproar, hon, I'll get us there safe and sound. We'll wait out the road conditions at Jerry's, where I doubt Bigelow would want to show his face. Then we'll get you all to Abbotsville. That sound like a plan to you?"

"It does, and I thank you for letting me know what you have in mind. You're always thinking, Mr. Pickens but, I declare, I wish you'd remind me of it every now and again."

By the time we got to the asphalt road that led to Mr. Johnson's place of business, Mr. Pickens had the car in low gear, steering carefully and more slowly than he was accustomed to doing. Mr. Johnson in his colorful car was inching along in front of us. I noticed the trees hanging over the road, beginning to sag with ice, while our tires crunched on the road.

I thought of something else to worry about. "What if Mr. Johnson loses power? We'll freeze to death out here in the country."

"He's got a generator. Now, listen to me, hon, you're paying me to do the worrying and I wish you'd let me do it. Believe me, I can do it better by myself."

"He probably can, Miss Julia," Little Lloyd said, adding his reassurance to Mr. Pickens's.

So I decided to let him. Unless I thought of something he might've forgotten.

Mr. Pickens followed Mr. Johnson as he turned into the lot at the Jerry Johnson's Racing place of business. Hazel Marie sat up and looked around, holding Mr. Pickens's coat around her shoulders.

"Wait'll I come around," Mr. Pickens said. "I'll walk you both to the door. It's not iced over yet, but there'll be slick spots."

But Hazel Marie and Little Lloyd got out on their own, holding on to each other as they made their way to the entrance, where Mr. Johnson waited for them. I managed to get across the front seat and hold on to the door until Mr. Pickens got to me.

"Hold on," he said, putting an arm around me. "We don't want to break anything."

I must say that steadying myself against his strong arm made walking on ice a comforting experience. Hazel Marie had missed something by not waiting for him, but young bones can afford to take chances.

Mr. Johnson stood, grinning, at the door. "Here comes Wonder Woman!" he bellowed, his voice bouncing off the walls. "I swear, Miss Julia, you're so good at finding things, I'm about ready to hire you, myself! Get on in here where it's warm and tell us how you found this good-lookin' woman. Was Bobby Bigelow there? Didn't see anything of mine, did you? Hey there, Little Boyd, thought you'd gone off and left us. You're one heck of a detective, and I'm ready to put you to work."

Little Lloyd softly corrected the name he'd been called without making an issue of it. Like me, he always appreciated hospitality in any form he could get it.

I declare, Mr. Johnson was more wound up, if possible, than he'd been before. I wondered if he needed medication, but of course worry does that to some people. Even though I didn't personally hold with superstition, I could understand his anxiety about his lucky charm. Lord knows, I'd suffered enough anxiety over Hazel Marie to sympathize with anybody who'd lost anything, especially something he believed, against all scientific evidence, would keep him in one piece on the racetrack. Now that I'd had some racing experience, I knew that he took his life in his hands every time he got in one of those cut-down trucks he had in his garage. I'd've found another line of business, if it'd been me.

There was only one mechanic in the garage, a man Mr. Johnson called Curtis, as we passed through on the way to the lounge. He waved at us and said he'd put the coffee on.

"I guess I've lost my mind," Mr. Johnson said, ushering us into the lounge, "but, with this weather, I sent most of the crew on ahead to Phoenix. I'm hopin' against hope, J. D., that you'll find my charm and make the trip worthwhile. If it don't turn up, I'm just gonna set down and bawl."

Hazel Marie looked at him with a frown on her face, not understanding where he was coming from. Mr. Johnson did take some getting used to.

As I headed for the coffee pot, Mr. Pickens assigned himself to take charge. "All right, Miss Julia, let's have it. How'd you and the boy know to go to the speedway?"

"Well, it was like this. Hazel Marie called Lillian this morning and told her she was in an RV, parked in a field at the North Carolina Speedway. Then we happened to call Lillian right afterward and found that out. Then Little Lloyd looked up directions to it on the computer. After that, it was simple. Too bad you had to go off somewhere and miss it all." I ignored his mumbling about needing to check out Bigelow's house and shop. "Mr. Johnson," I went on, "I hope you don't mind us using your electronic equipment, since it was in a good cause."

"Not a-tall!" he yelled, a wide grin on his face. "Wish I could've seen their faces when you showed up at the track."

"You should've seen us!" Little Lloyd broke in, loud enough to rival Mr. Johnson. "Miss Julia outran them all! When we got Mama in the car, they came after us in the RV, but she went around that track like Bobby Labonte!"

"That a fact?" Mr. Pickens said, his eyebrows raised halfway up his head. Skeptical, was what he was.

"Yeah! They spun out and wrecked on the number four turn, but we just kept on going!"

Mr. Johnson, though, was so astounded, he almost spilled his coffee. "Y'all lapped the track?" he bellowed. "Why, that thing's got a twenty-five degree bank on the third and fourth turn, and just about as bad on one and two."

"Yessir, we did!" Little Lloyd had to stop and get his breath. "And Miss Julia didn't wreck or anything!"

Mr. Pickens tried not to be impressed, but I knew he had to be. "Now, Ms. Puckett, Hazel Marie," he said, "we all want to know what happened to you."

Hazel Marie huddled up in his coat, as she took an easy chair and warmed her hands on the coffee cup I gave her.

"First off," Mr. Pickens said, "tell us about this boyfriend of yours."

"He's not my boyfriend!" she snapped, surprising me with this show of spirit. And relieving me of any lingering concern about having a church fund-raiser in my family.

"Sorry." Mr. Pickens favored her with one of his smiles, but it didn't register very high on her scale.

"Hazel Marie," I said, hitching up in my chair. "Tell us where you've been for the past two days and three nights. We've been out of our minds with worry, and you don't even know the half of it. Sheriff's departments all over the place have been looking for Bigelow and Wilson T., and you along with them and, on top of that, Mr. Johnson, here, is losing his livelihood because of those two. And something has to be done about it. So start off, and don't leave anything out."

She put a hand up to her forehead and rubbed it, shaking her head. "I didn't know what was going on, Miss Julia. It all happened so fast. When Wilson T. came by for me," she looked up, confused, "when was it? Wednesday night. We were halfway to Asheville when Wilson T. got this call on his cell phone. He turned around real quick, told me he had a business emergency he had to take care of, and off we went to his cousin's garage at Jessup Mountain. Well, when we got there, all these men were scurrying around, working on a racing truck. And Bobby Bigelow was in the offices, packing up files and papers and so on. Stacking them in boxes, like he was moving. He and Wilson T. talked and seemed to argue a little. I wasn't paying much attention, except I heard them say something about meeting in Phoenix and then going on to California. I kept telling Wilson T. that I was hungry and we were going to miss the movie if we didn't hurry up and leave. I couldn't understand why we had to be there in the first place. I mean, according to Wilson T., it's Bobby Bigelow's business, and he just enjoys being on the sidelines of a race team."

She stopped and looked up at Mr. Pickens, who told her something she didn't know. "The sheriff raided the place the next day. Bigelow must've known it was coming."

"Raided?" she whispered, then seemed to put two and two together. "That's why they got in such a hurry later on and, maybe, why Bigelow was so mad that Wilson T. had brought me along. See, something was wrong with their racing truck. The mechanics kept working on it while Bigelow and Wilson T. loaded the vans with the office stuff. Well, it got way up in the night and no sign of us leaving, and I started looking for a phone but they'd been packed up. I was real mad by that time and would've walked out if we hadn't been so far back in the woods."

"You were there all night?" I asked, recalling my own restless night. "What did you do all that time?"

"Begged to go home most of it," she said, frowning at the memory. "Wilson T. kept putting me off. Said he had to help Bobby and he'd take me home when the crew left. But they were still working on that racing truck, running the motor and tinkering with it, and Bobby Bigelow getting more and more upset and nervous. I finally dropped off to sleep on a couch for a while, and woke up when I heard Bigelow and Wilson T. arguing something awful out in the shop. Bigelow was mad because the race truck still wasn't right. Said they'd have to take it back to Rockingham where there was better equipment. See, I think they were planning to go on to Phoenix that night, and now they couldn't. Anyway, he gave Wilson T. some things to keep safe for him, and told him that they all had to stick together. And, and, he said that since they had to stay in the state longer than he'd planned to, they couldn't afford to let me tell anybody where they were. That's when I got scared and finally found somebody's cell phone and called home. And that's when they locked me in the RV, and that's when I knew I was really in trouble." She stopped again, her eyes getting bigger as something dropped into place. "Jerry Johnson!" She turned her big eyes on him. "That's *you,* isn't it? I heard them talking about you; you're the reason they didn't want to come back to Rockingham. Bobby Bigelow said he didn't want to see you until you were nothing but a blur in his driver's rearview mirror."

Mr. Johnson jumped up from his chair, so agitated he could hardly speak. A phenomenom, in itself. "I knew it! I knew they was trying to get at me." He whirled around and faced Hazel Marie. "Did you see anything that belonged to me? My lucky charm's missin', and I know they got it."

She leaned back away from his booming voice. "No, I don't know what they had. They loaded up their computers and boxes of papers, and what looked like rags and junk to me."

Mr. Johnson smacked his fist into his hand. "Thieves! That's what they are, just low-down, sneakin' thieves."

"As far as charms are concerned," Hazel Marie went on, "I do believe some are lucky. When Wilson T. snatched the phone away from me, I pulled one off my bracelet and threw it under a counter, hoping somebody'd figure out what was happening to me. And then there was that second one I left when we stopped at Gastonia where I tried to call again. I'd sure like to have them back, in case I need them again."

"I've got one, Mama," Little Lloyd said, plunging his hand in his pocket. "See, it's the one you left in the phone, and Deputy Bates has the other one. They worked just the way you wanted and led us right to you."

"Oh, I'm so glad to get it back," she said, the remaining charms on her bracelet clashing together as she reached for it. "I hated to pull them off, but I didn't know what else to do. Bigelow was so awful to me, I was scared to death of him, and he made Wilson T. watch me like a hawk. I was so mad at Wilson T. because he wouldn't stand up to him, just did everything Bigelow told him to and not taking up for me at all. Then I got him into big trouble. Bigelow was so mad he threatened to lock him up with me when I managed to make those phone calls." She smiled, pleased with herself. "More than once, too. I declare, Miss Julia, Wilson T.'s not real bright. I don't know why I hadn't noticed it before, dang his hide. Don't listen, Little Lloyd."

"No'm, I won't." Little Lloyd smiled, a dreamy look on his face, as he hung on her chair and every word out of her mouth.

"Why, that sorry thing," I said. "And he kept you locked up in that RV all this time?"

"Just about. We left Jessup Mountain right after I managed to call home, and they drove way out of the way, down into South Carolina on back roads. They were in sort of a convoy, with the RV, a transporter and a couple of cars. It took forever to get to Gastonia, where I begged Wilson T. to let me out for a little privacy. That's where I got to a phone again. Then we went somewhere out in the country around here, but they kept me locked up while they worked some more on the race truck. This morning, they decided they needed to do a practice run before leaving for Phoenix, and that's why we went to the speedway. Wilson T. let me out of the back room of the RV to walk around up front, and when he was watching them practice, I got his phone and called Lillian. When Bigelow found out that I'd made another call, he told Wilson T. that he was going to make him eat that phone if I got hold of it again. That's when you got there, Miss Julia, and just in time, 'cause they were ready to leave, and I might've never gotten home then."

"Yes, you would've," Mr. Pickens said, those dark eyes centered on her. "I'd've found you no matter where they took you."

I rolled my eyes, but neither of them noticed.

While we absorbed Hazel Marie's story, drank coffee and kept an eye on the weather, Little Lloyd wandered out into the shop, fascinated by the open hood of a race truck. He came back into the lounge, his eyes shining, and went over to Mr. Johnson. "Jerry, Curtis said I could ride with you in your Number 17 truck sometime. I sure would like that." Then, unable to contain himself, he reverted to proclaiming my driving skills again. "After going around that track with Miss Julia, I wouldn't be scared. Y'all should've seen her."

"It was nothing," I said, waving my hand. "Just a couple of turns around the track that we managed just fine. Though I can't say the same for Bigelow and Wilson T. Hazel Marie," I went on, getting to my feet. "I think we need to use the ladies'. Where is it, please, Mr. Johnson?"

He pointed toward the front of the building. "Go out in the hall, second door on your left."

I got to my feet, saying, "Come go with me, Hazel Marie." As I left, with her right behind me, I heard Little Lloyd begin again to give the details of our racetrack adventures, his voice high with the thrill of it all. There wasn't a sound from Mr. Pickens or Mr. Johnson all through his recitation but, as we went into the ladies' room, I heard Mr. Johnson yell that he had a good mind to put me in his truck at Phoenix. Fat chance, I thought. I didn't care to ride in a pickup, much less drive one.

As soon as we got the door closed, I sat Hazel Marie down and told her of the latest course of action by Brother Vern and how she now had less than ten days to answer the complaint he'd filed.

"Lillian and I've been keeping Little Lloyd out of sight so Lieutenant Peavey and Deputy Daly can't implement their snatch-and-grab order," I told her.

Tears welled up in her eyes, while her mouth tightened with anger. "Why can't Brother Vern leave us alone? Why's he doing this, especially now, with all this other mess Wilson T.'s got me into?"

"I don't know. But I'll tell you this, Brother Vern went to see Pastor Ledbetter Thursday morning, telling him that he'd been hearing uncomplimentary talk about you, and the pastor implied that he'd heard much the same. Now, wait, Hazel Marie," I cautioned her, as she started up at my news. "Don't get upset. You know how bad Abbotsville is for gossip. If nothing's going on, somebody'll make something up. But don't you worry, we'll put a stop to it. Anyway, that very afternoon Brother Vern filed his complaint, claiming to be acting in the best interests of the child, of all things." I studied on it for a minute, squinching up my eyes with the effort. "You know, I've been wondering what the pastor knew and when he knew it. He was awful worried about Wilson T.'s whereabouts and what was in, or *not* in, the building fund."

"He thinks Wilson T. embezzled the building fund? Oh, Lord, Miss Julia, how'd I get mixed up with such a man?" She buried her face in her hands.

"We don't know for sure that any money's missing, but we do know that Wilson T. put down a big bet on the Phoenix race. Ten thousand dollars' worth. Mr. Pickens picked the lock at his townhouse and found all sorts of incriminating evidence."

"Gambling! He's into gambling, too? What did I ever see in him? Here, he's as good as kidnapped me, brought Brother Vern out of the woodwork to threaten Lloyd, helped that sneaky cousin of his steal from Jerry Johnson, and all because he wants to *gamble*! I swear, I'd take his head off if I had my hands on him."

I smiled at the thought of Hazel Marie, as quiet and shy as she was, taking anybody's head off. "Well, the first thing we have to do is get you home, and how I'm going to drive up the mountain in this weather, I don't know. One more thing, Hazel Marie, nobody knows about the peril to Little Lloyd but Lillian and me. We didn't know who we could trust, so we've kept it to ourselves. That means that Mr. Pickens doesn't know squat about it, so don't let on. For all I know, he'd turn him over to the sheriff, and I don't want to take a chance on his willingness to evade the Law. Although he's certainly done so when it suited his purposes."

"Then we'd better leave before it gets any worse out there," she said, standing up and pulling Mr. Pickens's coat tighter. "I have to get home, so Binkie can help me fight off Brother Vern. Oh, Miss Julia, you'll testify for me, won't you? If it comes to that, I mean."

"You don't even need to ask. And it won't come to that. All we have to do is show up that thorn in the flesh for what he is, and prove that the child's best interests lie right where he is. I don't care what kind of gossip Brother Vern's passing on, you're a decent woman and every-body knows it."

Tears started streaming down her face. "I don't know what's wrong with me. I have the worst luck with men. Seems like the wrong kind just pick me out of a crowd, and I don't have enough sense to tell them apart." She stopped and looked at me, her face downright ashy-look-ing. "Oh, I am so sorry. I didn't mean to throw off on Mr. Springer. I know you don't want to talk about him, and I don't either, and I wouldn't hurt you for the world, Miss Julia. It just seems like I keep getting fooled by the likes of Wilson T. Oh, not that Mr. Springer was anything like him, but then there's Brother Vern who just waits for a chance to make trouble. And I've tried to live a good life, especially since you've been so good to us. I just try as hard as I can to make you proud of me, but nothing works out the way I want it to."

Well, it took me a second or two to figure out what to say to her. She was right, I didn't want to discuss Wesley Lloyd with her. It wouldn't've done either of us any good, but I had to admit that from her point of view he'd been a mighty poor pick. From mine, too, come to think of it. And I could see that she'd had bad luck with the men in her life, at least the ones I knew about. But I couldn't let her get down in the mouth, thinking she had some kind of curse dogging her when it came to men. That'd be as bad as Mr. Johnson putting such store in a lucky charm.

"Why," I said to her, "you just stop putting yourself down like that. I'll admit you've had bad luck so far, and I'm not excluding Mr. Springer. But you're not the only one as far as he was concerned. Your problem is that you've let the men do the picking. I say it's time you did some picking of your own. Take a hand in your own life for a change and things'll start looking up in the romance department."

Before she could agree with me, we heard the front door open and somebody walk through the hall, calling in a low voice to Curtis. I peeked out the bathroom door and nearly had heart failure. "It's Wil-son T.!" I whispered. "I can't believe he'd just walk in like nothing's happened."

Well, that little woman, who was as sweet and agreeable as any-body could want, built up a head of steam right in front of my eyes and stormed past me through the door.

She came to a stop in front of Wilson T. and let him have it. "What're you doing here? You followed us, didn't you?" she de-manded, her fists clenched by her side and her body trembling, she was so mad. "Well, it won't do you any good, because I don't want to see your sorry face again. So just go on back where you came from."

I stood by the bathroom door, waiting to see if Bigelow or any of his crew were coming in behind him, and wondering where Mr. Pickens was.

Wilson T., looking somewhat bedraggled from his vehicular accident, said, "If you've got it, Hazel Marie, just hand it over, that's all I'm asking. I never meant for you to get mixed up in this, but I've got to have what you took from Bobby."

"I don't know what you're talking about."

"Yes, you do." He took a step toward her, but she stood her ground. "Listen, I don't want to hurt you, but I've got to have it. Bobby made me come over here, and I can't go back without it. You know how he is. So give it here and I'll be gone."

"You're going to be gone, anyway, because I don't have anything of his. And you've got a nerve, just walking in here and acting like you didn't lock me up and lug me all over the state like a sack of potatoes!"

Wilson T.'s mouth tightened as he glared at her, doing a little fist-clenching, himself. I saw Curtis standing beside the truck he'd been working on, then he glanced out a back window as Mr. Johnson and Mr. Pickens passed by. I could see them talking, gesturing at the weather, completely unaware of the tense situation inside. Little Lloyd peeked out of the lounge, his eyes big at the sight of his mother and Wilson T.

"Be that way then," Wilson T. said. "We'll see what you say when Bobby gets hold of you. Let's go." He grabbed her arm and pulled her toward the door.

Before I could make a move, Little Lloyd streaked across the garage and made a flying leap for Wilson T.'s back, his arms flailing like a windmill. "Don't you hurt my mama! You get away from her!"

I got myself in gear and clutched a handful of Wilson T.'s overcoat, trying to pull him away from Hazel Marie. He shoved Little Lloyd aside and shook me off, neither of us slowing him down in his rush for the door, pushing Hazel Marie before him.

"Stop!" I yelled. "Mr. Pickens! Help!"

I grabbed the back of Wilson T.'s collar, pulling it tight enough to choke him, while Little Lloyd latched on to his leg. Hazel Marie screamed, as she twisted and turned, trying to break his hold.

Wilson T. shook his leg, sending Little Lloyd sprawling, and swatted at me. He pushed Hazel Marie against the wall, where she got enough purchase to slip his grasp. She turned and kicked and pounded on him, screeching at the top of her lungs, "Don't you hurt him! Leave my baby alone!"

His face red as a beet from the hold I had on his collar, Wilson T. grabbed her and shook her until her head flopped back and forth. "Give it here," he yelled, gasping for breath. "I know you've got it. Give it to me!"

I turned loose of his collar, took a firm hold of my pocketbook and started swatting him over the head with it. Wilson T. kept yelling, "Where is it!" and Hazel Marie screamed and scratched at him, while Little Lloyd kicked and hollered, "Don't you hurt my mama!" I yelled for Mr. Pickens, adding my two cents' worth to the din, at the same time getting in a particularly well-aimed whack, the jar of Metamucil in my pocketbook coming in quite handy as it clanked against Wilson T.'s head.

He released Hazel Marie and threw back his arm, sending me slamming against the front door. Before I could catch myself, my feet slid out from under me on the waxed floor and I flopped down on my backside with my legs spraddled out in a most shameful fashion. Sitting there slightly dazed with the suddenness of it, I felt myself being slid across the floor as the door was pushed opened behind me.

Mr. Pickens came barreling in, leaving me crumpled up between the door and the wall. I heard Mr. Johnson come at Wilson T. from the opposite side, yelling, "Dog bite it, leave that woman alone!" as he snatched Little Lloyd out of the fray. Mr. Pickens swung Wilson T. around and pushed him against the wall hard enough to put a dent in it. He had his hands more than full with Hazel Marie, though, because she kept going after Wilson T. She flew into him like a banty rooster, scratching and clawing at him, yelling, "I've had enough of you! You, you sorry excuse for a Christian! You're gonna regret the day you got me in this mess!"

"Hold on, hold on here," Mr. Pickens said, grabbing her around the waist from behind and holding her close.

"Turn me loose! He's got it coming and I'm gonna give it to him!" She tried to wiggle free of Mr. Pickens, but he had a good hold on her, which was probably the only thing that saved Wilson T. from serious injury.

My land, I thought as I struggled to stand up, having to turn over and hike my rear end up in the air so I could push off with my hands. It's the knees that go first, you know, and mine needed all the help they could get. But I wasn't worrying about my own ungraceful climb to my feet, being awed and amazed at Hazel Marie's display of fighting spirit.

She was wound up like a top and, if not for Mr. Pickens's arms around her, she'd've torn into Wilson T. again.

"Hold on now," Mr. Pickens said. "Let's get this straightened out. Who is this, anyway?"

"Wilson T. Hodge, that's who," Little Lloyd yelled.

"Bigelow's jackass is more like it," Hazel Marie said, struggling in Mr. Pickens's grasp.

Mr. Johnson switched his head around and let out a yell that echoed around his shop. "Bigelow! Is that egg-suckin' dog around here?"

Wilson T. didn't get a chance to answer. Hazel Marie balled up her fist and swung with all her might, landing a good one right on his nose. Wilson T. grabbed at his face and added his bellow to Mr. Johnson's. He looked ready to tear Hazel Marie limb from limb, and might've done it if Mr. Pickens hadn't put a hand out to hold him back. Mr. Pickens pulled Hazel Marie out of arm's reach, trying his best to calm her down.

Mr. Johnson noticed me hanging on to the door knob, trying to straighten myself up and catch my breath. He came over, bellowing right in my ear, "You all right, lady? Hurt anything?"

"Why, no, Mr. Johnson, thank you for asking. But I think I'd like to sit down for a minute."

He grabbed a chair, swung it behind me and shoved it against my knees, yelling, "Set it on down and rest yourself."

Wilson T. had pulled himself together by this time, and had regained some of his take-charge manner. "I don't know who you gentlemen are, but all I'm trying to do is get back something this woman's stolen."

Hazel Marie strained against Mr. Pickens's arms, trying to get at Wilson T. again. "You crooked, lyin', underhanded son of a . . . of a biscuit-eater!"

Mr. Pickens's eyebrows shot up at Hazel Marie's command of the language, and Mr. Johnson roared, "Whoa!" Then glaring eye-to-eye with Wilson T., Mr. Johnson bellowed, "You with Bigelow? You one of them thieves that robbed me? Huh? Huh? I want my lucky charm back and my disks and tools, and I want compensation for vandalizing my shop! J. D., you better call the cops, before I take somebody's head off here."

Wilson T. jerked away from him and straightened his suit coat down in an effort to regain his dignity. "I don't know anything about your shop problems. I was in Abbotsville up until yesterday, and I can prove it. Hazel Marie," he said, turning to her, "come on with me, and you can give Bobby's property back to him. I don't care what you do after that."

"What? What! I don't have anything to give to Bobby!" Hazel Marie was still so mad she could hardly catch her breath. "Get that through your thick head, and don't try to weasel out of anything. You may not've robbed anybody, but you took me off in that RV and wouldn't let me go."

"That was all Bobby's doing. You'll recall that he wouldn't let me leave, either. So if he's in trouble with the Law, it has nothing to do with me. I'm just a messenger here, trying to get back what you took from him. Then I'm washing my hands of it all."

Hazel Marie squirmed in Mr. Pickens's arms, trying to get at Wilson T. again. "Okay, okay," Mr. Pickens kept saying, trying to get her under control. Then to Wilson T., "She says she doesn't have what you're looking for, so leave it alone."

"I'm warning you . . . ," Wilson T. started, but that was the wrong thing to say to Mr. Pickens, as I had earlier learned.

Mr. Pickens handed Hazel Marie over to Mr. Johnson, who was frowning with the strain of trying to hear what everybody was saying. Then Mr. Pickens stepped up and got right in Wilson T.'s face. "Warn me again."

Wilson T. shriveled up at Mr. Pickens's challenge, to say nothing of his manly presence standing four-square and ready in front of him. I drew in a breath, hoping I wouldn't have to be a witness to an all-out dog fight. Which if it came down to it, Mr. Pickens would fix Wilson T.'s little red wagon good. There'd be a mess to clean up, though.

Wilson T. stared across Mr. Pickens's shoulder, unwilling to meet his eyes, and said, "I just want what belongs to Bobby. Make her take it back to him, and we're through here."

Mr. Pickens gave a short laugh. "*Make* her? Man, you don't know women. I'm not about to make her do anything."

I'd known all along that Mr. Pickens was a good man at heart.

Wilson T. then tried another tack. "Look," he said, finally meeting Mr. Pickens's eyes in an effort to talk man-to-man. "I have to warn all of you. She's taken something that belongs to Bobby, and it's valuable. You don't want to tangle with him, because well, let's just say that he'll get it back one way or another."

"What're we talking about here?"

"*She* knows. Hazel Marie, you don't know what you're letting yourself in for."

Hazel Marie's eyes blazed at him, as she tried to jerk herself away from Mr. Johnson. "I didn't know what I was letting myself in for when I met you, either! Get your sorry hide outta here, and I hope you and Bobby Bigelow rot in jail for the rest of your crooked lives!"

"Where is that sneakin' thief, anyway?" Mr. Johnson bellowed, turning Hazel Marie loose and rushing at Wilson T. "Tell me where he is."

"I don't know!" Wilson T. cringed against the auditory onslaught. "I swear I don't know. He told me to get back what she stole from him, and that's all I know."

"I didn't steal anything from him!" Hazel Marie cried, as Mr. Pickens grabbed her again.

"Where's Bigelow?" Mr. Johnson blasted the air like a thunderclap. "Where is he?"

"I don't know, I tell you," Wilson T. said, holding his arms in front of his face, scuttling away from Mr. Johnson's screwed-up face and blistering voice. "He's gone on ahead before the weather. . . . I'm supposed to go back to Abbotsville, the church, you know, my work. But I have to get back what she stole, please, that's all I know."

"You lyin' *thing,* you," Hazel Marie yelled. "Get outta my sight!"

"Good idea," Mr. Pickens said, keeping her uncommonly close to him. "Pack it in, Hodge. You may not've had anything to do with the robbery here, but the Abbot County sheriff'll want to talk to you." Then he spoke softly to Hazel Marie, "Come on now, it's over for now."

She went docilely enough, except for spitting at Wilson T. as she passed by. Mr. Pickens kept hold of her arm as he led her toward the lounge. Mr. Johnson got up in Wilson T.'s face again and, in his usual forceful manner, told him to take a hike and tell Bobby Bigelow that he was going to whip him to within an inch of his life. If Bigelow was ever man enough to face him, instead of sneaking into people's garages to tear up jack and steal what didn't belong to him.

Wilson T. made haste to leave, and I comforted myself with the thought of Lieutenant Peavey putting him on the hot seat when he got home.

"Come on, Little Lloyd," I said, putting a hand on his shoulder. "I declare, your mother made me so tired just watching her that I need to sit down awhile."

"She was something, wasn't she?" A note of pride filled his voice, and it warmed my heart to hear it.

Chapter 24

We got to the lounge in time to see Hazel Marie fling herself away from Mr. Pickens and stomp across the room to a chair. She flopped down, crossing her arms in a huff, still seething and steaming.

Mr. Pickens stood over her, his hands on his hips. "Man, lady, warn me before you get mad at me." He shook his head in admiration, a smile playing under his mustache. "You about put a permanent crimp in him."

Hazel Marie cut her eyes up from under her brows to give him a glare. "I would've, too, if you hadn't stopped me."

He laughed, earning himself another glare.

"I need to get home," she said.

"I'm working on it," he told her, but before he could let us in on his plans, Mr. Johnson came bounding in.

"What was that Hodge feller lookin' for, anyway?" he yelled, as Hazel Marie cringed from the blast to her eardrums. "Think it could've been my lucky charm? Ma'am," he said to Hazel Marie. "Did you see either of them with it?"

"No." She shook her head. "I didn't see anything like that. All I saw were disks and papers, and tools and motors and a lot of junk that didn't mean anything to me. The only charms I know anything about are the ones I dropped along the way."

Mr. Johnson just stood there with his head sinking lower, about overcome with the thought of it all. "J. D.," he said, slowly shaking his head, "I swear, son, if Hodge and Bigelow don't have it, where could it be? I was sure countin' on you gettin' it off of them."

"Mr. Johnson," I said, "it seems to me you're putting too much importance on something that can't possibly measure up to your own talent and knowledge and experience. I think your problem's all in your mind, and you ought to rise above it. Mind over matter, you know, even though I don't ordinarily hold with that Christian Science belief since I go to the doctor whenever I need to. But I think you ought to buck up and quit letting some little superstitious thing put you off so bad."

Mr. Johnson looked at me like I was crazy. "Ma'am, I 'preciate your advice, but I know it ain't no use me drivin' without it. I've tried it, didn't want to lean too much on superstition, like you say. But every time I drove without it, something bad happened. One time in the Powerstroke 200, this was a while back before I knew how bad I needed it with me, I blowed an engine. Very next race, I made a pit stop and went back out with loose lug nuts. Then on a qualifying run at the Texas Speedway, a Bigelow driver made contact when I was goin' high and he spun me into the wall. Tore everything all to hell and back, includin' my leg and collar bone, a coupla ribs and my truck. Took me out for most of the season. Man, I come outta what was left of my truck, hardly able to stand up, but I waited on the track till that driver come around again and throwed my helmet at him." He took a deep breath, reliving the experience. "Ever since I've had my charm, though, it's been clear sailing. I know it's superstitious, but that don't mean it don't work. Every time I have it with me, I blow the doors off everything on the track. And that's a fact.

"And now," he went on, looking down at the floor and shaking his head again, "just when I'm leadin' in points and got the championship all but sewed up, an' ready to move up full time in the Winston Cup scries, this has to happen. I been racin' more'n twenty year an' never been closer than I am now. J. D., they used to call me the Mark Martin of the Craftsman Trucks, 'cause I couldn't win the big ones. But I showed 'em last year, comin' in first three times, and this year I had a chance to do it again, and win on points, too. But there won't be no victory lane for this ole dog now. Might as well stay home, and let the young drivers have it."

"Don't give up, Jerry," Little Lloyd said. "Your fans are behind you. We're all pulling for you."

"Aw, that's real nice, Little Boyd," Mr. Johnson said. "I 'preciate it, but speakin' of fans, I got to ask each and every one of you not to let on to anybody about my lucky charm. I mean, people know I got one, but I'd never live it down if they knew how much I depend on it. I never wanted anybody to know and they wouldn't of, if that danged Bigelow'd kept his hands to himself. So don't nobody tell anybody, okay?"

"We can't, Jerry," Little Lloyd reminded him. "We don't know what it is."

"Well, it ain't much, I don't mind saying. Nobody but me'd look twice at it." He took a deep, shuddering breath and went on, "I'm just worried to death about the shape it's in by now. It was about wore down to a nub already, and it won't stand no rough treatment." He shook his head, overcome with his loss. "Thought it'd last a few more years anyway, and me and it'd retire together."

While Mr. Johnson bemoaned his pitiful situation, Mr. Pickens had commenced pacing back and forth by the window that looked out over the back of the garage. He glanced out of the window now and then, checking the weather, his hands rammed in his pockets while he enjoyed a few minutes of silence from Mr. Johnson. It concerned me that Mr. Pickens might be giving too much attention to Mr. Johnson's lost lucky charm, seeing as how he still hadn't gotten Hazel Marie home, which was what he'd been hired to do.

But, after watching him for a few minutes, I saw that he'd not forgotten her at all. In fact, the way his eyes kept glancing her way, sweeping all up and down her, I had to worry that he'd get distracted from his job in another way entirely.

I walked over to him and, lowering my voice, said, "Mr. Pickens, we need to work something out. I've got to get Hazel Marie home to straighten out some legal problems, which have nothing to do with our current ones, and she's got to do it as soon as she can or something awful will happen. We can't afford to fritter away any more time. The clock is ticking, Mr. Pickens. If you have a mind to take on Mr. Johnson's problem to the extent that you have to linger here, we'll just be on our way now."

He studied me for a minute with that penetrating gaze that almost unnerved me. "You looked out the window lately? It's a mess out there."

"Well, I know it but, between Hazel Marie and myself, we'll just have to manage. We can't afford to get iced in here for several more days. I'm telling you, you don't know what's at stake. I've got to get Hazel Marie home."

He frowned. "You mean there's more to this than Bigelow and Hodge?"

"There certainly is."

"Well, what?"

"If you must know," I said, edging closer to him and lowering my voice, "it has to do with her uncle, who's trying to get custody of Little Lloyd. He's sworn out a complaint against her, and at the most inopportune time, as you can see. And all because he wants the little bit of money in the child's educational fund." That's all I was willing to tell him of Little Lloyd's inheritance. Neither he nor anybody else needed to know that the fund would've educated every child in Abbot County, and then some.

Mr. Pickens twisted his mouth, making his mustache jump around, as he gave her another long look. "Interesting woman."

"Believe me, Mr. Pickens, if you find her interesting, you don't have a chance in the world of having any of it returned until she attends to the problem at home. That ought to be incentive enough for you." I hated to encourage him, knowing how susceptible Hazel Marie was to a man's attention, and knowing how quick he was to give it, but I had to use what I had.

"Won't give me a second thought till then, huh?"

"That's right. I know her, and what she's facing is going to take all her time and attention. Think about it."

"Oh, I am, and looks like I'm just gonna have to get you home one way or another." He smoothed his mustache with a thumb and forefinger, then touched my shoulder. "Tell me this, was she serious about Hodge?"

"Doesn't matter whether she was or not. She's certainly not now. I'll tell you this, Mr. Pickens, Hazel Marie's not had much luck when it comes to picking men. As you can see, she's in bad need of cheering up, and you're as good as anybody I've ever seen in that department. So, I'd appreciate it if you'd use some of those winning ways of yours in the service of a good cause, just to make her feel a little better. But it's to be only a temporary measure; I don't want you leading her on with false promises like she's already had too many of. But you're so good at what you do, I know you'll know how to handle it. I declare, Mr. Pickens, you certainly have a way with you when it comes to women."

Lord, I was laying it on thick, and he was eating it up, believing every word I said. What man wouldn't, since they all think they're God's gift? But he needed a spur or maybe a whip to get us on home, and I wasn't above giving him whatever it took to get us there. Meanwhile, I'd have to steer Hazel Marie away from him and warn her about his womanizing ways.

I looked around at Mr. Johnson, who was so woebegone as to be next to useless, then at Hazel Marie, who looked a million miles away, as she sat with her arm tight around Little Lloyd. He snuggled up to her as he watched the Weather Channel.

"I'm going to call Lillian," I said to Mr. Pickens, "and tell her we've got Hazel Marie back. I'll see how the weather is up there and, if the roads are halfway passable, I'm going to head out."

"Let me know what she says," he said, as he turned to look out of the window again.

Mr. Johnson gave me permission to use his phone and, when I got through to Lillian, it was all I could do to break in on her stream of information. Lieutenant Peavey and Deputy Daly had rung the doorbell before it was good light, looking for Little Lloyd; Coleman and Binkie had come by, worried about all of us; Sam had called three times, saying he was about beside himself not knowing where we were; LuAnne had walked over from the church after a counseling session to leave word that she'd made a doctor's appointment for Leonard, and Brother Vern had shown up on the front porch, telling Lillian that "whoever meddles in the work of those who are the called of God is doin' nothin' but danglin' over the fires of hell."

"Or something like that," she said. "He rantin' and ravin' to beat all I ever heard. You better get on back here, Miss Julia, they all goin' crazy on me."

When I told her that we had Hazel Marie and that all that was holding us up was the weather, she let out a shriek that even Mr. Johnson heard. "Them highways is still open," she told me, "I jus' heard it on the teevee. Backroads is gettin' bad, but y'all come on 'fore it get dark an' you be all right."

When I hung up, I walked back over to Mr. Pickens and gave him Lillian's weather report. "If we get started right away," I said, "we can be there before the temperature drops tonight and ices everything over. Mr. Pickens, we've just got to get home. Everything's going to you-know-where in a handbasket up there."

He gave me one of those little smiles that almost got lost in his mustache, and said, "Let me talk to Jerry a minute."

Well, a minute was all I was going to give him. I wasn't looking forward to slipping around on an icy interstate, but we had to do it.

Mr. Pickens hunkered down beside Mr. Johnson's chair and started talking to him. Mr. Johnson kept shaking his head and whispering loud enough for all of us to hear him. "Ain't no use, J. D. If I run at Phoenix, I'll just make a fool of myself. I don't wanta put my crew through all that 'cause we ain't got a chance in hell of runnin' in the top five. Not without my lucky charm, we ain't."

Well, I'd just about had enough of that, so I marched over to tell Mr. Pickens to leave him alone so we could leave.

Just as I got to them, Mr. Pickens said, "Look, Jerry, nobody but your own crew knows it's missing. Everybody else's gonna think your streak's still going. They'll stay intimidated, trust me on that."

Mr. Johnson shook his head. "I don't know, son. It's us that messes up when I don't have it."

"All right," Mr. Pickens said, "let me put it this way. We need you, and I still may be able to pull a rabbit out of a hat. You're all loaded up to go to Phoenix, aren't you?"

"Yeah, already sent most of the crew on with the backup truck, for all the good it'll do. With all the damage Bigelow did to us, I wanted them outta here. Number 17's in the transporter out there, ready to move out if anybody else came sneakin' around."

"Tell you what," Mr. Pickens said. "Instead of unloading and giving up, how about loading up Miss Julia's car and dropping us off in Abbotsville? That's not too far out of your way and, if you'll do that, I'll go on with you and find your lucky charm. If another crew's got it, they'll show up in Phoenix, right?"

"By dog, you're right!" Mr. Johnson looked as if he'd just gotten a new lease on life. "I ain't gonna find it settin' here, am I? That's where it'll be, out there where it'll do somebody some good. Come on, let's load 'er up."

"See, Mr. Johnson," I said, wanting to keep him encouraged, since it seemed the only way I was going to move Mr. Pickens was to light a fire under Mr. Johnson. "You just have to have faith that things will work out. Mr. Pickens has found what was lost for us, and he'll do the same for you. But, first, he has to get us home. And speaking of that," I went on, turning to Mr. Pickens, "just what did you mean by loading up my car? I intend for you to drive it, not ship it somewhere."

"Haw!" Mr. Johnson bellowed. "Just you wait an' see what J. D.'s got up his sleeve. I tell you, boys, my ole buddy's got tricks you ain't seen yet! Let's us get started on this, and you folks get ready to roll. Not gonna let a little sleet an' ice stop us now!"

He bounded out into the shop area, yelling and laughing and calling to Curtis. Mr. Pickens just stood there, looking pleased with himself.

"What're we going to do, Miss Julia?" Little Lloyd snapped off the Weather Channel and stood up. "They say there's another cold front right behind this one, and it's picking up moisture from the gulf. They're saying a winter weather watch is out for the mountains."

Before I could answer, Mr. Pickens put a hand on the boy's shoulder, saying, "We'll make it, and it's going to be the ride of your life. Let's go, ladies. Jerry's ready to roll."

Hazel Marie and I followed Mr. Pickens through the garage and on out the back door, our breath condensing in front of us as we hit the cold air. I was astounded at what was out there, and I'm here to tell you I'd never seen anything like it. We came out into an open-sided covered space, like a two-story double carport, with what looked like one of those huge, eighteen-wheeled moving vans parked underneath. It was painted the most awful shade of turquoise with JERRY JOHNSON RACING slashed across the trailer part in bright yellow, outlined in black and white. Garish, was all I could say for it.

As if that wasn't bad enough, there was Mr. Johnson wearing a jacket that was as close to Joseph's coat of many colors as I could imagine. It was of a shimmery turquoise material, nylon most likely, although it had so many decals, patches and emblems on it that you could hardly see the background color. JR LANDSCAPING was the featured advertisement, with SK POWER EQUIPMENT, somebody's motor oil, somebody else's service station and BUCKIE'S DRIVE-IN blinding my eyes. And to add to all that, there were black and white checks running up and down the sleeves. The man was a walking billboard. And Mr. Pickens wasn't much easier on the eyes in a borrowed coat, since Hazel Marie was still wrapped up in his.

Mr. Johnson had the whole back side of the trailer laid out on the ground and, before I knew it, Curtis came around the corner in my car and drove right up on the door and stopped.

"Watch this here, Little Floyd!" Mr. Johnson bellowed, though he hadn't needed to at all, for Little Lloyd was standing right beside him, watching the undertaking with his mouth open. As indeed I was, wondering what they were doing with the only car I had to my name.

Mr. Johnson pulled a lever or pushed a button or did something mechanical and, lo and behold, the back door of the truck began to rise, taking my car with it, until it was way up over our heads.

"What," I wheezed, trying to catch my breath, "what in the world are they doing?"

"It's a double-decker transporter," Mr. Pickens said, enjoying, I do believe, my consternation. "Jerry hauls his race truck on the top deck, and they're going to put your car right in behind it. Watch, now."

When the door got to the top deck, it stopped and the driver moved my car right on inside, anchoring it good and tight. Then he rode the door back down to the ground.

"Load up, boys!" Mr. Johnson yelled. "We gonna hit the road. Hey, Miss Julia, sorry I let my Winnebago go on ahead of us. You coulda rode in style, but you ain't gonna fuss about this, I guarantee you. Might not be too legal, but just keep the blinds closed and who's gonna know? Come on, now."

Mr. Pickens took Hazel Marie's arm and helped her into the lower deck of the trailer, while Little Lloyd followed her, eager to look around inside.

"Your turn!" Mr. Johnson bellowed in my ear. "Hop on in!" Between Mr. Pickens and Mr. Johnson, I found myself lifted up over the threshold and inside what looked like a garage on wheels. There was a narrow aisle between rows of cabinets holding every kind of tool and hose and machine you could think of. Mr. Johnson came behind us, closing and latching cabinet doors as he went.

"Keep on goin' to the front," he yelled. "I'll get y'all settled, then we'll head out."

"What is all this stuff?" I whispered to Mr. Pickens.

"Everything they need to repair or rebuild a race truck at the track. Would you believe they've got four motors ready to go if they need 'em?" He put his hand on my back as we moved toward the front.

Yes, I'd believe it. I saw enough plunder in that van to open a filling station, if you had a mind to.

About three-quarters of the way down the aisle, it took a little turn and went up two steps. We walked into a small sitting room, complete with aquamarine leather sofas built onto two sides of the space, a small table, and a wall of all kinds of electronic paraphernalia, including a television set, fax machine, telephone, computer and I don't know what all.

"My word," I said, astounded at the array before me. "Got a satellite hookup, too!" Mr. Johnson sang out. "Refrigerator's right under there with plenty to drink. The john's around the corner. Make yourselves at home, folks, and call me on the phone if you need anything. I'm gonna put this mother in gear and head for the mountains!"

"Mr. Johnson," I said, putting my hand on his arm as he started to leave. "Don't take any chances. That sleet's still coming down out there."

"Well, thank you for your worry, but a little sleet's never stopped me before. This here truck's got gears it don't even know about and enough tires to hold it on the road. I know you need to get home, and I'm gonna take you. And neither Bigelow's bunch nor a smokey's gonna stop us."

When he left, I asked Mr. Pickens what a smokey was. "Highway patrol," he said. Then we heard the door of the van being closed and latched, locking us inside the back side of something that looked like a circus truck, along with, according to Mr. Pickens, extra generators, engines, cool-down units, utility carts, pit carts, crash carts, tool boxes, nuts and bolts bins, body paint, oil lines, fuel lines, brake lines, springs and shocks. To say nothing of a racing truck and my car over-head, which were the only things I would recognize if I saw them.

I leaned down and looked out the window, seeing Mr. Johnson swing up into the cab. He started the motor, and I could feel the rum-ble of it under my feet.

"Sit here by me, Miss Julia," Little Lloyd said, "it might be kind of rough till we get on the interstate." The child was beside himself with the thrill of checking out our highly unusual conveyance.

I took a seat beside him on one of the sofas, noticing that Mr. Pick-ens took his right beside Hazel Marie. She was still looking down-in-the-mouth after considering the kind of men who'd been in her life. Little did she know that there was another of the same ilk sidling up to her again.

"Why," I said, rooting around on the sofa, "there're no seat belts." Then I hushed up about it, since that was clear proof we weren't sup-posed to be riding back there. "Hold my hand, Little Lloyd."

As the big truck pulled out from under the carport, I could hear the ting of sleet against the sides of the van. Looking out the windows, I saw sagging tree limbs, coated with ice, and began to have second thoughts as to the wisdom of our journey. But I closed the blinds as Mr. Johnson had told us to do, deciding that it was too late to back out now. And, of course, it was all for the best since getting home was what we had to do.

Mr. Pickens sat across from us, talking soft and low to Hazel Marie. She nodded now and again, occasionally giving him a sad kind of smile. I worried that he might be pulling out some of that manly charm he had so much of and which he used to get whatever he wanted. I'd seen him in action and, so far, had not seen any woman with enough immunity to resist him. Except me, of course, and I in-tended to see to it that Hazel Marie did, too. After he got us home, that is.

The truck lurched as it turned onto the main highway, picked up speed, and headed toward Charlotte. I hoped that Mr. Johnson was right when he said the thing could handle icy roads because, when I peeked through the blinds, there was hardly any traffic, and not a few cars and pickups stranded on the roadside and in ditches.

We were in the hands of the Lord and Jerry Johnson. I prayed to the one, and put my trust in the other.

"Mr. Pickens," I said, more sharply than I'd intended, for a sudden scary thought had occurred to me. "Have you given any thought to the fact that Wilson T. knows exactly where Hazel Marie lives and, if Bigelow can't find whatever he's looking for, he might come after her again? He and Wilson T. could be sitting there, waiting on us."

He nodded. "I've thought of it. But you said you needed to get there, so I figure we'll cross that bridge when we come to it."

I thought that through for a minute, then said, "But if you're going on to Phoenix with Mr. Johnson, that leaves us alone to deal with them. I don't like the thought of that."

"I'll talk to Peavey and some others I know. They'd like nothing better than to get their hands on Bigelow since their raid was a washout. They'll be watching out for 'em, so you'll be okay."

I nodded, reassured that Mr. Pickens was still thinking ahead on our behalf. The little room had begun to heat up, so I came out of my coat and helped Little Lloyd out of his. We had come into Charlotte by that time, as evidenced by all the stopping and going the truck was doing. The streets seemed some better, and as I peeked out the window I saw that the sand trucks were out and about, trying to make the streets passable.

About the time we got through Charlotte and back on the interstate where the riding was smoother, Mr. Pickens stood up and said, "I've got an idea to pass the time. Let me see if I can find some cards."

He rummaged around in several drawers and came out with a deck of cards and a round container that held poker chips. Not that I immediately recognized it as such, not having the gambling habit, but he announced, "Let's play some poker."

Little Lloyd was eager, surprising me that he knew how to play, and Hazel Marie hesitantly agreed. Mr. Pickens got them situated around the tiny table, wrote out what beats what on a scrap of paper for Hazel Marie's benefit, and said, "Come on over here, Miss Julia, and sit in with us. We'll play dealer's choice, but I'm ruling out strip poker, no matter what you say."

Well, I knew when I was being teased, but I had no taste for cards, especially the gambling kind. "Thank you all the same, but I'd rather watch, if you don't mind."

"Suit yourself," Little Lloyd said, doubling over with laughter, "Get it, Miss Julia? *Suit* yourself."

I smiled at Little Lloyd's quickness of mind, as Mr. Pickens grinned and rubbed his hand over the boy's head. He shuffled the cards, slapped them down in front of Little Lloyd and said, "Name your game, sport."

I made myself comfortable in the corner of the sofa, while they started their game. Hazel Marie sounded willing, but halfhearted at first, but gradually she got into the fun the other two were having. I began to doze off, lulled by the easy rocking of the truck as it made good time on the interstate. Mr. Johnson had certainly been right. So far, the heavy truck was doing just fine in spite of the road conditions. Fitting my head into the corner of the sofa, I drifted in and out of sleep, hearing bits and pieces of the game in progress.

"Hit me," Mr. Pickens said. "Dealer takes two. Everybody in?"

"Raise you one."

"I'll see you."

"I'm out."

"Chicken."

"Let's see what you're so proud of, Mr. Pickens." With a snap of cards on the table, Mr. Pickens said, "Pair of jacks."

"Ha!" Hazel Marie laughed. "Don't send boys to do a man's job."

Mr. Pickens picked up the cards, saying, "Loser says 'Deal, dammit, deal.' Five card stud, pairs or better to open." I heard the swish of cards and the chink of chips.

"Pot's not right," Little Lloyd said. "Oh, it's me. Sorry."

"Read 'em and weep," Mr. Pickens said. "What'll you have?"

"One," Hazel Marie said.

"Oh, me," Mr. Pickens moaned, "she's at it again."

Little Lloyd laughed. "You're really getting the cards, Mama."

Hazel Marie, sounding pleased with herself, said, "Well, you know, lucky in cards, unlucky in love. I'll see you and raise you two."

"Jesus," Mr. Pickens said. "I'm out."

"My turn," Little Lloyd said, gathering up the cards as Hazel Marie added to the stack of chips in front of her. "High-low, deuces and one-eyed jacks're wild."

I heard the snap of cards as he dealt, listened to their opens and raises and calls. After a while Mr. Pickens said, "Okay, boys and girls, down and dirty."

"See you," I heard Hazel Marie say, "and raise you three."

"Damnation, woman, what've you got over there?"

Hazel Marie giggled. "It'll cost you to find out." Right about then, I had a mind to put a stop to the game since it seemed to be getting out of hand. But, on second thought and a quick glance, I saw that Hazel Marie was smiling for a change, Little Lloyd was paying rapt attention, and Mr. Pickens was behaving himself. I let them alone and dropped on off to sleep.

I came awake with a start, feeling the truck gather itself as Mr. Johnson shifted gears. Separating the blinds with my fingers, I could see that we were just beginning the long climb up the mountain toward Abbotsville. Ice covered the sides of the road, and the trees were bent over so far they looked ready to snap. The dangerous stuff was still coming down. It would've been beautiful if we hadn't had to be out in it, risking life and limb with every turn of the wheels.

Well, worrying about it at this late date wouldn't do us any good, so I decided to call Lillian and tell her we'd soon be there. Think positively, I always say.

Using Mr. Johnson's telephone—Lord, I was going to owe him a mint—I called Lillian to announce our imminent arrival.

"If, that is," I told her, "we don't end up sliding back down the mountain. It's bad out here, Lillian, but I guess we couldn't be in better hands than a racing driver."

"What you talkin' about? Who you got drivin'? You mixed up in something you oughtn't to be again?"

"No, I am not. Don't give me a hard time, Lillian, I'm about worn out as it is. Now, Mr. Pickens and Mr. Johnson, and somebody named Curtis, a mechanic I think he is, are coming in with us so, if you don't mind, we might offer them some sandwiches or something."

"Sam'iches! They need more'n that. No, ma'am, I already got it on the stove. It'll be ready when you get here. And you better get on back here, 'cause that Lieutenant Peavy come by and say they gonna put out a warrant for Miss Hazel Marie, if she don't show up with Little Lloyd, and yo' pastor, he come over sayin' he know you don't want no new building, but he don't know you go so far as to tear down Mr. Hodge's reputation, and he think you owe the church something for doin' it."

I could've pulled my hair out in frustration when I heard that. I declare, every time I left town, the whole place went to pieces.

By the time I hung up, the poker game was over. The slant of the truck as it went up the mountain had the cards sliding all over the table, so we all just sat around and looked at each other. Although Mr. Pickens did most of his looking in Hazel Marie's direction, asking her if she was warm enough, did she want anything to drink, was she feeling all right, and on and on. All that solicitude would've gotten on my nerves, but she didn't seem to mind it. All I could think about was what was waiting for me when we got home.

Mr. Pickens picked up the phone and called Mr. Johnson, telling him what exit to take and giving him directions through the town to our house.

I hadn't realized that I'd been holding my breath, so to speak, until the truck leveled off as we reached the edge of Abbotsville. Peeking through the blinds again, I was relieved to see familiar landmarks, although they were considerably altered by a layer of ice. Parking lots were all but empty, except Wal-Mart's of course. There're some people who just can't stay away from that place, but not me. The first and last time I went, some old man came out of nowhere, grabbed my hand and grinned like an idiot, going on and on about how glad he was to have me there. You'd've thought he'd issued a personal invitation, when all he wanted was for me to spend my money. It beat all I'd ever seen, and I decided I could do without an official greeter and never miss it at all.

Mr. Johnson took it slow as he drove into town. It felt as if the truck was being eased along the empty streets and, when we crossed Main, I saw that the streetlights had come on in the early dark of the late winter storm.

Mr. Pickens was on the phone again, watching out the window, as he guided Mr. Johnson right to our door. Mr. Johnson pulled up on the street across from the house and parked with a whoosh of the air brakes. I looked out the side window to reassure myself that the house was still standing. After what Lillian'd told me, I wouldn't've been surprised to see one of those black-clad SWAT teams waiting for us, or some of Pastor Ledbetter's orange flags staking out my boxwoods.

Mr. Johnson and Curtis climbed out of the cab and came around to the back of the trailer to unlock the door and let us out. We gathered our coats, eager to be released from the cramped quarters. I, for one, was most anxious to see the last of long-haul trucking.

As we walked back through the aisle, sidling around the carts of racing equipment stuffed in every available space, Mr. Johnson lowered the back door of the trailer. He called it a gate, but it looked nothing like a gate to me. Mr. Pickens helped Hazel Marie down onto the street, then reached up to give me a hand.

Just as I was holding on to the side of the truck so my feet wouldn't slip out from under me on the icy pavement, Lillian came out on the porch.

For once in her life, she was almost speechless at the sight of that huge truck, its yellow running lights and red warning lights glittering in the glow of ice in the early evening. It made a picture, I'll say that for it, but I was more interested in getting in out of the slippery mess.

"My Jesus!" Lillian called, as Little Lloyd started across the street toward her. "What y'all been ridin' in? Come 'ere to me, sweet baby!"

She waited for him with open arms, having sense enough to stay on the porch and not risk the perilous stuff herself. After almost falling when he stepped up on the sidewalk, Little Lloyd made it safely to the porch where she nearly smothered the child in her apron. Looking across and seeing Hazel Marie by the truck, Lillian treated us and half the town to another shriek of welcome.

"Stay right here," Mr. Pickens said to Hazel Marie, cocking that finger at her. Contrary to my response to his finger pointing, she smiled at him. "I'll get Miss Julia in, then I'll come back for you."

He put his arm around me, telling me to test each step, and we started across the street. I glanced back to see Curtis raise the gate with Mr. Johnson riding up with it. By the time Mr. Pickens deposited me on the porch and started back for Hazel Marie, my car had been rolled onto the gate and was starting its ride to the ground. Wondering if the little thing would be able to get enough traction to be driven into the driveway, I stood with Little Lloyd and Lillian, who couldn't believe what she was seeing, watching the experts work. I declare, there's something to be said for professional drivers because, after spinning its wheels when it first hit the icy pavement, my car responded as nice as you please to Mr. Johnson's handling of it. He drove it across the street and right into the garage.

I breathed a sigh of relief to have things, to say nothing of people, back where they belonged. Curtis closed the gate of the truck and followed Mr. Pickens and Hazel Marie up the sidewalk and on into the house, where Lillian waited to welcome them. She could hardly contain herself to have us all safe again.

"Lillian," I said, "this is Mr. Johnson and Curtis, the best two drivers, I do believe, I've ever seen. And that includes you, Mr. Pickens, since you don't know how to slow down. I declare, I didn't have any idea the streets were as bad as they are, closed up as we were inside that truck. Mr. Johnson, I thank you for getting us home without a scratch."

"Aw, hell, 'scuse me," he bellowed, as Lillian's eyes widened from the shock wave. "Wasn't no trouble. Had to make the trip anyway. But I tell you this, I'm mighty glad to park that thing. Gettin' rough out there."

The warm smell of roast beef filled the house as we began shedding our coats. And something else was filling the Victorian chair by the gas logs burning in the fireplace.

"Sam!" I cried, stopped in my tracks at the sight of him. "What in the world are you doing here?"

"Waiting for you, Julia. When Lillian called to say you were on your way, I asked Etta Mae to drop me off here on her way to another client. I've been worried about you, woman." He had his leg propped on my needlepoint footstool, and I noticed that his cast had been changed to one that came only to his knee. I tightened my mouth at the thought that the Wiggins woman might've been instrumental in his partial recovery, to say nothing of his admission that he'd been with her earlier in the day. But I admit I was glad to see him.

After introductions were made and coffee and soft drinks offered and served—I didn't keep anything stronger than cooking sherry in my house—they gathered around the fireplace, while I helped Lillian in the kitchen. Sam had clasped my hand when I'd gone over to him, asking me to sit and recount how we'd found Hazel Marie and tell him about our truck ride. But with a house full of company, I didn't have time to go over all of it with him. Besides, between Little Lloyd's excitement and Mr. Johnson's loud talking, he was getting the gist of it.

Lillian had outdone herself with all the food she'd prepared, and we loaded the table down with dish after dish. Just as I went in to call them to dinner, the doorbell rang. The sound of it brought me back to reality in a hurry. Here, I'd been so taken up with ice and sleet and trucks and Sam and Mr. Pickens hanging around Hazel Marie, that I'd lost sight of impending danger to Little Lloyd. He wasn't safe until Hazel Marie appeared before a judge at a hearing and got a favorable ruling, which I had no doubt she'd get because I'd be there backing her up with lawyers and character references and my own personal testimony. But until that happened, those deputies could show up anytime, waving their custody papers, not caring a lick that Hazel Marie would be answering the summons bright and early Monday morning. They're so literal, you know.

I looked across at Little Lloyd, who'd been struck dumb by the sound of the bell. He sat there stiff as a board, his eyes popping open and his mouth pulled tight over his teeth.

"Little Lloyd," I said as calmly as I could, "Lillian could use some help in the kitchen."

He was up and gone in a flash. I straightened my dress, worn now for almost three days in a row, and composed myself to face a deputy looking to snatch and grab. And to throw something at Sam or Mr. Pickens if they made a move to help him.

I peeked out the window, then swung open the door, both relieved and exasperated. "LuAnne! What in the world are you doing out in this weather? Come in before you break your neck or freeze to death."

She came in with a rush of cold air, bundled up in her old fur coat, a head scarf with furry earmuffs over it and fur-lined boots. She looked like a little bear with all that ratty stuff she had on. "Oh, Julia, I'm so . . ." She stopped with a gasp at all the people in the room, who had turned to see who else was visiting.

"Oh, I didn't know you had company."

"We just got home, LuAnne. Now why aren't you home instead of running around in this mess? Here, let me have your coat."

She began to come out of all the layers she had on, whispering that she'd had to get out of the house and had come for some counseling from Pastor Ledbetter over at the church. He hadn't been there and while she waited, the time had gotten away from her and now she wasn't sure she could get home. "I'm afraid to drive in this, Julia, and I thought I'd just stay with you until the streets get sanded."

There was nothing for it but to make her welcome, though my hospitality was getting a bit strained. I took her coat and laid it on the chair by the door, wondering how I could sleep them all. Somebody was going to have to make his bed on a pallet, since it was a settled fact that nobody was going anywhere anytime soon.

"We're just about to sit down at the table. Let me introduce you, then we'll eat." Then without thinking of the consequences, I introduced her to Mr. Johnson, Curtis and Mr. Pickens as "my friend, Lu-Anne Conover."

After we were seated around the table, the dishes passed and plates filled, it occurred to me that there had been some unforeseen pairing up. Little Lloyd was being entranced again by Curtis's tales of mayhem on the racetrack; Mr. Pickens kept leaning in on Hazel Marie, his black eyes watching her every move so that he could hardly get his fork to his mouth; Sam claimed the chair next to me, taking the leftovers, I guessed, since the main dish in the form of Miss Wiggins wasn't there. And to my shock and dismay, Mr. Johnson had made a beeline to the place next to LuAnne, saying in his usual loud manner that good-looking women improved his appetite.

LuAnne's face was red as a beet from the attention he was giving her, as he told her in what passed for a whisper, about his racing career and how he knew she'd really like being on the circuit if she ever had a mind to follow it. She kept ducking her head, taking tiny bites of Lillian's good food, and cutting her eyes at Mr. Johnson. I heard her giggle even, which is not at all attractive in someone of her age and marital status. The woman was shameless. I knew in searing detail just what she'd been missing, and it seemed to me that she was in the process of making up for lost time. I just don't have any patience for people who can't exercise a little control.

"Sam," I whispered, "LuAnne's getting herself in trouble, the way she's flirting with Mr. Johnson. You'd think she'd know better, wouldn't you? I should've made it clear that she has a husband waiting for her at home."

"A little flirting never hurt anybody, Julia," Sam said, in that tolerant tone that could run me up the wall. I expected people to act like they're supposed to, but he didn't care if they just ran wild. He smiled at me and went on, "You ought to try it sometime."

"I'd think you'd've had enough of it by this time," I snapped. "Trifling with people's feelings is just plain, well, trifling."

Sam laid his fork on his plate, looked full at me and said, "Who's trifling, Julia?"

"Well," I said, unable to hold his gaze, "well, LuAnne, for one. Maybe Mr. Pickens for another and, well, you, Sam, and you know it." I pushed my chair back, unwilling to go any further with such matters at the dinner table, and said to the others, "We'll have coffee in the living room. Lillian, let's go cut the cake. LuAnne, I'd recommend that you call Leonard and let your *husband* know where you are."

As they began to get up from the table, Mr. Johnson walked over to Lillian and bellowed, "That was about the best meal I've had in a coon's age. How 'bout signin' on with me an' go on the circuit with us? We could use somebody who can cook this good." He put his arm around her, while she laughed at his goings-on. "Teach you how to change a tire, too! By dog, I'll even put you on the pit crew!"

LuAnne made sure, though, that he didn't pay Lillian too much attention, sidling up to him and suggesting that he tell her more about his lucky charm. "It's all just so fascinating, Jerry," she said. It made me want to throw up.

Mr. Pickens came over to help Sam to his feet, giving me a knowing smile as he did so. I declare, the man was showing himself, acting so nice for Hazel Marie's benefit. And Sam's, too, if the truth be known, because Mr. Pickens was quick to pick up on who was important to her. I determined to have another talk with Mr. J. D. Pickens, and soon. He needed to be cautioned again about leading Hazel Marie on and breaking her heart with those winning ways of his. He was entirely too free with spreading them around. Womanizers don't make good husbands. Believe me, I know whereof I speak.

I followed Lillian toward the kitchen to prepare dessert, being about fed up with all the carryings-on in the dining room. Just as I got to the kitchen door, the lights blinked, then went out.

"Whoa!" Mr. Johnson yelled, as everything went dark and people milled around, bumping into each other.

LuAnne screamed like she'd never been in a power outage before, and I wouldn't've been surprised if she hadn't latched on to Mr. Johnson. I heard her scrambling toward him. Of course, I couldn't see a thing. It was black as pitch: streetlights and the lights in the church parking lot were all out. The only flickering glow, dim as it was, came from the gas logs in the living room and gradually I could make out through the draperies the lights that'd been left on around the truck outside.

Little Lloyd was murmuring, "Mama, Mama, where are you?"

"Right here, sugar."

"My nerves are about to act up," he quavered. "Hold on to me, sport," Mr. Pickens said, right next to Hazel Marie where I knew he would be.

"Lillian, where're the candles?"

"They's some in the desk in the living room. But I'm lookin' for that flashlight that ought to be in this here drawer," she said, as I heard her feeling around for it. "I found it."

She flipped the thing on and handed it to me. "Them batt'ries 'bout dead," she said, as the weak light beamed a couple of feet, then took a downward swoop toward the floor.

"That's a light an' a half, ain't it?" Mr. Johnson roared. "Want me to go out to the truck an' get you a better 'un?"

"This'll do, Mr. Johnson," I said, threading my way through them as they stood huddled next to the table. "No need to risk breaking your neck when I'll have candles lit in a minute."

Just as I got to the living room, feeling my way by the feeble light, a heavy hand hit the front door. I nearly dropped the flashlight.

I hadn't heard a car pull up or a footstep on the porch. In the dark of the room and the silence that always falls when the lights go out, all I could hear was the whispery sound of sleet against the windows. And that BAM, BAM, BAM on the front door.

Chapter 27

Lord, it gave me a turn. What, I mean *who,* was out there?

LuAnne gave a screech, and even Hazel Marie began to moan under her breath.

Mr. Pickens said, "Calm down, everybody."

Lillian whispered loudly across the room, "Don't answer it, Miss Julia, it might be one of them UFOs. Where you at, anyway?"

Mr. Johnson cackled. "By dog, I been wantin' to see one of them things."

Sam said, "Wait, Julia, I'm coming," as I heard his cane scrape on the floor.

I couldn't do anything *but* wait, it scared me so bad.

BAM! BAM! BAM! again, shaking the door something awful, when there was a perfectly good doorbell right at hand.

Just as I was about to get my wits together, I felt Little Lloyd brush past as he broke out of the pack toward the middle of the room, his arms flailing in the air, jittering and carrying on in an absolute panic. "I'm *scared*! I'm *scared*!" he cried, jumping high and flinging his arms up on each "scared."

Mr. Pickens moved like a flash, wrapping the child in his arms as he squatted down beside him, crooning, "Hold on, sport, hold on to me. Hey, now, you forget I'm here? Who's gonna hurt you with J. D. Pickens around?"

I heard Hazel Marie gasp like she'd been stabbed in the heart, and I knew how she felt. Anybody who'd take care of a child, well, the rest of us would be safe with him, too.

And with that reassurance, I went to the door and cracked it open. Holding the flashlight straight up so the beam would catch the face of whoever was out there before it dribbled down in a nosedive, I peered through the narrow opening.

"Deputy Daly!" I cried. "You about gave me a heart attack!"

He stood there, so bundled up in a dark coat and a cap with earflaps that I hardly recognized him. "You folks all right? Deputy Bates asked me to look in on you, and I was on my way when this sector got knocked out."

Keeping the light in his eyes, I reached behind me and grabbed LuAnne's fur coat. With one sweeping motion, I flung it across Mr. Pickens and Little Lloyd.

Mr. Pickens said, "What the hell," but he didn't sound too surprised since I was the one who'd done it. I don't think Little Lloyd noticed, so wrapped up in Mr. Pickens's arms that one more layer didn't register with him.

"Why, yes," I told Deputy Daly, "we're fine, thank you. I'd ask you in, but I know you have a lot to do on a night like this. How many have lost power?"

"The whole south end of town's been out an hour or so, and now the west end's out. Probably some trees down somewhere, but Duke Power's got crews all over the county. Uh, but another reason I come by, Mrs. Springer, is do you know whose truck that is out there?"

"I certainly do. It belongs to Jerry Johnson, who is my guest."

Deputy Daly grinned through chattering teeth. "I thought so. Saw his name on it." My goodness, he was sharp.

"Anyways," he went on, "I'd hate to give *him* a ticket, I mean, he's a racin' legend and all, but I'm gonna have to ask him to move it off the street. Too dangerous out there with everybody slippin' an' slidin' around."

I didn't say anything about fools getting what they deserved if they took a mind to drive in these conditions. Instead, I said, "I don't know where we'll put it, my driveway certainly isn't big enough. But don't worry, Mr. Johnson'll know what to do. You just run on, Deputy, and we'll see to it."

" 'Preciate it, ma'am." He started to leave, then turned back. "Uh, ma'am, Lieutenant Peavey says we're still looking to pick up the Puckett boy since, you know, he's supposed to be in protective custody until the hearing. We'll be doing that as soon as things get back to normal. Pretty much have our hands full tonight, though, what with traffic lights out and folks running off the roads."

"Well, first things first, I always say."

"Yessum, me too. Y'all stay warm, now."

I closed the door, weak with relief that there was one thing that could be said for the current weather conditions. It took the mind of the Law off complaints and court summonses. All except Lieutenant Peavey, whose mind sorely needed something besides protective custody to occupy it.

"Mr. Johnson?" I called.

"I heard him. How 'bout that church lot over there?"

"Perfect. There's no way we'll have a service in the morning, so there'll be plenty of room. Now wait just a minute till I get some candles lit so we can see what we're doing. Mr. Pickens, I do believe it's time to come out from under *Mrs.* Conover's coat. It's not that cold in here."

Mr. Johnson and Curtis put on their coats, going outside in a blast of wintry air to move the truck. We watched the operation from the windows, hearing the roar of the motor and seeing the diesel smoke spume up in the falling sleet, mixed now with flakes of snow. I wasn't sure at first that the truck was going to move, as Mr. Johnson shifted gears and fiddled around in the cab. Curtis stood in the middle of the street ready to stop traffic, though there wasn't any, and guide Mr. Johnson into the church parking lot. With a lot of jerks and some spinning of wheels, the truck finally made the turn into the lot and Mr. Johnson pulled it around so that it was directly across from the house and parked neatly enough to leave plenty of room for other vehicles.

Lillian opened her mouth to say something, but I caught her eye and shook my head. Mr. Johnson couldn't be blamed for parking on a building site and running over the pastor's little orange flags. Who could see the things, covered over with sleet like they were?

By the time Mr. Johnson and Curtis came back in, stomping and discarding coats and gloves, Lillian and I had enough candles placed around the room to provide a semblance of light and warmth. Everybody gravitated toward the fireplace as the corners of the room began to cool off. Hazel Marie and Mr. Pickens took the sofa with Little Lloyd curled up between them. Mr. Pickens had his arm across the back of it, his hand much too close to Hazel Marie's neck. Mr. Johnson pulled a chair up next to LuAnne on one side of the fireplace, while Curtis sat beside them, his legs stretched out toward the fire. He squirmed a little to get comfortable, and looked ready to nod off. Sam sat next to the fire where he could rest his leg on the footstool, beckoning me to take the chair next to him.

I ignored him. "Lillian, let's get the kitchen cleaned up while we still have hot water."

Then, after seeing LuAnne put her hand on Mr. Johnson's and lean close to him, I said, "LuAnne, we could use some help."

She gave me a furious look, but she got up and followed us to the kitchen. We carried more candles with us and, I'll tell you what's a fact, it is not easy clearing a table in a rapidly cooling room with hardly enough light to wash a dish clean. But people had done it for centuries, so I guessed I couldn't complain about one night of it.

LuAnne and I brought plates in from the dining room, scraping and stacking them, while Lillian washed. I started hand-drying the silver, as LuAnne put things away. I'd closed the door to the dining room so we wouldn't be overheard since I'd decided to take the opportunity to remind LuAnne that she had a husband sitting at home with a disabled function, and that she ought to behave herself accordingly.

Well, come to think of it, maybe she was. But I didn't like seeing it done in my house.

"LuAnne, Lillian told me that you told her that Leonard was going to see a doctor. I hope things are better for the two of you now."

"He didn't go!" She threw a spoon in the drawer, slammed it shut and flopped down at the kitchen table. That was all the help we were going to get from her. I'd opened the floodgates. "He said he didn't *need* a doctor and got mad at me for making the appointment. And I did it because Pastor Ledbetter said it was my place to take care of my husband's health. Julia, I can't do it all by myself. If Leonard won't cooperate in *any*thing, and I mean *anything,* what am I supposed to do?"

She put her head down on the table and commenced to cry. I went over to her and sat beside her. "LuAnne, listen to me. I know it's hard, but consider the life of a widow or a divorced woman. If you leave him, you'll be no better off than you are now. In terms of doing without, I mean."

"Oh, Julia," she said, discounting my opinion entirely. "It's just beyond you to understand. *You* may be able to get along without the comfort of a man, but everybody's not like you."

Well, I'd known that for some little while.

I sighed and put my hand on her arm. "LuAnne, listen to me now, I'm saying this for your own good. I know you have your problems with Leonard, but you just can't throw yourself at the first man who's nice to you. It doesn't look good. And besides, Mr. Johnson's a good twenty years younger than you are."

"Fifteen!" she snapped. "And I'll have you know that age differences don't matter if two people find themselves in *tune* in other ways. Grow up, Julia. Jerry's giving me back some of my self-esteem, making me feel attractive and wanted and valued. A woman *needs* a sense of self-worth."

I just hate it when I have to listen to this modern babbling and carrying-on about self-worth and self-esteem, quoted straight out of some magazine with nothing on its mind but S-E-X. All about how to please, not your husband but your *partner,* of all things, or how he can please you or how to get in touch with your own feelings. You won't see me reading that stuff. I figured that if you have to get to know yourself through the half-educated, pseudopsychological ramblings of a freelance writer, you ought to stay ignorant.

But I said, "I know, LuAnne. It makes a woman feel good when a man finds her attractive, but you ought to remember that Mr. Johnson is a traveling man, and you know what that means."

"He's a race-car driver!"

"Truck," I corrected. "And he travels all over the country. Why, he's on his way to Phoenix now, and from there he's going on to California or somewhere. It wouldn't surprise me if he didn't have a woman everywhere he goes. He looks the type." And so did Mr. Pickens, but I didn't bring him up. He was next on my list to get a good talking-to.

"I don't care! All I care about is right now, right here! I *deserve* some consideration, considering what I've had to put up with for so long. My self-esteem is just about gone and, Julia, I tell you, I'm just about desperate. I don't know how you stand it."

Self-worth, self-esteem, I thought with exasperation, how about a little self-control? But I didn't think she was in any mood to listen to good advice.

I glanced over at Lillian, who looked awfully intent on scrubbing a pan, wondering what she was thinking. She was making out like she was deaf, dumb and blind, knowing that LuAnne treated her as if that's what she was. But I could've used some of Lillian's common sense in dealing with someone who was displaying no sense at all.

Then, surprising me no end, LuAnne sat up, wiped her eyes with the back of her hand, and said, "Ask Lillian, if you don't believe me. Lillian, a married woman has a right to have her husband's attention, doesn't she? Even the pastor said the husband is obligated to render unto the wife her due, and it's a settled fact that I am *long* overdue."

Lillian dried her hands on a dish towel and came over to the table. "Miz Conover, I know it not my place to be giving you no advice. You been a frien' of Miss Julia's for as long as I knowed both of you, an' I don't wantta butt in on yo' troubles. But I think I might know what got Mr. Conover in the shape he in."

"Oh, please, tell me if you do. Don't hold back, Lillian, I'll take help wherever I can get it." Which I thought was a little ungracious of LuAnne to say, but then she'd never shared my high opinion of Lillian.

"Well, lemme ast you this. Do he go to the bathroom a lot?"

"Oh, Lord, yes! He's up and down, in and out, going and coming all night long till I hardly get a wink of sleep."

"Then he got prostrate trouble. I know 'cause I seen it too many times, an' heard about it, too. That's what happens when a man get a certain age, they prostrate break down on 'em an' they goes and comes one way, but they can't in another. He need a doctor to ream it out, an' he be good as new."

I wondered just how good that would be, but obviously it'd pleased LuAnne at some point.

"He won't go!" LuAnne wailed. "I begged him for the sake of our marriage, and he won't do it."

"Then try it another way," I said. "Tell him it's for *medical* reasons, not marital ones."

"Yessum," Lillian agreed. "Tell him he got to take care of that prostrate, or it dry up on him an' he won't be able to do nothin' with it. He be in the hospital then."

"Could that happen?"

Lillian and I nodded in solemn agreement of Leonard's dire prognosis, although what I knew of such things was next to nothing.

"Then I'll do it," LuAnne said, straightening up and looking determined. "I'll take him in an ambulance if I have to strap him in and buckle him down. But, Julia," she went on, giving me a fierce glance, "there's nothing wrong if I treat myself to a good time tonight. I mean, the weather's bad and the lights're out, and things are different. If Jerry wants to flirt with me, I'm going to flirt right back because I might never get another chance. And I don't care what you say."

And, with that, she flounced out through the swinging door. And came back in on the back swing. "And another thing, Julia Springer," she said, her hands on her hips. "You've got a nerve lecturing me about Jerry when you've got something worse going on right under your nose. And what I'm doing doesn't even compare. So just clean up your own house before you start on mine!"

And out she flounced again.

Lillian and I stood there dumbfounded. "What in the world is she talking about?"

"They ain't no tellin', but it don't sound too good."

"Oh, well, she's just mad, and trying to get back at me. I'll straighten her out when I have the time. Let's finish these dishes; it's getting cold in here."

"I'll tell you the truth, Lillian," I said, after studying on LuAnne's outburst for a few minutes, "LuAnne's going to worry me to death. As if I didn't have enough on my plate already, she's just piling that much more on. The only good thing about it is, Mr. Johnson surely can't be taking her seriously. Fifteen years difference, my foot. She's old enough to be his mother twice over. Though I wouldn't say that to her face."

"No'm, I don't think I would either. He be gone pretty soon, so I don't 'spect she get in too much trouble."

"Maybe not, if I can keep them apart for the night. I declare, these racing people are something else, aren't they? And speaking of tonight, I've got to figure out how to sleep them all."

"You got to put some of 'em together, look like."

"Yes, and I'm giving it a lot of thought. I don't want any wandering around playing musical beds in the middle of the night. I'll just have to put people together who'll watch each other."

As we carried our candles back into the living room, I heard the clank and scrape of a snowplow on the street outside. Looking out the dining room window, I saw the bright lights of the big machine as it rumbled past, clearing a lane on Polk Street as a dump truck came behind, spreading sand.

"Looks like the sleet's stopped," I said to Lillian. "Let's hope we get power back soon. I'm getting chilled to the bone."

We went on into the living room, where everybody was still gathered around the fire. Little Lloyd had dropped off to sleep, his head against Mr. Pickens's chest and LuAnne's fur coat across his legs. Mr. Pickens still had his arm across the back of the sofa, but he'd progressed to the point of twirling a curl of Hazel Marie's hair, while he and Sam talked. There was nothing for it but to take Mr. Pickens aside as soon as I could and caution him about getting too familiar.

I forgot about that when I saw LuAnne stroking Mr. Johnson's arm. I pursed my lips and glared at Sam. There he was sitting right across from them where he couldn't help but see what they were up to, and he hadn't done a thing to put a stop to it. He looked up and smiled at me, like adulterous behavior wasn't going on in front of his eyes. He motioned to the chair beside him and said, "About time you two got in here. Etta Mae said she'd be by to pick me up about this time, so come on over here and talk to me."

"I doubt she'll be driving in this weather, Sam, regardless of the plans the two of you made. So you might as well plan on spending the night. I won't have anybody else trying to get you home, and you certainly can't walk. Now, listen everybody, there're enough beds if you're willing to sleep together."

Mr. Johnson sang out, "Got no problem with that!"

LuAnne giggled. If I heard "Oh, Jerry" one more time from her, I was going to lose my dinner.

Mr. Pickens leaned over and whispered something to Hazel Marie. I think she blushed, but I couldn't be sure. It might've been the glow from the fire.

Sam's eyes were sparkling. "Everybody's willing, Julia. Depending, of course, on how you pair us up."

I ignored their comments, as I considered my biggest current problem, which was LuAnne. With Mr. Pickens a close second.

"Hazel Marie, I'm going to put you and LuAnne in Deputy Bates's room. He won't be using it tonight." I figured that Mr. Pickens wouldn't be staging any raids with another adult in with her. And I knew Hazel Marie was a light sleeper, who'd hear LuAnne if she took to stirring around. "Sam, you need lots of room with that cast and you don't need to be trying to manage the stairs. Since Hazel Marie's room is downstairs and has a king-sized bed, I'll put you there. Mr. Pickens, there's plenty of room for you in with Sam, if you don't mind."

"I don't mind, but I can think of a better arrangement."

I let them have their laugh, and went on, "Mr. Johnson, you and Curtis can take Little Lloyd's room, on the right at the head of the stairs. Lillian'll be in her usual room, and Little Lloyd can sleep with me. Is that all right, Hazel Marie?"

She nodded, rubbing her hand over the child's side, wondering, I guessed, why I hadn't put him in with her. She'd figure it out, if she paid attention to what was going on with LuAnne and Mr. Johnson.

"Mr. Pickens, would you mind taking Little Lloyd upstairs? He needs to be in bed, and I'd suggest we all get in before the house gets too much colder."

It was barely nine o'clock by the time I led Mr. Pickens upstairs by candlelight, as he carried the sleeping child. When he'd put Little Lloyd down and I'd tucked in the covers, I turned to Mr. Pickens and said, "Mr. Pickens, as your employer, I need to have a talk with you. I want you to know that I appreciate how you're lifting Hazel Marie's spirits, she was in bad need of it, but I think you might be taking your job too seriously. I don't want her to be trifled with, so you can begin to slack off a little."

Those white teeth flashed and I thought I might sometime recommend shaving off that mustache so people could get the full benefit of his smile. On second thought, he didn't need any more advantages than he already had.

"What if I'm not trifling?"

"You and Sam! I declare, I don't know what else either of you'd call it."

"Let me tell you something, Miss Julia." And he had the nerve to start pointing that finger at me. "You've got to let people do as they're going to do, anyway. Quit worrying about everybody else, and pay some attention to Sam. He can't take his eyes off of you and, if that cast wasn't holding him back, you wouldn't get two steps out of his sight."

Well, that was just plain offensive. There the man was, in perilous need of counsel himself, and what was he doing? Turning it back on me, that's what. "I thank you for your advice, but you don't know everything that's been going on. Sam is as bad as you, taking on over every woman he meets, leading them on, playing with their affections and being, in general, just too careless with people's feelings, and I'll thank you to stop pointing that finger at me."

"What?" He looked at his finger, grinned and put it in his pocket. "Well, I'm not playing around, and I don't think Sam is, either."

"You just haven't seen that Wiggins woman and the way she flounces herself around in front of him, and you haven't seen the way he acts around her, either."

One eyebrow went up. "Make you jealous?"

"No, it does not. It's just that I don't need another man who's so easily distracted. But we're not talking about me, we're talking about *you*." I raised my finger and shook it right in his face. It was a point that needed to be made. "Listen to me now, and take it to heart. I want you to back away from Hazel Marie before she gets hurt again. I've seen you, Mr. Pickens, when you're engaged in your investigative techniques, and you just smother a woman with your smiling and your sweet words, whispering them up and making them laugh and turn red, and I'm not going to have you doing it to Hazel Marie. So let's get that straight right now."

His shoulders started shaking, and I realized he was laughing! There I was speaking as plainly as I knew how, telling him what he needed to know for his own good, and he was laughing at me.

He reached out and took hold of my finger, then he put an arm around me and said, "Miss Julia, you are some piece of work."

I declare, with that strong arm around me and that warm hand holding mine, I could've melted away right then and there. It was all I could do not to lean on his shoulder and enjoy, just for a minute, the feeling of being cared for even though I knew he was just being his usual womanizing self. But before I could stop it, while he stood there so close, smiling that warm smile, a vast feeling of loss and loneliness and, maybe, bereavement flooded my soul. If I'd met someone like him when I'd been of an age to take action, what would my life have been like? What would it've been like to've had someone with dancing eyes catch mine from across a room? What had I missed by not falling in love with a man who smiled and teased and was generous with hugs and touches? To say nothing of one with an overendowment of maleness? It didn't bear thinking about, because my time had come and gone, and all I had to look back on were too many barren years, years filled with *shoulds* and *ought to's* and hard looks and exasperated sighs. Sad and cold years, because I'd never delighted anyone the way every woman in the world delighted Mr. Pickens.

Well, it couldn't be helped.

So I disengaged myself from Mr. Pickens before I broke down and cried in front of him out of pure despairing misery.

"Come on, now," he said, his voice warm and reassuring, "let's go down before we wake that boy. I want to see you enjoy yourself for a change. You don't need to take on the problems of the world. Aren't you tired of looking out for everybody else?"

"Lord, yes. Tired to death of it, if the truth be known. But I'm the only one . . . I mean, they need me, or seem to, and nobody else. . . . Well, maybe I can try." I couldn't say anymore. I wanted him to leave so I could get myself together. I needed to have time to think things over, especially since he'd said almost the exact same words Sam had said when all this began. If Mr. Pickens and Sam thought the same way, well, wouldn't that mean that the two of them were alike in other ways as well? I mean in ways that made Mr. Pickens so aggravating and appealing all at the same time?

"You go on down, Mr. Pickens. There're a few things I need to see to up here. I'll join you in a few minutes."

He gave my shoulder a pat, smiled some more and said, "Anytime you feel things getting away from you, hon, just remember that I'm here for you."

He left then, and I was glad of it, having had more comforting than my heart could stand, being unaccustomed as it was to such sweetness.

I stood in the dark room, dimly lit by one fluttering candle, trying to get back to the here and now instead of bemoaning a past that couldn't be changed.

There was Little Lloyd, I reminded myself, a gift in my old age that was not given to many. And Hazel Marie, a sweeter woman you couldn't find anywhere, who cared for me and looked up to me. And Lillian, a rock and a bulwark against all the vicissitudes that'd come my way. And Sam. And Sam, who was always there for me.

At least, when Etta Mae Wiggins wasn't around.

Hearing the sound of a car motor on the street, I went to the window to see who could be out and about on a night like this. I always liked to know what was going on around me.

Pulling back the curtain, I could see enough in the glow of the lights from the north side of town reflecting back from the clouds to make out Pastor Ledbetter's sports utility vehicle turn into the church parking lot. I watched as the top-heavy machine managed the street well enough, but it spun and slid all around the icy lot before passing out of my view behind Mr. Johnson's truck.

"Now, what is he doing at the church this late on a Saturday night?" I said to myself, then realized that he was most likely going in to check on things, maybe to turn on some faucets. Which reminded me that I should do the same myself. There's nothing worse than frozen pipes and the resulting mess when they break.

As I turned from the window, a clanking, grinding noise coming from the other end of the street drew my attention. Peering out the window again, I saw another vehicle, this one long and low with the back end practically dragging on the pavement. Smoke billowed from the tailpipe, and the chains on the tires, one of them flapping loose against the fender, churned the sand and ice on the street.

"Well, my land," I said, astounded as I clearly made out the two-toned car as it turned into the parking lot and followed Pastor Ledbetter's tracks to the back entrance of the church. "If that's not Brother Vern, I'll eat my hat."

I stood transfixed by the cold window as various thoughts flashed in my mind. Why would Brother Vernon Puckett, ranting and raving television and tent revivalist, and Pastor Larry Ledbetter, silky smooth pulpiteer of the biggest church in town, be meeting together on a stormy night? There was only one thing in the world that Brother Vern and Pastor Ledbetter could be conspiring about, and that was their need for money—the one to keep his television show on the air, and the other to build a monument in my front yard.

Certainly the session needed to know that the pastor was up to something, and it couldn't be a meeting of like theological minds. They'd run Pastor Ledbetter out of town on a rail if he invited someone like Brother Vern to occupy the pulpit. Those two had to be getting their heads together for some other reason. And I figured I knew what it was. Something had to be done, and done tonight.

Lord, when the telephone rang, it scared me out of a year's growth. I dashed to it, snatching it up before it rang again and woke Little Lloyd.

"Yes?"

"Miss Julia," Pastor Ledbetter said, assuming that I'd recognize his voice, which I did but I resented the assumption. "Do you know who parked that truck in the church parking lot?"

"Why, yes. We had to get it off the street and there was plenty of room over there, so I thought . . ."

"It'll have to be moved. The contractor's stakes have been run over, and the weight of the truck is damaging the asphalt. Do you know what it costs to repair a parking lot of that size? I'm afraid you'll have to be responsible for that expense. I don't know why people assume that church property can be used for any purpose whatsoever."

"From the looks of it, pastor, the asphalt was due to be torn up anyway, so the truck's done nothing but help you out."

"Be that as it may," he said, after a pause in which he may've been trying to decide what to bring up next, while I about froze to death waiting on him. Then, remembering his pastoral responsibilities, he said, "I hope you can keep warm until the power's back on; everything at the church is out, too. If I can help you in any way, just let me know."

"I appreciate that, but I think we're in good shape, at least for a while. It's good of you to offer, though."

Then, as if he'd decided this was as good a time as any to get any number of things off his chest, he went on, "While I have you, Miss Julia, you should know that the talk about Ms. Puckett is getting worse. I've just recently heard that improprieties have resulted from her personal associations. You and I, and perhaps Ms. Puckett herself, need to get together and see what we can do to resolve this matter."

"This matter wouldn't've come to your attention by way of her uncle, would it? Who I happen to know is over there with you right now. That man is a nuisance, Pastor, and you'd do well to keep your distance."

"He's concerned about his niece, and he's only reinforced my suspicions that all is not as it should be where she is concerned."

Well, I'd about had enough of his implications and accusations about Hazel Marie, and it struck me that he was doing some of the same kind of implying and accusing that LuAnne had done when she'd lashed out at me in the kitchen. The pastor was right; the gossip about Hazel Marie was getting out of hand.

But before I could agree to a meeting, the pastor said, "I also wanted you to know that Wilson T. Hodge got back to town this afternoon after reporting in to his office in Charlotte. He just beat the weather and he called me as soon as he got in. He shares my concern about some, uh, discrepancies in the building fund. He's going to do an audit first thing Monday which, I'm sure, will put our minds at rest. I also questioned him about Ms. Puckett, and he said he had no idea where she is, so he's obviously had nothing to do with her disappearance. I certainly don't wish any ill to befall her, but it behooves us, Miss Julia, to disconnect her name from his before the building fund drive is irreparably damaged. I think you'll agree with me on that."

In spite of the patter of sleet against the window and the chill in the room, I could feel myself heating up. "Pastor, the building fund drive is the last thing on my mind, as I've made perfectly clear long before this. Now, I don't care what Wilson T. Hodge told you, because I'm telling you that he is up to his neck in a crooked business, and he just escaped getting arrested when the deputies raided that warehouse that was in the papers."

I wanted to shake my finger in his face. "So, you listen to me and learn something. Wilson T. Hodge can lie to you all he wants, but I happen to know that he was involved with holding Hazel Marie against her will. And another thing, you ask him, just ask him, about a certain wreck he was in when he had the nerve to chase her around a racetrack. And, furthermore, I know he's in trouble with his business partner, who is also his cousin and who is as crooked as the day is long. They're both into gambling on NASCAR racing and I don't know what all else, so you'd do well to audit that building fund. And here you are, worried over a little gossip about Wilson T. and Hazel Marie, when all she's been doing is trying to get away from him. He's the one who needs a talking-to, if you ask me."

There was dead silence on the line. Then he said, "Those kinds of accusations shouldn't be made lightly."

"There's nothing light about what I'm telling you. I know what I'm talking about."

"Well, Miss Julia, it sounds to me as if Wilson T.'s perfectly pure and good intentions are being twisted by the gossip-mongers into a potential scandal. And anything that soils him, soils the church by extension. Hazel Marie's uncle has reminded me of the kind of life she's led in the past, and that sort of thing could easily hurt the reputation of even the most godly man. You see?"

Yes, I saw. I saw that he wasn't giving one thought to one of his own flock, not one bit concerned about Hazel Marie's reputation or feelings, or what she'd just gone through, courtesy of the godly man he was trying to protect. In spite of the fact that he'd been counseling her for weeks on how to be a Presbyterian. The more I thought about it, the more affronted I became. The man didn't have a lick of sense, ignoring everything I'd told him about Wilson T. Hodge and doing nothing but blaming everything on Hazel Marie.

"Well," he went on with a deep sigh, "these matters are a heavy burden to bear. We just have to do the best we can with God's help." I couldn't help but feel a stab of compassion for him, even though he'd misidentified the name and nature of his burden. But anybody who pastors a thousand-member congregation of Presbyterians deserves a little pity.

Then he seemed to collect himself and went about dashing any smidgen of pity I had left. "Now, Miss Julia, that truck out there has to be moved. I'm just before calling the sheriff and having it towed. If the owner's visiting you, tell him it must be moved immediately."

"Oh, I'll tell him, Pastor." And tell *you* a few things, as well, along with that busybody, Vernon Puckett.

I hung up the phone, leaned over the bed to see if Little Lloyd was warm enough, then went to my closet. I rummaged around until I found my knee-high galoshes with the buckles I could never fasten. I pulled them on, letting them flap loose around my shins, put on an old heavy coat and wrapped a scarf around my head.

I clunked down the staircase, looking more like a bag lady than the most generous tither of the First Presbyterian Church, for which I'd never received proper credit in the first place. I grabbed the flashlight and headed for the door, paying no heed to the sudden attention I was attracting from those around the fire.

"Julia!" Sam called out, trying to rise from his chair. "Where're you going? Don't go out there; it's dangerous."

"Hey!" Mr. Johnson bellowed. "I'll get whatever you need. Come on in here by the fire."

"Miss Julia, what's wrong?" Hazel Marie was out of her chair and coming toward me, with Mr. Pickens right behind her.

Lillian said, "You know better'n to go out in that stuff. What's got into you?"

"All of you," I said, holding up my hand, "just leave me alone. I just got a call from Pastor Ledbetter, who is over at the church with, would you like to guess? None other than Brother Vernon Puckett! And I aim to get to the bottom of a few things this very night. So I'm going and that's that."

"Hold on, woman," Mr. Johnson yelled. "If you got a bee in your bonnet that bad, I'll go with you."

"Me, too," Hazel Marie said, pulling on her coat. "I'm gonna give that fool uncle of mine a piece of my mind. He's interfered in my life one too many times."

"Well, if that's the case," Mr. Pickens said, jamming his arms into his coat. "Sam, look after things. Jerry and I'll go with these two wild women."

And out we went, the four of us trekking across the vast expanse of the parking lot, with Jerry Johnson holding on to my arm, yelling "God dog it," every time his cowboy boots slipped on the ice, and Mr. Pickens mumbling words I won't repeat as Hazel Marie tried to keep him upright. She and I had hardly any trouble getting across. That's what a full head of steam will do for you, make you so mad that you just stomp on through a layer of ice and sleet and snow like nobody's business.

We finally reached the safety of the covered area at the back entrance, which some members called a porte-cochere at church, but a carport at home. As Mr. Pickens opened the door, we filed into the interior and stood bunched up together, absolutely blind in total darkness.

"Where's the flashlight?" Mr. Pickens asked, reaching for it. "Here it is," I said, clicking on the pitiful beam and handing it to him. "Maybe it'll last long enough to get us to the pastor's office, which is where I'd guess they are."

Mr. Johnson said, in what was for him a subdued tone—funny how a church can have that effect on a man. "Don't worry about the dark. They's likely to be some lightnin' pretty soon."

As Mr. Pickens swept the flashlight beam in front of our feet, we eased past the church kitchen on our right and came out into the echoing space of the fellowship hall. Folding chairs and tables lined the walls, waiting for Wednesday's covered dish supper.

"Lightning doesn't usually come with a sleet storm, Mr. Johnson," I said.

"Haw! It will with me inside a church. Likely to strike me dead."

That didn't warrant an answer, especially since Mr. Pickens held out his arm, stopping us, as he said, "Hold on a minute."

As we stood in the middle of the fellowship hall, I began to make out the feeble glow of light coming from the direction of the pastor's office. The low rumble of a man's voice reached us, one that I recognized as having the cadence of Brother Vern's television preaching style.

"Call out to 'em, Miss Julia," Mr. Pickens said, "so we don't scare 'em to death."

"It wouldn't be more than they deserve, to my mind." But I called out, as I struck off toward the office. "Pastor! We're coming in."

Chapter 30

We walked into the pastor's office, warmly lit by the yellow glow of a kerosene lantern and the beam of a heavy flashlight on the desk. That's all that was warm about it, though, for there was a definite chill in the air. Brother Vern looked twice his size in a quilted parka, as he stopped in midsentence and step when he saw us.

Pastor Ledbetter was sitting in his leather chair behind the desk, his eyes dark and sunken in his face. It was a settled fact that whatever Brother Vern had been holding forth on was not setting well with him. He looked stunned and, in spite of our unexpected appearance, unable to open his mouth. He just sat and stared into space. Whatever Brother Vern had been saying had clearly unnerved him. Maybe it took a preacher to get through to one of the same ilk.

Hazel Marie, however, didn't notice the pastor's stricken state. She centered in on her uncle, rushed straight at him, got right up in his face, and said, "What do you think you're doing? You're going behind my back to try to take Lloyd away from me again, aren't you? And you want Pastor Ledbetter to help you, don't you? It wasn't enough that you sent the sheriff to take my baby. You have to sneak over here in the dead of night and start telling tales in church, to turn my preacher against me! You are nothing but a sorry, underhanded excuse for a preacher, pretending to save people from their sins, when all you've ever been interested in is lining your own pockets. Well, let me tell you something. You're not getting your hands on my baby or on anything that belongs to him. Just get that straight right now!"

Mr. Pickens looked from one to the other of them, then when he realized what she was saying, he stared at her. "This is the one who filed the complaint?"

"Yes! He's claiming I'm an unfit mother!" she stormed. "And he's been trying and trying for I don't know how long to take Lloyd away from me. He just keeps on and on, making my life miserable, trying everything he can think of to get his hands on Lloyd's money."

I cringed inside, thinking it was the better part of wisdom not to announce to any single male in the world the inheritance held in trust for Little Lloyd. It was too tempting. But the damage was already done, although Mr. Pickens didn't seem all that excited by the news.

Instead, he turned a hard gaze on Brother Vern. "I've seen this lady in action, so I'd advise you to back off."

Brother Vern pulled himself up taller, got that inspired look on his face that came over him when he took it on himself to speak for the Lord. "This is first and foremost a spiritual matter of the direst consequences. It is my duty, as a minister of the Word of God and a leader of souls into the heavenly kingdom, to warn a fellow minister when he is in danger of the fires of hell. 'Brethren, if a man be overtaken in a fault, ye who are spiritual restore such a one in the spirit of meekness,' Galatians, six, one, and that's what I'm aimin' to do. Brother," he said, turning to Pastor Ledbetter, not in a spirit of meekness, as far as I could see, but in the spirit of thundering authority, as he gasped for breath. "I have come-ah to rebuke and exhort-ah, to caution and warn-ah, to put you back on the paths-ah of righteousness. Lissen to me, now, I'mah speaking from the Spirit-ah, put behind you the wiles of Satan-ah before you damage your soul-ah and the witness of this church-ah!"

Mr. Pickens reared back from the onslaught, and Mr. Johnson was uncustomarily quiet. His mouth was hanging open, though, as Brother Vern tore into Pastor Ledbetter.

"*What* is going on?" Hazel Marie demanded.

"Hold your peace, woman!" Brother Vern rounded on her, pointed his finger in her face and cut loose in her direction. "Hide your head in shame, beguiler of iniquity, and look no longer on the anointed of God!"

"What are you talking about?" She squared her shoulders and clenched her fists, ready to take him on. Mr. Pickens rested his hand lightly on the small of her back.

"That's what I'd like to know," I said, deciding it was time to take a hand in matters, since Pastor Ledbetter was looking more peaked by the minute. To say nothing of the fact that he hadn't said a word since we'd come in, an uncommon occurrence, in and of itself.

"This man-ah of God-ah!" Brother Vern cried, pointing the same shaking finger at Pastor Ledbetter. "Shame-ah has come upon him, through no fault-ah of his own. But," Brother Vern tempered his voice, leaned closer to the pastor and began to put on the posture of a counselor, "you have allowed it, Brother, I'm sorry to say. All, I'm sure, unawares. We never know in what form the tempter comes, do we? And he gets us in his snares before we know it, a-wrappin' and a-tanglin' us up till we don't know which end is up. That's why I come, brother, to reveal to you the vain and profane babblings of the multitude, and to warn you of the eternal peril you've got yourself mired up in."

The four of us stared at Brother Vern, trying to follow his line of thinking. No easy task, to begin with. But what he was ranting about now was simply beyond me. I couldn't figure out why Brother Vern was aiming his corrective remarks at Pastor Ledbetter. It was Wilson T. Hodge who needed the chastisement.

"Brother Vern," I said, speaking as sharply as I could. When a preacher is under the spell of the spirit, it sometimes takes a two-by-four to get his attention.

"Ah, Miz-res Springer." Brother Vern came toward me with out-stretched hand. "I wouldn't distress you with this matter for the world but, since you're here, I know I can count on you as a prayer partner for the sake of our brother who's being mocked and maligned by the ignoramuses of the world."

Allowing my hand to be grasped and pressed, I said, "I'm sure our brother appreciates your concern and your prayers." I glanced at Pastor Ledbetter who looked less appreciative than anybody I'd ever seen, but I was trying to get some sensible explanation for this unlikely confrontation. "But when I pray, I like to bring out the particulars. Just what are we so concerned about here?"

Brother Vern leaned over me, frowning with a worried look on his face. "You mean you haven't heard?"

"Well, no, but I've been out of town. I'm sure it has to do with Wilson T. Hodge, though, and I'm glad for your warning about him."

"Wilson T. Hodge? You mean," Brother Vern's voice dropped to a whisper filled with dismay, "do you mean to tell me, Sister Springer, that there's *two* men that's been entangled in this? At one and the same time?"

"I don't know about two. One's all I know about, and that's a gracious plenty. Considering what he's been up to, like stealing and gambling and such as that." Wilson T. Hodge could've been guilty of every sin in the book, for all I knew.

"Stealing! Gambling! Oh, Jehovah God, have mercy!" His face suddenly red with outrage, Brother Vern rounded on Pastor Ledbetter. "You are not fit to stand in the pulpit of the Lord! Cleanse yourself, Brother, and put away the evil that's overtaken you. I come in here to counsel with you and detract you from the path that's sucked many a man of God from the paths of righteousness. I know, oh, Lord, I *know*—get thee behind me, Satan—how the wiles of a woman can tempt us and destroy us and flat-out ruin our testimony. But, Brother, you are further along the slippery slope than I recognized, and I'm calling on you to repent and renounce this woman!"

"*What!*" Hazel Marie shrieked. "Do you mean *me*? I'm gonna knock you nine ways to Sunday, Vernon Puckett!"

"Wait a minute! Wait a minute." I moved between them, holding up my hand. "Brother Vern, do you mean to say that you think Hazel Marie and . . . and the *pastor* . . . well, my Lord." I was so undone that I needed to sit down. I mean, I didn't have much use for Pastor Ledbetter and his worldly ways, but this was too much.

In the silence that followed, Pastor Ledbetter looked ready to throw up, sitting there with his throat working, unable to get a word out of his mouth. Mr. Pickens's eyebrows were up around his hairline, and Hazel Marie stood there gritting her teeth at Brother Vern. Mr. Johnson finally broke the silence, "I b'lieve I'm gonna start goin' to church again. It's looking a lot more interestin' than I remember."

"Now see here, Brother Vern," I recovered enough to say. "I don't know where you're getting your information, but I can assure you that adultery is not in Pastor Ledbetter's reportoire. And certainly not with Hazel Marie."

I found it a little disconcerting to be defending Pastor Ledbetter, considering the woes and constant strife of the ordinary, day-by-day dealings I'd had with him, but I'm a fair woman. He had his faults, as do most people, but this was an accusation that shouldn't be laid at his doorstep. I mean, the man was an ordained Presbyterian minister.

"Well, I'm here to tell you, Sister," Brother Vern said, irritating me no end. I hated to be called *sister,* especially by the likes of Brother Vern. "When a man of God goes a-whorin' after strange women, it ain't no stretch to figger he'll be up to something else. Then you'll get your stealin' and your gamblin', and next thing you know, he'll have a woman a-preachin' in his pulpit."

Mr. Pickens just stood there, shaking his head. Even I was taken aback at how Brother Vern's list of sins had progressed from adultery down to women preachers, taking in most everything else in between.

"I never heard of such a thing," I threw at him. "You've got your sins all mixed up, as well as your sinners." And gotten me mixed up too, if the truth be known. I'd thought the gossip was about Hazel Marie and Wilson T. and, from the looks of him, so had the pastor. But Brother Vern had just named him the culprit.

"Let's just back up here a minute," I said, intent on setting Brother Vern straight. "I take it that you've taken it on yourself to counsel *my* pastor in *my* church because you've heard some gossip about him and Hazel Marie. Is that right?"

"Not only heard it, but know it's true." Brother Vern's confidence unnerved me. I glanced at the pastor, wondering what he'd been up to, and who with, because I knew it couldn't've been with Hazel Marie. I also wondered when he was going to come to his own defense. Unless he didn't have one.

Then it hit me that he'd been counseling LuAnne Conover day in and day out and, in her current state of mind, she was as susceptible as a woman could be. Lord, the very thought of LuAnne and Pastor Ledbetter together was enough to make me queasy. But that unsettling thought had to go on the back burner; I had my hands full, taking care of Hazel Marie.

"*How* do you know it's true?" I demanded, crowding Brother Vern's space. "You've seen him with her or some other woman? Is there a witness? Tell us just how you know."

"I know because I know the woman!" Brother Vern turned, pointed at Hazel Marie and thundered, "Down on your knees, woman, and pray G-*OD*-ah to forgive you for leadin' this poor, hard-workin' preacher astray! Along with that other man you been foolin' with."

Mr. Pickens was entirely at fault for not having kept a better grip on her. Hazel Marie flew at Brother Vern like she had springs in her shoes, backing him up into the corner by the bookshelf. Screeching and screaming and raking books off the shelves onto his head, she had him cringing and cowering and scrooching up in a ball trying to protect himself from the onslaught. I'd never seen the like before, not even when she'd lit in on Wilson T. Hodge.

Mr. Pickens had her by the hips, trying to pull her away while Brother Vern kept yelling, "Jezebel! Sodom and Gomorrah!" and the like. Which made absolutely no sense.

Mr. Johnson got tangled up in the fray when he tried to help Mr. Pickens pull Hazel Marie away, so his bellowing added to the din. Pastor Ledbetter remained in his leather chair, neither concerned about nor bothered by the ruckus in his office. I wondered if the man had been struck dumb. That can happen sometimes, you know, when you think you're doing fine, then find out everybody else is pretty sure you're not.

When Mr. Pickens finally got Hazel Marie off Brother Vern and was holding her close to him for fear of what she'd do next, I walked over to her. "Hazel Marie, calm yourself down now. I know Brother Vern deserves everything you can dish out and then some. But we're going to straighten him out right now. Mr. Pickens, don't turn her loose."

"I don't intend to," he said, pushing her tear-streaked face down on his shoulder.

"Hey, Brother Whoever-You-Are," Mr. Johnson boomed as he stood over Brother Vern, "I'd keep my head down, if I was you."

"Now," I said, "Brother Vern, we need a better reason why you think your own niece and Pastor Ledbetter have been . . . well, doing what you said."

"I know," he said, edging his way to his feet, but keeping his back to the corner, "everybody's talkin' about the two of 'em. I heard it all over the county. She's over here every night of the week, closed up in this office with him, and, Miz-res Springer, it don't look good. Everybody knows what kinda woman she is."

"No, everybody does not know what kind of woman she is!" I had a surge of anger fairly close to the one that'd flung Hazel Marie across the room at him. Rumors! Gossip! Whispers! Behind-the-hand talk! And easy to believe if your mind runs that way, which Brother Vern's did. Either because he was always looking for a way to get his hands on Little Lloyd, or because he'd at some time been in the same predicament with a woman himself.

"Pastor!" I clapped my hands in front of Pastor Ledbetter's face. "Wake up! Come to! Do something! Don't just sit there like you've been poleaxed! Tell this fool what you and Hazel Marie've been doing in your office. And," I rounded on Brother Vern, "it hasn't been every night of the week; it's only been two nights a week!" Which, I guessed, if anything had been going on wouldn't've been that major a point, but it needed to be made.

"Catechism," Pastor Ledbetter gasped. His face looked wet and clammy in the glow of the lantern. "I've been instructing her in the catechism."

Turning, I said, "You hear that, Brother Vern? These two who you've been so quick to condemn have been studying the Presbyterian creed."

"It don't hold a candle to the Holy Word of God," Brother Vern pronounced. "So look not upon church tradition for your salvation. As for me and mine, we'll soak ourselves in the Bible and nothing more."

"Theology!" I said, waving it away. "I'm not getting into that with you. This is a Presbyterian church, a creedal, catechizing denomination, and we'll study whatever we want to." Well, not exactly, of course, since we had to put up with the General Assembly.

After giving the situation a moment's thought, I said, "Brother

Vern, I think you're to be commended for your concern for a fellow preacher." Hazel Marie let out a noise that sounded like the gnashing of teeth. "Hold on," I said, "I'm not through. But, Brother, you went overboard and believed what you wanted to believe. You've slandered both your niece and my preacher, leaving yourself wide open for a lawsuit that'll wipe you out and ruin your ministry."

"Lawsuit? Did you say lawsuit?" Brother Vern was beginning to understand that I meant business.

"Yes, and I'll underwrite it. My advice to you is to get yourself to that judge first thing Monday and withdraw all those papers you took out against Hazel Marie. You are dead wrong about her, and a dozen people will testify to that fact. To your detriment, I might add." I took a deep breath and plowed on, determined to set him straight. "I'm telling you right now, that there's no way you'll get your hands on Little Lloyd because your complaint won't hold water in a bucket. I am going to have Pastor Ledbetter and every elder and deacon in this church testify to Hazel Marie's good name. And it wouldn't surprise me if that judge doesn't slap you with a fine for making false accusations and stirring up trouble."

"Well, I didn't make it up."

"I don't know if you did or you didn't, but you certainly passed it on. And there're enough like you in this town to create a considerable amount of havoc, which is what you've done." Then I had a flash of inspiration, recalling, in part, the Sunday School text of last Sunday. "And Brother Vern, if you need some Scriptural backup, listen to this: 'they learn to be idle, wandering about from house to house; and not only idle but tattlers also, and busy-bodies, speaking things which they ought not.' Timothy something or other, which is the word of the Lord."

Mr. Johnson chimed in about then. "Y'all ought to sue his britches off."

Brother Vern opened his mouth, but he couldn't come up with a verse to counter mine, so he retired from the field.

He turned and headed for the door, forgetting his flashlight. Then, getting in the last word, he said, "I'll be a-prayin' for you, Brother."

Chapter 31

"Same here," I said, as he disappeared into the dark of the fellowship hall. I hoped he'd be able to find his way to the door.

Mr. Johnson seemed to be having the time of his life, as he stood with his thumbs in his belt surveying the damage with sparkling eyes. He hadn't known what he'd been missing, being unchurched as he was. Mr. Pickens seemed unable to keep his hands off Hazel Marie, patting her and rubbing her back and whispering that he'd see that her uncle never got his hands on Little Lloyd, if she wanted him to. I declare, it was a poor time for him to be drumming up business.

"Miss Julia," Hazel Marie said, turning away from Mr. Pickens and covering her face with her hands. "I'm just so ashamed, my own uncle thinking I'd do such a thing with a preacher of the Gospel. It just made me lose control of myself. I know it wasn't ladylike, but I couldn't help it."

"Get a grip, Hazel Marie," I told her. "I'm proud of you. Meekness is all well and good in its place, but it wouldn't've done a lick of good with the likes of him."

Being well acquainted with the consequences of womanly submission, I didn't want Hazel Marie to suffer from it. A woman ought to take up for herself, if you ask me.

"Well, Pastor," I said, turning to the sweating man behind the desk. He'd taken out a handkerchief and was mopping his face. "My advice to you is that you reconsider all this counseling you've been doing. It's done nothing but get you in trouble."

"I . . . I can't believe it." He shook his head back and forth, bowed over the desk. He couldn't seem to lift it up and face us. "How could anybody think? . . . I'm a *pastor,* striving to live a life above reproach. Never have I been accused of such an ungodly act."

"I guess you haven't. But you've sure done a lot of accusing, yourself. Maybe now you know how it feels."

"What's that supposed to mean?" His head finally came up, and his voice regained some of its authority. "I've never falsely accused anybody, never been a party to gossip."

Well, that just took the cake. I leaned over his desk and let him have it. "Let me remind you, Pastor, it was not four days ago, right here in this office, that you passed on gossip to me about Hazel Marie and Wilson T. Hodge. Remember that? Remember how you were so concerned about *his* reputation? And how sure you were that Hazel Marie was the cause of it all? Where there's smoke, there's fire, you said. Now, come to find out that the gossip you heard *and* passed on was not about him and her at all, but about *you* and her. Where's the fire now, Pastor?

"And I'll tell you something else," I went on, about to pop with outrage. "You're as bad as Brother Vern. You assumed the worst because you'd already decided in your mind what kind of woman Hazel Marie is. You'd already decided that if she was in contact with any man, she had to be doing something wrong. You just didn't figure it'd come back on you, did you? Her relations with Wilson T. were honorable and aboveboard, being led on by him to think of marriage and home and family values and such as that, when all the time he was up to his neck in illegal activities. But did you blame him? Oh, no, it was Hazel Marie you jumped on with both feet. If there was gossip, it had to be her fault, didn't it? Well. Come to find out, now, that the gossip had nothing to do with him. It was all about you."

"I . . . I never heard a name," he admitted, wiping his hand across his face. "I confess I never heard a name, just that it was a man of the church, and he was the only one she was seeing, so . . ." He trailed off, because the full impact hit him square between the eyes. *He* was a man of the church; *he'd* been seeing her, and seeing her by himself behind a closed door.

Pastor Ledbetter's confession was interrupted by a loud, clanging commotion in the fellowship hall that seemed to go on and on. In the midst of it, we heard Brother Vern yelling, "God bless the God-blessed luck! Dang it all, somebody help me!"

Hazel Marie headed for the door. "What's that fool done now?"

"Hold on," Mr. Pickens said, grabbing the heavy flashlight. "Don't go out there in the dark."

"Oh, Lord," I said, laughing, because I recognized the metallic sounds. "He's run into the folding chairs."

And sure enough, when I followed the light in Mr. Pickens's hand, there was Brother Vern on his hands and knees in the midst of a dozen or more metal chairs, some of them still swirling around on the floor.

"Dang it all to hell and back!" he yelled. "Who put them cussed things in the way?"

"Gimme your hand," Mr. Johnson bellowed right back at him. "I'll he'p you up. We thought you was gone."

"I wisht I was," Brother Vern gasped, standing up and brushing himself off. "I got to the door, but they's a bunch of men swarmin' around out there."

Mr. Pickens clicked off the flashlight, surrounding us with the darkness of the hall. Hazel Marie drew in a sharp breath and clutched at my arm, while Pastor Ledbetter brought the lantern to the door of his office.

"Shut that thing off," Mr. Pickens said to him in such a way that the pastor did it with no argument. Totally in the dark, in more ways than one, we all stood where we were, waiting for Mr. Pickens to tell us what to do next.

Brother Vern spoke up, "What's goin' on?"

"Don't know yet," Mr. Pickens said. Then, "Hazel Marie, you and Miss Julia ease back into the office and call the sheriff. Jerry, if you can get out from those chairs, let's go to the door and see who's out there."

Hazel Marie and I felt along the wall until we came to the office door. Lord, I'd never been anywhere as dark as that place was. We bumped into Pastor Ledbetter, who still seemed dazed by his shattered reputation. He didn't make a sound as we moved him out of the way.

Feeling around on his desk, we found the telephone and, after some more feeling and counting of buttons, Hazel Marie finally got somebody at the sheriff's department. "We need help at the First Presbyterian Church," she said, her voice quivering. "There's a gang of men out in the parking lot and we don't know who they are or what they're doing and we're scared to death."

"They coming?" I asked as she hung up. "Soon as they can," she said. "They're all out on calls with this weather. Oh, Miss Julia, what if it's Bigelow?"

The same thought had crossed my mind, unsettling it to a considerable degree.

We heard the big door at the back of the church slam open, and a jumble of men's voices echoing in the fellowship hall. Then the whole place seemed to light up. Thinking at first that the power had come back on, I headed out of the office with Hazel Marie and the pastor right behind.

I could hardly see when I got out in the hall from the glare of headlights aimed inside. Somebody had pulled a car next to the porte cochere and switched on the brights. A group of dark figures, throwing long shadows in our direction, stood right inside the door, brought up short by Mr. Pickens and Mr. Johnson.

Just as we pulled back into the shadows, I recognized Wilson T. Hodge's voice. "She's here and we know it. They told us over at the house that she's here. Bobby's missing something valuable, and he just wants to talk to her."

"That's Wilson T.," Hazel Marie hissed next to me. I grabbed her arm and said, "Looks like he's brought an army with him. Tell me the truth, Hazel Marie, did you take anything from Bobby Bigelow?"

"Not a blessed thing," she said, quivering beside me. "I've never even been in his house."

"Then don't let them see you. Mr. Pickens'll get rid of them." I pushed her back toward Pastor Ledbetter and whispered to him, "Take her back to the office and stay there."

Well, I couldn't just stand there, watching from afar. So I picked my way through the scattered folding chairs by the glare of the headlights until I reached the dark side of the hall. Then nearly jumped out of my skin when Brother Vern loomed up in front of me.

"Who is it?" he whispered.

"I think it's a bunch of racing men who're mixed up in something worse than racing. They think Hazel Marie's got something we think they stole from Mr. Johnson."

"What?"

"Never mind."

I left him and snuck on closer, in case Mr. Pickens needed help.

About that time, Mr. Johnson's braying voice cut through the conversation by the door. "You sorry thief! Ever' sheriff's department between here and Rockingham's lookin' for you. And, Bobby, they got dead-level proof that it was you that robbed me blind. You got some gall comin' in here and accusin' a woman of robbin' you. I ought to whip your butt, boy, an' I'm just about to do it!"

"We don't know what you're referring to," Wilson T. said, in that sanctimonious way of his.

"Well, I'll tell you," Mr. Pickens said, just as calm and sure of himself as he could be. "Jerry, here, had his shop damaged and his lucky charm stolen, but you've not said what was stolen from you. If we knew what it was, maybe we could help you."

A soft, high-pitched voice from a dark figure, not much bigger than

Little Lloyd, answered him. "We just want to talk to the woman. Then we'll be on our way with no harm done."

If that was Bobby Bigelow, he didn't sound or look anything like the way I'd pictured him from all the stories of his meanness. From the looks of his dark outline, he was a little, sawed-off runt, even with an overcoat on. I'd had in mind a big, rough-looking man but, from the sound of his voice, he was quiet and mild mannered. Of course, those can be the worst kind, since you expect exactly the opposite from what you're likely to get.

"Let's get this straight right now," Mr. Pickens said, "Ms. Puckett is not available to you. I'd advise you to look elsewhere if you have a problem. In fact, I'd look closer to home, if it was me." And he looked Wilson T. up and down.

Smart man, I thought, get them distrusting each other.

"He knows *I'm* in the clear," Wilson T. said. "How many times do I have to say it? Hazel Marie is the only one who could've stolen it. So I know it's her. She's nothing but a thief, and a liar on top of that. HAZEL MARIE! Come out here!"

Poor Hazel Marie'd been called an adultress, a Jezebel and now a thief and a liar. All in one night, and I'd had enough of it. "Wilson T. Hodge," I said, coming out of the shadows into the glare of the lights. "You've got a nerve calling Hazel Marie names like that! Just get yourself on out of here. I don't know how you can come into a church, in the company of this, this criminal, even if he is kin to you. Don't think we don't know what you've been up to with him, breaking into Mr. Johnson's truck shop and tearing up everything and stealing valuable stuff and then placing bets on races you think you're going to win. And I'd like to know where you got the money to gamble like that, and I expect the pastor'd like to know the same thing. The sheriff's looking for all of you, and they'll be here any minute!" And I wished it was that minute, because I made out two more figures backing up Wilson T. and Bigelow. There was some shuffling of feet as I finished my onslaught on their characters.

Then the door behind them crashed open, and a small, back-lit person walked in, a head of blonde hair lit up in the headlights like a halo. My heart stopped as I tried to work out how Hazel Marie could've come in from outside when I'd left her in the pastor's office.

So softly that I barely heard him, Bigelow said, "There she is. Get her in the car."

The two dark figures in the background blended with the small one, while Mr. Johnson yelled "Whoa there!" and Mr. Pickens plowed in swinging the flashlight.

"Wait," Wilson T. Hodge called, "that's not . . ."

"What is this! Get your hands off me!" The voice was clear as a bell, loud, demanding and mad enough to spit fire.

My Lord, it was the Wiggins woman. Of all people I could do without, she was at the top of my list.

It beat all I'd ever seen. Although, to tell the truth, I couldn't see much. Just a roiling mass of people, struggling shadows, some trying to get Etta Mae out the door and others trying to keep her inside. Mr. Johnson's voice boomed out, yelling words that would've stopped anybody else in their tracks, and Etta Mae Wiggins just about equaling him in volume and vulgarity. And in a church, too. It was a wonder lightning wasn't singeing the hair of us all.

Bigelow and Wilson T. stayed on the sidelines, scrunched up in opposite corners away from the scuffle, which is pretty much what instigators usually do—start something, then stand back and watch. Wilson T. kept saying, "Wait . . ." "That's not . . . ," but nobody paid any attention to him.

I saw Etta Mae swing that big tote bag of hers against the head of somebody, knocking him into Mr. Pickens. Mr. Pickens gave him a mighty shove, sending him through the doors and out onto the porte cochere. That left the one Mr. Johnson was struggling with. Mr. Johnson pushed him against the wall and, while he was winding up for another blow, Etta Mae stepped in and did some real damage with a thick-soled boot. The poor man doubled over and started retching and moaning and gasping.

"Atta girl!" Mr. Johnson yelled, as he pushed the man, head-first, out the door. "Bring on the next bunch! Got us a fighter here!"

Mr. Pickens had Bigelow over in the corner, not laying a hand on him, but looming over him and penning him in so he couldn't leave if he'd wanted to.

Wilson T. hurried over. "We've made a mistake," he said, trying to smooth things over. "Look, let me talk to Hazel Marie. I'm sure we can straighten this out, if I can just talk to her."

"Hazel Marie doesn't want to talk to you," Hazel Marie said. I looked around to see both her and Pastor Ledbetter right behind me, standing in the glare of the lights. She looked ready to rip Wilson T. to shreds, while the pastor hung back, still mopping his face.

Seeing the pastor, Wilson T. quickly took a step back. "Larry," he said to him, "I don't want you to get the wrong idea. This is something separate from my work with your church. It has nothing to do with my contract with you. It's just a, well, a private investment enterprise with my cousin that I haven't had much to do with. It's gotten a little out of hand, I guess you could say."

"I guess you could," I said, disgusted at his attempt to clear himself. "Considering what all it's come to. To say nothing of defiling this church building by bringing such trash into it. I'll tell you this, I don't understand why winning a NASCAR race is so important that you'd be a party to hounding a poor woman to death."

Pastor Ledbetter moaned, hiding his face in his handkerchief.

Brother Vern was taking all this in. "NASCAR?" he said. "I'm a big racin' fan." Which was not a great addition to the discussion.

We heard the sound of a siren, several blocks away, but coming closer. Wilson T. plucked at Bigelow's sleeve. "You might better leave. I'll be all right. The pastor will vouch for me."

Bigelow stared at him for a minute, then jerked his arm away. Without another word, he pushed out the door and joined his men in the waiting car. It backed away from the porte corchere, taking the light with it. Then, as the driver hit the brake, it slid around in a circle on the icy pavement. We could hear the wheels spinning as it tried to get enough traction to head for the street. Two sheriff's cars turned in, light bars flashing blue streaks across the parking lot and our faces. They swerved and stopped in front of Bigelow's car, blocking it from the street. I wanted to watch what happened, because the dark bulk climbing out of one of the cars had to be Lieutenant Peavey and I would've liked to've seen him in some action that wasn't aimed at me. But I couldn't supervise everything, don't you know, and things were still happening inside.

"Larry," Wilson T. said, coming over to the pastor, "I can explain. It was all a mistake. I didn't realize what I was getting into. But it was a sure thing, Larry, although every investment carries some risks, you know that, but that building fund was just sitting there, waiting to make more than bank interest. I knew you were disappointed at the congregation's poor response, and, well, I thought a worthy investment would outweigh the risk."

Pastor Ledbetter just stared at him, so Wilson T. tried again. "We have a good start with the building fund drive, and I know you wouldn't want to jeopardize it at this point. If you'll just help me explain to the sheriff that I was a bystander, so to speak, I'll make sure the drive is successful, it's my business, after all and I'm good at it.

I'll see to it that you have a beautiful new building right out there for your congregation to use and enjoy for years to come."

"Bystander!" Hazel Marie screeched. "*By*stander! You're up to your neck in Bigelow's crooked business, Wilson T. Hodge! And I'm a witness, don't think I'm not. No use trying to wiggle out of it, after what you've put me through!"

"Ms. Puckett," Pastor Ledbetter started. I could hear the placating tone in his voice, so I knew he was picturing that building rising up, brick by brick, on the corner across from my house.

Brother Vern didn't miss a trick, especially where money was concerned. He sidled up to Wilson T., listening intently to what was going on between him and Pastor Ledbetter, and ignoring Hazel Marie all together. Wilson T. ignored him, in turn, taking the pastor by the arm and leading him into a corner.

"Say you're a fund-raiser?" Brother Vern asked, following them. Then as he stumbled into a wall, "Dag-nab it! Hold on, Brother, I wanta talk to you about beefin' up my teevee advertisin'. I got my 800 numbers, and I got my direct mailin' and my phone bank, but none of it's doin' the job good enough. What's it cost to hire you? You want a flat fee or do you take a cut of what you raise? I'd like that better, that way the ministry don't lose. Wait up, now, we need to talk."

"Enough!" I yelled, surprising myself. "Pastor, there's no need to huddle up with Wilson T. at this late date. I'd at least wait till you have an audit done, by an independent firm, I might add. Hazel Marie's going to do the right thing and tell the sheriff what she knows about Wilson T. and his cousin which, when put together with what the Rockingham sheriff knows, will mean big trouble for your fund-raiser. And that's going to happen whether that building goes up, down or sideways. And I'll tell you this, Pastor, if it's meant to be built, it will be, and you won't need Wilson T. Hodge's help. Predestination's what it's called."

"I need to think about this," the pastor said. "Pray about it."

"I'm sure you do," I agreed, distracted now by Etta Mae Wiggins running over to hug Hazel Marie.

"I've been so worried about you," Etta Mae said. "I came to take Mr. Sam home and when they told me you were over here, I just had to come see if you're all right."

That just ran all over me. Why did she think she had to come out on a night like this to take Sam home? Did she think she was the only one who could look after him? I just had no use for presumption, which she had a mortal plenty of.

Then the full import of her words hit me square between the eyes.

Sam's house had no power either, and it was more than likely that James had gone home. So how was Sam going to manage by himself in the dark with a cast on his leg?

The shock of her underhanded plan to spend the night with Sam stunned me so bad that I couldn't say a word, just stood there with my nerves thrumming away.

"I'm so glad you're back, safe and sound," Etta Mae went on, ignoring the presence of everybody else. "Honey, if anything happened to you, I don't know what I'd do. You've been my idol ever since we were in grammar school. We've all been worried to death."

My lip curled when she associated herself with those of us who'd made such an effort to find Hazel Marie. I say, we.

"I'm fine, I guess," Hazel Marie told her. "But are you all right? Did they hurt you?"

"Oh, don't worry about me, I'm okay. I didn't know what I'd walked into, I mean, you don't exactly expect to come into a church and get attacked, do you? But I had plenty of help." She gestured toward Mr. Pickens and Mr. Johnson, who were on their way out the door to add their two cents to whatever version Bigelow and Hodge were giving Lieutenant Peavey. "Who are they anyway? Friends of yours?"

Hazel Marie started explaining who they were but, when she said "Jerry Johnson," Etta Mae squealed like a teenager. Another big racing fan, I guessed.

"You really get around, Hazel Marie," she said, with a tinge of admiration and, perhaps, envy. Of all things.

"I don't know how I get into such messes. If it wasn't for Miss Julia, I don't know what I'd do."

Thank you, Hazel Marie, I thought, for the commendation. But it didn't help much, because I was trembling all over, still outraged by the Wiggins woman.

"Well, my patient's waiting for me," Etta Mae said. "I need to get Mr. Sam home and tucked in bed. He depends on me, the sweet ole thing."

She gave Hazel Marie a quick hug. Then, bless me, if she didn't stop in the porte corchere and hug both Mr. Pickens and Mr. Johnson, thanking them for coming to the rescue. From what I'd seen, Etta Mae Wiggins hadn't needed a whole lot of rescuing by anybody. As she moved out of the light, it flew all over me again that she was heading for my house. She'd just walk in like she owned it, I knew she would. Then she'd bundle Sam up and put him in her car and take him with her to his house. And would she just get him settled and leave him there? In the dark? With no heat? Feeling his way around with a cane? By himself, in the worst winter storm we'd had? NO, she would not.

I knew what she *would* do, though. She had every justifiable reason in the world for spending the night with him. Not that *she* cared about justifying herself. Women like that never do.

I stood there in the dark of the hall, vaguely aware that Mr. Pickens and Mr. Johnson were coming back into the church. I could hear them discussing the arrests they'd witnessed, with Mr. Johnson still bemoaning his loss. Over against the wall, Wilson T. continued to whisper to the pastor as he pled for understanding. None of it made any difference to me. I had more important things on my mind. *Sam,* in the clutches of that unprincipled woman.

"Peavey's coming in," Mr. Pickens said, opening the door for him and another deputy who were there to get statements or, maybe, to arrest anybody else who needed it. By the headlights of the sheriff's cars outside, I could see other deputies transferring Bigelow and his two men to the back seats of the patrol cars. It was a most satisfying sight, to say the least.

As Lieutenant Peavey and his deputy entered the dark church, the strong beams of their heavy flashlights swept over the pastor, Wilson T. and Hazel Marie, as well as Mr. Johnson and Mr. Pickens. I saw Lieutenant Peavey shake Mr. Pickens's hand, and heard the babble of voices as everybody tried to tell what'd been going on.

By this time, I was pressed against the wall of the kitchen, trying to determine how much danger Sam was in, and not intentionally staying out of the limelight. But that's the way it worked out. Besides, I figured the lieutenant would be in a better mood if I made myself scarce.

At Mr. Pickens's suggestion, the lieutenant agreed to adjourn to the pastor's study, where the lantern would give better light for the statements that had to be taken. As they moved out of the fellowship hall, nobody noticed that I wasn't with them.

So I stayed where I was, sick at heart over Sam's perilous situation, and no longer caring whether Wilson T. got what was coming to him or not.

This is not like you, Julia Springer. It was like a voice from out of the blue, and why not, since I was standing in a church? *Where's your gumption? Look at you: letting another woman move in where she has no business.*

Well, that did it. I'd let the same thing happen with Wesley Lloyd although, except for damaging my pride, what he'd done wouldn't've mattered a hill of beans to me. Go and stay gone would've been my response which, come to think of it, was what he'd done, with a little help from a heart attack.

I straightened myself up and pulled myself together. Sam wasn't Wesley Lloyd, not by a long shot, and Sam was worth making an effort for. So if it took a fight, then that's what Etta Mae Wiggins was going to get.

Standing there in the dark, I decided there was no profit in being the last word on proper behavior if it meant losing Sam. What would it matter if I was the one person in town who knew the *correct* way of doing things if that woman got her clutches in him? So what if some people didn't know Amy from Gloria Vanderbilt? Did I have to be the one who had all the answers? I mean, did it really matter in the scheme of things if I knew that a coffee is a morning entertainment and a tea is held in the afternoon? Who cared if I knew that open-faced cucumber sandwiches are correct in the summer and party-sized ham biscuits in the winter? And cheese straws anytime. Who cared if I knew white shoes are worn only between Easter and Labor Day, and that camellias should be planted on the southeast side of the house in our climate? What did it matter if I knew that "honor" should be spelled "honour" on wedding invitations? Or that the bride's family gives the flatware and the groom's family the silver service? Why had I ever exercised myself over people who didn't know which end was up?

None of it mattered in the face of this crisis. All that mattered now was that Etta Mae Wiggins was about to put Sam in a compromising situation, and that he wouldn't even know it until she'd sunk her hooks in good and tight. It was up to me to see that it didn't happen.

Chapter 33

I saw the flickering glow of the lantern as someone lit it in the pastor's study, heard the voices of Lieutenant Peavey and Mr. Pickens, and didn't give a rip if I wasn't in there to provide the details. I slipped out the back door, closing it softly behind me, and took my life in my hands to cross the sleet-covered parking lot by myself.

My galoshes flapped against my shins as I made my way toward Mr. Johnson's truck, looming like a behemoth between me and my house. Etta Mae was nowhere to be seen, so she'd managed the icy area without mishap. More's the pity, although I didn't customarily wish harm to anybody. But this was a special case, since she meant harm to me and mine.

As I reached the front of the truck, I steadied myself by holding on to the grill, resting while I looked across the street where Etta Mae's car was parked, and then up at my house. Blood pounded in my ears as I pictured what was going on in there in the dim light.

A shadow suddenly moved in front of me, scaring me so bad I nearly lost my breath and my hold on the truck.

"Who's that!"

"It's just me," Curtis said. "You all right?"

"Lord, Curtis," I said, gasping with relief, "you scared me half to death. What're you doing out here?"

"Got worried when those men came to the house looking for y'all. Then when we saw the cop cars, I came out to see what was going on, and to check the truck. Want me to walk you in?"

"No. No, that's all right. You keep on doing what you're doing, I'll manage." I walked out onto the sanded street where the footing was surer, not wanting to be held up on my mission.

Halfway across, I turned around with a sudden idea of how to turn Etta Mae's attention away from Sam. "Curtis?" I called. "Are you a race-truck driver, too?"

"No ma'am, I'm a fabricator."

"That'll do. She won't know the difference. Did you see that young woman come across just a minute ago?"

"Yes ma'am. She was in a hurry and didn't stop. Went on in the house."

"She's young, single at the moment, and somewhat attractive. At least, some people think so. Would you be amenable to distracting her for a little while? You could bring her out here and show her Mr. Johnson's truck, maybe. And, although I don't usually hold with such tactics, I think a little innocent dalliance might be called for. She's quite lonely, and could use some attention."

Even in the dark, I saw his quick grin. "I'm a married man, Miz Springer. For all of three months, so I better pass if it's all the same to you."

I threw up my hands and started again for the house. At least I'd tried for an end run; now I'd have to tackle her head-on.

When I opened the front door, I wasn't a bit surprised to see the little hussy sitting on the arm of Sam's chair. It just burned me up. I ignored Sam's call to me, as I took off my coat and head scarf; this was between me and Etta Mae Wiggins.

" 'Bout time you got back here," Lillian said, cocking her head toward Sam's chair. "I 'spect you about froze."

"No," I started, my mouth in a thin line as I thought that I was as far from being frozen as I'd ever been.

"Julia!" LuAnne jumped up from her chair. "What's going on over at the church? People knocking on the door and the sheriff over there, we were worried to death. Is Jerry all right? Where is he? When's he coming back?"

"Jerry's fine, LuAnne, sit down. Miss Wiggins took good care of him, didn't you, Etta Mae?" LuAnne narrowed her eyes, not liking that at all. "Sam, you should be in bed. Lillian, let's help him up. He needs his rest."

Etta Mae gave me an innocent smile. "Oh, there's no need of that, I'll be taking him on home in a minute. That's why I put chains on my car and followed the snowplow over here. Couldn't let my favorite patient get stranded, could I?" She reached down and patted his knee.

"I'd hardly say he was stranded. Besides, he doesn't need to spend the night by himself, with neither heat nor lights."

"Oh," she said, looking at me with wide-eyed innocence, "I'd never leave a patient in his shape by himself. I'll stay with him till James gets there in the morning."

"I hardly think that's advisable. Where's your cane, Sam? You're going to bed right here."

"Julia . . ." Sam started, but I hushed him with a look. I meant for him to stay out of this.

"He needs to be in his own bed," Etta Mae said, like only she knew what he needed. "He's got his pillows to prop his cast on, and a bedrail to pull up on. He'll be more comfortable there."

"Don't tell *me* where he'll be more comfortable." I could not control the surge of anger at the little know-it-all. "And I'd appreciate it if you'd get off the arm of that chair. It wasn't made to be sat on."

She jumped up like a shot, while LuAnne and Lillian looked at me with their mouths open. It certainly wasn't like me to be discourteous, but these were special circumstances. Besides, she started it.

Sam had the strangest expression on his face while this was going on, sitting there enjoying being fought over, as it was plain to see he was doing. I could've wrung his neck.

I marched over to him, paying no mind to Etta Mae who'd edged out of my way. I sat down on the footstool by Sam's wounded leg and said, "Sam, it's bad out there, and if you don't want that other leg broken, you'll stay here tonight."

"Well, Julia," he said, taking my hand, his eyes shining from the reflection of the fire, "if you put it that way."

I looked up in triumph at Etta Mae, only to catch the edge of a smile as she turned away. Now why would she be doing that when she'd just been put in her place? But saving face is important to some people, and I didn't care how she managed it. I had what I wanted.

Knowing I could now afford to be gracious, I said, "Have a seat on the sofa, Miss Wiggins, and get yourself warm before you have to leave. I certainly appreciate your dedication to your patients but, as you can see, Sam is well taken care of."

"Yes, ma'am," she said, just as docile as I could want. You just have to stand up to the likes of her.

Footsteps sounded on the porch, as Hazel Marie, Mr. Johnson, Mr. Pickens and Curtis came in with a lot of stomping and laughing and just plain noise.

"It's over, Miss Julia," Hazel Marie said, smiling as she came over to clasp my hands with her cold ones. "Or almost over. All that's left is to get to the clerk of court's office first thing Monday and make sure Brother Vern withdraws his complaint. When he's done that, the snatch-and-grab order for Little Lloyd will be thrown out. Then all I have to do is go in and sign the statement I just made to Lieutenant Peavey about Bigelow and Wilson T. I'll have to say that Lieutenant Peavey was real happy to hear my story. He was just as nice as he could be."

"Well, make sure you get your charm back from him," I told her. "I can't imagine he'd want to keep it."

"Oh, I will. It nearly killed me to damage my bracelet." She held her arm up so that the remaining charms jangled and sparkled. "I'm so relieved, Miss Julia, because Mr. Pickens took up for me and explained everything to Lieutenant Peavey. I'm out of it now, and Bigelow and Wilson T. were arrested and put in jail where they belong."

"Taken in for questioning," Mr. Pickens corrected her, "but they'll have some explaining to do, especially after the Rockingham cops get in the act."

Hazel Marie leaned close and whispered to me, "I tried to get them to take Brother Vern in, too, but they wouldn't." She gave me a wicked grin. "I'm going to tear him up if he doesn't withdraw that complaint, and he knows it. He won't have a congregation left by the time I get through telling the world what kind of preacher he is. He won't ever try to get his hands on Little Lloyd or his inheritance again."

"That's the spirit, Hazel Marie," I said, patting her hand. "And I don't think we'll have any trouble getting Pastor Ledbetter to testify to the good home you and I've provided for Little Lloyd. And if that's not enough, we'll have Mr. Pickens and Mr. Johnson testify to your good character. Why, it wouldn't surprise me a bit if the judge turns out to be a NASCAR fan, too."

She smiled and leaned her head against my shoulder until Mr. Johnson's loud mouth broke up the moment.

"Guess we took care of them," he announced, throwing his coat on a chair. "I wouldna missed it for the world. Now, I want to shake the hand of this little gal." He headed straight for Etta Mae, a big, goofy grin on his face. "Come'ere, you little honey, I got to get you in the light so I can see what I got. Might even have to give you a great big kiss. God dog, where'd you learn to fight like that?"

Etta Mae grinned right back at him. "Fightin' off men who're too big for their britches. Like you."

Well, that just delighted Mr. Johnson, and he showed it by grabbing her up and swinging her around, putting my furnishings and general decor in jeopardy. But wouldn't you know it, and I hoped Sam noticed, she'd turned her attention entirely on Mr. Johnson. Women like that will take up with any man within arm's reach.

LuAnne didn't like it. I could tell she was fuming at Etta Mae's sudden elevation in Mr. Johnson's esteem. Even though I had no use for Etta Mae at all, I had to be gratified that she was taking Mr. Johnson's mind off LuAnne. And LuAnne could tell she'd lost out to a younger model, you could see it eating at her. Jealousy is such an unattractive trait, don't you think?

"J. D.!" Mr. Johnson cried, turning away from his current interest. "Now you got these folks up to speed, when you gonna take up my case? We got to get on the road soon's the interstates're clear if we're gonna make Phoenix. But no use me goin' if my lucky charm's still missin'. I tell you what's a fact, I was hopin' Bigelow had it and we could wring it out of him. But don't look like he does, what with the way he's been lookin' high and low."

"Yeah," Mr. Pickens said. "He wouldn't've risked coming back here if he'd had it. He'd be in Phoenix by this time instead of the county jail. No, he doesn't have it, and Hodge didn't strike me as the type to hold out for long against Bigelow. I figure somebody else got it from them and has either gone on ahead or it's still around here somewhere."

He put his arm around Hazel Marie's waist, smiled down at her and said, "I'm good at finding things, though. Just look what I came up with on my last case."

That comment didn't seem to give Mr. Johnson any particular reassurance, and I can't say I blamed him. It was a stretch to compare Hazel Marie to any kind of lucky charm, to my way of thinking. But I wasn't ready to totally discount Mr. Pickens's investigative techniques, since they'd proven somewhat helpful in Hazel Marie's case. Although when you came right down to it, if it hadn't been for me and Little Lloyd he'd've still been looking for her.

I started to point this out to Mr. Johnson, but the lights flickered, came on, and the furnace clicked on in the basement. Everybody blinked and looked around, smiling at having our modern conveniences back at work.

Candlelight and open fires are all well and good in their place, but I could do without them in the ordinary course of events.

"Well, thank the Lord," Lillian said.

"And Duke Power," I added.

In the relief of having the power back on, everybody except Sam stood up, blinking in the brighter light, glad to be able to see what they were doing.

"Lillian," I said, "let's see if we can find something to eat. A little snack before we go to bed, and before Miss Wiggins has to leave, would be welcome."

I stood up, but Sam kept my hand, pulling me back down. "Hurry back," he said.

You know, it's not always the words, it's the way they're said that warms the heart. I tried not to let it show, since the Wiggins woman was still flitting around and who knew what she'd be up to as soon as my back was turned.

"Hold on a minute," Mr. Pickens said. Then, taking Hazel Marie's arm, he said, "I want to see you in the kitchen." Cocking that finger at me, he went on, "And you, too, Miss Julia. I want you, too."

His high-handedness affronted me, but I wanted to know what he was up to now, so I followed them through the dining room and into the kitchen. Mr. Pickens didn't let loose of Hazel Marie's arm, just marched her in and closed the door behind us.

"All right," he said, frowning but trying not to smile as he stared down at her. "Let's have it."

"What?" I asked.

"It's nothing," she said, turning her face away from him. "Really, it's not."

"What?" I asked.

Ignoring me, he got right up in her face, pointing that finger at her. "Don't put me off any longer, little girl. I know you've got something."

Now how did he know something I didn't? I looked from one to the other, trying to determine what was going on.

"Come on, come on." Mr. Pickens wasn't turning it loose. "What is it and where is it?"

"Well, it's . . . ," Hazel Marie started, stopped and looked at me for help, but I wanted to know as bad as he did. "Well, it's just so ridiculous, I'm ashamed to say. I mean, I don't know why in the world anybody would want it."

"Wait a minute," I said. "Hazel Marie, do you actually have something of Bigelow's?" I couldn't believe it. Here I'd been taking up for her when she'd been accused of stealing and taking what didn't belong to her. This was a pretty come-off, if you ask me.

"No, ma'am, I don't have anything of Bobby Bigelow's." Then she ducked her head and admitted, "I did take a little something of Wilson T.'s, but nobody could call that thing valuable by any stretch of the imagination. See, Miss Julia, I just wanted to get back at Wilson T., and it was the only way I could think of. I saw him take it out of its hiding place and look at it and rub his hand over it when he thought nobody was watching. Well, I thought, you know, I thought it was a . . . well, one of those weird things that some men get fixated on, like, well, a woman's foot or her underclothes. I don't know what you call it, a feet, a fet . . . some such thing."

Mr. Pickens said, "A fetish?"

I said, "A what?"

"Something with magical powers," Mr. Pickens answered, his eyes glued to Hazel Marie, the hint of a smile twitching around his mouth.

Magical powers, I thought. It seemed to me that there was more to a fetish than that, but I didn't pursue it.

"That's it," Hazel Marie went on, "and I knew it'd embarrass him to death if anybody knew about it, him being with the church and all. I was so mad at him for taking me off and doing everything Bobby told him to do, and keeping me from coming home, that I wanted to get back at him. I was going to show it to the pastor and the building fund committee, hoping they'd run him out of town and stop putting up that building."

Well, bless your heart, Hazel Marie, I thought. She'd been thinking of me all along, and that put a different light on any of her questionable actions, in my opinion.

"Miss Julia," she said, turning to me, a look of pleading on her face, "I know it's a sin to lie and steal, but I kept trying to think what you'd do in the same situation."

Well, for pity's sake, I thought, thoroughly taken aback.

"And," she went on, looking up now at Mr. Pickens, "I knew that Miss Julia would do whatever it took to make things turn out right. But this thing couldn't be Bobby Bigelow's, I mean, he's looking for something *valuable,* for the Lord's sake. What I took from Wilson T.

is not worth two cents, and I can't imagine him or Bigelow looking all over creation for it. But if it is, then they must be crazy, carrying on like the thing's a piece of gold or something."

"It's okay, sweetie," Mr. Pickens said. "Let's have it now, and I'll explain it to you."

She ducked her head and said something under her breath.

"What?" I demanded. "Look, Hazel Marie, we've been chased and manhandled and scared out of our wits because of whatever it is, and I'm tired of it all. So give it to Mr. Pickens, and let's wash our hands of it. And, frankly, I'd like to know what all the fuss is about."

"Wel-l-l," she said, her face getting redder by the minute. "It's what's left of somebody's . . . ," her voice dropped to a whisper, *"drawers."*

Mr. Pickens and I both just stared at her, our mouths open.

"Drawers?" he said. "You mean panties? Bloomers? What?"

"I don't know what it was to start with. There's not a whole lot left to tell."

"Let's see it."

"You'll have to turn around. I've got it on under my dress. Don't look."

I thought to myself he'd have the decency to step out of the room, but all he did was turn and face the door. "Go ahead," he said, and I reached over and put my hand over his eyes so he wouldn't be tempted.

I watched as Hazel Marie wiggled and twisted, reaching up under her dress and stepping out of a white elastic waistband that was rolled up on itself. You know how those things do. Then, smoothing her dress down with one hand, she dangled the ragged trophy over Mr. Pickens's shoulder.

"Here it is."

He took it, held it up, stretched it and turned it around so that I got more of a look at it than I wanted. The whole back end of what was once a pair of some man's underdrawers was gone. But hanging in the front was the unfortunate remnant of what had to be a placket. You know, the place of access.

"I hope that thing's clean," I said.

After letting me have a good look and taking one himself, Mr. Pickens leaned against the door and commenced laughing his head off.

"What's so funny, Mr. Pickens?"

"Oh, God," he laughed, straightening up and wiping his eyes. Then he sobered up right smartly, turned to me and said, "No wonder

Bigelow risked arrest to get this back. We're messing with serious stuff, here." And he doubled over, laughing again.

"I can't imagine what's so serious about the thing. It's just a rag, not even fit to polish silver with. Get hold of yourself, Mr. Pickens."

"If it's what I think it is, you better believe it's serious." He turned to Hazel Marie. "No telling how many people'd give their eyeteeth to get their hands on this, these, whatever they are."

"Oh, for goodness sakes," she said, waving it away. "Who would want such a thing, except idiots like Bigelow and Wilson T.? You wouldn't believe how careful Wilson T. was with it. He kept it all folded up in a velvet bag, treating it like it was the crown jewels or something."

She stopped, because Mr. Pickens had another laughing fit. He finally got himself under control, taking an inordinate amount of time to do so.

When he was able to speak again, he said, "How'd you get it away from him?"

"It wasn't hard. While we were at the racetrack in Rockingham, Bobby was so mad at Wilson T. for letting me get to a phone so many times that he was hardly speaking to him. And Wilson T. was following him around, trying to get back in his good graces, so I was able to find the bag. I took that thing out and put it on under my dress. Then I wadded up a handful of Kleenex and stuffed that in its place. Bigelow and Wilson T. were so busy fussing with each other and trying to get that race truck to run, they didn't even know it was gone. Well, until I was gone, too."

I stood there about ready to start tapping my foot. All this upset and turmoil for a pair of ragged shorts, it was more than I could comprehend.

"Well, I want to know why in the world everybody is so interested in a pair of worn-out underclothes," I said. "If Wilson T. and Bobby Bigelow needed some kind of magic fetish, they could've just torn up another pair. I tell you, the state of the world these days is just deplorable, what with one thing and another, and here grown men are running all over creation trying to find a pair of used boxer shorts. I'd've thrown those things away a long time ago, if it'd been me."

"This?" Mr. Pickens dangled the ragged thing in front of our eyes again, in spite of the fact that I'd seen all I wanted to of them. "This is Jerry's lucky charm."

"*That* thing?" Hazel Marie's eyes nearly popped out of her head, and mine weren't far behind. "You mean, that's what he's been looking for, and I had it all the time?"

I backed up to a chair and took a seat. Here, I'd had in mind a medallion or a rabbit's foot or a gold charm like Hazel Marie'd dropped all across the state. And all the while it'd been a piece of his intimate apparel.

"Thay Lord," I said. "I guess I don't understand the racing mentality."

"It's different, I'll say that for it," Mr. Pickens said, his mustache twitching again. "Look at these things. He's worn 'em so long, there's hardly anything left." He started laughing again, holding his hand over his eyes and shaking his head. "I know one driver who'll wear only a certain pair of shoes, and another who shaves a special way on race day. Another one has to pat the hood of his car three times before he gets in it. But Jerry . . . Jerry has his lucky shorts."

"One thing I'd like to know," I said, "does Mr. Johnson wear that rag by itself or does he put on a whole pair along with it?"

"You'll have to ask him, Miss Julia. I'm not sure anybody knows and, in spite of your curiosity, I'm not about to ask him."

"Oh, my goodness," Hazel Marie said, "he's going to be so mad at me."

"No, he won't," Mr. Pickens assured her. Then folding the rag carefully, he slipped it in his pocket. "Let's go tell him; then tomorrow, when I meet with Peavey, I'll make sure Bigelow and your boyfriend know Jerry's got it back. That'll change some odds, I expect."

Hazel Marie glared at him. "Don't you start on me again about any *boyfriend.*"

Mr. Pickens smiled at her, those black eyes shining. "Ex-boyfriend?"

"Not even that. He was just the only one available at the time."

As Mr. Pickens said something to the effect that somebody else might be available, I was thinking the less of her for trying to disclaim her earlier interest in Wilson T. Hodge. Then it came to me that she was most likely telling the truth. I knew she'd never been as enamored of Wilson T. as he'd been with her, which is as it should be, but she'd seemed so agreeable to his attentions that I'd thought it was just her way. Some women are born knowing that playing hard-to-get attracts men, who always want what they don't have.

Then it hit me that she might've been trying to please me, hooking up with a man of the church who had nice manners and a steady job and the preacher's respect.

I turned away from them, hoping the two of them wouldn't notice my momentary dismay, because it came to me that Hazel Marie had been looking for the so-called *decent* qualities in a prospective husband, without a thought in the world for whether she liked him or not. Just the way I'd done with Wesley Lloyd—looked on the outside and ignored what my insides were telling me.

If there's one thing I've learned, it's this: It doesn't matter how good a man appears to be, if you don't feel a little spark you'd be better off hightailing it away from him. One way or the other, it's not going to work. I don't mean that the marriage won't last. It can if you're of my generation, brought up to put up a front. And it could last if another man didn't come along to create an internal combustion. Like Mr. Pickens was wont to do. Or Sam.

"Now, Hazel Marie," Mr. Pickens said, just as serious and straight-faced as he could be, "I'm a little worried about you, seeing how you got so attached to men's underclothes. I wonder if I could interest you in some of mine?"

"Mr. Pickens!" I couldn't believe he'd be so forward.

Hazel Marie was equally shocked, but she quickly recovered as a smile spread across her face. "They'd have to be in better condition than that thing."

"Hazel Marie!" I gasped.

Neither of them paid me any attention, standing there looking at each other and smiling all over themselves.

"Sweetheart," Mr. Pickens said, as if they were the only ones in the room, "everything about me is in A-one condition. Trust me on that." Then he put an arm around her and drew me close with the other one. "Let's go tell Jerry to get ready for Victory Lane."

Chapter 35

Hazel Marie came to a stop in the dining room. "I don't think I can face Jerry," she whispered. "I mean, all this time I've had his lucky charm, while he was so worried about losing it. I just feel terrible."

"Don't worry about Jerry," Mr. Pickens said. "He'll be so happy to get it back, he won't care about anything else. In fact, he's liable to grab you up and give you a lip-smacking kiss." Mr. Pickens smiled at her. "Then I'll have to shoot him."

"Mr. Pickens," I said, "we're not going to have any of that, I'll tell you right now."

"Well," Hazel Marie said, a little smile playing around her mouth, "I think, if it's all the same to you, I'll just run up and check on Little Lloyd. So I'll be out of the line of fire from either of you."

She looked up at him again, and they stood there smiling at each other. Remember that spark I was talking about? Well, there were any number of them arcing between those two right there in my dining room. The whole situation should've made me uncomfortable, but it didn't. It made me walk on past and look for Sam.

He was standing by the fireplace, balancing himself with his cane. Waiting for me, I'd like to think. But whether he was or not, I went to stand beside him and take his arm. Staking my claim, so to speak, in case Miss Wiggins had any lingering ideas. Mr. Pickens and Hazel Marie had warmed me up to a fare-thee-well, and I wanted to share a little of it with Sam.

"Jerry," Mr. Pickens said as he came in, interrupting the whispering going on between Etta Mae and Mr. Johnson, "Got something for you. At least, I think I have. Recognize this?" He pulled the rag from his pocket and dangled it for us all to see.

Mr. Johnson came off the sofa in one bound, yelling, "My lucky charm! How the hell, oops, sorry folks, where'd you find 'em? J. D., I swear, buddy, you're the flat-out best there is!"

Well, that just polished Mr. Pickens's ego that much more, something he didn't need, what with his own high estimation of his abilities. He stood there grinning, so pleased with himself I could hardly stand it. Not that I don't believe in giving credit where it's due, but it just did me in that he'd figured out Hazel Marie's part in the mess before I could get around to it. Maybe he was as good as he thought he was, although I had my doubts considering how much help he'd needed from me.

"I'm good," Mr. Pickens said, in that smug way of his, "and that's a fact. But I had some help and I don't mind admitting it."

He walked over to me and had the nerve to point that finger in my face. "This is the one who kept me on the trail. Wouldn't give me a minute's peace, 'what're you doing now, Mr. Pickens?,' 'let's get busy, Mr. Pickens,' 'quit foolin' around, Mr. Pickens.' I swear, Miss Julia, if you'd take over my business, we'd make a million a year. How about it?"

"Oh, Mr. Pickens," I said, somewhat embarrassed by his teasing and the fact that everybody was laughing because, I suspected, they knew what he said was the truth. But somebody has to take over to get things done. "You're doing fine by yourself. But if you ever feel yourself getting slack, just come on over and I'll set you straight."

"You'll be seeing a lot of me, don't worry about that. I'm counting on help from you and Sam," he leaned down and whispered, "with Hazel Marie, and don't you start on me, Miss Julia, about leading her astray. I'm about to strain myself just getting her attention."

Sam started laughing, then he slipped an arm around me right there in public. "Tell you what, J. D., I'll help you get what you want, but I need some help getting what I want."

"You two," I said, pretending I wasn't pleased and hoping at the same time that Etta Mae was taking note. "I don't think either of you needs anybody's help. Except both of you could profit from keeping your eyes on the prize you want, rather than letting them wander to anything wearing a skirt. Just look at that, would you, and take a lesson."

I nodded toward Jerry Johnson, who'd hung his lucky charm around Etta Mae Wiggins's neck. That ugly placket hung down on her bosom like a pendant. Just the most vulgar thing you could ever hope to see, what with her prancing around showing it to everybody.

"You about raced the bottom outta these things," she said, laughing up at Mr. Johnson.

"I sure have," he bellowed, the sound waves echoing around the room. "My ex-wife got so mad one time that she threw 'em away. I had to go dig 'em out of a Dumpster, nearly fell in, too. They been washed and bleached so many times, they're about eat up. But they still work. Man, do they ever! Phoenix, here I come, I'm gonna lap everybody, goin' wide open, and end up cruisin' Victory Lane! See if I don't!"

In spite of all the bragging and flirting they were doing, I was pleased to see them carrying on with each other, since it was plain that Mr. Johnson was no longer giving a thought to LuAnne. Just as I'd predicted.

But LuAnne was just as bad in her own way as Etta Mae Wiggins. She'd turned her attention to Curtis, and the poor man's eyes were searching desperately for a way out, as she talked and hung on his every word. I had a good mind to send Mr. Pickens for Leonard, just to see what she'd do when he walked in. I declare, people act in the strangest ways when the lights go out.

But I was so content with myself, the way things were working out, that I decided to let her enjoy a little thrill. Even if Curtis wasn't appreciating it. It wouldn't hurt him to be nice to a needy woman.

Just for the evening, you understand. Tomorrow was another day, and I'd have to see to it that things got back to normal. I'd have to make sure that Leonard got himself reamed out, or whatever had to be done to him, so LuAnne would leave both me and Pastor Ledbetter alone. She needed to tend to her own knitting or, who knows, with all that counseling she'd been getting from the pastor, the next hot rumor would be about the two of them. And that'd lift the town off its hinges.

And speaking of the pastor, I intended to see that the building fund drive was stopped dead in its tracks. We didn't need a big activities building. Especially right in front of my eyes. That money could go to foreign missions or, even better, to home missions that could always use the help. And if the pastor wouldn't see it my way or, heaven forbid, if he spoke up for Wilson T. Hodge and got him off, I'd just get on the telephone to the session and the deacons and the Sunday School superintendent and the Women of the Church and go through the church directory. What I had to pass on to them wouldn't be gossip, it would be flat-out undeniable facts. There is a difference, you know.

As for Brother Vernon Puckett, the less said of him the better. But you know me, I didn't intend to let him fade into the woodwork only to pop up again when we least expected him. Twice now, he'd tried to get his hands on Little Lloyd, because that child's trust fund is an ever-present lure, blinding him and leading him on to the most outrageous acts of underhanded deceit and deception. I wondered if I made a quiet, but minimally generous, pledge to his television ministry, he'd leave us alone. I don't mind paying somebody off, if I get my money's worth.

But to more current problems. I'd have to watch Mr. Pickens and see how he conducted himself. If he was truly interested in Hazel Marie and, more important from my viewpoint, she was truly interested in him, I'd see to it that those black eyes of his stopped their wandering ways. I wasn't about to let her heart be broken, and I intended to make that clear to Mr. Pickens in no uncertain terms.

And speaking of broken hearts and the fickle men who caused them, Sam had some proving to do, himself. And the first thing he had to do was get rid of Etta Mae Wiggins. I didn't care if she was planning to meet Mr. Johnson at the NAPA 250 at Martinsville the same weekend as the Goody's Body Pain 500, whatever any of that was, that they'd been whispering about, I knew how handsome and attractive Sam was to women. If he as much as smiled at her, she'd be all over him again. What woman wouldn't?

Well, Hazel Marie and I would just have to make up our minds to watch our men. I hated the thought of that, although I will admit to the thrill of victory when I'd snatched and grabbed Sam away from Etta Mae Wiggins. A woman ought to be able to trust somebody. But if you happen to care about a man who can't help but draw other women to him, like Sam and Mr. Pickens, why, I guess you just have to be on your guard all the time and protect them from themselves.

"I think it's time we were all in bed," I announced. Then, as gracious as a winner should be, I turned to Etta Mae. "Miss Wiggins, you shouldn't be driving this time of night, so I'll offer you my bed. Of course, Little Lloyd's already in it, but he's a good little bedfellow. I'll rest down here on the sofa."

Sam drew me closer and said so that only I heard him, "I'll keep you company."

I looked into his kind eyes and smiled before I could help myself. I didn't give a thought to how it would look, even to somebody like Pastor Ledbetter who was so concerned about the proprieties that he couldn't see what he was stepping in himself. Feeling Sam's arm tighten around me, it didn't enter my head to worry about what people would say. After all, who would know and, at our age, who would care? They'd probably think we couldn't manage anything anyway.

But what they didn't know wouldn't hurt them, because I had in mind making a few victory laps myself and, from the looks of Sam, I didn't think he'd need a pair of ragged undershorts to keep up with me.